After a nursing career spanning more decades than she likes to admit, Barb retired to the coast of South Australia's stunning Fleurieu Peninsula with her beautiful and slightly neurotic Australian Shepherd, Shiloh.

Nestled between rolling hills and a panoramic coastline, she lives amidst the wetlands of an eco-village, free to write the fantasy books she loves and always wanted to read.

When not at her desk, Barb loves family get-togethers, playing sadly inconsistent golf, catching up with friends, and early morning walks along the beach to watch the sunrise.

The Brazen Dragon

by

Barbara J. Rosie

Book 1 in the Tangler's Web Trilogy

The Brazen Dragon

Internal map created by Leanbh Pearson.

IFWG Publishing International
Gold Coast

www.ifwgpublishing.com

For Greg.
In loving memory.

Acknowledgements

Quite a few years ago, I attended my first ever writers' weekend in Auburn, South Australia, hosted by Australian author Fiona McIntosh, and my love of writing was rekindled. The following year I attended one of her renowned five-day Masterclasses in commercial fiction and was inspired to begin my rather convoluted writing journey. To say that without Fiona's advice, encouragement and support over the ensuing years, this book would not have been written, never mind published, is no understatement. At her 2023 National Conference I was able to pitch The Brazen Dragon to Gerry Huntman of IFWG Publishing and was fortunate to be offered a contract for the Tangler's Web trilogy. I'm eternally grateful for her belief in me. Thank you, Fiona.

To my wonderful family, thank you for your support. Special mention to my daughter, Kate, for her feedback and love of the book, my sister, Sue, whose insightful comments are always spot on and very much appreciated, and my sister, Judy, for her review of the final draft. Love you all.

To my writers' group, the Writers of Rohan, especially Kate, Steve, Brydie, Sarah, Imogen and Steph: your comments, critiques and questions made for a much stronger story and made me a much better writer. Thanks, everyone.

Huge thanks to my friend Marcia Batton for her help in editing the book so it was fit for submission, and for pointing out inconsistencies, obvious to me only after she mentioned them. Your belief in the book and critical feedback were invaluable, thank you.

Last but not least, a big thank you to Gerry and IFWG and to Noel, my editor. I appreciate your faith in me and your suggestions in the final edit. Thank you both, so much.

Finally, I'd like to acknowledge the wonderful writing organisations we have access to in Australia. I've enjoyed many workshops and short courses, both online and in person, and all have helped me to hone my craft as a writer. Special mention to Writers SA, the Australian Writers' Centre and the Writers' Studio, I'd recommend them all to any aspiring writer.

Prologue

On the fourteenth night after first snowfall, a mist descended from the craggy peaks of Dragon's Doom. As cold and silent as angels' breath, it drifted with unnatural purpose to the valley below, shrouding the hamlet of River Glen in a gossamer haze. Here, it sought a particular knowledge. Tendrils of white seeped beneath doorways and through cracks in walls and down smoking chimneys to search every corner of every room. The name of the mist, like Magic, was long forgotten. From each dwelling, it gathered secrets and promises, dreams and desires, and the echoes of actions, both real and implied. The villagers slept on, unaware of the silent intrusion, or the faint crackle of old magic in the midnight air. If the mist disturbed their slumber at all, it was only that dreams suddenly sparkled with unfamiliar, vibrant colours or were threaded with long-forgotten melodies that swelled the heart with joy. When the villagers awoke, they remembered little, only a momentary longing for something so perfect, so impossibly beautiful, they knew it must have been a dream.

In a stone cottage by the bend of the river, the air was thick with grief and loss. As the Angel of Death gathered the soul from the body of a mother, lifeless on a pallet by the fire, the luminous cloud found its destination. In the midst of heartbreak and despair, the mist gave comfort and hope to the old woman tending the newborn babe, and in return, exacted a promise.

Chapter 1

Shardial, Capital of Cabarac.
Year ten in the reign of King Davic.
Fifty years since Plague end.

The brazen dragon crouched in the centre of the square, shimmering like tarnished gold in the autumn sun. Morag Poole stared at the bronze sculpture through the bars of her cage, then slumped against the wall, trembling. The instrument of her execution was both terrifying and beautiful.

The sculptor had captured the essence of the beast in magnificent detail: the curve of the spine, the fold of the wing, the hook of the talon, and the pattern of the scale. All perfect. If the sweep of the brow were a little shallow, the snout a shade too long, or the barbed tail too blunt, who could argue? Dragons had not been seen for generations. The creature had been damned and relegated to myth and legend, its wondrous magic denied. History had been changed in this kingdom, deliberately and callously, truth vilified reality ignored. The beauty and wonder of magic and all it had done to enhance the lives of the people of Cabarac was forgotten. Magic was now feared and despised. The woman in the cage knew this all too well.

The bronze beast waited. Bigger than a prize bull, it dwarfed the black-robed dispatcher, who watched as a boy lay kindling beneath its underside, in the space between muscled haunch and partially unfurled wing. To the rear of the dragon was a cart of cut logs. Beech and oak, chosen for their high heat and longer burn time. Morag knew this also, for she was a healer and wise to the ways of the forest. If she closed her eyes, the sights and sounds of this strange city disappeared and instead of the tall archways and domed roofs, she could see the snow-topped mountains and the towering firs of her home province. It was ironic, really, that Shardial owed its impressive architecture to magic and the Maladikkan invaders of long ago. It was testament to their skills that little had deteriorated in the last seventy years. The same could not be said for towns and villages in the outer provinces.

Nonetheless, Morag mourned the loss of her cottage nestled in the woodland, and the cold, crisp breeze that brought the call of the snow hawk and the scent of alpine flowers down from the mountainside. Never again would she pluck a small red apple from the tree and taste its sharp sweetness. Never again would she walk by the stream in summertime and feel the soft squelch of moss between her toes. All these things were lost to her now. Her execution was imminent. The dragon would bring her death.

The dispatcher stroked the snout of the bronze dragon with a gentleness that surprised her. Her body still ached from the torment he had inflicted. Her mind had tried to resist the memories, but now she forced herself to recall what had happened less than a week before. How had it come to this?

Three times, Morag Poole denied the accusation that she had used forbidden magic. Three times, the dispatcher rejected her claims of innocence.

Impatient for her confession, he had ordered his men to bind her to the ducking-stool fixed to the end of a plank. Fear stole her voice. She gripped the chair, suspended over the glacial waters of the river, white-knuckled and silent. The dispatcher signalled for the dunking to begin.

The shocking cold took Morag's breath as she hit the water. Heart racing, and with barely a breath to hold, she fought the instinct to inhale as her lungs screamed for air. The plank was raised quickly, however, and the dispatcher watched, arms folded, as Morag coughed and spluttered her denial.

Morag was better prepared for the second dunking and filled her lungs before she was plunged below the surface. The frigid blackness engulfed her, and her eardrums felt as though they were pierced with shards of ice. Just as Morag thought her lungs would burst, the stool was lifted clear of the river, and she inhaled great gulps of air as water streamed from her hair and robe. Goosebumps rose on numb flesh and her teeth chattered so violently she thought they might shatter.

"What say you now, Morag Poole? Do you still deny you are a witch? That you use magic?" The dispatcher's voice was as unforgiving as mountain stone.

Morag forced the words through lips as blue as the ink in her herbal. "I have only my healer's gift. The Eiran is not magic."

A cruel smile split the dispatcher's face, and he turned to the small crowd gathered on the riverbank. "The healer still denies her gift is magic. We will see. If she is innocent, she will die in the river. Only witches tainted with magic can survive."

"On my signal," he called to the soldiers straining to manoeuvre the plank. He dropped his arm and Morag plunged into the frigid depths of the River Glarice for the final time. She wanted to end the agony, to die and prove the dispatcher wrong. But he was clever in ways she had not yet fathomed, and as the bubbles of air leaving her mouth slowed, he brought her to the surface before she could drown.

Unconscious and perilously close to death, Morag hovered above her body in a dream state, her awareness linked to her corporeal body by the Eiran. She saw the shifting mood of the crowd, at first shocked and sympathetic, then whipped to anger and distrust by the words of the dispatcher, declaring her a witch. She had been the healer to the people of Brackenridge for thirty years, yet no one was brave enough to speak on her behalf. It pained her heart. Yet who could blame them?

Morag was confined to the cage of the prison wagon for the journey to Shardial, as though she were a wild animal. For three days she rattled around the back of the prison wagon, manacled hand and foot, drifting in and out of consciousness. But when the jolting of the wagon finally roused her, a new torment began. The dispatcher's young apprentice wasted no opportunity to make her last days as uncomfortable as he could. Small for his age, with the haunted eyes of a child abused for most of his life, he took pleasure in taunting and degrading her. His derision stopped short of physical harm only because the dispatcher had made it clear he wanted her alive when they reached the capital.

In front of King Davic and his court, the Healer of Brackenridge would provide the spectacle he so desperately wanted. The dispatcher had described her future with glee. Morag Poole would be the first person to be executed by the device he called 'Dragon's Breath'.

Near the end of their journey, at a bend in the road, Morag glimpsed the ramparts of Shardial, high on the hill. The walls that wrapped around the king's castle and the city it protected towered above the landscape, even from a distance, but nothing had prepared her for the sheer scale of the battlements as they passed through the traders' gates. The townsfolk were curious when they saw a woman behind the bars of the prison wagon, but all they did was mock and ridicule. Twice she was spat on. Unable to wipe away the gobbets of phlegm, she watched as they dried a sickly shade of green on the front of the thin shift that barely covered her nakedness.

The afternoon was unseasonably hot. Dust stirred by milling feet drifted on the breeze and parched Morag's already dry throat. Her hands had been chained behind her back and her shoulders throbbed. Her wrists were raw and bleeding where the manacles chafed against her skin. Morag was beyond caring. She prayed for the peace that death would bring.

The boy brought her evening meal of water and dry bread once the horses had been seen to.

"You stink like a pig." The boy sneered and held his nose between his fingers.

"Whose fault is that?" Morag held his gaze, and the boy was the first to look away.

Days before, he had shortened the chain between her manacles and a hook high on the wall so she couldn't squat properly over the bucket she used as a privy. Her robe had become so soiled she had begged the dispatcher to let her wash it. He hacked off the offending garment with his dagger instead, and left her dressed in her undershift, slashed to the thigh. The boy had watched, laughing.

"You're gonna die tomorrow, witch."

Morag closed her eyes and smiled. "Yes, thank the goddess."

"You won't be smiling tomorrow, Morag Poole. People all over Shardial will hear your screams."

"I know I will be welcomed into the arms of the angel, boy, which is more than you can hope for, unless you learn to soften your heart."

"My heart is as soft as it's ever going to be." The boy spat at her feet. "I'll be the greatest dispatcher Cabarac has ever seen! I'll gather witches like a fisherman catches a school of skipjack in his nets."

A shiver of goosebumps trailed down her arms and Morag knew the truth of what the boy said. He slammed the door closed, and she heard the key turn in the lock. She slumped against the wall of the wagon and moaned softly. She had no tears left.

Music drifted across the square and laughter was interspersed with gasps of astonishment, rousing Morag from an uneasy slumber. She eased her way up from the stool that her chains confined her to and shuffled to the bars. Lanterns flickered in the twilight, and above the heads of the crowd that filled the square, she saw flashes of flame from torches spinning high in the air. A troupe of performers was entertaining the throng with acrobatics and song. Soon the torches were spinning so fast they made a ring of fire, then acrobats began diving and tumbling through the circle as though the flames weren't even there.

A jester in brightly coloured costume, complete with fool's cap and bells, pranced by the cage a short time later with a gaggle of children trailing behind. He slowed his steps as he neared and then backflipped to land on his hands, balancing first on one hand and then the other before springing lightly to his feet only inches from the bars. He pulled a stream of brightly coloured ribbons from his sleeve with a flourish and tossed them high in the air for the children to scamper after. Furtively, he made the sign of the angel, so Morag would understand that he was a friend. Leaning close to the bars, he whispered to her in the language of old magic and Morag's heartache began to ease. She nodded her understanding, and the jester tumbled away in a series of handstands. Her soul was filled with a sense of peace. She closed her eyes and dreamed of home.

Trumpets heralded King Davic's arrival and roused Morag from her memories. The King and his entourage inspected the brazen dragon and then moved to sit in tented pavilions on the other side of the square. The dispatcher directed the boy to put more straw beneath the steeple of kindling, then bowed low to the King. Beckoning to two of the soldiers controlling the crowd, he strode back to the cage. The door opened, and her bladder emptied. Shamed by the betrayal of her own body, she choked back a sob. But what did a bit of piss matter? She was about to die.

The soldiers manacled her hands in front of her and pain shot through muscles stretched too long in one position. Dragged from the cart, she staggered and would have fallen if not for the soldiers gripping her arms. Morag heard the murmur of the crowd. A voice yelled out, "Kill the witch!" and the chant was taken up by the mob in a dreadful accompaniment to her faltering trudge to the dragon. The dispatcher raised his arms, and the crowd grew silent.

"Morag Poole is a witch!"

The crowd booed and jeered. He waited for silence.

"She is guilty of using magic. For that, she is sentenced to die. The witch says she is innocent! I say death to the plague bringer! What say you, citizens of Shardial?"

"Kill the witch! Kill the witch! Kill the witch!" the combined voices of a thousand outraged citizens thundered across the square.

The dispatcher raised his arms again. "So be it. The witch will die."

Morag heard nothing. She existed only in the space between

heartbeats. The dispatcher slid the pin from the barrel of a small door in the dragon's flank and the flap dropped down with a discordant clash. Morag's legs quivered. The soldiers tightened their grip. The inside of the dragon was hollow. Morag stared at the yawning emptiness and finally understood the manner of her death. It was an oven. Her heart pounded. She was going to be roasted like a goose at Midwinter's Eve. Darkness descended.

The boy slammed the door shut. The dispatcher held a torch aloft and nodded to the King.

"Death to magic! Death to the plague-bringer!" His voice was sharp with righteous indignation.

Morag roused as the door slammed into place. The metal cocooning her was cold against her skin, and she began to shiver. Her breath was loud in her ears, amplified in the dark confines of the chamber, as though she were the lungs of the dragon itself. The thought terrified her. Incense and aromatic scents assailed her nostrils. A waft of cool air stroked her feet, and she saw two pinpricks of light beyond her toes.

The dispatcher lowered the torch to the straw, and the dry stalks of barley caught the flame and ignited with a *whoosh*. The kindling twigs of birch and cedar followed, and the flame intensified. The boy fed the fire with more birch bark, and as the flames licked greedily at the belly of the dragon, he added the logs of seasoned oak and beech. The fire roared.

Morag felt a tremor beneath her buttocks and heard a bubbling sound, like water tumbling over stones in a stream. A pleasant heat spread along her hips and down her back and for a moment she relished the warmth. The tremor changed to become a vibration, the bubbling a waterfall. The warmth spread and soon became unbearably hot. Morag pressed her feet hard against the metal of the dragon's neck and tried to arch her back, but her shoulders started to burn. A hiss of steam erupted near her feet, scalding her toes. She pulled them back with a cry of alarm, cracking her knees against the metal.

The dispatcher paced around the dragon and paused at the snout. He cocked his head and listened. A rumbling echoed along the neck of the beast. The scent of incense mingled with the aroma of burning cedar and he bounced on his toes with anticipation. Secreted in the beast's floor and along its neck was a narrow cavity filled with water, rapidly transforming into steam. The dragon squealed and hissed as the steam was forced through the slits in its snout. He thrust the flaming torch to the sky and shouted, "Behold, the Dragon's breath!"

As the fire roared beneath the dragon, the intense heat seared Morag's back and buttocks to the metal. She tried to scream, but the air was so hot it parched her throat. Her lungs burned. Her eyeballs were so dry she could no longer blink. Locked in silent agony, Morag felt her skin blister and peel and her blood boil. She prayed to the Goddess of Light to let the angel take her. The words the jester had whispered suddenly came to mind and once again, a strange peace filled her.

The dragon's hide of burnished bronze glowed red in the heat of the flickering flames. The crowd fell silent as it hissed and snorted, as though it were alive and not made of metal. It seemed at any moment the beast would unfurl its massive wings and take flight. King Davic leaned forward, transfixed. The dispatcher and the boy stood triumphant at the head of the beast. The brazen dragon was a success. His promotion to Grand Dispatcher was assured. He stepped away from the boy and threw him his cloak. The dispatcher opened his arms wide as he walked in a slow circle to acknowledge the crowd, then bowed low to the King.

Morag was ready. She released the Eiran to the goddess. She heard the whisper of the angel's wings and the crackle of old magic. She saw the jester standing by her cottage in the snow. He opened his arms in welcome. The snow glistened with a brilliant whiteness as the body of the healer, Morag Poole, burst into incandescent flame.

A deep rumbling growled from the belly of the dragon, and the dispatcher pivoted at the unexpected change in sound. A spark flickered in the eye of the dragon. A white-hot flare blazed from its snout and arced straight towards his heart, engulfing him in flame. The boy's terrified screams echoed around the square as he watched the dispatcher burn brighter than any fire.

Chapter 2

River Glen, River Province.
Year sixty in the reign of King Davic.

Kira had never helped a man to die before, but Isaac wanted to have a death dream like his ancestors before him, and Kira had promised. She had visited him each morning for the last few days, wondering if each day would be his last; the angel was hovering over the old fisherman. The old ways lingered in his blood and Isaac wanted to be reunited with the one he loved most when he took his last breath.

There had been a time, over a century ago, when death dreams were common practice. Not now. Dream weavers had been banished with everything else magical, their skills disregarded and relegated to lore. People once again relied on healers to treat their woes. Kira had been blessed with the Eiran, and she would try to do this for him. Not actually kill him, of course, just ease his passage to the Goddess. It was a small distinction, but it mattered to Kira. The Eiran was meant to ease suffering, not cause it, and Kira would never abuse her healer's gift. She had done a great deal of soul-searching before she agreed, and even now harboured some misgivings.

Knowing what to do in theory was one thing, doing it was something different altogether. When Kira had told her grandmother what Isaac wanted, Agatha had been hesitant to teach her this uncommon skill. Not because she doubted Kira's ability, but never having given a death dream herself, was unsure of her knowledge. Nevertheless, Agatha's long friendship with Isaac and Kira's skill and natural reverence for her gift had swayed her, and she'd endeavoured to teach Kira all she would need to do.

Kira smiled to herself, Agatha didn't like to admit her age, but the tasks of village healer were falling more and more on Kira's shoulders. It was a responsibility she welcomed; healing was in her blood. She just hoped that using the Eiran in this way would not be a misuse of her gift.

Dawn was the best time to harvest the webs of the moon spider, and as Kira would have to walk through the forest to get to Isaac's, she decided to replenish her stores on the way. She pulled her scarf up over her chin as she left the warmth of her cottage, already ruing her decision to leave the baby squirrel she had rescued snuggled up inside the left hand of her warmest gloves. The moon was only two days into its wane, bright enough to give her a shadow and allow her to see the small clouds of her breath in the bitter night air. For the fourth morning in a row, she trudged along the narrow path to the river bend, the silence broken only by the crunch of leaves beneath her boots and the drone of frogs croaking a sombre, two-part harmony.

By the time Kira reached the small grove of gorse bushes at the forest edge, the sky was streaked with crimson and a thousand delicate webs glistened in the pale light like silken hammocks. Tiny beads of dew sparkled on the silver strands criss-crossed above the sheets of web suspended between the gorse, ready to confuse unwary insects and knock them down into the lethal, sticky trap.

While Kira felt a small pang of regret for destroying what it had taken the moon spiders all night to make, the densely woven webs were best harvested when they were fresh and at their most potent. She needed to collect them before they had a chance to trap their intended prey and contaminate the strands. Moving swiftly through the gorse, she murmured her apology to the spiders whose webs she stole before stowing the sticky threads into a copper pot. The gash on Isaac's head might have healed, but webs were always needed in a village where men worked with axes and knives.

The early morning chatter of birds serenaded her walk to the lake. The sun was barely visible through the trees and Isaac's cottage was easy to miss if you didn't know the path. It was surrounded on one side by dense woodland, the trees so tall the small dwelling was shrouded in permanent shadow. On the other side, the Lake of Shells stretched a half-league or so to the base of Dragon's Doom, gradually narrowing as it negotiated the rock falls and landslides to become the River Ryder once again. As Kira climbed the steps to the deck surrounding the cottage, she glimpsed a small wooden boat out in the centre of the lake, but it was soon swallowed by the swirling mist rising from the water.

She knocked on the door and went in. An old man lay bundled up in blankets on a pallet by the fire. His breath rattled in his chest as he laboured to breathe. The room smelled of stale piss and dried sweat. She longed to open a window and let in some fresh air but knew Isaac wouldn't have it.

"Well met, Isaac. It's me, Kira. I've just come to check how you are."

"Ah, the weaver of my dreams," he wheezed. "Come in, my child. I think this will be the last time you have to visit this old man." The effort to speak more than one sentence without a rest was too much and he began to cough. The rasping, gurgling, hack told Kira the build-up of fluid on his lungs had worsened. She put a hand to his head. The fever had taken hold. She eased him forward and rearranged the pillows behind his back, so he was propped up a little higher.

"Your cough sounds worse."

"It is. I felt the angel's wing brush my cheek twice through the night." Isaac paused to take a breath. "I thought there may have been a third, but I asked her to wait. The healer has promised me a death dream, I told her. When I have that, you can have me." He sighed deeply. Kira hid her apprehension with a smile.

"Let me make you more comfortable. Change your linens. Make you some willow bark tea."

"No need. My grandson is here now." Isaac nodded towards the lake. "Checking the nets." He coughed violently and hacked up some phlegm which he spat into a cup. It was streaked with blood. He slumped back against the pillows and reached for her hand.

"You've done enough, lass. I am ready. Jacob knows. He'll take me to the boat."

Kira nodded. She had done all she could to help the fisherman and he accepted his fate. He was older than her grandmother and almost as stubborn. Twice in the last few months he'd had dizzy spells while he was pulling in the nets and had fallen from his boat. The last time he'd gashed his head and nearly drowned. She had been able to save his life once, but her gift could only do so much. Isaac was dying. Kira looked out of the window. The mist had cleared, and the boat was heading back to shore.

"Jacob returns. He'll be here shortly."

"Good." Isaac's ragged breathing had eased, and his hand was growing cool. "My grandmother's herbal." He indicated towards the mantle with a lift of his chin. "On the shelf, there."

Kira managed to reach up and take the book from the shelf without letting go of his hand. The well-worn cover was made of tanned goat hide and embossed with tiny, gilded feathers, faded where the book had been handled over the years. A plaited thong was cunningly woven through the spine, long enough to wrap around the book twice over and tie securely. The book was surprisingly heavy, so Kira placed it on the bed, near Isaac's thigh.

"How beautiful!"

"For you." Isaac raised a bony finger and tapped the side of his nose. "Magic."

Kira's scalp prickled. Isaac's grandmother, Gwyneth, had been a simple hedge witch before the Great Divide and Kira was fairly certain the herbal would not have survived the purge that followed if it contained anything remotely magical. Her heart beat a little faster though; dispatchers still roamed Cabarac eliminating anything, or anyone, associated with magic. Kira squeezed the old man's hand and brought it to her lips. She shrugged away the thought that what she was about to do could be considered sorcery. Her healer's gift was strong, but she had always trusted Agatha's decree the Eiran was not magic.

"But your grandson?"

"No. She made me promise: give it to you." He smiled and nodded towards the errant brown curl that had managed to escape her braids. "The girl with the seasons in her hair, the forest in her eyes and magic in her touch."

Kira felt the tears begin to well. It was a strange thing to say. Isaac must be close to ninety; goodness knows how long it was since Gwyneth had passed. The only thing he said that made any sense was the colour of her eyes which were green, flecked with russet brown. Her hair, so curly that she rarely wore it loose, was a rich mahogany. Isaac's mind was beginning to wander. She hoped Jacob would make haste.

"My thanks and my blessings. I will treasure it always."

The hull of the fishing boat scraped on the stones lining the shore. Isaac squeezed her hand as his grandson entered the cottage.

"I would have the death dream Kira, if you please. I hear the beating of the angel's wings." The fisherman closed his eyes. His face had lost its feverish colour and had started to pale. Kira glanced at Jacob.

"Go ahead, lass. We've said all we needed to." He knelt on the other side of the cot and took hold of his grandfather's other hand.

Kira closed her eyes and concentrated on what Agatha had taught her. She summoned her awareness and let the Eiran guide her. In the space between his breaths, she found Isaac's dream spirit and linked her awareness to his. Immediately her mind was filled with the memories Isaac held dearest in his heart. They appeared to Kira not as images but as thousands of pin pricks of light, like multi-coloured stars in the night sky. She reached for the brightest of them all and the night fell away to reveal a meadow bathed in the soft, pink light of dawn.

A gentle summer breeze caressed the reeds at the edge of a small pond and the air was clear and perfumed with the scent of apple blossom. A slender woman in a long white dress turned towards them, an expression of puzzlement on her face. A circlet of wildflowers crowned her hair, which tumbled long and loose past her shoulders, almost to her waist.

"Nelly." Isaac's voice echoed in her mind with such love and longing that Kira felt his pain in her heart. "My love." The woman's eyes filled with joy, and she smiled and opened her arms in welcome. Kira felt a shift in Isaac's energy and when she glanced toward his dream spirit saw he was no longer old and frail, but tall, strong and youthful. He too opened his arms.

But Isaac could not move forward, tethered as he was to his earthly body. *Please.* Kira hesitated. Was she doing the right thing? *Please, Kira.* She had promised him, hadn't she? Kira placed her hand tenderly on the old man's chest and felt the shallow rise and fall of his ribs. She willed his wish be granted. Isaac sighed and did not take another breath. His heartbeat stuttered beneath her fingers. It slowed, then stopped. The angel brushed his cheek for the third and final time.

At the moment of his death, Kira urged Isaac's dream spirit forward into his lover's embrace. He strode towards Nelly, then caught her in his arms and crushed her to his chest. Their connection filled Kira with joy and released the small band of worry constricting her throat. She had given Isaac his death dream. The relief was like a hum that tingled from her scalp to her toes, and with it, a fleeting lightness, like a heavy weight had been lifted from her shoulders. Their image burned as bright as the sun for just an instant, and then was gone.

Kira crossed her hands, linked her thumbs, and pressed her hands to her chest in the sign of the angel. "Peace and eternal blessings, dear Isaac. May your nets always be full," she whispered. She opened her eyes and smiled at Jacob through her tears.

"Thank you, Kira." He brought Isaac's hand to his face and rested his forehead on it for a moment. Laying it back on the bed, he smoothed the bedclothes over Isaac's frail body. "Cranky old bastard he got to be in these last few years, but he loved his family, and we loved him." Jacob ran his hand across his eyes. "I'm gonna miss him somethin' terrible, Kira, and that's a fact."

He picked up the herbal on Isaac's bed and shook his head. "'Tis a poor gift for all you've done, I'm sorry, lass. Nowt but a lump of leather, really. We've all had a go at trying to untie the straps, but age and the damp has the better of us. The book's for show and not for reading, I'm afraid. He loved that old woman. Told us all sorts of tales about his gran when we was little. Ma used to scold his socks off, 'fillin' our head with rubbish,' she said. Still, Gwyneth were a healer, like you, and Granddad wanted you to have it, Kira, so it's yours."

Kira accepted the book from Jacob and felt a momentary light-headedness. She should have supplemented the Eiran with energy drawn from the fire. Too late now. She tucked the stray spiral of hair behind her ear and straightened her shoulders. "Thank you, Jacob. Er, could I trouble you for some water, please? I feel a little giddy."

But as Jacob went to fetch her a drink, Kira couldn't shake the feeling of remorse. She had done as Isaac had wanted, hadn't she? Ending his pain and suffering and fulfilling his dying wish should have salved her troubled conscience, but the reality of what she had done hit home. She began to tremble. The angel may have been hovering, but the truth lay beneath the sheet. She had just stopped a man's heart.

Chapter 3

Kira walked home with mixed feelings. Jacob's gratitude had helped ease her doubts and she tried to view what had happened a little more objectively. Knowing Isaac's death dream had reunited him with his wife, Nelly, gladdened her heart, and Kira felt privileged to have witnessed his special memory. And though she had agonised about helping Isaac ever since he brought the subject up, she had seen just how much it meant to him.

While many people experienced a dream or a vision at the end of their lives, to be sure that the dream was linked to a particular memory required the help of someone skilled in dream magic. In the olden days, before magic had brought the plague to Cabarac, it had been a dream weaver. Kira sighed. It was only because her healer's gift was so strong that she had been able to grant Isaac's request. If she was honest, she hadn't been sure that it would work at all. And despite her happiness in fulfilling his dying wish, she hadn't anticipated the impact on her peace of mind.

She had offered to stay and help with the death ritual, but Jacob assured her that his wife was on her way, and they would do the honour together. Isaac had wanted one last sail around the lake, and Kira left Jacob preparing the boat. He had wrapped up a rainbow trout that had been trapped in the nets for her dinner, with his thanks for Isaac's care. The herbal was stowed safely in her satchel. She quickened her pace as she crossed the bridge; Agatha would be wondering where she was, and Kira was desperate for a cup of tea and something to eat.

Agatha was not alone when Kira entered the grey stone cottage. An old man sat at the wooden table devouring a thick slice of bread smothered with butter and honey. Kira smiled. Eldred Tanglewood was one of her grandmother's oldest friends and a frequent, if erratic visitor. The renowned conjurer and master of trickery dropped by whenever he was passing through River Glen, sometimes for a meal, sometimes staying a week. His arrivals were nearly always a surprise. Even though he was getting on in years, his remarkable talents were still in high demand, and he travelled Cabarac widely and sometimes further afield to neighbouring kingdoms.

He dropped the bread onto the plate as Kira entered the kitchen, stood, and proffered a courtly bow with a grace and energy that belied his advanced age. As much as she wanted to confide in Agatha, she decided not to mention Isaac's death dream in front of him, because, despite a genuine fondness for the old man, his powers of observation could be unnerving, and she needed to restore some energy before she faced a barrage of questions. It would have to wait.

"Blessed be the day, young healer. We are well met, indeed. You've been harvesting webs, I see."

The webs were safely in her satchel. Kira glanced at her grandmother. *Did you tell him?* she asked in mind speech. Agatha shook her head.

"Don't frown, child. Your cloak is damp and stained with mud where you have been kneeling and there is a sprig of gorse snagged in the hem. The side of your cloak is streaked with silver where you have wiped the sticky threads from your fingers, and as any healer worth their salt knows, dawn is the best time to harvest the webs of the moon spider. Especially this close to a full moon."

Kira grinned. "Blessings to you, Uncle Tangler." She pressed her left hand against her heart and extended her right arm from the elbow as she bowed her head in the traditional healer's greeting. She and the old conjurer had played this 'looking game' since the day, as a child, she had asked him if he'd had hiccoughs because there were strands of dill stuck between his teeth. She studied him now.

His forehead was lined with wrinkles, and laugh lines radiated from his grey eyes when he smiled, but as always, he stood lightly on his feet. His travelling cloak was new and dyed an unappealing shade of nut brown, but the quality was evident in the cut of the sleeves as they flared gently at his wrists. The scent of rosemary and tarragon wafted towards her as he moved, and Kira guessed he may be about to start a long journey since the tarragon was too fresh to have been in his boots for days.

"I have fish for supper, Gran. The angel finally gathered poor Isaac, and Jacob gave me some trout as thanks for his care. Will you be staying, Uncle Tangler, or does your journey begin soon?"

The old man's eyes twinkled at the phrasing of her question. "You have reached eighteen summers, Kira, I think you are old enough to drop the 'Uncle', don't you? *Tangler* will suffice."

He raised his leg and made a figure of eight with his boot. "You can no doubt smell the tarragon. You have always had the knack for seeing more than just what is in front of your face. A skill that is underutilised and unappreciated. Fortunately for me!"

Kira laughed. Her first memory of him was at the Midsummer Fair, where she had watched, both enthralled and terrified, as he juggled half a dozen flaming torches while balancing on a tightrope. She had been only four or five at the time, yet the memory still gave her goosebumps. His concentration and athletic ability amazed her even now.

Tangler not only delighted the crowds with his juggling and acrobatics, but he amazed them with his sleight of hand as well. She wouldn't have been surprised to learn that he had been a pickpocket in his younger days.

Agatha placed a bowl and a steaming mug of tea on the table. Kira looked down at her diminutive grandmother and smiled her thanks.

"Final blessings to poor old Isaac. He will be at peace now." Agatha linked her thumbs and made the sign of the angel to show her respect. "Give me the trout, pet, I'll take it outside to clean it. You sit yourself down and get some food into you before Tangler eats it all. Have some porridge."

Kira handed over the parcel of fish and slid onto the bench opposite Tangler. She ate as quickly as the heat of the porridge would allow.

"To answer your question—I'm just passing through. I have a performance in Bishop's Crest." Tangler waved his arm in a westerly direction. "But I should be back in River Province before long. I'm to meet up with a group of troubadours and travel with them to the Northern province to entertain at Prince Rhicard's court. Unfortunately, not in time to see them perform here in River Glen at the next Merryman Ball. They're a talented group, in high demand." He looked at Kira and raised an eyebrow. "Do you attend the Ball?"

Kira grimaced. The Merryman Ball was the last ball of the year where young men could offer a token of betrothal to eligible young women. It was traditionally held over three nights, and villagers from all over River Province came to dance.

"Only as healer. Three nights of dancing can take its toll if people haven't prepared."

"I thought you enjoyed dancing, Kira?" Tangler raised the other brow to meet the first.

"Actually, I love to dance. But as the Merryman Ball is mainly about courtship, it seems rather pointless to dance with potential suitors when healers are not expected to marry. Also, this is a quota year, and since healers aren't included, it doesn't seem fair to compete for tokens with those who are."

For the last hundred years, young women risked being gathered for the quota and shipped to a foreign kingdom to pay off Cabarac's debt of obligation. The reason was buried in time, and no one seemed to question it. Not openly, anyway, especially since in River Province the rules differed slightly to the rest of the country. Other provinces had to send an ordained number of girls, but thanks to an agreement forged over eighty years ago by the man for whom the ball was named, only girls without a betrothal token were eligible.

"Indeed," said Tangler. "You have been fortunate in River Glen that Mayor Merryman had the foresight to obtain the King's promise all those years ago. The Crown Prince complains often that the numbers are down in River Province."

Kira nodded. "So we've heard. The High Sheriff visits next week to compile a register of eligible girls against the Record of Births. Agatha fears it does not bode well for the future."

Tangler gathered his beard in his fist and frowned. "I fear you may have more to worry about than a betrothal promise, dear child. The Grand Dispatcher is in the region. Piscator has a reputation for being over-diligent in his hunt for magic. He has scoured the other provinces and now he is here. Three girls in Corrick Hill are in prison awaiting his examination, and only last month two from River's End were executed in the brazen dragon."

Kira's breath caught in her throat. She spooned the last of the porridge into her mouth and put down her spoon.

"Magic? But surely there's been no magic in this land since the purge. Why on earth would he think that magic would return after more than a hundred years?"

"Dispatchers are as diligent now as they have always been." Tangler waved his fingers as though catching raindrops. "Blood magic is unpredictable. Even though it is rarely seen these days, there is always the possibility that it lays dormant in some bloodlines and will present unexpectedly. Evidence is scant, of course, and most people dismiss the thought, but there are many who have a hatred and a fear of magic."

Tangler paused and Kira heard a strange sadness in his voice when he continued. "You know why, of course. Sorcery was blamed for the plague which almost destroyed Cabarac, and therefore magic was banished. Those in power are determined not to go back to the old ways, so dispatchers are still sent to stamp out any hint of sorcery, real or imagined. More so, perhaps, since King Davic is so infirm. The Crown Prince ensures there will be no impediment to his succession. Piscator is a fanatic and unfortunately, Prince Thomac has assigned him to the Southern Provinces."

Tangler sliced another piece of bread and passed the plate to Kira. He raised his hand to rest a moment on her cheek, and she felt a surprising warmth at his touch. His voice, though gentle, held a note of warning. "It is said that even the healer's gift is frowned upon by Piscator. One of the women he executed was a healer, one in prison, also. You will need to take care."

"The Eiran?" Kira gasped as the air left her lungs in a rush.

"I'm afraid so, my dear."

"Pus and horehound!" she swore under her breath, clenching her fists under the table. Could what she had done for Isaac this morning be considered magic? Agatha had always told her that the Eiran was strong in her, that she had the healer's true gift. But Kira had always believed that magic was something arcane and dangerous. The Eiran was a blessing that she attributed to in-born empathy with the natural world. It helped her to treat illness and heal injuries. To save lives. Even so, Agatha had cautioned her to be careful in its use, as there were some who may not see a distinction. The strength of her gift was a secret kept between them both.

Kira glanced at Tangler. She was glad she had not spoken of the manner of Isaac's death, but the man saw everything. Nonetheless, if he only suspected how strong her Eiran was, she would not confirm his suspicions.

Kira pushed herself away from the table and straightened her shoulders. No use worrying about tomorrow when today had hardly begun. She frowned at this unwelcome news, then forced a smile.

"Thank you for the warning. It is sad to think people who are skilled in herblore and healing should be so persecuted. Hopefully, I will never clap eyes on the man. Can I get you more to eat?"

"No thank you, Kira. I have already stayed longer than I should. And I am sorry to have been the one to tell you such unpleasant news." He gulped down the last of his tea. "I will say my goodbyes to Agatha on my way out. But before I leave, I would like to gift you a small trinket to cheer you up. Hold out your hand, my dear."

"Oh, there's no need. It's not your fault," she started, but Tangler interrupted.

"Please. It would make this old conjuror very happy. Besides, I missed your last birthday, and your nineteenth will be here before you know it."

Kira nodded and held out her palm, but Tangler closed her fingers and turned her hand over, so the back of her hand was upright. She felt a tingling sensation around her wrist and then a cold heaviness that dissipated so quickly she must have imagined it. When she looked, she was wearing an intricately plaited leather bracelet, threaded with strands of silver. She ran her fingers across the exquisite workmanship, marvelling at the way the strands twisted and knotted around each other so seamlessly. Small beads of Haviland crystal clung to the silver like dewdrops. There was no catch that she could see, but from one junction of the threads hung a tiny silver cobweb.

"Oh, Tangler, this is beautiful, but I can't possibly accept such a..."

Kira looked around. She was talking to thin air. The conjuror had moved so silently she hadn't noticed him leave. His voice drifted through the open window from the garden beyond. "It's yours, my dear. Wear it well and stay safe!"

Chapter 4

Agatha snored gently as she dozed in her chair. Kira tucked a knitted blanket over her knees and stroked a whisp of silver hair back from her forehead. The wisdom and laugh lines creasing her face smoothed a little when she slept, but the faint smudge of blue beneath her eyes reminded Kira just how frail her grandmother was. Agatha would never admit it, of course, but age was slowing her down. She had smiled wistfully when Kira recounted Isaac's death dream. "'Tis a wonderful thing you did for him, pet. It's a shame we can't all have such kindness when we die."

After breakfast, she had left Agatha to her baking and gone to check on a woodcutter who had gashed his hand with the blade of his axe and almost severed a finger. Kira was pleased; there was no sign of infection, and the wound was mending nicely. He had promised a cart of cut logs for the fire as payment for saving his finger, for which Kira was very grateful.

She had come home to enjoy a bowl of mushroom soup flavoured with wild garlic and spent the next few hours replenishing her stock of herbs, making salves and tinctures, and cleaning the cottage. By mid-afternoon her back was aching, and Agatha did not need to tell her twice to get some fresh air into her lungs. Kira had waited until Agatha settled for her nap before collecting Gwyneth's herbal and heading outside.

Two gifts in one day. That was a rarity. Kira strolled down the path that meandered through Agatha's herb garden, the scent of rosemary, thyme, and lavender perfuming the accompanying breeze. It was warm for late autumn, as though summer had called in to wave a last goodbye before winter finally took hold. A short walk from the cottage, a grove of paperbark maple trees showed off their autumn colours. Leaves of scarlet, pink and deep crimson, glowed like bonfire embers in the afternoon sun. Kira chose a spot away from the shade and spread her blanket on a carpet of clover to enjoy this unexpected pretence of summer. But she knew the air would chill as the evening shadows lengthened, and the sun slid behind Dragon's Doom looming in the distance. Before allowing herself to inspect Gwyneth's herbal she checked everything in her mind room was in order.

One of the first things Kira had learned as a child was to build a memory room in her mind. In the beginning it was a rudimentary replica of her bedroom. Agatha had taught her to fill it with things she loved—the sunrise over the river with the mist rising like steam off freshly baked bread, the embroidered quilt from her bed depicting two stags fighting, her favourite doll, Agatha's oatmeal biscuits. It had taken hours and hours of practice, but gradually the images had stayed in the room instead of fading away like a dream, so that each time she entered she could see things exactly as she had left them.

As she got older, she filled her room with herblore, what plants looked like, what they smelled like, knowledge of what was poisonous, what was beneficial. Any new discovery, any detail she learned about healing and how the body reacted, Kira also stored in her mind room, so that, had the room been real, anyone who entered would see exactly what she wanted them to see. The room had expanded over the years to become a little cottage, diagrams of plants decorating the walls; the shelves were full of herbal medicine and the tools of her craft.

The room was a way to enhance her memory, Agatha had explained, a place to store her knowledge. Looking back, Kira wondered whether it was also a way to occupy a child curious about everything and full of questions. Still, it worked: she had an excellent memory, and it was especially helpful when she was healing. There were other memories stored in her room as well, private things, like the strength of her Eiran.

As she pondered over the day's events, Kira was thankful that Agatha had warned her to be cautious. Always careful never to draw attention to her gift, Kira used her knowledge and healer's skills first, but when an injury or illness was particularly severe, the Eiran was a blessing. Its effectiveness sapped a lot of her energy though, so she sometimes needed to supplement it with energy from something else, usually a fire. Kira understood Agatha's fear that some people may think it magic if they knew, so the times she had resorted to the Eiran were rare. Nonetheless, Agatha insisted those particular memories had to be hidden in a secret place, just in case anyone cared to snoop.

Kira had thought it would be extremely unlikely for anyone to be able to access her private thoughts, let alone her mind room, but had done as she was asked. On the floor of her mind room there was a knotted rug covering a trap door that opened to a dimly lit cellar. It was actually a ruse: the cellar contained nothing at all. The real hiding place was so well hidden that, on the few occasions Agatha had linked her awareness to Kira's and entered her mind room, she had never been able to find it.

Kira added dear Isaac to the list of those who had passed and stored the memory of his death dream in her secret place. Once she was satisfied that everything was in order, she shut the door and brought her awareness back to the present and the book in her lap.

The herbal felt heavy in her hands. Kira ran her fingers across the hide. She had been surprised at Jacob's description of the book back in the cottage, and even more so now that she could see it in the daylight. There was no doubting that the book was old, but the honey-coloured leather invited her caress, and the tiny feathers glinted in the sun as she turned it in her hands. However, the leather thong wrapped around the book was as stiff as old fishhooks and she couldn't even slide a fingernail inside the knot, so she wondered if, perhaps, Jacob was right, and it was too damp-affected. Yet the old herbal seemed to beckon to her, almost as though Gwyneth called from the pages. She trailed her fingers across the embossed gold, and as the tip of her forefinger pressed on the smallest feather, Kira could have sworn she heard a faint sigh of recognition. The book seemed to relax in her palm, and she was so surprised she almost dropped it. She glanced around quickly. She was alone.

The leather thong was now pliant in her hands, but still Kira untied it with difficulty. Her fingers shook and wouldn't do what she wanted. Finally, the knot gave way to her teasing, and she unwound the book from its tethers. She shook her hands to stop her fingers from trembling and opened the herbal. The scent of the forest wafted from the pages— old wood, rich earth, and damp moss lingered in the background of aromatic herbs and wildflowers. Kira closed her eyes, disoriented by the freshness of the fragrance. The sensation lasted only a few seconds, but Kira's pulse thrummed like she had run from spring to winter down the length of the forest. She breathed as deeply as she could and tried to slow the frantic beating of her heart. She entered her mind room and immediately felt more at ease. What had just happened? Kira knew Gwyneth had been a hedge-witch. Had she locked the book with a spell?

She opened her eyes quickly before she could ask herself the next logical question and concentrated on the book.

The pages were yellowed with age, but surprisingly well preserved. The edges were fragile in places where they had been handled most, the ink had faded in the early sketches, and the script was hard to read, but the hand drawn illustrations were easily recognisable. The first few pages were filled with drawings of plants, their names, and a brief description of their properties. The drawings were simple, obviously drawn when Gwyneth was young and inexperienced but rapidly improving to show more detail and nuances of colour. Kira was loath to turn the pages too quickly because the later illustrations were not only beautifully painted but incredibly lifelike. She could practically smell the scent of the flowers, birds and insects almost flew from the pages. She could have sworn she heard the trill of a nightingale and the drone of a bee.

Her scalp tingled. Books didn't do this. Her mind shied away from the implications, and completely enthralled, she turned another page. She was less than a quarter of the way through when the shadows from the trees blocked the light and made reading too difficult.

Kira used one of the leather thongs to mark her place and closed the book with a sigh. Gwyneth had obviously been a talented artist, but there was definitely something *other* about the herbal. Could it be magic? Kira stared at the gilt feathers on the cover, her mouth suddenly dry. The forbidden, dangerous magic people rarely spoke about, but which apparently must be eliminated at all costs, wasn't at all evident. There was no sense of evil, no feeling of impending doom. It was just a book. Kira laughed at herself. She just had a vivid imagination, that was all. Gwyneth must have been blessed with the Eiran as well—no doubt that was why Kira had been able to open the book to begin with. Satisfied with her reasoning, Kira smiled. Isaac had bestowed her a real treasure after all.

The air had turned chilly while she had been engrossed in the pages, and Kira shivered. She stowed the herbal back into her satchel and headed for home.

The trout was baking in the oven when Kira entered the cottage, and the scent of dill, thyme and lemon made her belly growl in anticipation. Potatoes and beans bubbled on the stove, while Agatha sat at the table sipping a mug of tea.

"Dinner smells wonderful, Gran. Have a quick look at Gwyneth's herbal before we eat. I'll just go and wash. Tell me what you think."

Kira placed the book on the table in front of Agatha and hid a smile. Her grandmother would love the illustrations as much as she did.

Much to her surprise, Agatha was serving dinner when Kira returned to the table.

"Such a shame about the water damage, pet. I remember my own grandmother telling me about Gwyneth's beautiful drawings. It's a great pity that the paint's so faded you can't even make out whether it's a rose or a toadstool. Still, as Jacob told you, it's a nice keepsake."

Kira swallowed. She looked carefully at her grandmother. Was she making a jest? She slid the book back towards herself and sat down. "How many pages did you turn?"

Agatha raised her eyebrows. "Enough to see there was little point. Why?"

Kira wasn't sure how to answer. Her throat was suddenly dry. She opened the book to the last place she had read. The growth cycle of the Chamomile herb seemed to blossom from the page, from tiny seedling to white-petalled flower. She held the book so Agatha could see it.

"What about this?"

Agatha squinted at the page. "It's a little clearer. What is it? A daisy perhaps?" She motioned to Kira to close the book and passed her a plate. "Don't be too disappointed, pet. The herbal is over a hundred years old, and I doubt whether Isaac thought to store it where it couldn't get damp. It's probably just as well; we both know the herbal is harmless, but if that dispatcher comes sniffing around he might think otherwise. Gwyneth was a hedge-witch, after all, so you'd best keep it out of sight, just to be on the safe side. Now eat your dinner before it gets cold."

Kira smiled at her grandmother and held her tongue. She bent her head over the plate and inhaled deeply. "Smells wonderful, Gran, thank you."

The fish was as delicious as she had anticipated. Agatha had smothered the potatoes and beans with butter and a sprinkling of chives, and regardless of her misgivings about the book, Kira devoured everything on her plate.

Kira found it hard to get to sleep. She had wrapped the herbal in a thin shawl, hidden it in an old travel bag and vowed not to look at it again. She didn't know what to do. For the first time in her life, she was keeping a secret from Agatha, and she wasn't sure why. Her grandmother had always had Kira's best interests at heart. She had raised Kira since she was a baby, teaching her how to use her talents when she'd realised her granddaughter was blessed with the true gift.

It couldn't have been easy, yet the old woman had never faltered in her devotion. Agatha was a skilled healer, but she only had a trace of the Eiran—enough to use mind speech and visit Kira's mind room—yet she had helped her granddaughter as best she could. Kira pummelled her pillow and turned over once again. Why could she not tell her grandmother about what she'd seen in Gwyneth's herbal? Surely the Eiran was the only reason she could see the beautiful illustrations. But if that was so, then why couldn't Agatha see them?

She mulled over her conversation with Tangler. Magic. He had warned her about the Dispatcher Piscator. Had he done it for a reason? She wished now that she had asked the old man a few more questions. She dreaded to think that she might have more magical ability than just being able to heal. Surely it wasn't possible? But if it was, then she was not the only person in danger. Agatha would be as well.

She couldn't bear the thought of causing Agatha any more pain. Kira's mother had died in childbirth, and though Agatha never talked about it, or blamed her in any way, deep down Kira had always felt responsible. She would have loved to know her mother's name, but the grief she saw in her grandmother's eyes tore her heart and she'd stopped asking questions almost as soon as she had begun. Losing a child was surely enough hurt for a lifetime.

Kira gave her pillow a final punch, pulled the blankets over her head, and decided, for the time being, to say nothing. The book would stay hidden.

Chapter 5

The evening of the registration had come far too quickly for Kira's liking, and the Lord Mayor had made it even worse by insisting the candidates had to get dressed up for the occasion. For the past few nights her dreams had been a curious blend of recent events and some of the illustrations from Gwyneth's herbal. Tiny spiders wove intricate webs of gold, strong enough to catch fish. Tangler balanced on his tightrope juggling flaming torches that turned into birds with feathers of fire. A chrysalis suspended beneath the leaf of a milkweed shattered like glass to free a glorious monarch butterfly. A boat drifted in the middle of a lake so still that there was barely a ripple. Gwyneth's herbal sang to her in the language of songbirds but when Kira tried to follow the melody, she found her hands tied by leather cords and her head covered in a hood of mist. She woke feeling restless and strangely apprehensive, and being seated in front of a mirror while Agatha fussed with her hair was not helping her nerves.

"Kira! Will you be still for just a minute? Your hair has a life of its own!" Agatha placed a warning hand on top of Kira's shoulder. Satisfied at last, she pinned a silver comb to the elaborate braid, and stood back to admire her handiwork.

"A minute must be a long time when you get to be your age, Gran, I feel like I've been sitting here for at least an hour," said Kira with a grin. "Besides, dressing up just to attend this registration is a nonsense, and you know it! I'm going to feel as out of place as a goat in a marketplace of prized milking cows." She rose awkwardly from the stool and swished the creases from the intricately embroidered skirt that covered not one, but three, petticoats.

"Nonsense or not, it's what the mayor has asked for. He wants to make a good impression on the High Sheriff. Everyone will be in their finest, not just you. The other girls won't be wasting the opportunity to show themselves off, let me tell you, even if it is from across the hall."

"Aye, that's true," said Kira, as she allowed Agatha to twitch at the pleats of her blouse. "Whereas, having neither brawn, nor beauty, I am fated to remain unattached. The farm lads will ignore me, and the guild boys will not think me decorative enough for their fancy halls, so there is little point, thank the goddess."

Agatha flicked the last fold of material into place and sighed. "Your dark hair and hazel eyes may not make you a dazzler in the traditional sense, but there's a rare beauty in your smile. "Tis a pity you don't use it more often. More importantly, you can dance."

Kira rolled her eyes and turned from the mirror to kiss the little woman behind her. "It doesn't matter anyway. I'd rather be kind than beautiful, and I don't intend to marry for years. If at all." She draped a warm shawl across Agatha's shoulders and linked arms. "Come on. Let's get this over with."

The Great Hall had been transformed. The usually austere oak-panelled walls were festooned with banners representing each of the ten villages in the River Province. Swathes of evergreen and ivy decorated the sills of all the windows and the scent of pine and sandalwood perfumed the air. Three elderly but talented local musicians sat at the back of the stage playing their fiddles loudly enough for people to hear without disturbing their chatter. The decorations and the music lent a festive air to what Kira suspected was going to be a somewhat sombre occasion.

The end of the hall was dominated by an enormous fireplace, which was almost equalled in height by the life-sized portrait of the most revered mayor ever to grace the Great Hall: Augustus Merryman, the man who had persuaded King Raymon to exclude young women who were betrothed from his biennial quota. At the time, the mayor had been derided for his decision to impose yet another restriction on the strict rules of courtship in River Province, but he had saved countless young women from the journey to White Haven and was considered a true visionary.

No one had expected the actions taken to end a war, and eliminate the plague that blighted two kingdoms, would have ongoing repercussions a century later, and so Cabarac was still indebted to the Legion Isles. Peace may have come at a high cost, but Kira wondered why it was that only young women were expected to pay the price.

Kira made the obligatory curtsey before his portrait and made sure Agatha had a seat, before making her way through the rows of chairs and the growing crowd of young ladies to stand with her friends beneath the silver stag banner of River Glen.

"Well met, Kira, you look lovely!"

Kira smiled at her best friend, Giselle, who was indeed the epitome of what a dazzler should be. Her fine, silky hair, the colour of a full moon on a dark night, was piled in curls on top of her head, but still she barely reached Kira's shoulder. Though her hair was fair, her brows and lashes were darker, and she had full lips and a slight upturn to her small nose. Elle, as Kira often called her, was exactly the type of girl the guild boys would be looking for. Kira smiled to herself, for Giselle's sweet expression hid a stubborn streak and a quick wit that may surprise them. Kira had seen those blue eyes flash with fury when she was crossed.

"Well met, Elle, you're looking a little ordinary, I'm afraid. If you don't make more of an effort for the ball, the boys will only be lining up one or two dozen thick to dance with you."

Giselle grinned at her friend as she punched her lightly on the arm. "Your wit is so sharp you might cut your tongue if you're not careful." She twirled as she spoke, and her skirt flared around her ankles, displaying the exquisitely embroidered silver stags chasing each other through golden oak trees.

"Oh, Elle, your skirt is beautiful. You've outdone yourself this time. If your plain face isn't enough to grab attention, then your needlepoint certainly will. Those guild boys will be fighting for a chance to give you a token."

The smile slid from Giselle's face.

"I hope so, Kira. My mother still misses her sister, Cassandra, who was gathered for the quota nearly twenty years ago. It's the not knowing that aches her heart. It's bad enough that women are used as this so-called tithe to the Legion Isles, but no one ever explains why! And why do the women never return?" Giselle took a deep breath, "I'm sorry. We all know that saying, 'as cursed as the Legion Isles', but who is more cursed? Them, or the women sent there? I know we're not supposed to question the need for a quota, but with three sisters behind me, my poor Mother will have to go through this dreadful uncertainty too many times."

Kira squeezed her friend's hand; the quota collection was such a part of life in Cabarac that people rarely challenged it. She was relieved to know that she wasn't the only one who felt bewildered by the need for such a thing, but this wasn't the place to discuss it.

"I understand, but try to think positive. You were offered half a dozen Tokens of Regard at the Midsummer Ball. It bodes well for the Merryman."

Giselle frowned. "Silver does not always guarantee a gold though, does it? I dance well enough, but I'm not as light on my feet as you, and beauty comes second to the dance. I don't know why we need to dance for three nights in a row, anyway. It's too much!"

Kira shrugged. "Tradition, I suppose. The reasons are hidden in the past somewhere. Don't worry, I'll make sure to cure your blisters and I'll give you some salts to soak your feet in each night." She glanced around the hall and spied a group of guild boys looking their way.

"Colac Procter either thinks you are the most beautiful thing he has ever seen or covets your skirt because he thinks you are dressed better than him. I can't quite decide which," said Kira, hoping to lighten her friend's mood.

"Where is he? No, don't look! Is he still looking? We danced well together, but you can't be sure. He also danced well with Freya Sands from Bridgefoot."

"Goddess of Light! Calm down. Yes, he still looks in this direction. Mmm, I think it's your skirt he covets though, judging by that frown on his face."

"Kira! You are such a—"

The strike of a gong reverberated through the hall interrupting what Giselle had been about to say. All the chatter subsided. Kira glanced back at the young men grouped on the other side of the hall. She knew all the boys from River Glen and many from the nearby villages. Freshly bathed and dressed in their finest, with their boots polished so they shone, they had scrubbed up well. As usual, the guild boys, dressed in their more elaborate garb, looked like peacocks in a hen house, but the boys who worked the river or the forest had also made a fine effort. Mayor Harbison would be pleased.

Giselle pushed her into position, and they lined up in single file along the length of the room, while the young men opposite did the same. The gong struck three times, heralding the arrival of the High Sheriff and his guards. Lord Callan made an imposing figure as he strode into the hall. He was younger than Kira had imagined, forty years at most, tall and broad-shouldered. Unlike his guards, he wore no polished breastplate, but a thigh length brocade jacket of deep red, with gold embroidery around the collar and cuff. A lethal looking sword hung from his hips.

Kira studied him with interest. This was not a man to give offence to. His air of authority came not from his sword, or the guards that accompanied him. It emanated from every pore. Within seconds the people in the Great Hall seemed diminished in his presence. Kira had the strange sensation that she was standing on the edge of a precipice. She felt Giselle's fingers brush against hers and gave them a quick squeeze.

Mayor Harbison was out of his depth, and it showed. His face was flushed, and Kira could see droplets of perspiration gathered across his forehead. He clenched the Staff of Office so tightly his knuckles were white. His robes were just a little too long and trailed on the floor, dangerously close to tripping him up. The mayor was a vain little man who didn't want to admit that he was three inches shorter than the previous Mayor, and so had refused to have the robes taken up. He wiped his hand across his forehead and quickly cleaned it down the back of his robe before stepping forward to greet the High Sheriff. His outstretched hand was pointedly ignored. Simply nodding, the black-eyed sheriff said, "Lead on."

This flustered the little mayor even more, and he was completely wrong-footed as Lord Callan swept passed. If not for the mayor's guard grasping his arm he would have fallen to the floor rather than performing a rather comical stagger. It was a measure of the formality of the situation that not one person in the hall laughed.

Lord Callan mounted the stage and began to speak before Mayor Harbison could join him. He wasted no time on pleasantries. "Greetings to the people of River Province. I speak on behalf of the Crown Prince in this matter and would have all here gathered, witness as the Royal Seal is broken."

One of the guards handed him a leather tube from which the High Sheriff pulled a rolled white parchment. Kira could see the seal of red wax at its centre. The Sheriff held the parchment in front of Mayor Harbison.

"Do you witness that this be the Royal Seal?"

The mayor nodded vigorously. "I so witness."

Lord Callan opened the seal with a crack and unfurled the parchment. He cleared his throat and began to read.

"I, Crown Prince Thomac, heir apparent to the Kingdom of Cabarac, do hereby revoke the decree made by my forbear, King Raymon, excluding River Province from fully participating in the biennial quota. It is evident to the Crown that this decree was unduly prejudicial to the other provinces, who have had to shoulder the burden of payments to the Legion Isles for over a century. This is a tithe that should be shared equally. As such, the River Province will participate in the quota, this year and in every subsequent year for the next ten years. Any maid not in possession of a token of betrothal at the end of the Merryman Ball will be sent to White Haven and thence to the Legion Isles. Regardless of this, a minimum of twenty girls will be needed to fill the quota from this day forward. This is my word, and my word is the law."

Lord Callan raised his head and gazed at the crowd. "The decree is signed by His Royal Highness, Crown Prince Thomac. I am here to do his bidding. Let the registration begin."

The silence was as thick as snow and just as cold.

Chapter 6

The fiddle-players broke the awkward, terrible silence with a gentle tune. The melody both soothed and lifted up the spirits as it swirled to each corner of the Great Hall, cloaking the urgency of whispered conversations.

"Well, that's put a hook amongst the fish, hasn't it?" muttered Kira.

"What are you going to do?" Giselle looked up at her friend.

Kira shook her head. "Register like everyone else, I suppose. What choice do I have?" She felt as though someone had slipped a silk scarf around her neck and knotted it tight against her throat. What she had told Tangler was true: she had been too busy with her studies to think about romantic relationships—healing and herblore were far more important than tokens of affection and betrothal promises. Kira had never had to worry about marriage or the quota as healers were customarily exempt from both. Until now.

Local dances were held all year in villages throughout River Province, but it was the four balls heralding the change in seasons which provided the framework for traditional courtship practices. At those balls, young men and women from every village in the province came to River Glen to dance and get to know each other. Silver tokens of regard could be given at any ball to signify interest, but it was only at the Merryman Ball, held at winter solstice, that the gold token of betrothal could be offered. There was little chance of that happening now. She enjoyed dancing as much as anyone but acknowledged that most of the boys would not have considered her as their potential life partner.

Anxiety gnawed at her gut. Even if one of the boys did offer her a token, would it be wise to accept it now, with the threat of a dispatcher in the region? If what Tangler said was true, even healers could be accused of magic and end up in prison. Or worse.

Giselle took her arm and found a gap towards the back of the line-up to register. Kira's thoughts were in turmoil. She was different to the other girls, and not just because she was a healer. Many were fair-haired and blue-eyed like Giselle, although certainly not as beautiful. Some were redheaded and brown-eyed, and others, a mixture of both. It was rare in River Province to see someone with her dark features. And she was tall. Though it was true that she'd had more physical contact with the village boys than most of the other girls—indeed, she had seen quite a few almost naked when she had tended to their wounds—it was not the same as dancing with them, with a view to courtship.

The queue was moving more quickly than she had anticipated, they were almost at the registration table. Kira glanced across to the other side of the Great Hall; the other queue had only five boys left in line. She risked a quick look over her shoulder and estimated at least a dozen girls behind her. The odds were not good.

A quiet sobbing interrupted her thoughts. It appeared Kira was not the only girl upset about having to consider marriage or the quota. The mayor's niece, Jenna, had long felt called to the service of the Goddess of Light and was due to join the order known as the Sisters of the Flame as a novitiate. Jenna had talked about becoming a nun for as long as Kira could remember, and Jenna loved to talk. Growing up, Giselle had often suggested that Jenna should practice her vow of silence, just to give their ears some respite.

"Jenna has been refused permission to enter the order. She is eligible like everyone else," said Giselle under her breath. "If Lord Callan refuses a nun, I don't hold much hope for a healer, do you?"

"No, I do not," replied Kira. Her imaginary silk scarf tightened even more. The front of the queue moved inexorably closer. Giselle registered first. Kira stared at the bent head of the High Sheriff and swallowed.

"Name?"

"Kira of River Glen."

Lord Callan looked up. "No last name?"

Kira shook her head. "I will take the name Stillwater when my grandmother passes on."

Lord Callan nodded and wrote her name. Kira was thankful that he was familiar with the custom, and she did not need to explain that her mother had died giving birth, and that she had no father's name to claim.

"Kira is our local healer, Lord Callan," said Mayor Harbison, who was hovering behind the High Sheriff's shoulder.

"Healer? Indeed? You are young for such a thing, are you not?"

Kira bowed her head and chose her words carefully. "Yes, My Lord. Agatha, my grandmother, is teaching me. I am still learning."

"You are too modest, Kira," interrupted the mayor. "She's one of the best healers River Glen has ever had. It would be a pity to lose such a talent to the quota."

Lord Callan placed the quill in the ink pot with care, then cracked his knuckles. Kira watched as the colour drained from the little mayor's face. The sheriff looked Kira in the eye and said dryly, "Then she had better hope she gets an offer of marriage, hadn't she."

"**E**dalyn's Flame! I thought the High Sheriff was going to punch the mayor right in his interfering little nose," exclaimed Giselle as they waited for the final tally. "He'd already tried to plead Jenna's case and got knocked back. Why on earth would he risk Lord Callan's wrath and ask again? Is he witless?"

"Lord Callan does not strike me as a man set to brawling with minor dignitaries, Elle. I think he is cold and calculating, not someone who would let his temper rule his good sense."

The gong sounded before Giselle could reply. The room was silent before the reverberation had reached the end of the hall. Once again, the High Sheriff took to the stage.

"Registration in River Province is complete. There are one hundred and seventeen unmarried males over the age of eighteen and one hundred and thirty-two females. This means that at least fifteen girls will not be offered betrothal. As per the Crown Prince's decree, another five will be needed to fill the quota." He paused and looked to every corner of the hall.

"The Merryman Ball will be held in two weeks and will take place over three nights as usual. I will say this to the boys—there is no expectation on you to Promise. This is a matter for you to decide. If you do not feel ready, then do not offer a Token. This is how it has always been, and it should be no different now. Betrothal is a serious matter and marriage is for life. Broken promises are not tolerated, so you must be sure in your affection.

To the girls I say this: the tithe you may have to pay is an honourable one. The Legion Isles have suffered much in bringing peace to our land, and the quota is the only way we can repay their sacrifice. I will return in two weeks to oversee this matter and escort the quota to White Haven the day after the Ball."

He nodded once to the mayor and bowed low to the crowd before saluting.

"Peace be with you."

"Or else the land shall suffer," the villagers murmured in reply.

The silence lasted only until the door closed behind Lord Callan, then the hall erupted.

"I've got to find Agatha," Kira said to Giselle. "I'll speak to you tomorrow." She hugged her friend and made her way through the crowd of increasingly angry and vocal villagers to find her grandmother. Agatha wiped her eyes and blew her nose as Kira approached. Agatha was more vulnerable than she allowed others to see, and it was rare for her to show distress publicly. Kira felt a jolt of dismay. She rearranged the shawl across Agatha's shoulders and took her arm. "Come on, Gran, let's go home."

Agatha raged about the Crown Prince and Lord Callan and what she would like to do to them most of the way home. Kira longed for silence to think, but she knew her grandmother needed to vent her wrath, so she pretended to listen, nodding and saying "Mm" now and then.

Her thoughts darted about like fish in a stream. What was she to do? Agatha was in her winter years, and while not exactly feeble, a recent illness had shown Kira that her grandmother was more frail than she appeared. Who would look after her if Kira was sent away? Would she get a token? Did she even want one? She would have to dance better than most of the other girls to have a chance. How would the village manage without a healer? How would Agatha manage without her? There was one question she dared not think about, because the answer filled her with dread. What happened to the girls in the quota when they reached the Legion Isles? No one seemed to know, or if they did, they certainly never told.

Chapter 7

Kira ran her fingers back and forth over the soft fabric of the shawl, soothing her nerves with the repetitive movement. The herbal was wrapped inside, its weight heavy on her lap. She arranged herself more comfortably in the bed and contemplated her options. She was reluctant to open the book again, but she needed something to take her mind off the ball. The first night had been enjoyable—every dance was progressive so that each girl had a chance to perform with a different partner. By the end of the evening, she had danced with all the boys at least once and she had learned two things: she was taller than half the boys there, and she wasn't attracted to any of them. The second evening had been enjoyable in a different way. The first few dances had again been progressive, but the others were by invitation, and Kira was twice surprised—firstly that she had danced all but one, and secondly that she had been offered two silver tokens.

Her fingers worried at the edge of the shawl. Giselle was right— silvers did not mean a gold would be offered, only that the boy was interested. Such a strange concept, but it was the way courtship had always been done, and for the most part it seemed to work. Marriages built on foundations established at the dance lasted the longest. That was her dilemma now. She had always believed that tokens were generally given because there was at least a spark of attraction between a couple, a glimmer of possibility for a future together, but in her case she wasn't so sure. The first one had come from the woodcutter's son who, though an excellent dancer, was otherwise clumsy and whose cuts and bruises she had tended more often than she cared to remember. He had talked less of any future they may have together and more of how important it was to keep a healer such as herself in the village.

The other was from Owen, Jacob's son, also a wonderful dancer, but who was so painfully shy that he had barely spoken. What little he had communicated made her feel as though he was only offering the token as his thanks for caring for Isaac. While she was grateful to both, she wondered if either really saw the woman behind the healer, and what confused her even more, was why it should suddenly matter.

Under different circumstances, if it meant she could stay in River Glen, she would accept a gold token from either of them, and do everything she could to make the marriage succeed, but another problem loomed. One that Kira was reluctant to even contemplate, despite it overshadowing everything else. The dispatcher had been seen in another village. The Eiran was strong in her and if Piscator was persecuting healers for their gift, would it be fair to put another person in danger? Kira sighed. She wouldn't have had to worry about this at all if the Crown Prince hadn't made that stupid decree!

Her hands slid the shawl from the herbal and Kira was again struck by the sense of recognition she felt when the leather touched her palms. She undid the cords and ran a fingertip across the embossed feathers. The book shuddered in her hands, and startled by the sensation, she dropped it in her lap. A waft of cool mountain air caressed her face, and she was momentarily blinded by a golden flash of light. She blinked and watched, astounded, as a bright red feather drifted in front of her to land gently on the open page. Despite the warning prickle of her scalp, Kira could not look away. She was mesmerised by the detail in the painting. Two birds faced each other mid-air, one gold, one red. The long tail feathers swirled down the page and entwined and changed to flame as the feathers touched. Each held a black, taloned claw towards the other, but the glint in their eyes hinted at desire, not battle. She stared at the words written beneath the flaming feathers.

Vemaerisi or Fire Birds.

Kira shivered as she experienced a peculiar sense of disorientation. Books referencing the rare and beautiful creatures had been destroyed a century ago because the fire birds were both magical and dragon kin. The birds had been relegated to creatures of myth and rarely spoken of—few people knew or even cared that the Vemaerisi had ever existed. Indeed, Kira had only heard of them because of a fairy tale that Tangler told her, and yet looking at them now, they felt as familiar as the robin redbreast chirping outside her window. She knew why: they were the birds in the strange dreams she'd had after she had opened the herbal. What she didn't know was why the book had opened to this very page or why this strange feather had suddenly appeared. If she read further, if she turned the page or touched the feather, what might she discover? Could it really have something to do with…*magic*? She nibbled the inside of her lip as she considered the implications. What would happen to her if Piscator ever found out? Caution battled curiosity and lost.

The feather covered the writing on the opposite page. Kira reached her fingers towards it and hesitated. *Goddess! It's only a feather*, she scolded herself, but was still reluctant to touch it. She blew on it gently instead and it drifted onto the bedclothes. Nothing happened, and she laughed at herself. *Idiot!* As she read Gwyneth's beautiful script, her heart began to race. Not only had the magical fire birds actually existed, they had once nested in the mountains that surrounded River Glen, and according to Gwyneth, had shared a special bond with the villagers. Indeed, the courtship customs that the villagers followed were in some way connected to the mating ritual of the Vemaerisi. Kira was stunned. Was it true? She tried to turn the page to read more, but the herbal frustrated her attempts. Kira groaned. Damned book. Why give her only half a secret?

She reached for the feather and picked it up gently by the quill. A breast feather, she surmised, as she compared it to the painting of the magnificent birds. She ran her fingertip across the velvety softness of the vane and was startled to find that the feather changed from red to gold. It was too much. A hundred-year-old feather, still intact and able to change colour. She was filled with a sudden sense of dread as reality hit. Magic again. She dropped the feather back onto the page and closed the book with a snap. Once again the herbal was relegated to the bottom of the old travel bag.

As she dressed for the Merryman Ball that evening, Kira chose the same green skirt and pleated blouse that she had for registration. The previous two nights she had worn her best healer's robes and cinched them at the waist with a wide belt embroidered with wildflowers. Agatha had braided her hair in the elaborate style expected for the dance, but tonight Kira had chosen a simple hairstyle that started as tiny braids around her face before joining at the nape of her neck to form a thick plait that reached almost to her waist. Agatha didn't argue. Kira suspected her grandmother was putting her disgruntled mood down to nerves and decided not to enlighten her. Not only was she worried about the ball and the dispatcher, but now that damned herbal as well.

Agatha had baked a fish pie for the supper that would be shared by everyone at the halfway break, and the tantalising aroma was making Kira's stomach growl.

"There's some pie filling left over if you're hungry," said Agatha as she picked up Kira's satchel and slipped it over her shoulder. With Kira dancing each night she had taken on the responsibility of healer at the Ball.

"No thank you. I'm too nervous to eat. Besides, I had some cheese and bread not that long ago."

"Have you decided—" began Agatha.

"No," Kira interrupted, more harshly than she had intended. "Sorry. No. I don't want to count my chickens. Let's just see what happens tonight." She wrapped her shawl over her shoulders and placed the pie in a basket. "If you're ready, we may as well get going."

Once again the Great Hall was beautifully decorated. The evergreen and ivy that surrounded the windows were threaded with rust-coloured giddy-leaf and fragrant, orange flowering ginger. Circlets of wildflowers decorated the walls in tones of lavender and blue, but Kira hardly noticed—except for the violet-blue flowers on the bracts of hyssop which perfumed the air with a peppermint scent when she brushed passed the foliage.

Agatha took the basket from her and patted her arm. "Go and find Giselle. I'll put this on the table and find a seat with my friends. And don't look so serious! Try to smile."

Kira nodded. "Yes, Gran."

Giselle was beaming when Kira found her.

"Well met, Kira!" she said and grabbed Kira by the arm, pulling her closer to the wall.

"Well met, Elle. Why the glum face?" she teased.

Giselle's grin got even wider. She beckoned Kira close. "Colac Procter just asked me to keep the last dance for him. He's going to offer a gold! I'm happy and excited, and just so relieved!"

Kira embraced her friend. "Elle, that's wonderful. And I'm happy for you, too. He must really be keen to show his hand so early."

Giselle bounced up and down on her toes. "Yes! He saw that Ewan Rochester gave me a silver last night and wanted to make sure I knew his intentions before Ewan had a chance."

"Ewan is a fine boy, too. I thought you danced well together."

"We did, and he is lovely," Giselle admitted, "but Colac's family are Masters in the Tailor's Guild, and I would have a lifetime's supply of beautiful materials and threads. Colac was rather impressed with my needlework, and our common interest in sewing and tailoring is just as important as developing an affection for one another."

Kira agreed and hugged her friend again. At least one of them had a secure future. Giselle had a rare talent for needlework and her skills were in high demand. She released Giselle from her embrace as Jenna and some other girls from the village joined them.

"Not a word," whispered Giselle.

The chatter washed over Kira as the musicians began to tune their instruments. Tangler had been correct: the groups' reputation was well deserved. The troubadours were dressed in elaborate performance gear, the bright colours rivalling the guild boys, but rather than embroidered vests, they wore leather jerkins. Unlike village boys, minstrels were in service to their art until they were twenty-five years of age, and it was highly unusual for them to pledge to marry before then. Life on the road was difficult for a single man, and doubly so for a family with no regular income. Despite the uncertain life, musicians and entertainers were well respected if they had a talent and welcomed into villages throughout the Kingdom.

Kira knew that Tangler performed all over Cabarac for both princes and paupers, without fear or favour. Travelling minstrels had a strange sort of prestige—no nobleman wanted to get on the wrong side of a bard for fear of his reputation being besmirched across the length and breadth of the country. Minstrels kept the villagers informed about what was going on in other provinces, as well as the capital Shardial, and usually without the bias that came from the Crown's official messengers.

What would it be like, she mused, to have the freedom to travel throughout Cabarac doing something you loved? For the first time in her life, Kira was conscious of the possibility of a very different future to the one she had imagined would be hers. Was she to be betrothed to a man she barely knew and had no feelings for? Or worse, sent to the Legion Isles for Goddess-knows-what. She didn't even want to contemplate an encounter with the dispatcher. Oh, to be a troubadour, she thought wryly.

There were six talented musicians in this particular troupe who called themselves the Rainbow's End. The lead vocalist was tall and blonde-haired. He had a rich tenor voice and a comic wit about him. Some of the verses in 'The Ballad of the Royal Fishing Line' were perilously close to scandalous, but sung with such humour and charm that the poison was sucked from the sting. He was a skilful mandolin player as well. There were two brothers, alike enough to be twins, with red hair and even redder beards. They played both zink and gemshorn with such wonderful harmonies it sounded like angels singing, and played the fiddle with equal skill.

The other minstrels were also excellent singers. There was a drummer, who sometimes played the harp, a bald-headed lute player with a long, plaited beard, and a tall man who played only the finger cymbals but danced and somersaulted his way around the stage with an easy grace.

The good-looking mandolin player looked up from adjusting the strings of his instrument and winked. Kira blushed and bent her head. She had caught him watching her several times over the past two nights, but musicians were notorious flirts and had a reputation for being fickle with their affections. She glanced at him from beneath her lashes, but he had already shifted his attention and was blowing a kiss to Giselle. *Typical.*

They certainly knew how to play a tune though, Kira had to grant them that. Even the traditional melodies they played had extra flourishes, and the harmonies when they sang had been wonderful. She decided that no matter what happened tonight, she would enjoy the music and make the most of the dance. It might be the last time.

The chatter around her dwindled to silence and Kira became aware of the sound of footsteps behind her. She turned to see Lord Callan approach. He stopped and bowed. Kira was almost too surprised to reciprocate, but remembering her manners just in time, she dropped a curtsy.

"Kira," he said, eyes narrowed in an assessing stare.

"Lord Callan." Kira clasped her hands in front of her and looked at his boots.

"My wife and son have not long arrived, and the boy is unwell. I would ask that you call and see him in the half-way break. If you would be so kind."

Kira looked up. "Certainly, Lord Callan. I can go to see him now if he is sick. I don't mind."

Lord Callan smiled briefly. "There is no need. The break will do. My guard will let me know if his condition worsens. Enjoy the dance. I would not rob you of the opportunity to receive a token." He touched a finger to his forehead and strode across the hall to join Mayor Harbison at the mayoral table.

Giselle hurried to her side. "Is all well?"

"Yes, fine," Kira said with a nod. "Save me a plate of food in the break, if you don't mind. Lord Callan would have me check on his son. Hopefully it's little more than a chill."

Owen Fishlock linked arms with Kira and danced her through the complex steps of the Fisherman's Net, a lively reel, with eight pairs of dancers in each formation. Faster and faster they twirled, until the hall blurred. Owen was a good dancer, though, and made sure she kept her feet. As the foot-stomping climax of the dance ended to thunderous applause, Kira clung to his shoulder, breathless and exhilarated and waiting for the room to stop spinning.

Before they could move, the doors of the Great Hall were flung open and a dozen soldiers marched in. From her position beneath Mayor Merryman's portrait, Kira saw Lord Callan's guards spring to attention in their various vantage spots around the hall. Lord Callan rose to his feet as the applause stuttered to silence. He flicked his fingers behind his back as he straightened, and Kira noticed that the guards who saw his hidden command repeated the gesture so quickly that if Kira hadn't been watching closely, she doubted she would have seen it. Soon all his men were on high alert.

Lord Callan, however, seemed unperturbed. He strode to the centre of the dance floor and waited. Owen grasped Kira's hand and pulled her back to the side of the hall. The soldiers continued their slow march until they stopped about ten paces from the High Sheriff.

A black-robed figure materialised from the centre of the column of soldiers looking, thought Kira, like a shadow without a body. Not an ounce of flesh was visible, and even as he moved towards the High Sheriff, he seemed to float rather than walk.

"Dispatcher Piscator, I presume," Lord Callan said dryly.

Kira went cold.

Chapter 8

The shadow drifted close to Lord Callan and spoke so softly that it was impossible for anyone but the High Sheriff to hear. Whatever was said obviously displeased Lord Callan, as his head jerked back, and his sword hand twitched.

"Now? You want to do this now?" he hissed. "This is selection for the quota, not some—"

Lord Callan stopped speaking as a thin, bony hand reached out and touched his tunic, and Piscator whispered again.

"Very well. But make it quick." He stepped back from the dispatcher and bowed. His fingers flicked again, and Kira saw the guard closest to the door slip out.

"Apologies to the people of River Province. The Merryman Dance will be interrupted momentarily while Dispatcher Piscator examines the participants for signs of magic. Young ladies, please line up on this side of the hall. Gentlemen on the other." He turned to the table he had just vacated. "Mayor Harbison, perhaps you could join us?"

A murmur of concern rippled through the crowd. Owen touched her arm and whispered, "Take care."

As Giselle took her place next to Kira, she let out a gasp. The last soldier held the chain of a barrel-chested stag hound with some difficulty. Giselle had been terrified of large dogs ever since she had been attacked by one as a child. Kira reached for her shoulder and gave a reassuring squeeze. "Remember to breathe." She thought that perhaps she should take her own advice and took some calming breaths of her own.

Kira scanned the villagers for Agatha as the little mayor walked reluctantly across the floor but couldn't see her. She longed to use mind-speech but dared not. If Piscator somehow sensed the use of the Eiran, she would put them both in danger.

The soldier brought the hound to the dispatcher and handed him the chain. The dog immediately stopped straining at its bonds and sat at Piscator's feet. Lord Callan strode to the end of the line. "Come, Piscator. Let's get this done so the people of River Province can continue their festivities."

Piscator strolled down the line of young women, inspecting them with the intensity of a chief cook at a fish market. Occasionally, he fingered a silver pendant that hung from a long chain around his neck. Kira ran her tongue over dry lips. The hound put its nose to the floor and began sniffing around the skirts of the first girls in line. Soon its sniffing intensified and then the dog growled threateningly at a sweet girl Kira knew slightly from a neighbouring village. Her father raised pigs and there was always a faint aroma of cured ham around her. The dog raised up on its hind legs and barked aggressively. The girl stumbled back and began to cry.

Piscator clicked his fingers and the dog sat. He motioned to the High Sheriff and whispered something.

"Mayor," said the Sheriff, his voice timbred with irritation. "Piscator informs me his hound smells magic on this girl. Did you think it would not notice such a thing?"

There was no way to answer such a question. The mayor bowed low, beads of sweat forming on his brow. The dispatcher placed his hands on either side of the girl's head, then pulled them back as if scalded. Two of his soldiers immediately stepped forward and grabbed the terrified girl to drag her away, as her plaintive wail of denial echoed around the hall.

Kira was horrified. Was no one going to help her? Where was her family? A tide of righteous indignation rose to her throat, and she clenched her teeth at the injustice of the man. There was not an ounce of magic in that girl. How could he not know she was innocent? She took a deep breath. "But—"

Say nothing! The warning rang in her mind as loudly as if someone had yelled from across the room. Kira was startled into silence. Only she and Agatha used mind-speech and never had she heard it so loud or so clear. Who had spoken? Would Piscator sense the Eiran and think it magic?

She had no chance to ponder that thought as the dispatcher and his hound drew closer. She could feel the perspiration gather at the back of her neck and concentrated on slowing her breathing. The hound stopped in front of her and Giselle, and began to sniff at Giselle's skirts. Piscator's face was shadowed by his hood, but his breath was foul, as though he had a rotten tooth. The dog growled deep in its throat. She could feel Giselle trembling beside her and prayed she would hold her nerve. The dog growled again and tensed its muscles. Kira used her awareness instinctively.

Hush now.

The hound whined softly and sat at her feet. For a panicked moment, Kira wondered if she had spoken the words out loud. Goddess of Light, Goddess of Light, Goddess of Light, she was so frightened she couldn't think of the words that came next. The High Sheriff turned to the guard that had materialised at his shoulder. He was taller and even more broad across the shoulders than Lord Callan. Kira was sure he was the guard who had left the hall earlier. As they spoke the dispatcher focussed his attention on Kira. The dog lay happily at her feet. He clutched at the silver medallion hanging round his neck. Kira caught a quick glance of the unusual black stone at its centre before it was covered by his nail-bitten fingers.

"Who is this?" he hissed.

"K…K…Kira," stammered Mayor Harbison.

"She is the local healer, Piscator, and I have just been informed that my wife needs her services." Lord Callan turned to his guard and nodded. "Take her to Lady Lydia."

The guard saluted and reached for Kira's arm. The staghound leapt to its feet and snarled, teeth bared.

"Call off your hound, Piscator. If my man gets so much as a scratch, the animal will taste the steel of my sword."

Kira was bustled away by the guard, so she couldn't hear what else was said. She looked around the hall frantically. Where was her grandmother?

Agatha was waiting at the door. She thrust Kira's leather satchel and a cloak into Kira's hand as she was hurried out of the hall. Kira had no idea how Agatha knew she had need of her satchel but was relieved to have it in her possession.

"Thank you!" Kira held up the bag. "My healer's herbs," she said to the guard by way of explanation.

Be wary, child, warned Agatha in her mind. *Be wary.*

The night air hit like a snowball to the face after the warmth of the hall. Kira struggled to hold the satchel and pull on the cloak as she was marched rapidly in the darkness. She caught the toe of her boot on the edge of the path and stumbled. The guard shot out a well-muscled arm to stop her from falling.

"Oof," she gasped. "Thank you." It was like being saved by the limb of a tree. She wondered if the ground might have been softer.

The guard made a non-committal noise in the back of his throat that sounded like a cross between a sigh and a growl. He took hold of her elbow and urged her forward with the pressure of his fingers. Kira had to trot to keep up with his long-legged stride, but fortunately the inn was only a few minutes up the road.

Once inside, he directed her to a flight of stairs, releasing her elbow to propel her up the steps with his hand on the small of her back until they reached the landing. There was a single door and he rapped three times with his fist before stepping back and standing at attention. The maid opened the door and gave a little squeak. "Flame it, Ned. You fill up a doorway like no other!"

The guard bowed. "Your pardon. I bring the healer for Lady Lydia."

Kira was taken aback. His voice was deep and surprisingly cultured. He beckoned her forward and closed the door behind her. The maid took her cloak and hung it from a hook on the back of the door.

"The healer's here, M'lady."

"Lady Lydia?" The room was dimly lit, and Kira hesitated.

"Come in, please. What is your name?" A thin, pale-faced woman rose from a stool by the fire, and even in the flickering candlelight Kira could see her eyes were bleary and red-rimmed from lack of sleep.

Kira bowed her head. "I'm Kira, M'lady. Lord Callan sent me."

"Oh, thank the Goddess!" The woman beckoned to Kira. "Please, help my son. I think he's dying."

A child of about seven was curled up on a small cot near the hearth. Kira leaned over and stroked his cheek. It was cold and clammy despite his proximity to the fire. His breathing was shallow and laboured. Lady Lydia was right to be concerned.

"What happened?" Kira opened her satchel and searched through the contents.

"He fell off his pony four days ago. Landed on a log. I just thought he'd bruised his ribs, but yesterday he came down with a fever. Tonight, he's so cold. He's sleeping all the time. I'm afraid he won't wake up. Please help him." The woman started to weep.

"Bring the lamp closer, please. I need more light."

A cold draft swept around the room as the door opened again. Kira glanced up from her examination of the boy and was surprised to see Lord Callan. She could hear the heaviness of his breaths and wondered if he had run all the way from the hall.

Kira pulled down the blankets and began to lift the boy's undershirt. A calloused hand grabbed her wrist and twisted. A spasm of pain shot along her arm to her elbow.

"You can heal him?" Lord Callan asked gruffly.

"He is gravely ill, My Lord. I fear the angel hovers."

"The mayor says you are the best healer he has ever seen. That must mean the Eiran is strong in you. Is it so?"

Kira heard the desperation in his voice and knew that the High Sheriff loved his son. But Piscator was in the hall this very minute, checking people for magic. If she admitted to an ability the dispatcher had persecuted healers for having, would Lord Callan hand her over? She could be dragged off to who knows where, like that poor pig farmer's daughter. Kira hesitated only briefly; the first rule of healing was to do no harm. If she denied she had the Eiran, the boy would surely suffer. She glanced up at Lord Callan and saw the fear in his eyes.

Kira nodded. "It is so, My Lord."

He let go of her wrist and brought his hand to his heart. "Save my son and I will not speak of it again. You will be protected from the quota. Do what you need to do."

The sheriff strode to the window and deliberately turned his back. Kira lifted the boy's shirt again.

A dark purple stain blossomed over most of his lower back. He made no sound as she rolled him gently from his side to his back. She placed her cheek on the boy's chest and listened to the uneven stutter of his heart. Herbs alone would not save this child. He would be dead before morning if she did not call the Eiran. Kira hesitated. She had never tried to heal someone this close to death and this young. What if her healer's gift wasn't as good as Agatha said it was and the boy died anyway? And if she did use the Eiran and healed the child, would the High Sheriff keep his word? Agatha's warning rang in her ears, but no matter the danger, she could not let a child die. Even one belonging to the High Sheriff.

"Fill three bowls with hot water from the fire kettle." She handed Lady Lydia three small bags of dried herbs. "Finger balm, birch, and chamomile. Sprinkle a thimbleful of one in each bowl. You must stir them gently, never let the water still. And I will need an empty bucket."

Kira rubbed her hands with a salve of comfrey leaves and Lady's mantle, then rested her palms lightly over the bruise, hoping the chore she had given to Lady Lydia would divert her attention. She closed her eyes, concentrated her will on the heat from the fire, and gathered the energy. Kira focused her awareness on the child and let the heat flow gently from her fingers. The healing warmth spread like molten gold. In the corner of her mind room, Kira conjured the silver thread, just as

Agatha had shown her, and secured it to her awareness so she could find her way back. She allowed her awareness to follow the heat as it seeped through the boy's bruised skin, soothing his aching muscles.

She moved cautiously through a red mist, and into the pool of dark blood that was causing the pressure on his lungs, searching for the leaking blood vessel deep in his chest. She used her awareness like a sponge to absorb the blood and was able to see the tear in the vein. Delicately, she wrapped a gossamer thread around the tear and willed it to seal.

A splinter of bone protruded from the muscle between his ribs. She eased it from the festering mess, absorbed the pus and macerated flesh, and then seared the wound. Two of his ribs were cracked, but the bones had not been displaced, so Kira wove a web of gossamer around them to help them mend and reduce the inflammation in the muscle. Slowly she withdrew her awareness, taking care to check for any damage she may have missed. Though the healing had taken only about twenty minutes, it felt more like three hours to Kira and the fatigue was instantaneous.

Opening her eyes, Kira immediately felt ill. "Bucket!" she gasped, and purged the contents of her stomach into the vessel. She passed the bloody, purulent mess she had absorbed from the boy's injury to the shocked maid. "Best throw it on the fire."

She checked the sleeping boy in front of her. Already his colour was better, and his breathing easier.

"Sponge the finger balm over his bruising morning and night. Give him sips of birch water every couple of hours for the next few days. It will help his pain and keep his fever down." Her voice croaked with exhaustion.

"And the chamomile?"

Kira took the bowl. "That's for me." She swallowed the tea in one long draught.

Lydia grabbed her in a fierce embrace. "Thank you. With all my heart I thank you. We are forever in your debt, Kira of River Glen."

She risked a glance at the High Sheriff. He was standing stiff-backed, still facing the window. But Kira saw the tremble in his shoulders and his hand wipe his eyes in the reflection from the glass. She tiptoed quickly across the room, averting her gaze, certain the man would not appreciate her witnessing any show of vulnerability.

The door flung open as her hand reached for her cloak and the dispatcher strode into the room, effectively blocking her exit. Kira took a step sideways and lowered her head.

"Most people knock before entering, Piscator." The High Sheriff turned to look at the dispatcher. The colour was high in his cheeks, but his tone was mild.

"Forgive me, My Lord," said Piscator, "but I am not 'most people'."

Kira was surprised at the raspy quality of the dispatcher's voice. It was like a boy on the edge of puberty whose voice had not quite broken. She kept her gaze on the floor and tried to ignore the headache that was beginning to form behind her eyes.

"Indeed," said Lord Callan. "What do you want, Piscator?"

"Not *what*. *Who*. I want *her*," he rasped.

Kira's head snapped up at that.

"I see. And why do you want this girl?"

"Magic."

Kira felt her stomach clench and prayed the chamomile tea would stay put. Lord Callan finally moved from the window to stand next to his wife, pausing only to throw another log on the fire.

"Explain yourself, man. I am sick of trying to drag information out of you one syllable at a time." The High Sheriff had not raised his voice or changed his tone from one of mild boredom since the dispatcher had entered the room, but Kira could sense the anger coming off him in waves and wondered if it was as obvious to the others, or whether it was just due to her heightened perception. From Piscator she sensed nothing but an unsettling black emptiness.

"The hound sensed something about her. I can smell magic in this very room."

"You are mistaken," said Lady Lydia with a calm strength. "She is a simple healer who came to look at Mica. She rubbed some salve on his ribs and prepared a couple of herbal remedies for me to use. No doubt that's what you can smell."

Kira heard the dispatcher's sharp intake of breath.

"I am rarely mistaken, Mistress. You will forgive me if I do not simply take your word in this matter. I will test the girl for myself."

The High Sheriff touched his wife lightly on her arm to forestall her reply.

"And my word, Piscator?"

"Many people have given their word, My Lord. As much as I would like to take yours, I am beholden to the Crown to eradicate magic. How could I be sure that the girl has not bewitched you into believing that she has no magic if I did not test and find out? If she is devoid of power, she has nothing to lose. And nor do you."

Kira felt the sweat gather at the back of her neck and quickly opened the door to her mind room. She stowed the memory of what she had just done into her secret hiding place and prayed that since Agatha had never been able to find it, Piscator wouldn't either if he probed her mind that far. The thought of him delving into her most private thoughts sickened her. Kira raised her chin and looked at the dispatcher. "I have no magic but my healer's gift, sir."

Piscator snorted.

"There are some women who claim the Eiran is a divine power bestowed by God himself. Yet many loyal to the Crown believe it is a remnant of old magic, that healers risk bringing back the sorcerous plague that caused the near destruction of Cabarac. What say you, Kira of River Glen?"

Kira knew she was between a rock and a hard place and chose her words carefully. Not only was the dispatcher fanatical about the eradication of magic, it seemed, but his use of the masculine deity rather than the Goddess told her he was a follower of the Vengeful God.

"Sir, I will leave it to you to decide. I would deny that my talent is one of magic, but neither would I claim to be blessed by the hand of the divine. All I know is that my grandmother's grandmother was a healer, as is she, and like my maternal forebears I am also graced with the ability to heal."

"Hah! We shall see." If Piscator was offended by her remark, Kira was unable to tell from his expression, still shadowed by the cowl of his hood. His tone of voice was dulled by the reediness of his speech and Kira tried not to grimace at the scent of his foul breath. She was starting to feel light-headed. She needed another draught of chamomile tea, some nourishing food, and a short nap to restore her balance after the healing.

Piscator placed his hands on top of her head. Kira stilled a small shudder of revulsion. With her senses still open and on high alert, she could feel the innate wickedness of the man and the malevolence he felt towards not just magic but women in general. Instinctively she opened the door to the room in her mind and retreated her awareness to the far corner. His energy hovered in the doorway, but made no move to follow, and Kira realised with a shock that the dispatcher had very little power of his own. Piscator was just a woman-hating fanatic with a dangerous obsession for ridding the world of magic. It seemed the dog and his laying on of hands were little more than theatre.

But then Piscator dropped one hand and clutched at his medallion. Kira felt a peculiar flicker of energy brush her awareness, and the room began to spin. Piscator swore underneath his foul breath. "Dragon's blood!"

Kira heard him call to the High Sheriff. "This woman has magic. Arrest her!"

The curtains closed and the room went black.

Chapter 9

Kira woke to the smell of fresh hay and stale vomit. A pale light angled through the bars of a small window, and from the cold and the quiet she guessed it was early morning. Her hip and shoulder ached. Her hands were frozen, and she couldn't even feel her feet. She peered around groggily. A massive oak door with a square of steel bars confirmed it. She was in prison. She had vague recollections of being deposited none too gently on the floor of the cell, then someone had tossed a blanket over her. She was about to ease herself up onto one elbow when she heard the small iron grate behind the bars of the door slide open. She closed her eyes and lay still.

"The witch still sleeps?" Piscator's reedy voice floated through the bars.

"Out like a light."

"Good. Put one of our men on guard, Scarrow. That local prison guard is not to be trusted, even if he could be found." Kira could hear the fury in his tone and dared not move. "No one is to be admitted until I return. No one."

The grate slammed shut. Kira lay quiet and tried to take stock of what was happening. She was thankful that though her thoughts were foggy, her head no longer throbbed. The healing had taken more energy than she had been prepared for, and not being able to replenish her stores with tea and something nourishing to eat had allowed the inevitable migraine.

She hoped young Mica had survived the night. The dispatcher had accused her of using magic, she remembered that much. She brought her fingertips to her forehead and rubbed her brow. Was it true? Was her gift more than just the Eiran? If it had helped her to save a life, then surely magic was a good thing.

Kira eased herself up and tried to massage some feeling into her numb toes. The blanket was too thin to provide much comfort. She pulled her cloak around her shoulders and blew into her cupped hands. The warmth of her breath was welcome but fleeting. Thoughts chased themselves around her head like leaves caught in a drain. Where was Agatha? Was her grandmother safe? Did she know what had happened?

Agatha? Kira tried to reach out with mind speech, but she knew from experience that unless her grandmother was within earshot of normal talk, it was useless.

She thought of the stronger voice that had entered her mind last night to warn her at the dance. Who had it been? So much had happened in the last few hours, she hadn't given the voice a second thought. There were no other healers in River Glen, so where had it come from?

Now was not the time to dwell on it, she realised, as the tread of boots on the flagstone floor interrupted her thoughts. Kira scrambled backwards so her back was against the wall and drew her cloak around her, heart pounding. The key jangled in the lock and the door swung open with a creak.

"Kira?" Lydia's voice was gentle in its enquiry.

Kira looked up with a start. "My Lady? Is Mica well? How does he fare?"

"Yes, Kira. He is more than well, thanks to you. But you are in grave danger because of your blessed skills. Lord Callan argued strongly on your behalf with that abominable dispatcher, but Piscator thinks himself above the law. My husband despises him. If he argued too much in your favour, Piscator would have thrown accusations that he was sympathetic to the use of magic, or that you had bewitched him. The dispatcher is a dangerous enemy to make in these times. Though we all swore that we had not seen any sign of magic, Piscator was adamant. Even when the Lord Mayor and your grandmother spoke on your behalf he would not listen. I'm so sorry, Kira. He would see you burn."

Kira's headache returned with a vengeance. She stared at Lydia. "Burn?"

"Not if we can help it. I know Lord Callan granted you release from the quota, but it will be your only means of escape. You must come with me now. There's no time to waste. We have only minutes before the guard returns. Take off your clothes. Quick as you can."

Kira felt as though she was moving through deep water. Her limbs were slow and heavy. Lydia pulled the cloak from her grasp and tossed it onto the straw. Her beautiful skirt followed and then her blouse, and with it, the sour smell of vomit.

"Make haste, Kira. Put these on." She thrust a pair of wide-legged travelling breeches, a shirt and a thigh-length tunic at Kira, and as the girl dressed, piled up the straw into a vague body-like shape and covered it with the discarded clothes and blanket. Lydia threw a thick blue travelling cloak over Kira's shoulders and pulled up the hood. "You'll find a belt in your bag with your other clothes. Follow me!"

The urgency of Lydia's whispered commands finally penetrated the haze that had been clouding her thoughts. She fastened the clasp of the cloak at her neck and followed. Lydia locked the door and hung the keys back on a hook above a small table and an empty chair. A small lantern glowed on the centre of the table, casting enough light for Kira to see her satchel and a travelling bag on the ground beneath.

"Get your bags," said Lydia as she grabbed the lantern. "This way. Piscator's man will return soon. I must get you to the carriages and return to the room to check on Mica. Lord Callan will escort the quota to White Haven. Mica and I will travel to Prince Rhicard's court tomorrow."

"What of Piscator?"

"He prepares to leave as we speak and will return in a few days with the brazen dragon. He was in a fine temper this morning; something raised his ire, but I don't know what. It has worked in our favour as he will be nowhere near the town square as the quota leave. We can only hope you will be halfway to White Haven and safe before he discovers you are gone, and he will never suspect you left with the quota."

Kira followed Lydia along a dark passage. She felt as though she had ridden the River Ryder down Traitor's falls in a rudderless boat and was now caught in the rapids below. She had no sooner evaded one rock when another loomed in its place. She was not sure 'safe' was the word she would have chosen.

"Agatha?"

"Your grandmother sends her love and her blessings. But for her safety and yours she must not be seen near the quota carriages. One of the dispatcher guards watches her cottage. No one can know where you are until you are far from here. You did not receive a Token last night, so the other girls in the quota will not be surprised to see you in the carriage, but you must stay hidden from view until you are well away from River Glen."

Kira stumbled but didn't fall. She reached for the cold stone of the passage wall and scraped her knuckles along the roughness as she ran. No. She wasn't dreaming. She was in danger. Agatha was in danger. The people of River Glen. The High Sheriff and Lady Lydia. Everyone. Because of her. Because of the magic she wasn't supposed to have. She slowed her pace and stopped.

Lydia was waiting at a heavy oak door just ahead. The village square was on the other side.

"I should go back. It's not fair to put so many in danger."

"It's too late, Kira. The boat's too far from shore to turn back."

"But…"

Lydia gripped her hard, above the elbows. "But what? You'd rather let Agatha watch you burn in the brazen dragon?"

Kira shook her head. "No, of course not!"

"Then you need to decide. Now. You saved Mica's life. Yours is worth saving, too."

Lydia let her go and opened the door enough to peek around the side. She glanced back at Kira. "Yes or no?"

Kira breathed through the tightness in her chest. Why was she even hesitating? "Yes."

"Good." Lydia nodded once, then checked outside again. She pulled a white kerchief from her pocket and waved it twice.

"What are you doing?"

"Signalling Lord Callan. He will send the driver of the last coach on an errand. But still, we must hurry. They begin loading shortly." She pulled at the fur trimming the hood of Kira's cloak so that it covered her face and took her hand. "Come."

Kira bowed her head and slouched her shoulders and allowed Lydia to lead her across the cobblestones to the last carriage in a line of five. The square was eerily quiet. As was customary, no one was admitted in the square to farewell the quota. Each girl was permitted to be accompanied to the Guild Hall by her family, but she left alone through the line of guards to the waiting carriage.

Lydia opened the door of the last one and motioned her in.

"Twenty girls make up the quota. You will share this carriage with another three. You must hope that in their distress and anxiety they do not realise that you were already here."

Kira clasped her arm before she could close the door. "Thank you, My Lady. Although, my thanks do not seem to be enough for the risk you take. You are kindness itself. Please tell Agatha. Tell Agatha I…" Kira was flooded by anguish and loss and couldn't speak.

"I will tell her, Kira. Be brave, child." She pulled a leather flask from the bag across her shoulders. "Here. It's cold but it's wet, and Agatha said it will help. Quickly! Your driver returns. Take care and good luck."

Kira grabbed the flask and crouched low on the seat. Of all the things that had happened, not being able to say goodbye to her grandmother distressed her most of all. Wary that once she started to cry she may never stop, Kira uncorked the flask instead and took a tentative sip. Chamomile and mint tea. She gulped enough to ease her parched throat, then lifted a corner of the green velvet curtain and peeked through the tiny gap. A line of guards protected the parade of young women, as one by one they made the solitary journey from the guild hall to the waiting carriage. All wore the same dark blue cloak that Lady Lydia had given her. Some of the girls were strong and made their way unassisted to the carriage, but most were not. Their sobs could be heard throughout the silent courtyard. Kira choked back a sob of her own. After she had watched two of the carriages being loaded, Kira could no longer bear to look and dropped the curtain.

Her fingertips smoothed the material back in place and she was surprised by the richness of it. Kira turned her gaze to the rest of the carriage. The padded leather seat was surprisingly comfortable. The interior was lined with a polished wood and the frame of the windows carved with oak leaves and acorns of a darker timber. Kira frowned. The inside of the carriage was the opposite of what one would expect from the plain black exterior, quite luxurious in fact.

The vehicle lurched forward, and Kira felt her mouth go dry. She took another gulp of cold tea and reached for her bag to stow the flask inside. Suddenly conscious of how cold she was, she searched her bag. Agatha had packed her warmest clothes and her stout travel boots. She pulled off the light boots she had worn to the dance and thrust her feet into a pair of woollen socks and then into the sturdy boots. Her toes began an agonizing tingle as they began to thaw out. She found her vest and fastened it over her tunic, then cinched a wide leather belt around it. Her gloves were there, too, and Kira pulled them over her chapped and bloody fingers, then put her cloak back on. She stowed the bag and her satchel on the shelf above her head and risked another peek around the curtain.

The carriage lurched again, and Kira saw they had drawn level with the line of guards. Lord Callan strode from the carriage in front and waited with his back to the window, blocking her view. She could hear the approach of the first girl by her plaintive moans. She sounded like a mewling cat.

"Cabarac is honoured by your sacrifice," said the High Sheriff in the detached tone Kira remembered from the previous night.

The mewling stopped. The door opened and Lord Callan's dark eyes met hers. He nodded once and turned to offer his arm to the girl behind him. Kira held her breath. The girl half climbed, half stumbled into the carriage and Kira instinctively thrust out her arm to steady her. The girl looked up in surprise.

"Kira?"

"Jenna. Well met, I'm sorry to say."

"Oh Kira! I'm so pleased you're here." Jenna slumped on the seat, threw her arms around Kira, and began to sob in earnest. Lord Callan reached over them to deposit Jenna's bag on the shelf.

"Keep the curtains drawn until you are past the outskirts of town. There are two guards assigned to each carriage. One of them will let you know when you are permitted to open them. We will stop to eat and attend to the horses at Chain of Ponds. We will not stop before then. Is that understood?"

Kira nodded. "Yes, My Lord."

Jenna sat up and wiped her nose. "Yes, My Lord."

"Good. Make it clear to the other girls." He held Kira's gaze. "Your grandmother sends her blessings and her regrets that she was not able to give you these personally." Lord Callan pulled a small package from beneath his cloak and handed it to Kira. "I also regret this." He smiled so briefly that Kira was unsure whether he did at all. "The scent of oatmeal honey biscuits has been plaguing me for the last two hours. You are fortunate that I am a man of great self-control."

Kira lifted the package to her nose and inhaled. "Indeed, My Lord. Thank you."

The High Sheriff bowed stiffly and closed the door.

Jenna stared at Kira open-mouthed.

"Who would have thought Lord Callan had a sense of humour?"

Kira nodded. "Who indeed?" But she had understood that his words had more than one meaning and was grateful for the hidden apology. Her stomach growled loudly. Agatha must have been up half the night baking. She opened the package and offered it to Jenna.

"Would you mind if I ate? I've had nothing since before the dance last night."

"Go right ahead. Not for me though, thank you. My mother practically force-fed me porridge this morning." Her eyes filled with tears again. "I ate to make her happy, but I really didn't feel like it. However, if we don't stop until Chain of Ponds, I'm glad I did. That's a good four-hour ride from here."

Kira stuffed the biscuit into her mouth and savoured the taste of honey and cinnamon on her tongue. Before she could chew more than a couple of times the door opened again, and a girl Kira thought she recognised from a nearby village entered. Kira didn't know her name. The newcomer stared at them silently for a few seconds, then gathered her cloak around her, pulled the hood as far over her head as she could, and sat in the opposite corner of the coach, making herself as small as possible. When Jenna tried to speak to her, she turned her head to the wall and tugged the edge of her hood even further, so her face was completely obscured.

Kira raised her brows at Jenna and shrugged. "Give her time," she whispered. The guard had dropped the bags on the floor of the carriage, and since the girl made no move to do so, Kira hoisted them to the shelf above her head. The girl didn't move, but Kira thought she heard a muffled "thank you" from beneath her hood.

She had just sat down when the door opened again and a voice said firmly, "Thank you, I can manage."

Kira froze. She stared at the hands clutching at the bag the owner was trying to lift into the carriage. *Pus and horehound, it couldn't be!* Jenna reached across and helped lift the bag. The girl looked up in response, the edge of her fur-lined hood framing the delicate features of her wonderful, familiar face.

"Giselle?"

Her friend grinned, jumped into the carriage and onto Kira's lap and hugged her so tightly she could barely breathe.

Chapter 10

Once Giselle had composed herself, Jenna moved across to the other seat so Giselle could sit next to Kira. Giselle wiped her eyes and blew her nose. She looked up at Kira and said, "I'm glad to see you."

Kira tried to gather her scattered thoughts. Giselle was the last person she expected to see.

"What happened?"

Giselle shrugged, a grim set to her jaw. "Boys can be such fickle creatures, can't they?"

Jenna moved uncomfortably in her seat and frowned. Before she could say anything, Giselle flicked the fingers of one hand towards her, as though shooing a fly. Kira's belly rumbled and before she could beg anyone's pardon, Jenna said, "She hasn't eaten since before the dance. Lord Callan just gave her some biscuits from Agatha."

Giselle turned to face Kira and patted her knee. "Well, then, you eat first, and I can fill you in on what happened after you left. Jenna, let me know if I forget anything." She addressed the other girl, "And you too, er, I'm sorry, I don't know your name. I'm Giselle."

There was a brief silence. "Mevis. Mevis Carter from Bracken Ridge." She turned to face the others but didn't pull back her hood.

Kira recognised the name. Her father, Digby, was a mean-spirited man who hauled stone from the quarry to the dock at Ryder Bridge. He was as dour as the rocks he carried.

As the carriage began to move forward, Giselle settled herself into the corner and began to fiddle with her braid.

"Piscator was not happy after Lord Callan sent you to his rooms, Kira, but Lord Callan insisted he continue his testing so the Ball could recommence. The dog started sniffing again and after that very tall, broad-shouldered guard came back, Lord Callan left. Piscator made a show of pretending he was in charge, but whenever that awful animal started to growl it would suddenly stop and scratch its fleas or lick its balls. Once it even lay on its back for a belly rub. You couldn't see Piscator's face as it was hidden by his hood, but the expressions on his soldiers said it all. They had never seen the hound act like that before, I'm sure."

Jenna agreed. "The mood changed in the hall, and people began to whisper, and some even laughed, although I was still terrified and was just praying that it would all be over soon. When the dog went to cock its leg on the mayor, it was the final straw for that dreadful dispatcher, and he told the soldier to take it outside. I was so relieved, I just wanted to drop to my knees and give thanks to the Goddess. Piscator is a vile man. Lord Callan may be hard and very strict, but he's not like Piscator. He's just evil. I could sense it as soon as he came near me!"

Kira had the same opinion and nodded her agreement as she chewed.

"It was strange," said Giselle. "As soon as the dog was taken away, Piscator seemed to lose some of his authority. His soldiers were still there of course, but I think he could sense the change in the crowd and without the hound and Lord Callan to back him up, he made quick work of inspecting the rest of the girls. He didn't even look at the boys, which seemed very unfair, but we were glad to see the back of him, nonetheless!"

"And what of Annie Trotter? Do you know what has become of her?"

Giselle and Jenna looked at each other and shook their heads. "No," said Giselle, "not a word."

"Aye. I know." Mevis spoke so quietly that Kira barely heard her. She pulled the hood back from her head, revealing a purpling bruise beneath her left eye.

"Her poor dad was beside himself, so he was. He came to our house, because my mother is his sister, and wanted to borrow some money to bribe the prison guard. Uncle John says the guard is a soft touch, always on the lookout for more money because he likes a drink and loses all the time at the dice. But my dad was having nothing to do with it, wouldn't give him his hard-earned coin, even with the promise of free pork for a year. My mam was crying and pleading with him, but he wouldn't budge.

"Anyways, I went and got my earnings from cleaning the Mayor's house and doing their big laundry. Coin that I had been saving for the last couple of years, for a dowry, you know, if ever I was asked. I gives it to Uncle John, because I didn't get a token, so I'm hardly going to be needing it, am I? My dad gives me a backhander and says he should have got that money for all that he'd done for me, which is a total of nothin' let me tell you. He's a tight-fisted old so-and-so, wouldn't give you the shite from his boot…" She took a deep breath and blinked several times as though startled she'd finally said out loud what she'd always been thinking.

"Anyways, Uncle John takes off. My dad goes to hit me again, and Mam clocks him in the back of the head with the kitchen skillet. He was still passed out on the floor when we left this morning."

"Fish and pickles!" said Jenna, wide eyed. "And Annie?"

Mevis grinned, "My Auntie gave the thumbs up to my mother as we came to the Hall this morning. I'm thinking that Annie and Uncle John are on their way to family in Bishops Crest. Good luck to them both."

Good luck indeed, thought Kira. Piscator would be doubly angry when he returned to find both his prisoners gone. Kira went cold. She remembered Piscator's anger and hoped with all her heart that it wasn't because he had learned of Annie's escape. She wrestled with her conscience momentarily, before deciding that since she didn't know for sure, she would say nothing. Mevis deserved some hope. They deserved to know the truth about her own predicament, but perhaps not all the unpleasant details.

"So what happened after Piscator left the Ball?"

Giselle waved her braid around, "Mayor Harbison told the minstrels to start playing and we all started dancing. Not with as much enthusiasm, I must admit, but that nice looking singer, you know, the one with the blonde hair, he sang a very funny ditty about little men with big dogs, and that perked us all up. Lord Callan came back before the last dance, and then all the girls without a token were asked to line up by the stage. Nineteen girls did not get a betrothal promise, and he said that would do. When you hadn't returned, I wondered if the twentieth would be you."

Kira looked at her friend closely. "You didn't get a token? What happened to Colac Procter? And Ewan Rochester—he was also keen, wasn't he?"

Giselle shrugged. "I guess Colac changed his mind."

Jenna squirmed in her seat. "That's not quite true, though, is it?" she blurted out. Giselle threw her a glance that could gut a fish. "Well, it's not," Jenna continued. "Colac did give you a token, but you gave it back. I saw you."

"What! Whatever for? You were so excited about his promise. You said you and he would make a good team," said Kira, bewildered by her friend's actions. "Why on earth would you give up a secure future for this?!" She gestured around the carriage.

Giselle pursed her lips. Two spots of red burned her cheeks. "I was wrong. He wasn't a nice person at all." She glared again at Jenna, then turned to look at Kira. "I had already told Ewan that I would be accepting Colac's token, so naturally he didn't offer me a gold." Her eyes filled with tears, but she brushed them away angrily. "Colac Procter said some things which made me think that we would not be as well suited as I thought. Please do not ask me what they were. I have no desire to repeat what he said." She reached out and laid her hand on Kira's arm. "I'd much rather hear what happened to you."

Kira knew better than to argue with her friend. She was as stubborn as a mule. Kira smiled and hoped that once Giselle was over the hurt, she might reveal what Colac could possibly have said that was bad enough to reject his token.

"Yes, Owen Fishlock asked me if I knew where you were," said Jenna with an apologetic glance at Giselle. "I told him you had gone to help Lord Callan's wife, at least that's what Uncle Will—I mean Mayor Harbison—told my mam. I think he was going to offer you a gold, Kira. He was very disappointed and hardly danced the rest of the night."

Kira blinked. "Well, that is a surprise. He barely spoke to me when we danced. I thought he just gave me a silver as thanks for looking after his grandfather, Isaac."

"So, what happened? Where were you? I thought you were going to see Lord Callen's son." said Giselle.

Kira hesitated. "I did. His name is Mica. He was most unwell."

"Dying, Uncle Will said to Mam this morning," Jenna interrupted.

"You are a fountain of information, Jenna," exclaimed Giselle. "Is there any gossip you haven't heard?"

Jenna flushed and sank back in her seat. "Sorry."

Kira nodded. "He was gravely ill. Thankfully, I was able to save him." She wondered what else Jenna had overheard. "I was on my way back to the ball when Piscator arrived and accused me of using magic." She paused, unsure of what to say next. Jenna saved her the trouble.

"He threw her in prison!"

"Jenna!" both Mevis and Giselle scolded her. "Are you alright?" continued Giselle. "Did he hurt you? How long did you have to stay there?"

Kira's throat tightened. "I'm fine. I stayed all night. Lord Callen's wife came to me this morning and brought me here."

"Well, that's some thanks for saving the life of her son!" exclaimed Giselle. "You'd think she could show a little more gratitude than having you carted off as part of the quota."

"Oh, she did," whispered Kira. "She did much more than show her gratitude. Lady Lydia risked her life. It was either leave River Glen as part of the quota or stay and face the brazen dragon. Piscator wants me dead."

Saying the words out loud somehow made it all very real and Kira was overcome by a wave of emotion. Everything that had happened in the last twenty-four hours—the ball, the healing, Piscator, prison, the quota, and worst of all, not being able to speak to Agatha—suddenly hit with unexpected force. Kira began to tremble. Her teeth chattered and she was unable to speak. Giselle pulled off her cloak and threw it over Kira as Jenna fished in her bag for a knitted shawl. Mevis looked hesitant for a moment, then took a small flask from her pocket and offered it to Kira.

"Have a swig of this. It's my dad's whisky, so it is. Tastes awful, but it'll warm you up and knock the shock away."

Kira managed a gulp with Giselle's steadying hand, coughing as the liquor burned her throat.

"Goddess!" she croaked as she wiped the tears from her eyes. Mevis was right, however, and her trembling stopped. She ate another biscuit and washed it down with a mouthful of tea.

"Feel better?" asked Giselle a few minutes later.

"I do, thank you all." She removed Giselle's cloak and handed it back and gave Jenna her shawl. She may be part of the quota, and facing an unknown future, but she was extremely grateful to be sharing the carriage with friends like these.

An hour or so later, Kira rested her head against the side of the carriage and peered through the gap at the end of the curtains. The hills in the distance were topped with white, a stark reminder that winter would soon arrive. The trees lining the road were a profusion of reds and oranges that would normally have inspired Kira to get out her paints and capture the autumn display, but their beauty barely registered. Her mind was still trying to process all that had happened in the last few hours. Giselle was curled in a little ball on the seat beside her, using Kira's lap as her pillow. Kira moved a strand of hair from across Giselle's cheek, tucking it behind her ear. Giselle was so deeply asleep she didn't move. Faint smudges of blue dipped beneath her lashes and Kira guessed it was because her friend hadn't slept much the night before. She wondered what had really happened at the ball but didn't want to pry. She hoped Giselle would confide in her eventually.

Jenna and Mevis slept like mirror images of each other on the seat opposite, hips touching, heads in the crooks of their elbows against the carriage wall. Kira envied them. The steady clop of the horses' hooves and the gentle sway of the carriage should have lulled her as it had the others, but sleep eluded her. All she could think about was her grandmother. Would Agatha be alright? What would happen when Piscator returned and found Kira gone? Would Agatha get the blame? Who would look after her? Her grandmother was held in high regard not only in River Glen but in the surrounding villages. Kira prayed that the community she had served would keep and protect her. As for herself and the other girls, who knew what lay in store for them. A lifetime of servitude? Pleasure girls in the brothels of the Isles? Or, as Jenna was convinced, human sacrifice to the dragon that guarded the gate of the abyss into which magic had been banished a hundred years ago?

Exhaustion finally overcame her overactive imagination and allowed Kira some respite from her dark thoughts.

Chapter 11

By the evening of the fourth day of travel, even Jenna had run out of things to say. Kira was quietly thankful: discussions of what their future held were pointless, and Jenna's fanciful notion they were to be dragon fodder bordered on the absurd.

Lord Callan had established a strict routine. The quota had to be up and having breakfast by seven o'clock, and they were to be inside their carriages and on the road by eight. Conversation was restricted to the girls in their own carriage and their two guards. Ned and Jock were the guards assigned to their carriage. Ned was as taciturn as he was tall, or as Jenna liked to put it, the strong, silent type. Fortunately, Jock was his opposite. Small and wiry with close-cropped grey hair and a short salt-and-pepper beard, he had a ready smile and a jovial disposition, and could often be heard whistling or singing as he rode. He was generally the first to offer his hand when they alighted from the carriage and tried to keep their spirits up with his easy banter, whereas Ned rarely spoke to them and seemed to have a permanent crease between his brows.

Although Ned was much younger than Jock, the older man seemed to defer to him, and even Lord Callan treated him more as an equal than a guard. His silence intrigued Jenna, and she took any opportunity she could to ask probing personal questions. He usually answered with a growl, which, depending on the inflection, could mean yes, no, or maybe, but when she'd asked him his age he'd replied, "Older than my first name but younger than my last," and she'd been the one to growl. Kira estimated his age to be about twenty-five or twenty-six, but his attitude was that of a man much older. Giselle decided he was quite good-looking in a rugged sort of way, even though she had to crane her neck to look up at him, and Mevis thought that his grey eyes were kind and had remarked more than once that his hair was the colour of her ma's treacle toffee. Kira took little notice. She much preferred talking to Jock.

The weather had not been kind. It had been unseasonably wet, with either light, constant drizzle, or torrential downpours, meaning they arrived later than expected at the Pine and Pike, their accommodation for the night. The first three nights had been spent in hostelries, four girls to a room, which Kira had found slightly disconcerting as she had not shared a room since she was a child. Unlike the other girls she had no sisters, and, unaccustomed to listening to other people sleep, had slept poorly herself. When she had finally drifted off, her sleep was plagued with strange dreams and nightmares about being burned alive.

The Pine and Pike was more of a tavern than a hostelry, and Lord Callan warned them all to keep to themselves and not talk to any strangers. The tavern was well prepared for their arrival. A sturdy wooden table, long enough to seat ten girls either side, had been stationed against the far wall. Several smaller tables were positioned in front so the guards could screen the girls from any tavern patrons who might care to look.

Jock escorted them to the table and indicated they should sit at the end.

"I'm to ask if you'd like venison stew, or baked salmon for your dinner. We need to get the orders in quick. They've got entertainment here tonight."

"Ooh," said Jenna clapping her hands. "I'll have the salmon, please. Are we going to be able to watch, too?"

"Only if you're good and finish up your plate," replied Jock with a grin.

"Salmon, too, please," said Giselle. "Do you know who it is?"

"I do indeed." Jock looked at Kira and raised his brow. "And you, lass?"

Kira decided she couldn't face yet another baked salmon and chose the venison. Mevis agreed and ordered it as well.

"It's the Rainbow's End. Those lads that played at your ball."

Kira exchanged a look with Giselle. She wasn't sure whether they needed to be reminded of the night they had all lost their freedom. Aware that her lack of proper sleep was making her more irritable than she cared to be, Kira decided to take a leaf from Jenna's book and try to be a bit more positive. She smiled at Jock and said, "That'll be lovely."

As they waited for their meals, Kira looked along the table at the girls from the other carriages and recognised the same look of trepidation she often saw on her reflection in the carriage window. She found herself wondering again what the future held for them all. Her musings were interrupted by the arrival of their food.

The venison stew was full of chunky potatoes, onions and carrots, and flavoured with garlic, thyme and bay leaf. Kira's belly rumbled as soon as the delicious aromas reached her nose. The meat was so tender it fell apart as soon as she speared it with her fork, and Kira thought it was easily the tastiest meal they'd had since they left River Glen. She was wiping up the gravy with the crust of her bread when she felt someone watching her. She looked up and met Tangler's gaze across the room.

"Tangler!" She started to stand up, but remembering Lord Callan's orders, quickly sat back down. Tangler waved and indicated he would come to her, and then pointed to where Lord Callan was sitting with Ned and Jock. Kira watched Tangler approach the men and was surprised to see that Lord Callan greeted him like an old friend. They spoke briefly, then Lord Callan glanced over his shoulder to where Kira and the others were sitting. He looked back to Tangler and shook his head.

"Is that your Uncle Tangler?" murmured Giselle. "What's he doing here, do you know?"

Kira nibbled at her bottom lip. "Yes, it's Tangler alright. He did tell me when I last saw him that he was meeting up with the Rainbow's End to travel north to Prince Rhicard's court. I suppose that's why he's here."

"Not to mount a rescue, then?" said Jenna, who, Kira decided, had the best hearing of anyone she had ever met.

"I doubt he even knew I was part of the quota," said Kira, and she glanced back at the table. Tangler sat down heavily on a spare stool and raked a hand through his hair.

"I think he might, now," said Giselle. "I think Lord Callan just told him."

"Either that, or he told him that Piscator wants to see you burn."

"Jenna!" Mevis and Giselle censured their friend with one voice.

Jenna raised her hands. "Well, he might have," she said defensively.

After a few minutes of animated conversation, spoken so quietly that even Jenna could not hear what was said, Tangler and Lord Callan shook hands. They both stood and approached the quota table.

"Well met, Kira. I did not expect to cross paths with you so far from home," said Tangler, his voice thick with concern. He hooked a stool from a nearby empty table with his foot and sat down.

"Well met, Tangler, and in truth, nor did I."

"Lord Callan has told me what happened and though I deeply regret your misfortune, I am very glad you are safe." The old man searched her face. "Are you well?"

Kira nodded. "I am recovered, but I worry about Agatha. I didn't even get the chance to say goodbye. You know how frail she has become these last months, and with winter coming…" Her voice became husky with tears, and she couldn't continue.

"Try not to fret, my dear. Agatha is well-regarded in River Glen. The villagers will make sure she wants for naught; you can be sure of that. And I will check on my oldest and dearest friend as often as I can, I promise."

Lord Callan cleared his throat. "Though I wish I could grant you more time, I cannot. Once the quota has been gathered, no further contact with family is permitted. Since you were robbed of your farewells, Kira, I granted Tangler this small favour. But it is not fair to the other girls to allow prolonged conversation, I'm sorry."

He placed his hand on Tangler's shoulder and addressed the quota. "Master Tanglewood and the Rainbow's End have asked to travel with us as far as Mount Leopold. There are reports of robbers and cutthroats on the roads, and since there is safety in numbers, I have agreed. The rules are unchanged. You will speak to no one but your guards and the girls in your carriage."

Tangler squeezed Kira's hand and stood. "All will be well, my dear, don't worry."

But all was not well. That evening a cold front swept down from the north bringing wild winds, hail as big as acorns and torrential rain. Lord Callan conceded there would be no travel for the quota the next day. Rain lashed the windows of the inn and the howling gale rattled the roof timbers with such ferocity Kira was sure the roof would be blown off altogether. The only good thing about the delay was that they were permitted to sit at small tables in the great room, which was kept warm and cosy by the heat of a roaring fire.

The innkeeper had supplied each of the tables with a deck of cards, since he had no other patrons to deal with, and Kira and Giselle had spent the morning quite pleasantly, teaching Mevis and Jenna how to play Hook, Line and Sinker. The bruise on Mevis's cheek had faded to yellow and she was finally starting to join in with their chatter.

They had just finished the last hand when Jock entered carrying a tray. He motioned for them to clear the table and set down four bowls of steaming vegetable soup and a basket of crusty bread rolls.

"Here you go, lasses. Ned'll bring you a pot of tea, shortly."

Kira murmured her thanks, and not for the first time, pondered the strangeness of their situation. Though the quota was quite clearly under guard, they were never treated like prisoners. Their guards spoke to them courteously and with respect, their accommodation had been comfortable and their meals nourishing, and ofttimes delicious. Lord Callan was strict and expected his rules to be obeyed but was mindful of their comfort and safety.

She wondered whether it was just a ruse to gain their trust and co-operation, or a genuine concern for their welfare. Either way, it worked. Her friends now talked less about their future on the Legion Isles and more about which of the minstrels was better looking in the Rainbow's End. The group had been sitting at a long table on the other side of the room for most of the morning, tuning instruments and mending costumes, and were now also eating lunch. Kira studied them as she ate her soup and listened to her friends' chatter.

Farren, the mandolin player and main singer, was clearly a favourite with his blonde locks and twinkling brown eyes. He had an engaging smile and expressive face, which he used to great effect when he sang. On the surface, he seemed happy-go-lucky and quite the flirt when he performed, but Kira noticed a much more serious air about him as he chatted to Tangler.

"Aye, Farren is nice looking, so he is," said Mevis, "but I wouldn't say no to a tumble with that brown-haired fella—I think his name is Hugo. He's a might taller than I would like, but he's got fetching eyes and lovely hair."

"Mevis!" Jenna stared at her friend, wide-eyed. "You haven't even danced with him. How could you think about a tumble?"

Mevis groaned. "What pond have you been livin' in, Jenna? Did you not see the man struttin' about at the ball dancin' and doing summersaults? He'd have the moves, to be sure."

Jenna blushed. "Well, the twins aren't bad looking, though I'm not sure which is which or even what their names are. I think they begin with D."

"Do you like them because they're gingers, like you?" teased Giselle.

"No." Jenna's hand went straight to her braids.

"The one with the curly hair is Donald," said Kira, "and the other one is Declan. His beard is a little darker." She shrugged when the other girls looked at her. "What? They're not identical, are they?"

Giselle laughed. "You said that as though you were describing the difference between a mushroom and a toadstool. I suppose you know the names of the other two as well?"

"Yes," Kira admitted with a wry grin. "The one who plays the drum and the harp is Ralph, and the short one with the bald head and long beard is Parr."

"I bet you could tell us what they were all wearing at the ball, as well, couldn't you?" said Giselle. "You can remember the oddest things, Kira."

Kira was relieved she didn't have to answer as Ned appeared at that moment with a pot of tea, cups and a plate of shortbread biscuits. The tray looked tiny in hands more suited to swordplay than domestic chores, and Kira wondered if perhaps his silence was due to resentment rather than natural reticence. She watched him discretely as he collected the empty bowls and was surprised to see a flicker of amusement cross his face when Jenna asked if he had weather like this where he came from. As usual he answered with a growl.

The wind howled for most of the night, but the rain had stopped before midnight. The road to Mount Leopold was wide and made of packed stone and as Lord Callan wanted no further delay, he deemed the day fit for travel. The quota set off at eight o'clock precisely, and as usual Kira's carriage was last in line. Today, however, they were followed by a wagon, similar in design to a traveller's caravan. The members of the Rainbow's End had affectionately nick-named it 'Pot'.

The wild weather had taken its toll. Twigs and small branches littered the road, made slippery from the mud that had washed from the banks alongside. Travel was further slowed by the waterlogged holes that now pockmarked the surface, frustrating Lord Callen even more. He sent Tangler and Farren to check what lay ahead. The quota was stopped for the third time in as many hours when Tangler returned. Kira heard the weariness in Lord Callan's voice when he spoke.

"Please tell me this road improves. Three times a carriage has become bogged or stuck in a pothole disguised as a puddle."

Kira motioned to the others to be quiet and pressed close to the window. Through the narrow slit between curtain and glass she could see the men talking. Tangler was partially obscured by Lord Callan's back, but she could see that the old man's face was creased with frustration, as he gathered his beard in his fist.

"The news is not good, I'm afraid. The road is damaged but still able to be used. Unfortunately, we met three riders on the road who all told us the same story. The pass to Mount Leopold bridge remains blocked to all but people on foot or on horseback. There is no way the carriages can get past the rocks!"

"Damnation! Prince Thomac was notified of the rockfall four weeks ago. The debris should have been cleared by now." Lord Callan's tone was matched by the stiffness of his back. "These roads were built by the Maladikkan invaders centuries ago and lasted the whole time they occupied Cabarac. Prince Thomac is in charge for five minutes and it all goes to hell!"

"It seems the Crown Prince would rather spend his coin in the Western Provinces," said Tangler. "I hear the Summer palace is benefitting from a much-needed refit."

"Bollocks!" hissed Lord Callan. "That bloody monstrosity had a king's ransom spent on it only two years ago. What's wrong with the man!"

Tangler shrugged. "You know the answer to that as well as I, My Lord. It does us no good to ponder the prince's folly now. You have a decision to make. Turn back, take the long way round or take your chances crossing the old bridge at Marybank."

"Marybank?" Lord Callan slapped his thigh. "That's little more than a cattle crossing. Will it even take the weight of a carriage? No, there must be another alternative."

Tangler stroked his fingers down the length of his beard. "I'm afraid not. If turning back is out of the question, then it is Marybank or an extra three weeks of travel at the very least. Mason's Crossing is the next bridge big enough and that's ten days on from Leopold, unless you want to go over the mountain."

Lord Callan flexed his sword hand. "Very well. Winter is too close upon us to waste more time than we already have. Marybank it is." He turned on his heel and began shouting orders to his men.

Kira sat back and stared at the others.

Jenna spoke before she had a chance. "Mount Leopold pass is blocked. We are to cross the river at Marybank," she said, wide-eyed.

"What? That rickety old bridge? Even the goats hesitate to cross there," said Giselle.

"Oh, it's not as bad as it looks," said Mevis with a reassuring smile. "My Uncle John uses it quite often when he's taking his pigs to the markets in Crystal Brook, so he does. Mind you, he always complains that he ages ten years between one side and the other, but he says it's safe enough."

Not entirely comforted by Mevis's words, Kira nibbled at her lip. "I suppose it's better than an extra three weeks of travel."

The detour took hours longer than expected. The vicious storms that had lashed the nether reaches of River Province in the last few days had left their mark all along the trail that led to Marybank and on to the bridge. Felled trees were common, and mudslides had spread rocks as big as a man's head onto the road. The locals had cleared the debris as best they could, but occasionally the road was blocked by boulders the size of a small boat, and the carriages had to waste more time negotiating the unsealed path that had been fabricated around them. Twice, the girls were forced to leave the carriage to lighten the load and lay beds of branches beneath the wheels to stop them from becoming bogged in the muddy verge. The mountain wind was bitterly cold, and dark clouds gathered above. Lord Callan's patience was at breaking point.

The detour had meant that Tangler's troupe now led the caravan and Kira's carriage was next in line. Evan, their driver, pulled the carriage in alongside Pot when they arrived at the bridge mid-afternoon. The girls scrambled out to have a look while the rest of the quota caught up. Kira looked dubiously at the bridge. It was narrow and seemed far too fragile.

Since the larger and more popular Leopold Crossing had been constructed twenty-odd years ago, it appeared little to no maintenance had been done on the old bridge, and many of its timbers had started to rot. Some had disappeared completely, and the handrails reminded Kira of the teeth of a broken comb. The river flowed with greater intensity than she would have imagined for a crossing. Broken tree limbs and branches were caught between supporting pillars fleetingly before being dislodged in the swiftly moving current. Larger logs defied the river, however, and embraced the ancient timber pillars for far longer than seemed possible.

"The river's not usually this turbulent here," said Mevis. "I'm guessing the rock falls upstream have caused a funnel, so the water flows faster."

"Back in your carriage!" barked Lord Callan as he rode up to the front. He waited until they were all back inside before turning to converse with Tangler. Kira pressed her ear to the window again and heard Tangler offer to cross first since their wagon was almost certainly heavier than the quota carriages. She watched as Tangler walked the fifty yards to the middle of the bridge, testing his weight on the boards that formed the deck.

The old man completed his appraisal, then with a lightness that belied his age, he ran back to the waiting travellers.

"There are some areas of concern, My Lord. As you see, the side rails are non-existent and some of the boards have started to rot. We will need to cross one carriage at a time. I think it would be safest if the girls alight and walk across, but the wind is strong and with nothing to hold onto, I think they will need their guards' assistance."

Lord Callan groaned. "Very well. We will need to go as quickly as possible. Those clouds are looking ominous." He looked around hesitantly. "We will cross carriage by carriage. I do not want the entire quota stuck on one side of the river if we cannot get the transport across. Nor do I want to risk sending all the carriages across first."

Kira glanced at the sky. Heavy, grey clouds were looming and already the afternoon seemed darker. She looked at Giselle and pulled a face. "It seems we will cross first. However, it is not all bad—I think the last carriage will be getting a drenching."

A roll of thunder sounded in the distance. Seconds later, the sky lit up over the mountain and the thunder rumbled again.

"Fish and pickles!" Jenna thrust her head out of the carriage. "I think we're all in for a soaking. We'd better put on our cloaks."

Tangler looked at the sky and back to Lord Callan. "We could go back to Marybank and try again in the morning?"

Lord Callan shook his head. "That track will be nigh on impassable once the rain hits. I do not want to risk the carriages getting bogged. We'd be safer waiting here. Let us try now. The inns at Crystal Brook are known for their hospitality, and the stables are a higher quality than in Marybank. If we are to be delayed, then at least let us do it in comfort. Crystal Brook is less than an hour's ride once we reach the other side."

"As you wish, My Lord." Tangler bowed his head and indicated to his troupe to move forward. Donald and Declan dismounted and led their horses across first. Hugo and Ralph followed. Kira clasped her hands under her chin and sent a silent prayer to the Goddess. A hundred paces had never seemed so far.

Tangler looked up at Parr, who had offered to drive their wagon across.

"Watch the deck near the middle," he advised, "a few planks are rotting, and there are a few missing close to the end. I think maybe Farren should walk between the horses; the wind is picking up, and they will be nervous enough crossing this poor excuse for a bridge. Find some shelter under the trees and set up the tent. I think we will all need a hot drink."

Parr grinned. "These old girls will be fine, Tangler, never you mind. We didn't just pick this breed for their pulling power; they're canny beasts, gentle and willing. It'll be their weight, not their temperament that might be the problem. Don't you worry, we'll take it slow, I wouldn't risk it if I didn't think all would be well."

Farren nodded, "I'll come straight back once our wagon is safely on the other side. I think all the horses will need to be led across." He rubbed a hand up and down the dappled grey nose of one horse then the other, before offering them both a chunk of apple.

Once he'd seen that the others had reached solid ground, Parr flicked the reins, and the horses took the strain and plodded forward. Farren took his place between the horses and picked his way carefully across the boards, talking to them and stroking their necks all the while.

Lightning cracked the sky and the clouds grumbled. Lord Callan stood in his stirrups and looked back to the mountain pass. "The last quota carriage approaches, thank the Goddess. Pray this rain holds off, Tangler. We'll follow your advice. Evan will drive the empty carriage across. Ned and Jock will accompany the girls behind if you and Farren could lead the way."

"Yes, My Lord. We'll come back for the other carriages once these girls are safe on the other side." Tangler gathered his cloak more securely around him and opened the carriage door.

He grinned in surprise to see them all cloaked up and ready. "Well done, my dears, well done."

They huddled at the start of the bridge, marvelling at the calm strength of the horses as the wagon pitched from side to side on the uneven boards of the deck, the raging river so loud they could barely hear the shouts of encouragement from the men on the other bank. Finally, Parr waved to indicate they were across. Farren scurried back, his curls blown straight by the strengthening breeze. Tangler embraced him briefly and patted his back. "Well done!" He moved to grab the bridle of the one of the horses pulling Kira's carriage and began murmuring words of reassurance to sooth the fractious beast.

Farren grinned and turned to the girls, "It's not as bad as it looks, I promise you. Be brave and show those other girls how it's done. Ned and Jock will keep you safe."

He joined Tangler and took the bridle of the other horse and began to sing a lullaby, but the words of his song floated away on the wind before Kira could make out his tune. Her stomach was churning and when she looked at the others, saw her apprehension reflected in the faces of her friends.

"If the horses and wagons can make it across, then surely the bridge can take our weight, don't you think?" she said, as much to reassure herself as her friends. A wail of anguish floated from one of the carriages behind them.

"Sounds like Lord Callan has just delivered the news," said Jock, who had just tethered his mount next to Ned's at the back of the carriage. "The journey won't get any shorter by thinking about it. Let's go."

"Will your horses be safe by themselves?" asked Giselle.

"Aye, lass. They're bred for battle. Crossing a bridge won't worry them."

He stood with his hands on his hips. "Now, who's coming with me?"

Mevis and Jenna quickly linked arms with Jock. More to escape the intimidating bulk of Ned than eagerness to be first to cross the bridge, thought Kira, as Jock wasted no time moving forward.

Ned waited until the others had gone about twenty paces before offering his arms to Giselle and Kira. "Hold on tight. That wind is fierce, and it'll be even stronger when we reach the middle."

Kira threaded her arm through Ned's and grasped her cloak. The wind caught her hood and swept it off her head, and she felt her braids loosen. She reached over her shoulder to grab the hood and pulled it more securely over her head, holding tightly to the fur to make sure. The muscles in Ned's arms tensed and he said, "Ready? Let's go."

It was as though their footsteps on the bridge triggered the storm's fury. A finger of light raked across the clouds as thunder echoed down the valley like a volley of drums. Kira felt her skin tingle. The first icy drop of rain landed on her nose when they were almost halfway across the bridge. By the time they had gone another ten paces it was pelting down. Her cloak whipped around her legs and the wind tore her hood from her grasp. She didn't bother trying to retrieve it but clutched Ned's forearm instead. She hoped Giselle was holding tight.

"The carriage has cleared the bridge," Ned's deep voice cut through the howl of the wind. "Tangler returns."

"Make haste but watch your step," shouted Tangler. "The boards are loose up ahead, as well as slick with the rain."

Kira bowed her head into the wind, thankful for Ned's sheltering bulk. Beneath her feet she caught glimpses of the snarling, turbulent river in the gaps between the weather-worn timbers and tightened her grip on his arm.

Freezing rain stung her cheeks and Kira could hardly see in front of her. She squinted her eyes against the onslaught and saw Farren making sure Jock and the other girls made it safely across. He turned and the wind seemed to blow him back towards them.

"I'll take Giselle," he yelled, "the wind strengthens!" He gathered Giselle from Ned's protection and sheltered her under his arm, shielding her as best he could from the wind's fury. Kira clung tight to Ned. Only ten paces to go. Lightning cracked the sky and the air around them sizzled as thunder roared above her head, loud enough to set her ears ringing. A spear of intense blue light impaled the bridge behind her. The old timbers shattered. The force of the impact propelled Kira forward and she stumbled. A bolt of pain shot down her leg as her knee twisted awkwardly, yet Ned somehow managed to keep them both upright. He yelled at Farren and Giselle to keep going, then Kira felt Ned's arm beneath her thighs as he swept her off her feet and cradled her against his chest. "Hold tight," he growled, and carried her the last few paces over the bridge.

They joined Farren and Giselle, who were sheltering beneath an oak tree and turned to look back at the bridge. The acrid smell of scorched timber filled Kira's nostrils. A gaping, black hole in the timbers of the bridge hissed in the rain. Steam rose from the blackened wood, despite the deluge. Her heart sank. There was no way any other carriage was going to get across.

Chapter 12

She heard Ned's growl of frustration and glanced up at him. "Bollocks. We'd better check the damage, Farren," he muttered grimly, then looked down at Kira, "Do you need me to carry you to your carriage first?"

Kira shook her head. "I'll be fine, thank you. I can lean on Giselle if I need help." He set her down gently and waited until she had her balance before striding off.

The storm receded almost as fast as it had come. By the time Kira had limped to the carriage with her arm across Giselle's shoulder and they had stripped off their wet cloaks, the rain had eased to a drizzle and the thunder echoed far in the distance. Jenna and Mevis, having escaped the worst of the weather, were horrified to learn what had happened. Reassuring her friends that she had suffered only a sprained knee took almost as long as the bridge crossing, but finally they were satisfied. Farren supplied them with towels from the troupe's wagon and told them that Donald and Declan would soon have a fire going with their supply of dry wood.

"Come over to Pot when you are dried, and we'll brew you some tea." He flashed Kira a smile, saying, "Ned told me you'd hurt your knee. I'll check Tangler's chest for some willow bark."

"My thanks, Farren, but there's no need to rob Tangler," said Kira, returning his smile. "I have willow bark in my satchel."

"Very well," he said, bowing low with a flourish of his hand. "We shall look forward to your company soon, ladies." He exited with a wink and a wave.

"He's such a nice fellow, isn't he?" said Jenna.

"Yes," Giselle and Mevis spoke at the same time.

Giselle caught Kira's eye and grinned. "Like sunshine on a rainy day," she said, and tossed her another towel.

Kira was surprised to see Tangler warming his hands by the fire when she ducked under the canvas shelter that extended from the roof of the wagon. Raindrops clung to his beard and gradually let go to fall on his boots with a plop.

"Come close and warm yourselves, my dears. The water has boiled, and the tea is brewing." He indicated four small wooden stools by the fire. "Take a seat, take a seat."

Once they were all seated, Tangler took a small pan from the stones around the flames and set it down next to Kira. "For your willow bark, my dear. I can make you a poultice when we get to Crystal Brook." Kira smiled at him gratefully and stirred the willow bark into the steaming water with a clean stick that Tangler handed to her.

Farren clambered out of the wagon with a wooden tray laden with bread and cheese and some sliced apple. "Not the greatest of fare, ladies, but it should take the edge off your hunger until we get to Crystal Brook."

Kira's stomach growled loud enough for them all to hear and she gave an apologetic grin. "Your pardon. I guess I must be hungry."

"You could deny your hunger till the nets are full, Kira, but your stomach will always tell the truth!" Giselle teased and prodded Kira with her elbow. "We haven't eaten since breakfast, and I don't know about you, but I am famished!"

Tangler grasped his beard and nodded his approval as the girls tucked into the simple fare. "Eat up, my dears, and while you do, I will tell you our plans."

Kira took a quick gulp of her tea. She had barely given the rest of the quota a passing thought since she left the bridge. What would happen to them now? To all of them? She nibbled on a piece of cheese and focussed her attention on what Tangler had to say.

"Understandably," he began, "Lord Callan is not a happy man. The bridge is quite unsafe"—the girls all nodded their agreement—"and the other carriages are unable to cross. His quota is now split, and he cannot be in two places at once. Therefore, he will stay with the larger group and escort them to the next safe crossing after Mt Leopold. He cannot spare more guards to watch over you, much to his chagrin, so the troupe and I will travel with you to White Haven. The supremely capable Jock and Ned will remain as your guards and Lord Callen directs you to do as they say. Their words will be his."

Tangler looked at each of the girls in turn to emphasise the gravity of the situation. "It is too dangerous for you girls to go back across the bridge to join the others, and even if you managed it, I fear squeezing an extra body into each of the remaining carriages would make for extremely uncomfortable travel. Particularly since the journey will be extended by at least another three weeks." He paused and sighed. "However, I have been told that I must allow you to choose. If you would prefer to rejoin the quota, say so now and we will endeavour to make the crossing as safe as possible."

Kira could think of only one thing worse than crossing the bridge again, and that was to be separated from Giselle and the others. She waited for them to speak first.

"There is no way I am going across that bridge again," said Giselle firmly.

"No, no, no," agreed Mevis, shaking her head. "Once was enough for me, so it was."

"Fish and pickles! Absolutely not," said Jenna.

"I think you have your answer, Tangler," said Kira. "Looks like you're stuck with us!"

"Take off your cloaks," cautioned Tangler as they neared the inn at Crystal Brook. "Not everyone would know that they signify you as part of the quota, but it is best to be sure. Many wealthy families hire guards to protect their coaches from robbers in these parts, so Ned and Jock will not seem out of the ordinary. Nonetheless, as soon as we have eaten, I think it best that you retire to your room. We'll make an early start tomorrow."

The inn was grubbier than their previous accommodation, but the stew was surprisingly tasty, and a fire blazed in the hearth of the dining area, providing a welcome respite from the evening's chill. Tangler seemed to be on good acquaintance with the barkeep, and after a long chat slid onto the bench at their table.

"We won't be singing here tonight, lads," he said in a low voice. "Terry says there's a half dozen Lancers propping up the other end of the bar, and he doesn't want to keep them around any longer than he has to. Not fond of the Prince's men is our Terry."

"I still can't tell the difference," said Jenna, waving her fingers towards Jock and Ned. "I know you are the King's Guard, but why are you different to the others?"

Jock exchanged a look with Ned. "The King, despite his infirmity, is the nominal head of the King's Guard. He also has a personal garrison called the Castle Guard, who are loyal only to him."

"Thank the Flame," muttered Tangler with an apologetic shrug at Ned. "Well, it's true. If not for them, Prince Thomac would be on the throne already. Captain Blackwater has been a blessing to the King."

Ned made a non-committal growl at the back of his throat. "Time and place, Tangler," was all he said, however. Jock looked between the men, then continued his explanation.

"The High Sheriff commands his own platoon of soldiers. At the time of the quota, he has a detachment guarding the quota carriages, while the rest of the platoon continue their usual duties." He pointed to the breastplate both he and Ned wore. "The red cross on the gold shield signifies we are part of the King's Guard. The green laurel behind signifies we answer to the High Sheriff."

"So, the black lance through the red shield on the cloaks of those soldiers indicate that they belong to the Crown Prince?" asked Jenna.

"Correct," said Jock. "That's why you'll sometimes hear them referred to as Lancers instead of the Royal Guard."

"What about Piscator's men?" asked Giselle. "Is he like the High Sheriff with his own detachment of men from the Crown Prince?"

"Aye, well done, lass!" Jock beamed at her. "Their cloaks are lined with red to distinguish them from the Royal guard."

"So, who has the most authority, then? Piscator or the High Sheriff?" asked Mevis.

"Hah!" said Tangler, slapping his hand down on the table. "Depends where in Cabarac you happen to be. Not so many years ago the High Sheriff would answer only to the King and his word was law. Now, it seems Prince Thomac has taken on the collection of the quota, and Lord Callan must now answer to him. There have been other, subtle shifts in the balance of power, and dispatchers, or more particularly Piscator, claim more authority than they ever had a right to."

Kira was surprised at Tangler's candour. It was a side of the old man she had rarely seen and wondered about the hint of bitterness she heard in his tone. She felt certain it had a history longer than her recent misfortune. She sipped on her tankard of honey mead and rubbed her knee. It had been a long and tiring day, and she for one would be glad to finally rest her head. The warmth from the fire and the poorly lit room made it hard to keep her eyes open.

"Where do we go to from here?" asked Giselle, trying to stifle a yawn and not being entirely successful.

"Bed, by the sounds of that," said Farren.

"Yes. But I meant in the morning," she said, yawning again.

"The easiest route takes the low road from here to Roseberry and then to Tunbridge. We can take the ferry across to Watervale and then to White Haven. Three or four days at most." Tangler ran his fist down his beard.

"What a pity we can't go via Woodville," said Jenna. "I could show the girls the Priory of the Flame." She looked at Kira. "That's where I would have taken my vows."

"Yes, it's a pretty route in summertime, my dear, and the view of the priory across the lake is quite spectacular, but the road gets flooded in winter, and after the rain we've had, I wouldn't like to risk it." Tangler shrugged an apology. "Besides, it would add a day or two onto our journey. What do you think, Ned? Jock?"

Jock nodded. "Aye, though the priory itself is not quite a day's ride from here, it's the road on to Woodville that'd be hard going for the horses if the ground is too muddy. It's the high road, you see. The road has a gradual incline which is not evident at first, especially if you are riding in a carriage. The land on that side of the ranges sits a lot higher than this."

Ned stiffened suddenly. "Flame it. Lancers approach." He turned to Kira and with a muttered apology pulled her onto his knees and pressed her against his chest. The metal of his breast plate was hard against her cheek but the cold shock of it gave her the presence of mind to bring up her hand to cover the rest of the insignia. She felt something brush against her leg and saw that Farren had slipped under the table and was now seated in her chair with his arm over Giselle's shoulders. Kira couldn't have moved even if she had wanted to; Ned had one arm across her back and her head cradled in his other hand. She inhaled a strangely masculine combination of sandalwood and cinnamon and tried to calm her thudding heartbeat.

"Laughter now, boys," said Tangler, and Kira heard the men chuckle appreciatively, as though Tangler had just told them a joke. She was able to squint between Ned's fingers and saw two soldiers come to a holt behind Tangler.

"Ah! Tis the Prince's own guards," he exclaimed and raised his tankard. "Welcome, my good men. Would you care to join us for an ale or two?"

Kira clutched at Ned's sleeve. What was Tangler playing at?

"Aye, don't mind if we do, that's very kind of you."

Kira felt Ned's arms tighten around her. "Take my seat. My wife's had a wee bit more honey mead than she's used to, and I'd best get her up to bed." He stood up and hoisted Kira a bit more comfortably in his arms. "Don't wait up for me, lads. Nice to make your acquaintance, Master Tanglewood."

Ned carried Kira up the stairs and didn't put her down until they were safely in the room.

"You're heavier than you look," he said as he deposited her on the bed.

"Thanks," said Kira, caught between indignation and relief. "Why on earth did Tangler ask the soldiers to join us? It was evident the way he spoke before that he thinks little of the Crown Prince or his men."

"Have you not heard that expression 'Keep your friends close and your enemies closer'?" He strode over to the door and opened it a crack. "The soldiers would not expect a man with something to hide to invite them to drink at his table. Tangler will glean far more information from them than they will from him, I assure you."

Kira was less surprised by what Ned had to say than by how many words he had taken to say it. She didn't think he'd spoken so many words on the entire trip. Certainly not to her and the other girls. He was quick to return to form, however.

"I can hear Farren and the other girls coming up the stairs now. Be ready for an early start tomorrow." He raised a hand in quick farewell and slipped out of the door without so much as a backward glance.

Kira heard the mumble of conversation outside the door and then Giselle and Mevis joined her on the bed as Jenna locked the door.

"Well," said Giselle, "our travelling companions certainly know how to think on their feet, don't they? I imagine that not every place they play appreciates their talent as much as we did. They spouted lies to those two lancers with so much conviction that even I was fooled."

"It was amazing, so it was," said Mevis, nodding her head in agreement. "Jenna and I are Jock's daughters, don't you know. Accompanying our cousin and her betrothed to Tunbridge, so we are."

"Betrothed?" said Kira with a grin.

"You can raise your brows all you want, Mrs Ned the guardsman's wife, the wink he gave when he took you up to bed left no one in doubt as to what he was going to do when he tucked you in!"

"Giselle!" The heat rose in her cheeks as the others giggled in agreement. "Ned? Well, he must be a better actor than he is a talker, that's all I've got to say."

Jenna grabbed a log from the crate by the hearth and tossed it onto the fire, "I must admit, I wasn't too sure about what sort of protection a group of musicians could really give us, but I was impressed by the way they handled things tonight. I've been wondering why everyone seemed to consult Tangler before they made a decision, but he had those two soldiers baited and hooked before they realised he'd even tossed in the line."

A soft tap at the door silenced them all. Jenna put her ear to the door and whispered, "Who is it?"

"It's me, Parr. Tangler sent me up with a pot of willow bark and some cabbage leaves to wrap around Kira's knee."

Jenna opened the door a few inches, and only then did Kira see the poker in her other hand. Parr poked his hand and half a cabbage through the gap, "It's only me, lass, I promise. Tangler apologises that he can't come himself and fix you a poultice. He asked if you would try the cabbage leaves instead; good for swelling he tells me." Parr placed his goods on the table once Jenna had let him enter the room. "I'm to tell you that Farren will sit up alongside of Evan when you set out in the morning, and that Ned and Jock will ride with you as is usual."

He pulled the leaves from the cabbage as he spoke and crushed them with the heel of his hand. Once he was done, he pulled a roll of clean rag from his pocket and set it alongside.

"Unfortunately, you will have to leave before sunrise to stay true to the story he told the soldiers, just in case they are still hanging around. Jock will wake you in plenty of time and fetch your things." He glanced at the girls and shrugged an apology. "Sorry, it can't be helped. Evan will pull over, once you reach the edge of Chetwynd Forest, and wait there. We'll be an hour or so behind you."

Kira looked over her cup at Giselle. "It's a tangled web he weaves, is it not?"

"Indeed," said Giselle. "And as the weaver, I suppose he gets to choose who gets up with sparrow fart and who gets to lie in."

Parr hastened to reassure them. "No, no, not at all. It's far safer for you to leave first. If the soldiers decided to check your carriage and stop you from leaving, we wouldn't know until it was too late."

Giselle patted him on the arm, "All is well, Parr. Just because we see the truth in your plan does not mean we accept it graciously. Tell Tangler we'll be ready."

Parr gave them a wry grin as he left the room. Mevis locked the door behind him as Jenna and Giselle began applying the cabbage leaves to Kira's knee.

"I've heard that cabbage leaves are good for breasts when the mother stops nursing, but I didn't know they worked on knees, too," said Jenna doubtfully, holding the leaves in place as Giselle wound the bandage around Kira's knee.

"They help reduce swelling and redness, so I would think it might work on joints as well," said Kira, already feeling more comfortable with the coolness from the leaves and the support from the bandage. "I'll sleep on the couch tonight, so I can prop my leg up on the armrest." She sipped her tea as the other girls pulled blankets and pillows from the beds to make her more comfortable and then settled into bed themselves.

Kira contemplated the day's events as she waited for sleep to overtake her. Being separated from the rest of the quota was hardly ideal and having to make their own way to White Haven was slightly terrifying. Jenna was right, though: both the guards and their travelling companions knew what they were doing. Ned may be the most taciturn man in all of Cabarac, but if it wasn't for his quick reflexes on the bridge, she might well be sleeping in a watery grave. Quick to think and quick to react. Kira supposed you couldn't ask much more of someone trying to protect your life.

Chapter 13

The late night and pre-dawn start had taken its toll, and Kira's eyes grew heavier with each rhythmic sway of the carriage. The others were already dozing, but Kira felt an uneasy tension in the air and despite her tiredness, was unwilling to close her eyes. The distant snow-capped mountains she glimpsed between the trees glowed pink in the early sun, but the road was still heavily shadowed, adding to her sense of foreboding. She pulled her cloak a little tighter around her shoulders and shifted her leg to a more comfortable position as she stared out of the window. The cabbage poultice had certainly helped.

Nothing seemed to be going well on this journey. She had thought that yesterday's terrifying experience on the bridge had been the salt on the fish, but then Farren told them this morning that the Lancers had been looking for Annie Trotter. The news cast a pall of melancholy over them all, especially Mevis, who had retreated back into her shell and had not spoken since. Kira watched her friends as they slept. What would have happened if it was her the soldiers had been looking for? More conscious than ever of the danger her presence brought to the carriage, she wondered if they would reach the safety of White Haven before she was caught in Piscator's net.

Her contemplations came to an end as they rounded a bend in the road to find a large tree branch blocking their way. Ned reined in his horse alongside the carriage and stood in the stirrups to look around.

"I don't like this," Kira heard him mutter to Jock. He saw her watching and raised his hand abruptly. "Stay in the carriage."

The carriage rocked slightly as Farren jumped down from beside Evan. Ned shook his head. "We've little choice but to move it. Either that or turn back."

Farren jogged over to the tree and back again. "The limb and the tree both bear scorch marks. I'm thinking the lightning struck more than just the bridge."

Ned growled, "Stay with the girls, Evan." He dismounted and stood next to Farren and Jock, who had already tethered his mount. "Let's make it quick, then."

Kira watched as the men reached the fallen branch and was just about to poke Jenna to stop her snoring when her attention was caught by a movement on the other side of the road. Four men materialised from the bushes, swords in hand.

"Trap!" yelled Ned.

Evan slapped the reins against the horse's backs and as the clang of sword meeting sword rang out, he steered them down a narrow track into the forest. Kira's heart pounded in time to the hoofbeats.

"Elle! Jenna! Mevis!" Kira's frantic call woke her friends. "We are attacked!"

Kira heard a high-pitched whistling sound and then the roof and body of the carriage were peppered with sharp thwacks.

"Get down," yelled Evan. "Down on the floor!"

Everything seemed to happen in slow motion. The colours around her melted into a tawny brown but her friends seemed to glow with a light of their own. Elle was a bright buttercup yellow, and Kira pushed her from the seat and down to the floor. Jenna was the colour of bluebells, and she grabbed her arm and pulled her on top of Giselle.

The thwacks came again. Louder this time, and with it the sound of splintering wood. Kira felt her face begin to sting. She heard Evan's agonised cry of pain and threw herself on top of her friends, screaming for Mevis to follow. "Mevis! Get down! Get down!"

Kira reached behind her and grabbed Mevis's leg, "Mevis! Come on! You need to move!"

Mevis moaned softly. "I can't."

Kira looked up at her and the breath left her lungs in a whoosh. "Goddess of light." The bolt of a cross-bow arrow protruded from Mevis's chest, pinning her to the seat.

"I can't, Kira." Her face drained of colour and her head dropped to the side.

"Mevis!" Kira's pulse throbbed in her ears. She was so frightened she could barely breathe.

Jenna whimpered beneath her, "Goddess protect us, Goddess protect us."

She could feel Giselle trembling beneath her right arm and dropped her forehead to rest on her friend's shoulder. "Hold on," she whispered, "hold on."

Kira flinched as another rain of arrows pounded the carriage, and she braced herself over her friends like a shield. She felt splinters of wood land on her back and cocked her head to check the damage. A single arrow had penetrated the seat where Giselle had been seated only seconds before. A wave of nausea tightened her gut.

Mevis hadn't moved. Her head lolled towards her shoulder. A small trail of blood trickled from her nostril to her ear. There was very little blood around the exit wound. Had her heart stopped beating? Kira closed her eyes and let out a small moan of anguish.

The carriage lurched and rocked as it tumbled along the uneven path, the trees so close that the tips of the branches scraped its sides. Kira clenched her hands on the metal struts of the seats, uncaring that her injured knee was taking a pounding on the hard wooden floor. They jounced along for what could only have been a few minutes before Kira felt the carriage slow and finally stop.

Kira heard the thundering hooves of an approaching horse and prayed the rider was a friend, not foe. "Don't move, don't move," she hissed.

The door of the carriage was wrenched open, and Kira twisted her head to see who it was. A stranger glared at her, sword in hand. He pulled himself up onto the step with a snarl. Kira thrust her good leg back as hard as she could, and her boot smashed into his knee.

"Aargh, you sarding bitch!" The man staggered back and raised his sword. Jenna screamed. Kira reached for the door. Her eyes met his and he lunged towards her. Evan yelled and the man hesitated and looked up. Kira's cloak was splattered with blood and brain as Evan's axe cleaved the top of their attacker's head and he crumpled to the ground. Evan tumbled from the driver's seat and landed with a thud.

Kira scrambled across the floor and looked outside. Evan lay, unmoving, across the body of their attacker. She hesitated. Jenna's horrified moan and plea to 'shut the door, shut the door!" compelled her to act and she slammed the door shut.

The frantic jolting had loosened the arrow and Mevis was slumped across the seat. Kira knelt on throbbing knees and placed her cheek against her chest. Nothing. No breath. No heartbeat. Her throat tightened. Her hands clenched the fabric of Mevis' cloak. She tried desperately to link her awareness to hers. Too late. Mevis was dead. What use was the Eiran if she couldn't help her friend? Her heart ached, but there was no time to grieve yet. She choked back her tears and made the sign of the angel.

Jenna helped Giselle back up to the seat and they clung together, staring wordlessly at Mevis. "What do we do? What do we do?" hissed Jenna.

Kira had no idea.

Outside, someone groaned, then swore.

"It's Evan!" Kira opened the door and jumped down next to him. Evan had managed to roll onto his side and was struggling to sit up. The sleeve of his jerkin was covered in blood. In contrast, his face was as white as snow. She put her arm under his back and eased him upright.

"What do you think you're doing?" Ned's voice barked from behind the trees. "I told you to stay in the carriage."

Kira did not want to cry, but she was overcome with relief, grief, and a whirlpool of other emotions she couldn't identify. Evan patted her on the back with his good hand as she sobbed. "Go easy, Ned. You're scaring the poor lass."

Ned growled, "Are you well?"

Kira wiped her eyes and her nose on the back of her sleeve. She looked up at him and shook her head. "No," she said with a sniff. "Well at least, I am. But Mevis…Mevis is dead."

"What!" Ned strode over to check as Giselle and Jenna climbed out of the carriage white faced and wide-eyed.

"It's true," said Jenna. "One of those arrows went straight through her chest."

"Yes," said Giselle, her voice quavering with emotion, "and if Kira hadn't acted as quickly as she did, I would have been next."

Jock and Farren exchanged a look as they emerged from the trees.

"Mevis? Poor wee lass." Jock hastened to Jenna and Giselle as Farren bent down to check on Evan.

"What happened?" He pointed to the blood darkening Evan's sleeve.

"Arrow got me too. Lost the reins. Lucky the path was too narrow, and the horses stopped of their own accord. That bastard," he indicated to the body at his feet, "got in the way of my axe as I fell off the seat."

"Who were those men?" asked Jenna, still breathy with fear. "Have they gone?"

"Horse thieves." Jock spat on the ground; his disgust obvious to all. "Four of the wee shites kept us occupied while another couple stole our mounts. We had to choose between finding you and chasing them. You won." He had an arm around both Jenna and Giselle's shoulders and gave them a reassuring squeeze, even though his tone had suggested it was a close call.

"What happened to this one's horse, then?" said Farren.

"Reckon the archer was riding pillion. Took off when his mate's scalp was split."

"Probably thought it would take too long to untether two horses from the carriage by himself." Farren checked underneath the carriage as he spoke. "Fortunately, we have the horses, but this carriage isn't going anywhere. The axle's cracked. This wheel would have come off if you hadn't stopped when you did."

Kira tried not to dwell on poor Mevis and concentrated on what she could do to help Evan. She asked Ned to get her satchel from the coach and used the water from Farren's waterskin to wash the wound. The arrow had grazed his forearm about halfway between his wrist and his elbow but fortunately had missed the bone.

"Lucky you were wearing those leather gauntlets, or this would have been a lot worse."

"Luckier still, that I got whacked in the head by a branch that knocked me sideways, or I would be sharing the same fate as that poor lass inside. I reckon that arrow was meant for me."

Kira's throat tightened. She quickly sprinkled dried comfrey and yarrow into the wound, teased some blood moss from the clump she found in her satchel and packed it on top, and wrapped a roll of clean rag firmly around it. She looked Evan in the eye and nodded. "All done."

"Thank you."

Farren and Jock had unhitched the horses as she worked and were now discussing with Ned what was to be done next.

"There were too many arrows to be just the one bowman. Crossbows take longer to load, and you can see, there are fletched arrows here too." Jock plucked an arrow from the woodwork and snapped it across his knee. "It's not safe to stay here. They could be back any time, if not for him, then the horses."

"We'll take him into the trees and cover him with branches," said Ned.

"Somebody has to ride back and let Tangler know. The Rainbow's End could fall into the very same trap."

"Easier said than done, Farren," said Evan. "There's no saddles. You'll have to cut the reins to make them short enough to thread through the bridle. Neither of them are used to having a rider on their backs."

"Flame it, Evan. Give us some good news."

"I didn't say they wouldn't. Just that they're not used to it."

Farren took out his knife and began sawing at the lead rein.

Ned paced about, then squatted down to go through the stranger's pockets. He straightened and blew out his cheeks. "Nothing. Even his sword is a hacked-up piece of rubbish."

"Rubbish or not, if Kira hadn't given him a donkey-kick to his shins, one of us might not be sitting here now," said Jenna as she blew her nose.

Ned exchanged a look with Jock and raised his eyebrows. Jock nodded.

"Very well," Ned said with a sigh. "Farren, you and Evan ride back. Keep a lookout for those horse thieves, mind. Jock and I will take the girls. We'll take the forest paths and head east towards the priory. Tell Tangler to take the priory Road and stop when he reaches the lake. We won't make it that far, so you'll have to work back through the forest to find us."

Kira helped Evan get to his feet and as he joined the other men, she hunkered down next to Jenna and Giselle.

"I'm sorry," whispered Kira.

"Sorry for what? Saving our lives?" Giselle was incredulous.

"If I wasn't with you, Tangler wouldn't have had to worry about Piscator or the lancers and make all these ridiculous plans. You could have all left the inn at a reasonable time and this would never have happened. Mevis would still be alive."

"Kira, I swear you would take the blame for a change in the weather! Not everything bad that happens is your fault. You just heard Evan say the arrow was meant for him, do you blame him for ducking at the right time?"

"No, of course not."

"Then don't blame yourself. You have even less reason to than him."

Kira knew what Giselle said made sense, but still found it hard to forgive herself. If only she had reacted more quickly. If only she could have used the Eiran before Mevis had taken her last breath. If only she hadn't had to join the quota to escape Piscator. If only…if only…

Chapter 14

They buried Mevis beneath a larch tree near a stream where the ground was soft and easy to dig. Ned and Jock had dug Mevis's grave, shallower than was usual, as time was of the essence, and they also had to hide the brigand's body in the woods. Kira and Giselle collected as many smooth rocks and pebbles from the water's edge as they could carry, while Jenna chanted the funeral dirge for souls buried far from home. Kira's knee throbbed from the pounding it had taken on the floor of the carriage, and more than once gave way as she scrambled up the bank, but she ignored the pain and reached the top to empty her sack. Together they laid the stones in the sign of the Goddess, a crescent moon with three stars, to complete her interment and honour her death.

"Make haste, lasses. We can't tarry here, and if Tangler and the others don't make it back with horses, we'll be tramping through the woods in the dark."

Kira nodded. "Our thanks for the time you spared, Jock. Mevis will lie in the arms of the Goddess tonight because of your kindness."

"Aye, and thanks to your quick thinking, Kira, we are not," said Giselle, with a break in her voice.

Jock acknowledged their words with a wave of his arm. "Pick up your bags, lasses. We go now. What you can't carry, leave behind. Ned and I have as much as we can manage. Our sword hand must be free at all times." He motioned them forward with a nod of his head, "You follow Ned, and stay close. No talking. If you have a problem, raise your hand. I'll be at the rear. On you go."

Ned turned. "If I tell you to move, do it quickly and without question. If we have to leave you for whatever reason, do not come out of hiding unless you hear either Jock or myself say 'Cabarac'. Is that clear? He turned back without waiting for an answer and strode down the path.

Kira had threaded the handles of her travel bag through the strap of her satchel and hefted it, so the strap sat across her shoulders and the bag rested against her back. It was uncomfortable, but it meant she could have her hands free to grasp the branch that Ned had fashioned into a staff to help support her aching knee.

The path wove between groves of oak and larch, narrowing as they moved deeper into the forest. A fine, misty rain penetrated the canopy above so that gradually their cloaks grew damp and intensified the afternoon chill. Kira's knee throbbed with every step. She gripped the staff tighter and tried to concentrate instead on the sounds and smells of the forest. The steady murmur of the distant river was a comforting reminder of home. Home. Would she ever see it again? Guilt gnawed at her heart. Maybe Mevis's death wasn't her fault, but she couldn't help feeling some responsibility.

It wasn't fair to the others to have them put in harm's way like this. Magic may be a death sentence for her, but she should not allow her dilemma to imperil the others. She would never have agreed to leave with the quota if she had realised what was in store.

Kira hitched the straps of her satchel, so they rested more comfortably across her shoulders, and concentrated on the path ahead. The rain had eased but the sky that was visible above the trees remained a foreboding grey. She swallowed hard against the lump in her throat as she trudged behind Giselle and tried not to think of a life without her dearest friend. The throb of her knee was a distraction from the pain in her heart, so she focussed her attention on that instead and allowed the agonising hurt to serve as punishment for her part in their awful predicament.

They tramped through the forest for another two hours, stopping only for water and to adjust the belongings they were carrying. Giselle and Jenna had each offered to share some of Kira's burden and lighten her load, but she declined.

"Thank you, but you have enough of your own to carry."

She saw the glance exchanged between her friends and knew they were worried about her. "I'll be alright when we get to the priory," she said, "I just need some willow bark tea and a poultice on my knee. I'll rest up tonight and tomorrow it'll be fine, you'll see."

"I hope your treatments are more effective than your lies, Kira, or your reputation as a healer is surely undeserved," said Giselle, eyebrows raised. "Give us your bag at least. Jenna and I can carry it between us."

"But—"

"No buts, my friend. If the shoe was on the other foot, you'd have done it for us ages ago. You saved our lives, you goose, it's the least we can do."

"I can manage—" Kira started to say.

"Shut up!" Giselle interrupted again. "I don't want to hear it. Now hand over that bag, you goose, and let's get going."

Startled into compliance by her friend's scolding, Kira eased the burden from her aching shoulders and handed the bag of clothes to Giselle. Ned helped Kira to put her satchel back in place as her friends each took a handle of the travel bag.

"The path is a bit wider through here, don't worry, lass," he whispered as he adjusted the straps. "By the time it narrows again, Tangler will be here, you mark my words."

"Thank you," she said, her voice thick with emotion.

Less than an hour later, Kira heard the whinny of a horse in the distance. "Behind the trees. Quick now!" Ned hissed in an urgent whisper as he ushered them from the path and into the undergrowth.

"Stay low. Don't move. Jock and I will make sure it's Tangler. Stay quiet."

Kira watched as the two guards crept along the edge of the path and then melted into the trees. She sent a silent prayer to the Goddess they would meet Tangler and not those horse thieves, and rested her cheek on the wet grass. Giselle lay on the ground not a yard away. Her expression was hard to read in the disappearing light, but Kira could hear the uneven panting of her breath. She reached out her hand and Giselle grabbed it tight.

"All will be well," whispered Kira. "We'll be at the Priory in next to no time." Giselle pursed her lips and closed her eyes, nodding.

"I hear horses," hissed Jenna.

They lay in silence as the sound of hoofbeats and the jangle of tack grew closer.

"They should be here, somewhere," said Jock. "It's us, lasses. You can come out."

The girls didn't move.

"Ha! You've taught them well," said a voice Kira would recognise anywhere. "Come out, you brave girls. Cabarac salutes you."

Kira gripped Giselle's hand even tighter. She locked eyes with Jenna and shook her head.

Tangler called out again. "You're safe, girls. Hurry now. It will be dark soon and the path to the priory too hard to find."

The silence was as heavy as a blanket and though Kira felt the weight of it, a lesson had been learned, and Ned's warning had been clear. Either he or Jock had to say the safe word.

Finally, Ned spoke. "Cabarac."

Jenna leaped to her feet. "Here! We're here. Kira needs a hand."

Before Kira could object, Tangler and Farren were at her side. "I'm fine, really," she started to say, but her knee gave way as soon as she tried to put any weight on it, and she sat back on the grass with a thud.

"So I see," said Tangler.

Kira bristled at the amusement in his tone. "The grass is wet."

"Yes, it is," he said kindly. "All the more reason to allow us to help." He turned and nodded. "Farren." They each hooked an arm beneath her armpits and hoisted her up. A spasm of pain shot down her leg and she gasped. Lying on the cold, wet grass had done her knee no favours. Tangler took a flask from his saddle bag and offered it to Kira. "A little medicinal concoction from the north," he said with a wink. "It'll warm you up and ease the ache in your knee."

Kira took a swig. The liquor burned the back of her throat, and her eyes began to water but before she could complain a delicious warmth spread throughout her body and the aftertaste on her tongue was an odd combination of honey and cloves. She took another sip, then handed the flask back to Tangler. "Thank you."

He vaulted onto the saddle and took the reins from Ned, who stepped forward and lifted her off her feet like she weighed no more than a sack of flour. He tossed her onto the back of the horse to sit behind Tangler. She looked around for her friends. Giselle was behind Farren, and Jenna was being given a leg up behind Jock. Ned began gathering up their belongings and stowing them on the saddle of the other horse. He nodded to Tangler. "Let's move."

Tangler undid the cloak he was wearing and with a flick of his wrists managed to fling it over Kira's shoulders. She felt its warmth immediately. "Hold tight, my dear, we'll be there before you know it." Kira clasped her hands around his waist and lulled by the steady rhythm of his heartbeat beneath her cheek, and whatever he had given her to drink, felt herself drifting.

She dreamed. Not of firebirds, but of grey owls with white faces and kind eyes. They lifted her from the horse and flew with her up the steps of a small castle, high into the turrets where the walls were covered with tapestries and the floors with thick rugs of deep red. They took her robes and lowered her into a copper tub filled with hot water perfumed with lavender and rose. They unbraided her hair, and she tried to protest because she had promised Agatha that no one should ever see her hair loose, but the owls didn't listen, and they washed her clean and dressed her in a soft white linen sleeping shift and then laid her on a cloud to sleep again.

When Kira woke, a woman in a grey habit was standing at the end of her bed watching her. Kira blinked. The bed was a magnificent four-poster, with intricate carvings around the columns and foot. Above her head was a highly detailed tapestry of a snowy owl in full flight with a staff clenched in its talons. She glanced around at her unfamiliar surroundings. The light from several lanterns emitted a soft glow around the bed, but the room beyond was in darkness.

"Well met, Kira. May you always be blessed with the Light of the Goddess."

"Well met, Sister. As I am blessed, so shall you be," Kira replied with the traditional greeting that was rarely used outside religious celebrations. She eased herself into a seated position and gathered her hair into her fist.

"You have beautiful hair, Kira, though I think, for your sake, and for ours, it may be prudent to secure it in a braid. Its unruliness could be a little disconcerting for some."

"Yes, Sister." Kira felt her face flame and lowered her head. "I'm sorry." She quickly plaited her curls and twisted the braid around her head, tucking the end into place.

"Do not apologise for your heritage, my dear. The Valethrix blood thrums in your veins, that much is evident. Whether this will be a blessing or a curse, I fear, will depend on you and the choices you make," she said cryptically. Kira stared at her blankly. She had no idea what the nun was talking about. Her stomach growled.

"Forgive me, my dear. I brought you a tray. The others have eaten and have also gone to bed, but I thought you may be hungry when you woke." She picked up a wooden tray from the table in front of the bed and placed it on Kira's lap, removing the silver cloche with a flourish. "Potato, leek and bacon soup. Bread and cheese. I will send you some more willow bark tea shortly. How is your knee?"

Kira flexed her leg. The pain had been reduced to a dull ache. She looked up, surprised. "Much better, thank you. How did...?" Her voice trailed off. Too much was happening, maybe she was still dreaming. "Thank you for the food, Sister."

"Eat up, Kira. All will be well. Come and see me in the morning. I think we will have a great deal to talk about, you and I."

Kira paused with the spoon halfway to her mouth. "Yes, Sister. Erm…who shall I ask for? I'm sorry, I didn't catch your name."

The nun smiled. "Sister Evangeline is my name. Or just ask for the prioress if you forget. I'll answer to both." She left the room and closed the door with barely a click.

Chapter 15

When Kira woke again the sunlight was streaming through the window and onto the wall that she had been unable to see in the darkness the night before. On the thick grey stone was a silver shield depicting the sign of the Goddess. Beneath the crescent moon flew an owl, similar to the tapestry above her bed. Radiating from the circular shield were wooden staffs tipped with silver or gold and studded with coloured stones that glinted brightly as the light touched them. The military display seemed at odds with the beautiful tapestries in the rest of the room until Kira realised that most of them depicted nuns in battle stance, wielding staff or flame. With a jolt of surprise, Kira realised that the Sisters of the Flame must be guardians.

Before she could process the information, there was a knock at the door, and she heard Giselle's voice. "Kira, are you awake?"

Her friend didn't wait for an answer and opened the door. She ran across the floor and jumped on the bed, throwing her arms around Kira and giving her a hug.

"Well met, Kira! Are you well? I told Sister Evangeline that you are usually up at the crack of dawn, so you were bound to be awake at nine o'clock and probably hungry for your breakfast, so she said we could come and visit you and bring you some food, so here we are!" Giselle finally ran out of breath and let go of her friend. Jenna was standing in the doorway, holding a serving tray. She grinned at Kira. "Well met, Kira. Your breakfast awaits."

"Well met, my friends. I'm so pleased to see you. Thank you!" Kira eased herself into a sitting position and accepted the tray from Jenna.

"How's your knee?" she asked.

"Much better. I don't know what the Sisters put on it, but it hardly aches at all. The swelling has gone down, but the bruising has started to show. I really should get up, I'm hardly an invalid!"

"Have your breakfast first," said Giselle. "Sister Evangeline wants to see us all when you have eaten and dressed."

"She's so lovely. Not at all what I expected a prioress to be. I'd love to be able to stay. I've wanted to become a Sister of the Flame for as long as I can remember," said Jenna with a sigh.

"I didn't realise they were guardians," said Kira between mouthfuls of porridge.

"It's not spoken about much since the Purge," Jenna nodded. "Not all nuns who represent the Goddess are guardians of course, but the Sisters at this priory have been protectors of the Eternal Flame for more than a thousand years. To the outside world they are like any other religious order, but the nuns here are all trained to fight. There are secrets within these walls that need to be protected at any cost." Jenna's face suddenly flushed as though she realised she had said too much.

"How do you know so much about them?" asked Giselle.

"We have had Sisters of the Flame in our family for generations," said Jenna with a touch of pride. "It's sort of a tradition. We don't talk about it. Well, not about them being guardians, anyway." She looked at Kira's empty plate. "If you've finished, I'll take your tray to the kitchen and let you dress. Elle can show you the way to the Chapel. I'll meet you there."

Kira gulped down the last of the tea and allowed Jenna to collect her dishes. "Thank you."

Kira listened to Giselle's account of their arrival at the priory as she washed and dressed and redid her braids. Her knee was turning purple, but apart from feeling a little stiff, the intense pain was gone, leaving a dull ache she hardly noticed. There were a few tender spots on her face, but since the bathroom had no mirror, she was unable to see why. She suspected that Tangler had put a potion in the drink he had given her, because she had no recollection of their ride through the forest, and only her strange dream about the owls, which she realised must have been the nuns.

"I'm ready." Kira ran a fingertip over the sore spots on her face. "What have I done here?"

Giselle grimaced. "You did nothing. You got a few splinters from the roof of the carriage when the arrows struck, remember?"

Kira would never forget. She bowed her head and sighed deeply. "Poor Mevis."

"Don't you dare say again that it was all your fault!" said Giselle fiercely. "You saved our lives back there. We'd all be dead if it wasn't for you. The Sisters told us that they have removed the splinters and you won't have any scars to mar your beautiful face."

Kira rolled her eyes. "Shall we go?"

Their footsteps echoed on the flagstones as they walked down a long corridor. Unlike her bedchamber, the walls were sparsely decorated and only with the more traditional religious artefacts and paintings associated with the Goddess and the Eternal Flame. The expanse of grey was interrupted by tall, arched windows overlooking the forest and mountains in the distance, and a large lake beyond a walled garden below. Kira would have loved to stop and admire the view, but Giselle quickened her pace as a bell tolled twice. "End of guidance," she said over her shoulder. "Don't know what it means, exactly, but Sister Evangeline asked that we meet her after guidance, and that it would be marked by the bell."

She turned to go down a flight of stairs, "Do you need a hand? Can you manage down the steps with your knee?"

Kira grabbed the railing. "No, thank you, it's fine."

At the bottom of the stairs the passage ran in two directions. Giselle glanced left and right then pointed to the left. "It's this way. See that door with the sign of the Goddess? That's where we have to wait. Jenna is already there."

The door opened as they approached, and about a dozen nuns exited the Chapel beyond in single file, heads bowed. Kira's nostrils twitched. She stared at the women as they filed past. Guidance was most definitely not sitting in the Chapel whispering devotional prayers. Their faces were flushed, and a sheen of perspiration covered their skin. The scent of hard work lingered on their clothes, and Kira realised with some surprise that their grey habits were not robes at all, but more of a tabard, slit to the thigh. Beneath the tabard she glimpsed wide-legged trousers, gathered at the ankle.

Kira turned back towards the door and found Sister Evangeline watching her. Her face was glowing, but her voice was steady when she spoke. "Well met and blessings to you all." She nodded towards the backs of the retreating nuns and smiled. "There are many ways to serve the Goddess. Some of us require guidance for not only the heart and the soul, but the body, also." She invited the trio into the chapel with a wave of her hand. "Please. Come in."

Kira stood in the oak doorway, transfixed. The chapel was narrow, with small wooden pews on either side of the aisle. There were only ten rows. The ornate wooden altar in the nave was carved with scenes depicting the four seasons. A statue of the Lady Edalyn stood to one side holding a lamp in one hand with a coronet of stars on her head, as was traditional in places of worship. Unlike other statues Kira had seen, however, the Lady held a staff in the other hand and a round shield similar to the one on the wall in her bedchamber, hung from the crook of her elbow.

But it was the stained-glass window dominating the small chapel which drew her eye. Lady Edalyn stood beneath a crescent moon, in front of a forest of green, with the Flame in a brazier at her feet. On her left shoulder perched a large grey owl, and on her outstretched right palm sat an open book. Kira stared at the window and tried to swallow the lump that had formed in her throat. It was breathtaking.

The prioress broke the silence as she spoke, "The window is beautiful, is it not?" She glanced at it briefly, then continued, not expecting an answer. "I am aware that one of your travelling companions was delivered to the arms of the angel yesterday. Before we talk further, I wondered if you would like to light a flame in her memory. At the Aurora Cantus this morning, the nuns chanted the blessing for the dead and each lit a candle to help her soul find its way to the Goddess. You are welcome to add your candle to theirs." Sister Evangeline motioned towards a tiered table filled with miniature lanterns. Kira followed the others and waited as they each took a small candle, lit it from a flame sitting in the centre of an ornate silver bowl, and placed it inside an empty lantern.

Kira's hand trembled as she held the candle wick over the flame. She took a steadying breath and the flame finally caught. *Eternal Blessings, Mevis, I am truly sorry. Please forgive me.* Kira felt Giselle's hand on her shoulder and smiled down at her friend. As they moved from the table the clouds parted outside and a beam of light shone through the glass, bathing the walls and floor of the nave in brilliant colour.

"I think Mevis is letting us know she sits in the glade of the Goddess," whispered Giselle. Kira nodded. The sentiment was lovely. She hoped it was true.

Sister Evangeline had overheard, it seemed. She smiled sadly.

"Before the purge, I could have spoken freely of the Lady Edalyn and the role magic played in her quest for the Eternal Flame. For now, let us say what you have been taught to believe is true, and the window represents The Lady, The Flame, and the Book of Truth. Ultimately, she represents all that is good about the Goddess of Light, and for the time being that will suffice. If, in the future, you desire to learn more, all you need do is ask. Do not seek the knowledge, however, if you are not prepared for the challenges that the answer may bring."

Judging by Giselle's puzzled frown, Kira was not the only one confused by the cryptic nature of Sister Evangeline's statement. She nibbled the inside of her lip thoughtfully. The prioress beckoned and turned towards a door to the left of the altar. A whiff of honey and new-mown hay wafted in the air as the door opened and for the first time Kira noticed the garlands of woodruff suspended around the walls of the chapel. She glanced again at the window and gave in to the urge to make the sign of the angel as she met the Lady's gaze.

The room they entered was more of a library than a study. The floor-to-ceiling shelves that lined the two longest walls were crammed with books. *There must be thousands of them,* thought Kira. If the Chapel had taken her aback with its simple beauty, the sight of the books touched Kira's heart in a way she could never have anticipated. She felt as though they beckoned to her, begging to be read. It was disconcerting, to say the least. Just when her head felt it might explode with the voices that sang in her mind, Sister Evangeline clapped her hands and said "Enough." The books quieted immediately. Kira smiled at the prioress in relief and received a quizzical smile in return. Giselle was gazing around the room in wonder. She loved reading almost as much as Kira, yet was evidently unaffected by the call of the books. Kira swallowed nervously against the dryness of her throat.

Towards the back of the room was a small wooden table and four comfortable looking armchairs with gilded legs. The table was set for morning tea. Sister Evangeline invited them to sit and took a thick cloth from a hook on the fireplace to wrap around the handle of a kettle warming on the hearth. She poured the steaming water into a silver teapot and the scent of chamomile and mint perfumed the air. When the tea had steeped to her satisfaction, she filled the porcelain cups and handed one to each of the friends.

"Firstly, let me welcome you to the Priory, I know this is an unexpected detour on your journey to White Haven, and ultimately the Legion Isles, but I hope you will find your time here beneficial. The Priory has always offered sanctuary for those in need. Its ability to protect meets even the exacting standards of your guards, Ned and Jock." Sister Evangeline raised her eyebrows and gave a wry smile, "They have agreed that you will be safe here while they go with Tangler to procure more horses and arrange for your carriage to be repaired."

Jenna's face lit up. "You mean we actually get to stay here?"

"For a few days at least, perhaps longer. I have given my word, however, that you will be in White Haven to meet with Lord Callan and the quota."

"Oh," said Jenna.

"Don't be too disappointed, Jenna. Unfortunately, incidents such as the attack you experienced yesterday are becoming all too common. It seems priorities have changed at the Palace; the Royal Guard pursues harmless young women with greater fervour than it does horse thieves and brigands. The Crown obviously believes a hint of magic is of greater concern than the loss of life or property, or indeed the repair and maintenance of roads and bridges."

Kira was taken aback by the bitter note in the prioress' otherwise deliberate way of speaking. Tangler wasn't the only one unimpressed with Piscator and the Royal Guard.

The prioress sighed deeply and continued in a more even tone. "The mountains that surround River Province are not just an inconvenience for travellers such as yourselves. Much of what happens in Shardial, and in the provinces that border our Capital, reaches us slowly. This is not such a terrible thing. The panic that grips the population when the King sneezes twice before breakfast, or the Crown Prince's horse throws a shoe on a Tuesday, when on Monday a magpie flew over his head, fortunately runs out of legs well before we need to suffer such folly."

Kira kept as still as she could. She had never heard anyone speak like this before, certainly no one in authority.

"Tangler has informed me of the actions of the Dispatcher Piscator, in River Glen and other villages in River Province. His methods are abhorrent, and I condemn them without reservation. Unfortunately, these are not isolated incidents. There have been rumours of increased prosecutions throughout Cabarac, and while not all dispatchers serve as cruel a punishment as Piscator, executions are on the rise. I will not burden you further with the political orchestrations stirring trouble in Shardial right now; you young women have had to deal with more than your fair share of strife already. It saddens me to think that it may be safer for you all in the Legion Isles, but regardless of the future, you need to be better prepared. I think we can help you with that."

Sister Evangeline paused to take a sip of her tea and Kira mirrored her action, feeling like she had swallowed a spoon of dry oats. She wasn't sure that she liked the direction the prioress' words were pointing.

Chapter 16

Sister Evangeline opened a small drawer on her side of the table and placed three leaves of paper and a small silver inkwell and matching pen in front of her.

"Before I elaborate, I would like you to meet someone." She smiled and quickly wrote a few lines on each page. She folded the messages in half after blotting the ink and handed one to each of the friends.

"Read the words to yourself and remember them. Please do not share what you have read."

Kira opened the page and read the elegant black script.

The woman you are about to see was so severely beaten by her drunken husband that she can hardly walk. She has lost the sight in one eye and can barely see from the other, rendering her almost completely blind. She has no other family to take care of her.

The prioress rang a small bell and a few minutes later the door opened, and a middle-aged woman staggered into the room. She limped painfully towards them with one arm outstretched as if feeling her way. She stopped a few feet from the table, head bowed, body swaying slightly.

"On the count of three, I would like you to hold up one finger if you think this woman should be in prison, two fingers if you think she should be in an asylum and three if you think she should stay in the priory. One, two, three."

Kira was surprised to see that she was the only one to hold up three fingers. Giselle held up one and Jenna two.

"She should be in prison," exclaimed Giselle.

"She should be taken to an asylum and kept there until she is cured," said Jenna.

The girls all spoke at once.

"Her husband is the one who should be in prison, not her!" Kira couldn't believe what the others were saying.

"There's no cure for what she has done!" Giselle was adamant.

"Her poor husband loves her. Why would you separate them when she is so ill?" Jenna looked between them; her brows furrowed in bewilderment.

The prioress clapped her hands for silence.

"Giselle, perhaps you can tell us why you think this woman should be imprisoned?"

"She spends all her money on fortified wine and neglects her children. Two have starved to death. She fell into a ditch dead drunk, and the baby drowned."

"What?" interrupted Jenna. "No, she has been ill with winterfever. Her poor husband found her wandering half naked in the snow. She has severe frostbite on her feet and suffers with hallucinations."

Kira was impressed. "You gave us all a different description. Yet each could account for the way she moves. We all have our own version of the truth."

"Indeed," said Sister Evangeline and waved her hand in the direction of the woman, who now stood tall, steady, and clear-eyed. "You were all given information you believed to be true, and her actions confirmed it for you. And yet, as you can now see, the truth is something else entirely. Meet Sister Eloise, Mistress of the Staff, and expert in disguise."

The nun inclined her head. "Well met, and blessings, young travellers. Sister Evangeline has informed me of your predicament, and I hope we can give you respite for the brief time you are here. I hope you can see why Sister Evangeline gave you this little exercise. Not everything you are told will be the truth, so do not be too quick to accept everything on face value. Be sure of its worth. Think on this in the future and remember how easily you were deceived by a few lines on a piece of paper written by someone you thought you could trust."

Kira exchanged a look with Giselle. It was a powerful message delivered in a way that made it easy to understand. And remember.

Sister Eloise took a cup from the sideboard and poured herself some tea, then stood with her back to the fire and studied them over the rim of her cup as she blew on the hot liquid. She was straight-backed and alert and had a completely changed demeanour from the woman who had first entered the room.

"Sister Evangeline and I both think that it would be best if you receive some training while you are here."

"Training?" said Giselle with a note of challenge in her question.

Two spots of colour bloomed on her pale cheeks. "Your pardon, Staff Mistress, I did not mean to sound rude. I'm afraid I am a little rattled…" She shrugged and gave a little wave of her hand that somehow encompassed all that had just happened.

"There is no need to apologise, Giselle. You have all been through a great deal. All the more reason to begin training. Rest assured, you are not training to become a Sister of the Flame," Sister Eloise said with a smile. "I will be teaching you the basic art of self-defence. You may be young women, but there is no reason for you not to be able to defend yourselves when the need arises. As you recently discovered, there may be occasions when you do not have guards to protect you, and you should know some fundamental countermeasures, should you be attacked."

Kira felt her heart sink. *What countermeasure was there for an arrow through the chest?*

Giselle stared at Kira for a few seconds. "Excellent," she said. "I think that is a particularly good idea. Women have had to rely on men for protection for far too long. Who knows what we will encounter in the Legion Isles? I will be glad of some knowledge. What say you, Kira? Jenna?"

Kira raised her eyebrows. What Giselle said rang true and Kira acknowledged her friend's good sense. "I say that I agree. Who knows what manner of man we meet on the Legion Isles? Hopefully, some with better manners than here in Cabarac."

"Yes, I hope so, too," said Jenna. "I felt quite helpless in the carriage yesterday. I would like to think I could do more than scream and yell 'shut the door' if ever we were attacked again."

"Excellent. No time like the present, so we will begin as soon as Sister Evangeline has finished with you."

"I have finished," said Sister Evangeline with a smile. She clasped the crescent in her fingers. "I did not want to cause distress with my words, only point out that what is happening to you is part of a much larger tapestry." She looked at them all, but Kira felt what she said next was aimed directly at her. "You do not need to feel you are at fault for anything that has happened. You are not to blame."

Kira wasn't sure what to think. She let the others walk ahead and took a few calming breaths before opening the door to her mind room. It reminded her so much of home and Agatha she was overcome with a wave of nostalgia so powerful it made her heart ache. She needed time to process what she had learned. Little news from Shardial reached River Glen unless it came in the form of a decree such as the one that had changed her future. What Sister Evangeline had told them was disturbing, but was she really telling the truth? Or was she testing them? She closed her mind room and hurried after the others.

Sister Eloise was waiting at the bottom of the stairs. She led them down a short corridor and through a heavy oak door. Kira glanced around the room in surprise. Despite being windowless, the chamber was brightly lit, and the air was fresh.

"Welcome to our guidance chamber," said Sister Eloise. "It's part of the catacombs beneath the priory. This is the area where novices learn the basics of the staff. There are other rooms where other skills are practiced. For now, this is the only chamber you will use." She pointed to a bench that ran half the length of the room, "You will find training tunics there on the bench. I think they should fit. The material is lightweight and easy to move in but still looks enough like traditional garb to fool prying eyes, in the unlikely event that someone enters the chamber uninvited."

The tunics were similar to the outfits Kira had seen the other nuns wearing when they filed out from the chapel: pale grey trousers gathered at the ankle, a white top made from the finest wool she had ever seen, and an ankle-length darker grey tabard that belted at the waist. It was remarkably comfortable, if a little cool.

"You may feel a little chilly to start," said Sister Eloise, as though she had read Kira's thoughts, "but by the end of our session, you will be glad you are not wearing anything heavier. Now… Before any exercise, we must warm up our muscles. First, we stretch. Then I will teach you about the staff."

The next three hours flew by, and it did not take the friends long to break into a sweat. Kira's exercises were modified slightly to protect her healing knee, but to compensate she put extra effort into the upper body drills. By the time they broke for lunch, Kira was able to hold and wield the staff correctly and could confidently stand in ready stance. Though her muscles ached with the unaccustomed exercise, she hadn't given a single thought to the traumas of the last few days.

Sister Eloise was a strict but patient teacher, and informed them that she would train with them for three hours a day until they had to leave the priory. Not every hour was to be devoted to work with the staff, however. She would also instruct them on how to hit with the heel of the hand, elbow and knee, and the areas of vulnerability to aim for, such as the eyes, nose, throat and groin.

"You will need to practice every day to become proficient in the staff, but also to develop your reflexes." The staff mistress smiled grimly. "You will be able to see for yourselves how hard you train."

Kira had no idea what she meant until a couple of days later, when she noticed the large bruises that had formed on her upper arms, not from her opponent's weapon, but from the constant striking of her own staff against her body when she practiced the diagonal strikes. Jenna's bruising was even worse, as she threw herself into the training with such enthusiasm that Sister Eloise had to warn her not to overdo it. Kira hoped their training wouldn't be needed on the Legion Isles, or anywhere for that matter, but each night was thankful for the effort she put in when she fell asleep almost as soon as her head touched the pillow.

Chapter 17

After training on the fourth day, Sister Eloise congratulated them on their progress. "As a special treat, I would like to introduce you to one of our most beloved nuns, Sister Marguerite. She has been in service to the Flame for longer than anyone here at the priory, and she would like to speak with you. I will meet you at the entrance to the courtyard opposite the dining hall after lunch."

The small courtyard was bathed in the afternoon sun. A large apple tree grew to the side, near an ivy-covered wall, its leafless branches a stark contrast to the green creeper. In summer, the canopy would provide a welcome dappled shade, thought Kira, but the early winter frosts had already stripped the leaves and they carpeted the cobblestones in faded shades of autumn.

Despite the sunlight, the air was still crisp and the tiny figure sitting on one of several wooden benches in the centre of the courtyard was cocooned in a woollen knee rug and a thick shawl. As they approached, Kira could see that the old woman's eyes were covered by a thin strip of gauze tied around her face, which was deeply tanned and as wrinkled as Agatha's. The nun raised her head.

"Ah, Sister Eloise. Blessed be. You bring me hot cocoa and visitors," she said in a surprisingly clear and melodic voice. "What a treat!"

"I have indeed, Sister Marguerite. Would you like me to introduce them to you?"

"Oh no, my dear Eloise, where's the fun in that?" she exclaimed cheerfully and extended her hand to receive the mug of cocoa. She cradled the mug and brought it to her nose. "Ooh, lovely. I smell Sister Dulcima's excellent malted whisky if I'm not mistaken. Thank you. A double treat. Now you run along, Sister, I'm sure these young girls will keep me company while I sup."

Sister Eloise grinned. "Certainly. I'll come and rescue them in half an hour, shall I?"

Sister Marguerite cocked her head as though listening to a distant conversation. She shook her head. "No dear, I think I will need longer than that. I'll ring the bell."

Kira noticed a small silver bell on the arm of the seat. The curved handle of a walking stick rested alongside.

"Pull up a bench, my dears. Sit opposite me so I can get a good look at you," she laughed at herself. "I may not be able to see how beautiful you all are, but I can sense your auras as clearly as you can read a book." She paused as the girls manoeuvred the bench into position.

"Sit yourselves down. That's it."

Unlike the other nuns, Sister Marguerite wore a knitted bonnet that fastened under her chin with long tasselled straps. Wisps of white hair peeked from beneath the bonnet where the gauze blindfold slipped under the straps. Kira guessed that the elderly nun was even older than Agatha, but her voice betrayed neither her age nor her infirmity.

"My name, as you have been told, is Sister Marguerite. And, as you can see, I am blind. What Sister Eloise will not have told you, because that is my story to tell if I choose to do so, is that I am a seer."

Kira felt a knot form in her stomach. A seer? She rubbed her thumb across the corner of the armrest and concentrated on the rough texture of the wood against her skin as she waited to hear what Sister Marguerite would say next. She inhaled deeply and was rewarded with the delicate citrus fragrance of winter clematis and glanced around to find the glossy green foliage of the climber trailing over a decorative arch. She was surprised to see that the white bell-shaped flowers were already in bloom, weeks earlier than she would have expected. Ever since she had opened Gwyneth's herbal, the world had seemed just a little off kilter and Kira wasn't sure she was ready for any more revelations.

The little nun continued her chatter, apparently unaware of Kira's apprehension. She waved her hand towards Jenna, who sat at the other end of the bench.

"I see an aura of blue on my left, here. Surely someone devout of heart. What is your name, my child?"

"Jenna. Jenna Lustrum, Sister."

"Ah, Jenna. I know many of your aunts. Your family do wonderful service to Lady Edalyn. You would like to follow in their footsteps, I think."

Kira closed her eyes. The seer saw Jenna's aura as blue? Perhaps it was coincidental, that she, too, had seen Jenna as blue back in the carriage when they were attacked. She opened them again and glanced between Jenna and Sister Marguerite.

"I would indeed. I was preparing to become a novitiate when I was gathered for the quota. I have prayed to the Goddess and to the Lady every day since to deliver me from my fate in the Legion Isles. If it wasn't for Giselle and Kira, I don't know what I would have done. But I feel blessed to be here at the priory, even if it is to be for a short time," said Jenna, her voice beginning to break.

"Fret not, dear Jenna. Would you allow me to take your hand?"

Jenna knelt at Sister Marguerite's feet and placed her right hand on top of the nun's. Sister Marguerite covered it with her other hand and raised her head, as before, as though she was listening.

"Ah, The Shield. For you, the path is straight and true if you follow your heart. The choice you make will be difficult and will mean separation from your friends. Your journey will have its own hardships and danger, but the reward will be great. If you choose instead, the path of least resistance, your life will be comfortable, but unfulfilled."

She patted Jenna's hand, "Choose wisely, my dear."

Jenna stared at the old nun for a few seconds, then bowed her head. "Thank you, Sister."

Giselle nudged Kira in the ribs and mouthed, "I hope mine's better than that."

Sister Marguerite faced Giselle and smiled. "And who is the girl with the aura of sunshine and buttercups?"

Kira felt a little sick. She nibbled on the inside of her lip and watched as Giselle slid from the bench and onto her knees.

"I am Giselle Threadgold, Sister Marguerite." She placed her hand onto the nun's open palm, "And I hope that your foretelling does not reduce it to mustard and dead leaves!"

Sister Marguerite chuckled. She covered Giselle's hand with hers and tilted her head. The smile faded from her face. It was a long minute before she spoke.

"The Vessel. The road you travel is fraught with danger. Remain steadfast in your vows and all will be well. Falter, and dark times befall many. Four times you will be faced with death before true happiness is yours. But remember that the choice you made before this journey even began is the very thing that will save you in the end. With sacrifice comes reward. Blessings to you, Giselle."

Giselle sat back on the bench, her eyes bright with unshed tears.

Kira frowned at her friend's white face. Giselle patted her lightly on the knee and shrugged. "Mustard and dead leaves," she whispered.

"And lastly we have a young woman who is a healer, if I'm not mistaken. Although your aura swirls with other colours besides the traditional forest green that I associate with healers." Sister Marguerite patted the seat next to her, "Come and sit here, child, I sense your knee would not thank me if it rested on the cold cobblestones."

Kira inhaled deeply and took her place. She flexed her fingers several times and pressed her palm to the nun's. A strange tingle ran up her arm, as though she had plunged a hand half frozen with cold into a bowl of warm water.

"My name is Kira of River Glen."

"Ah, I see," said Sister Marguerite, her previous cheery tone replaced with one that was much more subdued, sombre even. "Cause and effect. The Lock and the Key." She paused, "You will feel, at times, like the weight of the world is on your shoulders, Kira of River Glen, but you must listen to your heart and seek solace in your gift. Trust in your teachings and know that it is sometimes necessary to sever an arm to save the body. Destruction is sometimes required in order to heal. You, more than most, will have to make impossible choices. Lean on your gifts, and do not, for a minute think you make them alone. Keep your friends close."

Come and see me tomorrow after you break your fast, Kira. I have things that I need to show you. Come alone, if you please, and tell no one.

Kira answered both in her mind and out loud. "Yes, Sister. I will."

"Fish and pickles," said Jenna with a sigh. "Do you think Sister Marguerite is a wee bit addled? I mean no disrespect, but 'The Shield, the Vessel, the Lock and the Key?' Really? Do you think this is another one of Sister Evangeline's tests? Are we supposed to believe what she said or… or…" She slumped on the bed and massaged her temples. "I don't know what's going on anymore!"

Kira understood Jenna's dejection, but she was more concerned about Giselle, who had been unusually quiet on their walk back to Kira's bedchamber. She poured a glass of water from the pitcher on her table and handed it to her friend. "Is something amiss?"

Giselle smiled her thanks and shook her head. She sipped the water, then cleared her throat. "I think the foretelling had a ring of truth, don't you? Despite the strangeness of her words, I felt her sincerity as she spoke. I don't think she was trying to fool us."

Kira sighed. "No, unfortunately, I don't think she was."

"But I don't want to go anywhere without you," said Jenna, wiping away a tear. "I mean, I've always wanted to take my vows, but you are my best friends. I don't want us to part."

Kira sat on the bed and put her arm over Jenna's shoulders.

"Before you start apologising again," said Giselle, with a nod towards Kira, "I'll tell you this. My father's sister had the intuition. She often knew things before they happened. Little things, like the change in the weather, or if someone was with child. Occasionally she would get a premonition about something bad that might happen, but she always said that what she saw was only a possibility. If the circumstances changed, then so would the outcome. If not," she shrugged, "then it would come true."

"I didn't know that," said Kira, wide eyed.

"No," replied Giselle with a note of apology in her voice. "Like Jenna's family, it is something we keep very closed lipped about. We all have secrets we need to protect from the people who might not understand. You are not as alone in this as you might think, Kira. I'll bet many families in River Glen would be wary of the likes of Dispatcher Piscator."

Kira was lost for words. For most of her life, and certainly in the last few weeks, she had felt the burden of secrecy. She realised, of course, that everyone had secret thoughts and dreams that they wished to keep private, but it had never occurred to her their secrets might also be dangerous. The tension she wore like a scarf suddenly seemed a little less restrictive.

Giselle joined them on the bed and took hold of Kira's hand. "Sister Marguerite was right, Kira. You don't have to face whatever the future holds alone. You have a special gift, and it helps people. Just because some people are afraid of it, doesn't make it bad. Stop blaming yourself for what happened to Mevis. Remember, you saved the life of a child, and you saved our lives, too." She nudged Kira with her shoulder and smiled ruefully. "Besides, if the foretelling is true, my life will be in danger three more times, and I think it will be your magic that saves me!"

Magic. Giselle had said the word out loud. Kira swallowed against the painful lump in her throat.

"Why do you look so shocked?" Giselle asked gently. "Are you surprised that we know this?" She tilted Kira's chin with her finger. "Or is it… Don't tell me you didn't know yourself!"

Kira sighed and shook her head. "Not until recently. Well, that's not exactly true. I've always known I had the Eiran, but I didn't consider it magic. Not the type of magic to get me killed, anyway. I think I know different now." She smiled, unused to the lightness her confession had brought to her heart. "But how did you know?"

Giselle raised her eyebrows. "Your hair. Do you not remember the scalper?"

Kira went cold. Goosebumps rose along her arms. The memory was distressing, yet oddly, she remembered very few details. She recalled a stranger in the woods, being very frightened and then Agatha and Uncle Tangler comforting her. Tangler? Why was he there?

"A scalper? Don't see them in River Glen very often. The girls there wouldn't want to sell their hair," said Jenna, running her hand over her braids.

"No, and that was the problem, I think. This man had no takers, and he was desperate for hair, had a special order for a blonde wig, he told me. Kira and I were picking mushrooms in the woods, and he tried to get me to give him my braids for a bag of toffee and a rag doll. When I refused, he grabbed me and tried to cut my hair anyway."

"What! How old were you?"

"Six or seven, I think."

"What happened? How did you get away?"

"Kira. She grabbed a stick and whacked him across his back, and when he lunged at her I was able to wriggle free. He grabbed Kira instead and took his knife and sliced off her braid."

As Giselle spoke, the cloud that had fogged her memory suddenly cleared and Kira was able to recall in perfect detail what had happened. She stared at Giselle.

"He threw me to the ground and picked up the stick," she whispered, "and told you to let him cut your hair or he would beat me with the stick."

"Lady Edalyn!" breathed Jenna. "What a monster. What happened next?"

Giselle's eyes filled with tears. "He did. He did hit her with the stick. Just so's I'd know he meant what he said. I was terrified, but before I could move, Kira's braid suddenly burst into flame in his hand and the scalper ran screaming to the river."

"We ran all the way to the cottage," said Kira. "Agatha put me to bed and Tangler took Giselle home."

"My father and some other men went looking for the scalper. They found his campsite, but there was no sign of him. My mother didn't exactly not believe me, but she thought I might have been embellishing the tale."

"Why in the name of the Goddess would she think that?" exclaimed Jenna.

Kira touched her braid with her fingertips. "Because when Giselle and her mother came to see me the next morning, my hair had grown back to the length it was before."

Giselle squeezed her shoulder. "If it wasn't for the bruise across Kira's back, I'm not sure I would have believed me, either. Agatha reassured my mother, I remember that. She made up some tale about the scalper tripping and landing in the fire, and us being so scared, things had jumbled up in our minds. You were so quiet and so sad for weeks, Kira, do you remember? My mother made me promise not to speak of it to you, so I never did."

Giselle took a sip of water. "I never forgot it, though. And for the longest time I thought it was because you had magical hair." She laughed. "You never wore your hair loose; it was always in a braid. My mother said it was because it was so curly, but I thought it was to keep the magic from flying away."

Kira sank into the steaming water of her bath and allowed the scent of rose and lavender to soothe her battered senses. Giselle's revelation had shaken her more than she let on. Why hadn't she been able to recall the incident with the scalper before now? For someone who had always prided herself on her memory, the realisation was unsettling, to say the least. Why hadn't it been in her mind room? She felt adrift in a rudderless boat. So much was happening that was out of her control. So much had changed in such a few short weeks. She longed to talk to her grandmother. Agatha had always told Kira that the Eiran was stronger in her than in anyone she'd ever met, but if there was another magic in her too, why not tell her the truth? So many secrets. She held her breath and slipped beneath the suds.

Chapter 18

A howling gale, and rain pelting against the window, woke Kira. She grabbed a shawl from the end of her bed and padded across the room to look at the storm. Through the rivulets water running down the glass she could see the trees in the garden below bent against the wind, and the sky filled with ominous, dark grey clouds. She hoped the storm would not delay Tangler and the others. If she was unable to ask Agatha for answers, then maybe he could supply some. She ran her fingers over the bracelet he had given her. It was odd; some days she forgot she was even wearing it, and then she would look down and there it was. She shivered and hastened to get dressed. Her clothes had been placed in a cedar chest, and she rummaged through them to find the thick woollen jumper that Agatha had knitted for her birthday. She held it to her nose and inhaled deeply, trying to find any lingering scent that Agatha may have left behind.

She had her meeting with Sister Marguerite to deal with this morning. Her stomach growled and Kira rolled her eyes. Breakfast first.

The prioress joined them at the breakfast table just as Kira finished the last of her oats.

"Blessings to you all," said Sister Evangeline, inclining her head. "I was hoping that perhaps you would like to do some chores to ease the burden on the sisters and pass the time, since it is such a miserable day outside," she added, after they had returned her greeting. She continued without waiting for a response. "Kira, our apothecary, Sister Catherine could use a hand, but before you go there, could you deliver this to Sister Marguerite please, since you will pass her room on the way?" She handed Kira a small package wrapped in brown paper and tied with string.

"Giselle, I hear your needlework skills are exceptional, so I wonder if you would assist Sister Victoria in the sewing room. And Jenna, we will be having extra guests tonight, so I am sure Cook would appreciate a helping hand in the kitchen. Sister Eloise will see you all after lunch to continue your training."

Whether it was by coincidence or design, Kira wasn't sure, but she was glad that she didn't need to find an excuse to meet Sister Marguerite alone. She drank the rest of her tea and made her way to the seer's room.

The door was opened by a plump-bodied nun with deep blue eyes that sparkled with good humour. She balanced a wooden tray between her hip and her outstretched arm, beckoning Kira inside with a nod of her head. "Ah, well met and blessings to you! You must be Kira. I'm Sister Catherine. You'll be coming to see me, I believe—well, you will if Sister Marguerite lets you out of her clutches! Don't keep her too long, Maggie," she tossed over her shoulder as she exited the room, "I have a list of jobs for her!" She winked at Kira and closed the door without waiting for a reply.

"Well met, Kira, and blessings to you. Come in my dear, take a seat."

"Well met and blessings to you, too, Sister Marguerite." Kira glanced around the small room as she sat in the armchair opposite the little nun. The walls were painted the colour of clotted cream and sparsely decorated with paintings of the Lady Edalyn and wooden carvings of the crescent moon and its three stars. Above the narrow bed was a tapestry of an owl flying through a circle of flames. Kira thought of her bedchamber upstairs and was taken aback at the contrast. Her room was almost opulent compared to this.

"You are staying in the guest chambers, Kira. Most of the nuns have rooms like mine. The prioress' is a little bigger, of course, but that is as it should be." Sister Marguerite chuckled as she heard Kira's gasp of surprise. "I'm sorry, my dear, your thoughts are easy to read when you are this near. You need to shut the curtains, so to speak."

Kira blinked. "I'm afraid I don't know how to do that, Sister, I'm not sure what you mean."

"Ooh, I can see there are many things you are unsure of, my dear. It must be very confusing for you. First things first. You have a mind room?"

Kira felt her mouth go dry. "Er, yes. Yes, I do."

"Very good. Imagine you are inside your room, and I am trying to peer in the window. You do not want me to see what is inside, so you close the shutters. Can you do that?"

Kira entered her mind room and immediately felt more at ease. She sensed a presence at the window but instead of the nun, she saw only an orange glow, like summer clouds at sunset. Kira fastened the shutters together and the light disappeared. She brought her awareness back to the nun's room.

"There you are. Easy, wasn't it?"

"Yes. You can't read my thoughts now?"

"No more than you can read mine." Sister Marguerite smiled. "You have much to learn, Kira, and I fear very little time to learn it. Tell me, what do you know of your mother?"

The nun's words were gentle, but unexpected, and Kira felt them like an arrow to her heart.

"My mother died giving birth to me. My grandmother raised me."

"You feel her loss deeply, I can tell. It is hard for a girl to grow up without a mother. And your father? What do you know of him?"

Kira shifted in her seat. Her fingers found the little spiderweb charm hanging from her bracelet, and she rubbed it between her finger and thumb.

"I know nothing of him, either. My grandmother said he died before I was born. Agatha was both mother and father to me. She has done everything for me, taught me how to use the Eiran, my healer's skills, everything. I love her dearly."

Kira's throat tightened. She longed to know more about her mother but had stopped asking when she was old enough to recognise the pain and anguish it caused Agatha. In her heart, Kira blamed herself for her mother's death.

Sister Marguerite nodded. "And she loves you equally, I am sure. Agatha Stillwater has done well to keep you safe for the past eighteen years, Kira. It is neither her fault, nor yours that you find yourself in this predicament now. She did what was needed, and I can sense that you are a kind and responsible young woman. There are, however, certain truths that should be revealed to you now that you are of age. I am not the person who should be telling you these things, of course, but for your own safety and that of your friends, it falls to me. Some may argue that the timing is not right, but I saw the need in my foretelling yesterday, and I trust my gift more than anything else."

Kira felt the hairs stand up on the back of her neck. The nun's voice was calm, soothing, even, but despite her peaceful demeanour Kira dreaded what she was going to say next. Somehow, she knew the seer's words would change her life forever.

"Give me your hand, child." Sister Marguerite held out her right hand. "I feel that showing you the truth may be more palatable than hearing it spoken."

Kira reluctantly placed her hand on the nun's upturned palm. Her skin was warm and soft, and she felt a sensation of comfort and connection as Sister Marguerite placed her left hand on top.

"You are trembling! Fear not, Kira. The gifts we receive from the Goddess are to be treasured, not feared. I would like to share my gift with you now, but if you choose not to accept, I will not force it upon you."

Kira straightened her shoulders. Better to know the truth and be prepared, than to live a lie in ignorance. She nodded, then remembering the nun was blind, said, "I am ready."

Sister Marguerite smiled. "Picture your mind room and enter it. When you do, imagine there is a door, a secret door you have never seen before, and wait for my knock. When you open it, link your awareness to mine. You will have access to all my foretellings, but the one you need to see will be shown to you. Keep hold of my hand. Look for the owl. You will be safe."

Kira entered her mind room for the second time. It was just as she had left it. She pulled back the rug and opened the trap door to the empty cellar. A small wooden door was centred on the far wall. Kira joined her awareness to the silver thread tethered to her corporeal body and waited for the knock. On the third rap she opened the door and was almost blinded by the whiteness. She felt the nun's awareness beckoning and linked her own to it.

She stepped into a white passageway that ran in two directions, further than she could see. Every few feet a door appeared, as white as the walls of the corridor, but she could see no handle, lock or hinge. After she had passed about a dozen doors she stopped. The next door was made of oak and was as familiar as the back of her hand. Agatha's cottage. Kira was overcome with such a feeling of homesickness and longing that she could barely contain herself. She reached for the doorknob and as the door swung open, what she saw was so completely unexpected that her senses reeled.

An owl appeared and as soon as she acknowledged it, she was flying. On the back of the owl. Or was she inside it? Kira didn't care; it was exhilarating. High above the rooftops of River Glen she soared. Through the treetops covered in snow, over the River Ryder, now a dark ribbon gliding between the white slopes of the mountains, and beyond. She saw the moon reflected in the deep waters of the Lake of

Shells, and only then did Kira realise that night had fallen, and she was in darkness. She became aware, then, of the sound of beating wings, the rhythmic pulse of air and then an eerie quiet as the owl glided noiselessly above the forest. In the silence she heard a scream. The bird swooped down to the treetops, closer and closer until Kira could hear the clash of swords and the heavy grunts of men growing weary with fatigue.

By the light of the full moon, two men fought in the glade below. It seemed to Kira that the older man had the advantage; he was more experienced, wielding his blade like a seasoned soldier. His strokes were economical, his thrust and parry almost effortless. But as she watched, Kira noticed that the younger man battled with far greater desperation, and she thought that his determination might just give him the edge.

The owl turned its head and focussed its gaze on a shadow in the undergrowth. Kira saw a figure crouched against the trunk of a large oak. She heard a gasp of pain and a woman fell to her knees, clasping her belly. Her cry distracted both men, but it was the younger man who recovered first and slashed his blade across his opponent's throat. The blood arced across the snow once, twice, and the old soldier dropped to the ground.

"Aeldra!" The young man ran to the woman's side. "Aeldra, my love. Does the child come?"

"Not yet," she gasped, "but soon, I think. We must hurry!"

In the distance, Kira heard the baying of a hound. Too far away for human ears, yet the woman seemed to sense the danger. "Talek, they come! I fear the dogs have our scent. We need to go."

The young man stood and glanced around. "Can you spare me your cloak?" He searched the ground for the cloak the soldier had discarded before their battle. "You take this one. I'll backtrack and try to confuse the scents. River Glen is but a league away. The healer's cottage is on the outskirts near the river."

Kira expected the woman to protest, but she unclipped her cloak and pushed back the hood. Her hair tumbled loose down her back and seemed to sparkle like moonlight on the river when she moved. But the young man quickly bundled her up in the soldier's cloak. He bent his head and kissed her deeply, then thrust her from him. "Hurry, Aeldra. I will meet you at the cottage as soon as I can."

The owl took to the skies and Kira glimpsed them both set off in different directions. She longed to follow the woman but knew this story was hers only to observe. The owl soared high above the tree line, halfway up the mountain to perch on a rocky outcrop. The night sky seemed blacker than it ever had before and the moon and the stars brighter in contrast. Kira wondered if it was because she was so high up, or because of the owl. Then she saw a thick mist descend from the craggy peaks of Dragon's Doom and knew that it was neither.

Kira and the owl circled high above a stone cottage by the bend of the river and waited for the mist to end its search. Kira looked down and knew that the cottage was Agatha's, yet the trees in the garden were not full grown and the orchard and herb gardens less than half their current size. The owl drifted down to the roof of the cottage and then, somehow, they were inside and perched on the rafters. Kira's heart ached to see her grandmother so distraught.

Agatha knelt by the fire cradling a newborn. The air was thick with grief and loss, and Agatha bowed her shoulders with the weight of it. On a pallet in the corner of the room, the body of the young woman lay lifeless on sheets still damp and glistening red. Kira was overcome with a strange sadness. She had done no more than observe this young woman named Aeldra, but she was filled with such a sharp anguish she thought her heart might shatter. But before she could give in to her tears, the air around them shuddered, and a whisper caressed her cheek. Kira's awareness was flooded with warmth and love and welcome. She heard the trembling note of a perfectly plucked harp string. The angel of death had come to gather another soul.

Kira felt another shift in perspective, and now not only could she see what was happening from above, she had insight into Agatha's thoughts and emotions.

Agatha feels the sting of failure as sharp as a lash. In her heart she knows the woman was already weakened by her journey through the snow, but still feels responsible for her death. A lifetime of herblore and healing has amounted to nought. She tried desperately to save both mother and child, but the afterbirth wouldn't pass, and the bleeding wouldn't stop. Agatha stifles the sob that tightens her throat. She is bone weary, but the babe needs her attention now. Groaning as she rises to her feet, she stretches the kinks from her back and eases down onto her rocking chair with a sigh.

The poor mite is barely breathing. The thought of another death fills her with dread and a band of worry tightens across her chest. Agatha inhales deeply and pushes away the fatigue. She will do all she can. She straddles the babe face down along her arm and cradles her head and shoulders with her hand as she supports her tiny jaw with her fingers. With gentle but firm strokes, she rubs her other hand up and down the baby's back.

Agatha whispers to the listless babe, "Come on, my beauty, take some big breaths for me. Don't you let me break my vow. Breathe deep, my darling girl."

Her wrist is painful. Four half -moons are etched deep in her skin, where the mother had gripped Agatha's arm so tightly she had drawn blood.

"Save my child," she had begged, even as the angel hovered. Agatha had promised, but it was only when the woman took her last breath that her hand fell away from Agatha's wrist.

She sends a prayer to the Goddess of Light, and any other gods that may be listening, to give the child the strength and the will to live. The seconds seem to stretch to hours before the baby finally coughs and begins to cry.

Agatha wraps the babe in linens scented with lavender and warmed by the fire and nestles her close. She slumps back in the chair and closes her eyes. The child breathes easily now and sleeps in her arms.

Agatha is too exhausted to notice the mist. It oozes through the hole in the roof stuffed with yew twigs and old rags to keep out the snow. The mist coalesces and swirls across her shoulders to cocoon the pair in a gossamer blanket. Agatha is startled by the unexpected warmth. Her heart starts to pound as her body is suffused with well-being and an energy she hasn't felt in years. Old magic? It cannot be. A frisson of trepidation quivers along her spine, and yet she is not afraid. An ancient voice rumbles in her mind like distant thunder, and as she listens, her heartache is both eased and intensified. For the second time that night, Agatha makes a promise that she doesn't know if she will be able to keep. The babe stirs in her arms and opens her eyes. She strokes her finger gently across the baby's cheek. "Your name will be Kira, as your mother wanted, because you are strong and brave and true."

The mist retreats to whence it came, leaving in its wake the smell of rain on a summer's day, the taste of fresh baked bread and the glow of a winter sunrise.

"You will need to be, dear child, you will need to be," Agatha croons, and the illusion fades as quickly as the mist.

Kira felt the pull of the present and knew she had to leave the scene of her birth. She turned to gaze once more on her mother's face, but like the mist, Aeldra's body had disappeared.

Chapter 19

Kira trembled so violently her teeth chattered. She was flooded by a turbulence of emotions where past and present swirled together in a whirlpool of pain and loss, anger and forgiveness, love and understanding. Sister Marguerite pulled a knee rug from the bed and handed it to Kira. "Put this over your shoulders." Her fingertips traced a familiar path across the top of her nightstand and she pressed a button. The top drawer slid open, and she reached in and pulled out a small flask of amber liquid. She held it out towards Kira. "Sister Dulcima's finest malt. I find a little nip helps me to sleep. Have a swig. It'll warm you up and settle your tingles."

Kira uncorked the flask with difficulty. Worried she would spill the contents with her shaking hands, she took a gulp as quickly as she could. The whisky caught the back of her throat as she swallowed it but had the desired effect. Within a few seconds her shivers had stopped, and a delicious warmth had settled in her belly.

"Are you well?"

"I'm not sure," Kira said shakily. "I have never experienced anything like that before. It was both wondrous and heartbreaking."

Sister Marguerite steepled her hands and tapped her forefingers against her lips. "As difficult as it may have been, you can perhaps appreciate why I chose to show the foretelling rather than try to explain it to you."

"I can." Kira pulled the blanket a little more tightly around her shoulders. "But perhaps, past-telling might be a better name for it."

Sister Marguerite nodded her agreement. "Indeed. However, your future is very much rooted in the past, and you needed to see this to better inform the choices you will soon be forced to make. I need to speak of such things, but first tell me if you have questions you would like to ask."

Kira was silent for a moment. The storm outside was abating and so was her distress. "Aeldra was my mother?"

"She was."

"And Talek my father?"

"Yes."

"Did he escape from the people who were chasing them?"

Sister Marguerite shook her head. "I'm sorry, child. He led them to the river. All that was recovered was his sword and your mother's cloak. The soldiers believed that both your parents had drowned. That is why no one searched further, and your birth was not discovered."

Kira pressed the heels of her hands against her eyes. "I see. Thank you." She cleared her throat. "Do you know why the soldiers were chasing them?"

"Magic," she said. "Your mother was a descendant of Valethrix, weaver of the ethereal web and, at the time of Lady Edalyn, the most powerful magician in Cabarac. Aeldra was a talented dream weaver."

Goosebumps rose along Kira's arms. *A dream weaver.* No wonder she had been able to give Isaac his death dream so easily. She must have some of her mother's magic in her blood. Did Agatha know?

"My grandmother, did Agatha know?"

"Agatha Stillwater kept her vows as she had promised. There was no way of knowing whether you would inherit Aeldra's magic, or any other. She did her best to keep you safe from harm. She showed great courage when she accepted a stranger's child as her responsibility, and I believe she loves you as much as if you were her own."

"She does. And I love her equally." Kira's throat tightened and she felt the tears form, but this time she didn't brush them away. She grieved for the mother and father who gave their lives so she might live, but mostly she grieved for the little woman who saved her. All these years Kira had blamed herself for her mother's death, but she understood now that Agatha's reluctance to talk about it was because she also blamed herself.

"I think perhaps you have much to think about, Kira. It may be best to go to Sister Catherine now and distract your mind by keeping your hands busy. After you have finished your training this afternoon, I think you would benefit from a chat with Sister Evangeline. She has a prodigious knowledge of Cabarac and its history, and many other things besides. I will discuss what you experienced this morning with her, so she will no doubt be able to answer any questions that occur to you between now and then." Sister Marguerite adjusted the gauze strip that covered her eyes. "I, too, have much to think about, but I think a short nap may be in order first."

She brushed away Kira's offer to help with a kindly wave. "No, dear, you run along. Come back and see me in a day or two. Sister Catherine awaits."

Kira saw that the little nun was safely on her bed before she closed the door. She leaned against the cool wall of the corridor and took a few calming breaths before stowing the memory of what had just happened into her mind room. She had much to think on.

The Apothecary's dispensary was a wonder of a different kind. The fragrances and bunches of drying herbs and wildflowers suspended from the rafters were so familiar that Kira's heartache began to ease. The scent of new-cut hay and honey floated from bunches of woodruff. Pots of lavender and violet decorated the window-sill and pomanders lined the lower shelves of a bookcase so that as she browsed the tomes, aromatic herbs and spices wafted from beneath the pages.

The room was long and narrow, the outer wall split by a tall, arched window in keeping with the rest of the priory. Kira imagined that on a summer's day the room would be filled with light, but today grey clouds still blocked the sun and although not as heavy as the earlier storm, a persistent drizzle still fell. Several lanterns illuminated the work area, and a heavy iron candelabra rose from the floor, with a dozen or so thick candles flickering in the slight draft from beneath the door. The flames flickering in the tiny fireplace were barely enough to keep the chill off the room but kept the fire kettle bubbling for Sister Catherine's endless supply of chamomile and mint tea. Kira supped on a mug now, nibbling on a honey oat biscuit almost as good as Agatha's.

She had cleaned and re-labelled row upon row of jars and bottles and dusted the shelves with her usual diligence while Sister Catherine documented the stock in a leather-bound ledger. The apothecary nun had asked many questions about Kira's healing practices, nodding with approval at her answers and occasionally beaming with delight when Kira could tell her about the medicinal uses of unusual herbs she named.

Sister Catherine rearranged her collection of mortars and pestles before topping up her mug with tea. "I have enjoyed your company and your help very much, Kira. Tis a pity you will not be staying with us. I could use someone with your skills, especially as winter is nearly upon us. We had many succumb to winterfever last year. Not just in the priory, but in the neighbouring villages as well."

"Thank you, Sister, I know too well the ravages of winterfever. River Glen was struck with it, too. Even my grandmother suffered. A mild case, thank goodness, but even so, it laid her up in bed for a week." She cradled her mug between her hands and stared into the pale-yellow liquid, savouring the notes of apple and mint despite her deep concern. "It is my dearest wish that no such ills befall her this year."

"I will enquire about her wellbeing through Jenna's family and ask that they keep a check on her, though I am sure that the village will take care of her needs as well. From what you have told me, your grandmother is much loved and respected in River Glen."

Kira acknowledged to herself that it was true. Agatha would be well looked after. She had served the people of River Glen for decades, and that dedication would be well rewarded. The village net was tightly woven and cast wide. She would be safe.

Chapter 20

Kira smeared the last of the chicken and vegetable broth with the crust of her bread and popped it into her mouth with a sigh of satisfaction. "That was delicious!"

Jenna grinned. "Thank you. I peeled the vegetables myself. Wait until you see what is for dinner tonight. Smoked haddock kedgeree and steamed pudding for afters!"

"Did you enjoy your time in the kitchen?" asked Giselle with a knowing smile at Kira. Jenna had spent the last half hour talking non-stop about her morning. She had told them in three different ways what was on the menu for this evening's meal.

"Yes, I..." She caught the look between Giselle and Kira and paused. "Sorry, I know I keep rabbiting on. Go on, Elle, tell us about your sewing. Oh, but before you do, I've just got to tell you this." She glanced around and, seeing some novitiates seated at the other end of the long table, beckoned her friends closer. She leaned forward and lowered her voice. "Tangler and the others return to share the meal tonight. He has news of the quota and of Piscator."

Kira stared at Jenna in disbelief. "You thought that peeling vegetables and smoking fish were more worthy of telling than Tangler's return?"

Jenna's face flushed as she winced apologetically.

"Jenna!" said Giselle before she could answer. "How do you know what news he has, anyway?"

"I overheard Cook talking to the gardener. Did you know that they are the only married couple that live in the priory grounds?" She hastened to continue at Giselle's hiss of frustration. "Well, their son is named Bendon, and he went along with Tangler and the others to help Evan, because his arm is still in a sling from when the arrow, well, you know what happened..." Her voice trailed off.

"Yes, we do," said Kira. "Go on."

"Well, Bendon returned mid-morning to let the prioress know that the rest of them would be here late afternoon."

"And?" said Giselle. "What about the rest of the quota? And Piscator?"

"That's it. That's all I heard."

Giselle tossed her napkin at Jenna and groaned. "Come on. We'd better change and get ready for Sister Eloise. I'll tell you about my wonderful morning sewing as we walk." She reached up to brush the top of Kira's head. "Don't know what you were doing with Sister Catherine, but something has dropped on your braid. Looks like blue bottle."

Kira fell in step beside her and ran her fingers over the braid. "No idea," she said with a shrug. "I don't remember seeing any cornflower dye, but the light was poor in the back shelves."

"Maybe your hair *is* magical," said Jenna, waving her fingers around her head. "I thought I saw red strands after we were attacked. The next morning it was gone so I put it down to blood from the cuts on your face. But, maybe not…"

"Jenna!" Giselle admonished her friend. "I know we are in the priory, but you really shouldn't say things like that away from the privacy of our rooms. You never know who's listening."

Jenna had the grace to look shamefaced. She lowered her voice to a whisper, "I'm sorry. I was having a jest, but you know…after what you told us yesterday…it could be true."

Kira frowned. Jenna had tied the hook to the line. After what she had learned this morning, she thought her friend was almost certainly correct.

Kira practiced her exercises and staff work with an enthusiasm that rivalled Jenna's, and earned praise from Sister Eloise. "You have all improved greatly in this last week. So much so, that I think it is time to choose a staff of your own. Even though the time approaches that you must leave the priory, the carrying of a staff when travelling is not so unusual as to cause comment from others."

Kira felt a jolt of dismay at the nun's words. Though she had always known their stay was temporary, the reminder was distressing. She still had so many questions.

Sister Eloise led them down a short corridor and then a longer flight of stairs. The labyrinth of tunnels beneath the priory were vast, bigger than the priory itself, thought Kira. The nun took a set of keys from her pocket and unlocked the massive oak door set into the stone. The room was about the size of Kira's bedchamber, but the light from the lamps wasn't bright enough to illuminate it all, and the high domed ceiling remained in shadow.

"We allow novitiates to choose their staff from this room," said Sister Eloise. "They belonged to guardians of the past, but once they have taken their vows, they are free to have one made to their own specifications or keep the one they have. Some are made specifically for fighting, others are more ornate and ceremonial, but all of them become a weapon in the right hands. Please," she said, sweeping her arm around the room, "make your choice with care. Take your time."

Kira stared at the walls, open-mouthed. Dozens of silver and bronze shields adorned the upper portion of the walls. In the purpose-built wooden racks beneath stood hundreds of wooden staffs. Some were highly decorative, with seams of silver or bronze twisting down the length of the wood. Others were tipped with metal or studded with gems that glittered in the lamplight. Jenna went straight to the racks holding the fighting staffs and began testing them for weight and balance.

Kira walked slowly around the room trailing her fingers across the polished wood, and was startled to discover that images flashed into her mind when she touched some of the older timber. A nun's face, a battle, a field of flame, a chapel pew, an enemy's death. Instinctively, she knew that these were the staffs belonging to guardians of a different time. A time of war. A time when magic was as commonplace as fish for dinner. A time when the last memory of the nun who held the staff was imprinted in its core. She dropped her hand from the last staff she touched, reluctant to intrude on such intimate memories. How could an inanimate object keep something so alive? But she knew the answer. Didn't Gwyneth's herbal do exactly that?

"You are having trouble selecting a staff?" The serene voice of the prioress startled Kira, even though she spoke quietly.

"Oh! I'm sorry, I didn't see you. Well met, Sister Evangeline."

"Blessings, child. No doubt because your eyes were closed. Perhaps it may be easier for you to look at the staffs before you touch them?" She glanced at Jenna and Giselle on the other side of the room. "If you wish to learn more about the old guardians, there are easier ways that are not quite so emotionally draining. You are, perhaps, feeling a little fragile with all that you have learned today."

Kira felt the heat rise in her cheeks. That was one way of wording it. "Yes, Sister. I was hoping to come and talk with you later. I have a few questions, if you don't mind."

Sister Evangeline smiled. "I'm sure you do. Come and see me in an hour." She nodded towards a rack by the end wall. "I think you'll find that the staffs over there are a little more suited to you."

"Thank you, Sister." The prioress made her way to Jenna and Giselle, who seemed to be comparing staffs. Kira hastened to the other rack, prepared to grab the first one she saw and join her friends. They were much more ornate than what she wanted, however, so much so that she thought they might draw unwanted attention. A much plainer staff rested at the end of the rack. Only the first hand-span was decorated, a few swirls of metal spiralled around the oak shaft to join in three places at the bronze cap. She thought it would suit her well.

"Kira! Have you chosen yet?" Jenna called. "Do you need some advice?"

"No, all is well. I have one, thank you." Kira touched the staff with her forefinger and was relieved that no image flashed in her mind. But as she grasped it in her fist and removed it from the rack, a familiar shiver of recognition trembled along her arm. She looked more closely at the swirls of metal and was not surprised to see that they were replicas of the golden feathers that adorned Gwyneth's herbal. What did surprise her was that she somehow knew, with absolute certainty, that the name of the staff was Seren.

In the time it took Kira to walk across the flagstones to the others, she had decided two things: there was more magic in Cabarac than she had been led to believe, and the nuns of this priory were more than just Guardians of the Flame. She had a hundred other questions swimming around her mind but was too overwhelmed to sort through them now. She would ask the prioress later.

Jenna pirouetted in front of her and lunged forward with her staff, stopping an inch from Kira's chest. "What do you think? Isn't she a dazzler?" She came to attention and held out the staff for Kira to examine. Jenna had chosen a hickory staff, longer than those that they practiced with, which meant that she would sacrifice flexibility for greater reach. But Jenna was quick on her feet and had found she had a natural aptitude for fighting and anticipating what move her opponent would use. Kira looked at Giselle. "Would you hold Seren for me, please?"

"Seren? You've given a name to your staff?" Giselle took the staff and nodded in admiration. "It's lovely."

Kira took a deep breath. "No, she told me her name. It was not mine to choose."

"Oh!" said Jenna. "Can you tell me if mine has a name?"

Kira held out her hand and grasped the hickory shaft. It had little embellishment apart from a bronze flame set into the wood in the very centre. A vision appeared as others had before, but without the visual clarity. She seemed to be in a cave or underground vault, the darkness absolute apart from a flickering blue flame on a stone carved like a book. The image vanished almost as soon as it appeared, but Kira was left with the impression that the staff had belonged to a seasoned fighter.

"Ailith," she said as she handed the staff back to Jenna. "Its name is Ailith."

"Ailith! I like that. Thank you."

Sister Evangeline and Sister Eloise were deep in conversation by the door, but both looked up as Jenna spoke the name. The prioress glanced between Kira and the staff, and she frowned as though puzzled. Sister Eloise touched her on the sleeve and drew her back towards the wall, so they were angled away from the girls.

Giselle offered her staff to Kira with a solemn smile. "Don't ask me why I picked this one. But you can tell me its name if it has one."

The staff was short, barely reaching past Giselle's shoulder, but Kira saw at once what had drawn Giselle to it. If Jenna's staff was made for fighting, then Giselle's was for ceremony. The oak shaft was decorated top and bottom with a fine silver filigree that reminded Kira of stag horns. The carved handle was the head of a deer. About a foot from the head two bands of silver, the width of her thumb, sat close to each other.

Kira grinned. "It could have been made for you." She took the staff and was relieved to find that she had no reaction when she touched the wood. It did offer a name, however.

"Rhan," she said softly. Fate.

"Well, Rhan is more than just a pretty thing," said Giselle as she took back the staff. "Have a look at this." She rubbed her thumb across the deer's head and the staff split in two at the silver bands. A wickedly sharp blade, only a finger's length, protruded from the shorter shaft. "It's a dagger!"

"Yes, I can see that," said Kira with a laugh. "Very clever."

"Sister Eloise showed me what it could do after I had chosen it. She said it was a very apt pick."

Kira agreed. There was so much more to Giselle than most people realised. Too often they would see only her beauty and sunny disposition and ignore what lay beneath. Like the staff, she had hidden talents. She was sharp, clever, and stubborn.

Chapter 21

"Come in."

When Kira entered Sister Evangeline's study, the prioress was standing with her back to the fire cradling a mug in her hands. Kira was more aware than ever of the quiet strength and dignity that seemed to emanate from the prioress. Her hands were broad, the knuckles scabbed in places, like she was used to manual labour, but the ink stains on the side of her long fingers revealed she was a scholar as well. She had asked Kira to bring Seren with her and waved her closer to the fire.

"Take a seat, my dear. Just prop your staff against the back of the chair." She took a small pan of milk from the hearth and poured it into a silver jug. "My secret indulgence." She smiled. "Have you ever tried spiced cocoa?"

Kira shook her head. The delectable aroma of cinnamon, honey and pepper mingled with an unfamiliar, earthy, bittersweet scent as the steam wafted from the jug. Sister Evangeline poured the rich brown liquid into a mug and handed it to Kira. She blew on the cocoa, revelling in the scent, then took a tentative sip. The flavours danced on her tongue, and she looked up at the prioress with delight. "It's delicious!"

Sister Evangeline's eyes sparkled. "I know. I have found that I must limit my intake to one mug only once or twice a week. Too much of a good thing is quite often bad for you."

Kira nodded. Agatha had made that very point when Kira overindulged on quince pies at a summer fair and was sick most of the way home. She hadn't eaten a quince pie in the last ten years. She placed her mug down on the table in front of her and looked at the prioress.

"I would ask you, Kira, do you think magic is a good thing or bad?"

Kira sat up a little straighter in her chair. She felt the weight of Sister Evangeline's words and did not want to hurry her reply.

"I find that a difficult question to answer. For most of my life I have believed that magic is…not exactly bad, but something to be feared. If it has enhanced the Eiran and my ability to heal people, then I would say it is a good thing, yet because of it I am persecuted and sentenced to death. And that is not a good thing."

"Sister Marguerite tells me that you did not know your mother, or that she was a dream weaver?"

"I did not. Sister Marguerite showed me in a foretelling this morning." Was it only this morning? Kira felt her heart start to race. She reached for her mug and took a gulp of cocoa.

"Sister Evangeline, a great deal has happened in the last few weeks. Some of it you know, but much I have told no one. I don't know who to tell, to be honest. At first the burden was a small one, but I feel it getting heavier by the day. I would have carried the load alone, I think, if not for events here at the priory. I think perhaps the Sisters of the Flame know a thing or two about magic, and maybe you could help lighten the load. Can you help me?"

Sister Evangeline smiled. "I told you when you first arrived that all you need do is ask, Kira. Sister Marguerite has hastened what I hoped would be a more gradual understanding of your heritage, but I fear the time you have here is shorter than we first thought, so it's probably just as well." The prioress made herself comfortable in the armchair opposite Kira, "I can offer you information and understanding. However, your magic differs considerably to those of us who are blessed by the Flame, so I am afraid I am unable to teach you what you will need to control it."

Kira frowned, "I need to control it? I am not sure what you mean."

Sister Evangeline leaned forward and picked up a few pieces of kindling from a basket on the hearth, then tossed them on the fire. The flames licked around the dry timber and grew taller. She glanced at Kira, then picked up a log which she also placed on the fire. The flames, already flaring, danced along the dry bark, crackling greedily. Within a few moments the crackling changed to a roar and the flames blazed in the hearth. The heat that emanated from the fire was almost scorching in its intensity, and Kira drew back her legs.

"Consider the fire to be your magic. Fire is one of the most useful tools we have, yet it can also be one of the most destructive. Feed it too little and it is easily extinguished, too much and it can blaze out of control. You need to be aware of the right fuel to use and the right time to add it. Think of your magic in the same way. Many a cottage fire has been started because people have not taken care of the hearth. Do you understand?"

Kira sat back in her chair. She understood the fire allegory but wanted to liken her powers to a candle rather than a blaze. *No*, she thought, dismissing the comparison almost immediately, *that is a truth you told yourself.* She thought on the previous lessons the nun had taught her. What were the facts?

"I think I need to start at the beginning. The day I gave Isaac Fishlock his death dream."

And so, Kira recounted all that had happened from the time of Isaac's death to the time of Mevis'.

"You feel responsible for the death of your friend?" The prioress frowned.

"I am certain that if not for me, the travelling arrangements would have been different, and the carriage would not have been attacked in the first place."

"That's a long line to cast, Kira, yet I sense you feel a deeper responsibility than that."

Kira bowed her head, "I couldn't save her. I have the Eiran. What good is a healer's gift if it cannot save a life?"

"Ah, I see." Sister Evangeline nodded. "But even the most powerful magic cannot bring someone back to life, Kira. You must know this."

"I do," she whispered. "But the thing is, I didn't even try to save Mevis. Not when there might have been time. Perhaps I could have saved her, but I didn't try."

"No, you chose to protect your other friends instead," Sister Evangeline admonished her gently. "Would you have given their lives for hers?"

Kira looked up and brushed away her tears. "No. No, I would not."

"Then you made the right decision. Sister Marguerite tells me you will face many such choices in your lifetime, dear child, so be guided by your heart. That you feel so deeply about these matters speaks of your good nature. Do not let others take advantage of this. If you do not learn how to control your gift, I fear that others will try to use it for their own ends. Be wary of this."

"I thank you for the advice, Sister Evangeline, but before I learn to control it, perhaps you could explain exactly what it is and why it has suddenly appeared." Kira's voice rose with every word, and she fought to regain her composure.

Sister Evangeline raised her eyebrows, but she held out a hand as though she was placating a fractious horse. "I will try, my dear, I will try." She stood and walked to Kira's chair and picked up the staff.

"The staff told you its name, as did the others. This is because you have the Valethrix blood. Dream weavers have an affinity with both spirit and memory. It is something you are born with, and it is magical. It is unlike our gift"—she placed a hand on her chest—"which is given if we are chosen to be blessed by the Flame. In the minds of those who do not have such gifts and therefore distrust and even despise those who do, there is no distinction. Magic is magic. For a thousand years, ever since the Lady Edalyn ventured into the darkness and was bestowed the Flame by the Goddess of Light, the Guardians have protected her gift. Those who earn the right are taken to the chamber and if considered worthy will receive the blessing. The staffs that spoke to you belonged to the sisters who served the Flame, and as you gathered, preserved their last memories in their core. You could see this because you are a dream weaver."

"But—"

The prioress held up her hand. "I cannot explain our gift to you. That is only for those who are chosen. Even the nuns who serve the Flame but who are not chosen, or do not care to be, do not know the secret of the Flame. But whether you are born with a gift, or have it bestowed upon you, I believe that ultimately the gift comes from one source, and that is why the priory has always given sanctuary to those in need. At the time of the purge, many books and valuable objects pertaining to magic were secreted in the caves beneath the priory. In return, the priory has not only a sacred protection, but a mystical one as well." She ran her hands down the length of the staff and sighed, "Seren did not belong to a guardian, or even a nun, but to a very dear friend to the priory. She was a healer, as you are. Her name was Willow."

Sister Evangeline handed Seren back to Kira. "I'm sure she would be thrilled to know that her staff is now in your hands."

"Thank you." Kira felt a quiet pleasure in knowing that Seren had also belonged to a healer and that it had chosen her. But still she wanted to know the answer to her questions. She looked at the prioress expectantly.

"I cannot tell you much about your magic, only that at the age of eighteen your potential becomes evident, and your power rises accordingly. Any bindings that may have been placed upon you..." She paused at Kira's jolt of surprise. "Don't look so shocked, it will have been done to keep you safe. Any such bindings will have weakened sufficiently for you to begin responding to objects that you have a magical affinity with. Gwyneth's herbal is one example, the staff is another."

Sister Evangeline fingered the crescent hanging from her neck and frowned.

"Like all dispatchers, Piscator wears a medallion around his neck and at the centre is a shard of dragon scale. This is how they test for magic. It is likely that the shard responded to your power. In you, it recognised the dream weaver magic, the same magic that enhances your healer's gift."

Sister Evangeline divided the last of the cocoa between their mugs and took another sip. "Sister Marguerite told me that not only did you see her foretelling, but your other senses felt it too. Most people would not have experienced the vision as you did, but the dream weaver magic is strong in you. Depending on how your magic continues to manifest, you will need to learn to guard against certain things."

Kira frowned. "What things?"

"Books will call to you, particularly those with a kinship to your magic. You might touch a grave and know the manner of the one who died. You might read the thoughts of someone who brushes past you. Your magic may rise to protect you when your life is threatened. You might be asked to weave a dream and make a nightmare instead."

"Stop!" Kira jumped up from her chair and began pacing. "That sounds terrible, more like a curse than a gift! Tell me how to control such things. Please. All I want is to be a good healer. I do not wish to cause harm to anyone. I do not want to read the thoughts in someone else's head."

"Sit down, Kira. I only tell you this so you are aware of the possibilities. There may be others, depending on the strength of your gift, and you should know how important it is to learn control. You will be able to do much good as well. But, unfortunately, I have not the skills to teach you."

Kira slumped back in her chair. It was all very well to be told she needed a teacher, but time was running out. She would be leaving for the Legion Isles soon. If she remained in Cabarac, Piscator would surely find her and have her executed. His brazen dragon would devour her and her magic. She massaged her temples and looked up at Sister Evangeline. "And where do you suggest I start looking for someone to teach me these things? You said I don't have much time."

"Oh, you don't have to go searching, my child. Tangler returns, and will be here for dinner tonight. He'll know what to do."

Kira stared at Sister Evangeline. Tangler? What on earth did he know about controlling magic?

Chapter 22

Kira scanned the length of the guest table through half-closed eyes as Sister Evangeline gave thanks for the meal and proclaimed the evening blessing. The fellows from The Rainbow's End were there, and Ned and Jock sat either side of Tangler. She had hoped to speak with him before the meal but hadn't had the opportunity. Kira clamped down on her disappointment and took closer stock of the men. Parr didn't seem to be there, and where was Evan? She hoped that his arm was mending.

"Blessed be," Sister Evangeline concluded the prayer.

"Blessed be," the response echoed around the dining hall.

Evan is well. He and Bendon are eating in the kitchen with his father.

Kira looked up in alarm. Mind speech? She recognised the voice as the one that had warned her at the Merryman Ball. She glanced around at the people seated at her table, but all were concentrating on the tureen of soup that Jenna had just placed in front of them. She flicked her gaze over at the men seated at the guest table once again, but they too were busy with the meal. Kira had never used mind speech with anyone but Agatha and Sister Marguerite. She didn't even know if she could *speak* to someone when she didn't know who they were.

Try it.

Who are you? she demanded.

No need to shout, said the voice. *I'm just here.*

Your pardon. But who am I speaking to? Kira felt the heat rise in her cheeks. The men with Tangler were all drinking their soup. No one looked her way, but Farren raised his head and winked when he caught her eye. Farren? Surely not.

Hahaha. A chuckle.

Please. Tell me your name.

Why? It is not important.

But you know mine. I think it only fair. What may I call you?

Mmm. Sir?

Kira clenched her fists. She would not answer until she heard a name. But now she had at least confirmed that the voice was male.

Master?

She picked up her spoon and began to eat.

My Lord?

She turned to Giselle, "Could you pass me some bread, please?"

Your Royal Highness, Prince of all that is wonderful?

She dunked the bread in her soup and stuffed it into her mouth and tried not to smile.

Kindly leave my head and return when you have learned some manners. If you do not tell me your name, I shall call you Llyr.

The mythical king of the ether? 'Tis a much nicer name than my own. Llyr it shall be. I bow to the Lady Kira and will see you on the morrow.

The voice left her mind as quickly as it had entered. Kira gave a little growl of frustration, which had Giselle looking at her in concern.

"Is something amiss?"

"No, no, I am fine." Kira reassured her friend, while berating herself for not closing the shutters of her mind room as Sister Marguerite had instructed her. Then again, she had not expected that her thoughts could be read so easily. This was all new to her. She was determined not to look at the men again until after she had finished her meal.

After the kedgeree, which was every bit as delicious as Jenna had promised, Giselle nudged her in the ribs and nodded towards the guest table. Tangler was deep in conversation with Ned and Jock.

"Our guards have dressed for the occasion, did you notice? Ned looks like a man rather than the trunk of a very large tree," she whispered. The lamplight glinted in the metal studs of Ned's jerkin, and Kira realised that both he and Jock were dressed in linen and leathers rather than their usual mail byrnie and quilted undershirt.

"'Tis a pity he doesn't smile more often," chimed in Jenna, who had overheard Giselle's remark. "Even Lord Callan has more of a sense of humour than dour-faced Ned. He always looks so grim."

"I guess disposition takes second place to guarding," said Kira. "I'd rather have someone with their wits about them but is close-mouthed, than a happy-go-lucky sort who would rather whistle than fight."

"Jock manages to combine the two," said Jenna.

"True," Kira agreed, "but I guess responsibility lays more heavily on some than others."

Both Tangler and Ned chose that moment to look over at Kira and her friends and Jenna gasped.

"Fish and pickles! Do you think they heard us?"

Giselle shook her head. "Don't be silly. We're too far away for that."

Kira folded her napkin with care. From the dangerous glint in Ned's eye, she wasn't quite so sure. Tangler ran his fist down his beard and stood up. He patted Ned and Jock on the shoulder and spoke a few words more, then made his way to their table.

"Well met, Kira, Giselle, Jenna." He bowed to them each in turn. "Sister Evangeline has told us much about your stay here, and I am glad to hear you are faring well. I have a great deal to tell you, but we are all weary from our journey and I hope that you will excuse me from talking tonight. Perhaps tomorrow after breakfast would be a more suitable time?"

Kira examined his face. The light from the wall sconce behind her illuminated the shadows beneath his eyes and the lines on his face were more deeply etched than was usual. It was clear that he had hardly slept for days. There was no way she could disturb him with her questions tonight; tomorrow would have to do.

"Of course. You look like you could sleep for a week. We can see you in the afternoon if you prefer?"

He smiled, and for a moment the old Tangler was back. "As tempting as your offer is, my dear, we shall meet after breakfast. Sleep well and I will see you on the morrow. Sister Evangeline has offered the use of her study while she takes the novitiates for guidance."

Kira sat on the windowsill of her room and gazed into the night, cocooned from the cold by the quilt from her bed. The storm clouds had finally passed, and the moon lay on its back high in the sky, its pale light reflecting only on the very top of the mountains where the snowfall was heaviest. Despite the uncertainty of their situation, Kira felt a strange sort of contentment. She had visited her mind room after she got ready for bed and replayed the memory of her foretelling at least a dozen times. She knew her mother's voice and her face. She had seen her father's bravery and how much he cared for his wife. Aeldra and Talek. She knew their names. Most importantly, she had seen that her birth had not caused her mother's death. The guilt and grief that once filled a dark corner of her heart had been replaced with love and understanding.

Still, she had been unable to sleep. An old wound from the past may have started to heal, but in healing one wound another had opened. As much as she wanted to find out more about her dream weaver magic, the very fact that she had it put her in danger. If Piscator learned more of her power, he would double his effort to find her, she was certain. The priory and all it held would be in peril if he found her here, and she wanted no more deaths on her conscience. No matter what Sister Evangeline said, she would always feel responsible for Mevis.

Her mood shifted as her thoughts turned to the quota and the ever-present threat of the unknown. As much as she tried not to dwell on it, their journey to the Legion Isles loomed closer by the day. Could the danger that awaited them there be any worse than what she was facing here in Cabarac? She rested her head against the windowpane and watched the moon and the mountains disappear as her breath clouded the glass. *If only it was that easy*, she thought, *then I, too, would vanish in a cloud of mist.*

Kira was awoken by a tapping on her door. "Kira. Are you awake?" Jenna called from the passageway.

"Yes. Come in. What's wrong, have I overslept?" Her head felt full of wool and her voice croaked like a marsh frog.

"No," said Jenna as she entered the room, "but I was helping in the kitchen again this morning and I thought you might like a cup of tea. And I also found this." She waited as Kira sat herself up in the bed and then held up a hand mirror.

Kira was more in need of a hot tea than a mirror, and reached out her hand for the beverage. "Thank you, and well met, Jenna, but why?" She gestured towards the mirror, which was a lovely thing, made of ebony and inlaid with diamonds of lapis-lazuli.

"So you can see your hair," tutted Jenna, as though it was the most obvious thing in the world. "So you can see when it changes colour and change your hair style accordingly." She sat on the edge of the bed and held the mirror so that Kira could see her reflection.

"Ever since you told me about your hair, I've been watching closely to see if it changes. And it does! Remember how I saw a red streak in your hair after we were attacked, and then Giselle noticed the blue streak yesterday? Well, they may have faded, but sometimes, when the light catches your hair, some strands still show up in different colours. I've seen green ones, too."

"No," said Kira doubtfully.

"Yes!" Jenna nodded and took the cup from Kira's grasp. "Come over to the light and I'll show you." She pulled back the quilt from the bed, leaving Kira little choice, but to follow. Jenna grabbed her by the elbows and shuffled her into place so that the beam of sunlight that angled through the glass struck her hair. She held up the mirror. "There, bend down a little. Stop! There, can you see? Just to the left of your parting?"

She took the mirror from Jenna and moved it around her head. Jenna was right. Strands of her hair gleamed red and blue and green where they were touched by the sun. Kira's heart skipped a beat. She dropped her arm and stared at Jenna. "What am I going to do?"

"Oh, don't worry. We've got it sorted. Giselle will be here in a moment."

Kira shook her head. Giselle?

There was a rap at the door and Giselle entered without waiting for a response. She had a basket looped over her arm.

"Well met, Kira. I hope you don't think we are presumptuous, but we took a page from Sister Evangeline's book and decided to offer a solution and not just point out the problem." Giselle grinned and indicated that Kira should sit on the chair, "Now I know you don't like to wear your hair down. But I think we need to see the extent of your coloured locks, don't you?"

Kira couldn't speak. She sat on the chair and accepted the cup from Jenna, sipping the tea as Giselle untied the ribbon from her braid. Freed from its bonds, her hair cascaded over her shoulders and down her back. She closed her eyes when her friends gasped.

"Goddess of Light! It's beautiful." Jenna gathered a handful of hair in her fist, then let it fall through her fingers. "It's so silky. How can your hair be so curly, yet so smooth and shiny? You have no knots or tangles or...or..."

"No wonder you don't wear it loose," said Giselle, "it's almost as though it has a life of its own. People would not stop staring."

Kira grimaced. "I know. It's always been very...healthy."

"That's like calling a whale a minnow," said Jenna, laughing.

"We had better get a move on," said Giselle, inspecting Kira's scalp. She caught the coloured strands between her fingers and slid them down the length of the hair.

"That's interesting. The green is longest and reaches almost to the end. There is a strand of silver here, too, almost as long. I didn't notice it before. Then the red and the blue."

Kira groaned. "Sounds as though there's a carnival tent in my hair."

"Actually, it's not as bad as it sounds. Each strand of colour is made up of only ten or twelve hairs. With clever braiding we should be able to disguise most of it. And…"—she reached into her basket and pulled out a handful of material squares—"offcuts from my sewing. Sister Victoria gave them to me. I was going to make a quilt. But instead, we are going to wear them on our heads." She folded the material across the middle to make a triangle and handed one to Jenna, then took another and laid it over her own head and tied the ends at the back of her neck, under her braid. "See? It's a hair kerchief."

"Amazing," said Kira, swallowing the lump in her throat, "but why are you wearing one?"

"You are such a goose sometimes, Kira. If we all wear one, then you don't stand out. I'm going to embroider some of the others, so they aren't all so plain. Maybe put some fancy ribbons on, too." She glanced at her reflection and nodded. "Yes, it will work. Now, let us see to your braids and get down to breakfast."

Kira felt her self-consciousness dissipate as soon as she walked into the dining hall. No one noticed their headwear, or if they did, no one cared. Farren and Hugo were the only two at the guest table and they had finished their breakfast and excused themselves before Kira and her friends served themselves porridge. Farren flashed them a grin and a wink as he passed the table, and even the normally reserved Hugo managed a wave.

Kira turned to Giselle to ask for the milk and was surprised to see a blush forming on her cheeks. Giselle ducked her head to hide her embarrassment but not before Kira saw the smile that played on her lips. She reached across her friend and grabbed the jug. "Hot milk?" she asked, careful to keep any hint of teasing from her tone. She would not reward Giselle's kindness with a taunt. But she thought she might know which of the two minstrels had aroused Giselle's affection.

Chapter 23

Tangler, Ned and Jock were studying a large map on the desk in Sister Evangeline's study when the girls entered. They had weighted the edges down with heavy glass paperweights on three corners and a painted wooden statue of the Lady Edalyn on the other. Jenna gasped and cast her eyes around the room. She picked up a brass candlestick from the mantle and replaced the statue with care. Tangler threw her an apologetic glance, but Ned and Jock did not raise their eyes from the map.

"Here." Ned tapped his forefinger on the chart.

"Aye, I think you're right," said Jock with a sigh of resignation.

Tangler tugged at his beard. He looked at Kira and frowned, but when he spoke his voice was gentle. "'Tis a good thing I am skilled as both a conjuror and a juggler, for I fear I will need to keep many balls spinning in the air for this trick to work."

Kira's breakfast churned uneasily in her stomach. What now?

He pulled some stools around the table and indicated that they should sit.

"Tell me, girls, can any of you sing?"

Kira was taken aback by his unexpected question and unsure how to respond. Giselle had the voice of an angel, but Kira whistled far better than she could sing, and she could barely whistle. But Jenna had sung the funeral dirge for Mevis very sweetly, she recalled. "Giselle has a lovely voice, without a doubt," she finally replied, "and Jenna also. But me…not so much."

"Let's put it this way," said Giselle casting a fond look at her friend. "If Kira had to sing for her supper, she'd go to bed hungry."

"Mmm, 'tis as I remembered, unfortunately," said Tangler with a shrug. He paced back and forth several times between the fireplace and the desk. "Never mind, you dance very well, I believe, so it will still work."

"What will?"

"The art of deception, my dear. One hand points this way, the other that." He waved his hand around and suddenly the brass candlestick appeared in his fist. When Kira looked back at the table, the statue of Lady Edalyn was once again holding the corner of the map in place.

"Fish and… How did you do that!" Jenna almost fell from her stool as she looked between Tangler and the statue in complete bewilderment.

"Sleight of hand, my dear Jenna. The conjuror's stock in trade. Hopefully my next trick will work just as convincingly."

"It is still a risk," said Ned, his voice deep with concern.

"That it is," agreed Jock, "but I think we have little choice in the matter. It'll work if we can get everything in place in time."

"Can you please stop talking in riddles and tell us what is going on!" Kira slapped her hand on the table hard enough to make Lady Edalyn jump. Giselle placed her hand on top of Kira's and gave it a gentle squeeze before speaking.

"We have had a great deal to contend with since we left River Glen, Tangler, Kira more than anyone. Plain speaking would be appreciated, whether the news be good or bad."

Kira shot Giselle a look of gratitude. "Your pardon, Tangler. I do not mean to sound rude, but I am beginning to feel a bit like a pawn on a chess board."

"No, it is me who should apologise, my dear. My head is so full of bluff and double bluff that I sometimes forget to speak plainly." He nodded towards Giselle in acknowledgement. "I will stick to the facts as best I can."

He counted each fact with his fingers as he spoke. "Firstly, Lord Callan and the quota have crossed the river safely at Mason's Bridge, but the poor weather has added more time to their journey. He sent a message back with an old friend of mine to tell me that he expects to reach White Haven in ten days' time.

"Second, Dispatcher Piscator is furious that his prisoners escaped." Tangler hesitated and glanced back to Ned, who nodded once. "I am sorry to have to tell you this, but Annie Trotter and her father were discovered on the road to Bishop's Crest. They were executed where they stood."

Kira felt the room tip. Giselle reached for her hand and grabbed hold tight.

"May she rest in the Glade of the Goddess." Kira heard Jenna's whispered prayer and clasped her other hand in hers, as well. She forced herself to look at Tangler. They had asked him to speak plainly; they couldn't choose which words he spoke.

"Although Piscator has no proof that you escaped as part of the quota, he has sent his men to White Haven just in case, with orders to check every carriage before the quota can board the ships that will take them to the Legion Isles." He gathered his beard in his fist and tugged. "We have done our best to plant seeds of untruths wherever we have travelled, knowing that people will often embellish a lie in the retelling. And even if Piscator grows wary of rumours and gossip, he sends men out to investigate, nonetheless. Unfortunately for us, he has heard that the priory is hosting some unexpected guests. He will be here in three days to see for himself."

It felt to Kira like all the warmth had been sucked from the room. Goosebumps rose along her flesh and her heart started pounding. She looked at Giselle and saw the colour drain from her face.

"Three days? Where will we go? What will we do?" Kira hated how panicked her voice sounded and tried to calm herself. She took a few deep breaths and tried to focus on what Tangler was saying.

"As much as Sister Evangeline would like to hide you within the walls of the priory, there are many secrets and ancient artefacts here that she guards as well. Things we cannot risk being revealed or destroyed. Piscator knows nothing of these things, he is hunting only one thing." Tangler looked Kira in the eye and held her gaze. "You, Kira."

Her eyes filled with tears, but she did not look away. "Yes. Yes, he wants only me. I don't want anyone else to suffer because of this magic I have inherited."

"Don't say it!" Giselle interrupted. She jumped up from her stool and stood with her hand on her hips. "Don't you dare say that you will sacrifice yourself to save us! Do you think that would be the end of it? Look what happened to Annie Trotter and her father. Piscator is a vile and vindictive man. Do you think he will be satisfied with only you? He will want everyone who helped you escape to suffer!"

Giselle reached out her hands and grasped Kira by the arms. "We are your friends. I love you like my own sister. More, probably," she grinned, and her voice returned to its usual volume. "I don't know that I would wear this attractive headwear to please one of them."

Kira pulled Giselle into her embrace and held her close. "Thank you," she whispered when she had composed herself. She fished a rag from her pocket and blew her nose. "Thank you, dear friend."

Tangler cleared his throat. "We have a plan which I believe will keep all of you safe. Would you like to hear it?"

Giselle sat back on her stool and nodded as she wiped her eyes.

"The carriage in which you were attacked has been taken to the village and repairs made. It will arrive at the priory today and will get a fresh coat of paint. Tomorrow, Sister Eloise and three other nuns will leave in the carriage and journey to Bishop's Crest. They will be disguised as members of the quota when they pass through villages along the way, but if Piscator or his men chance upon them, they will of course be Sisters of the Flame on their way to the priory in Bishop's Crest."

"Hugo and Declan have offered to ride with them for protection. Disguised as quota guards, of course. Hugo is almost as tall as Ned, and with a bit of extra padding across the chest and shoulders, should fool any who care to look. Bendon will drive the carriage."

Kira glanced at Ned. He sat with his arms folded across his chest, his attention on Tangler. It would take more than a bit of padding to expand Hugo's shoulders to the width of the guard.

Tangler gestured as though he was juggling. "We left Pot in the village of Woodville a day's ride from here and continued on horseback, so the wagon was not seen anywhere near the priory. We will leave the same way and meet up with Parr, who stayed to make a few modifications and tend to the horses. You girls will become part of the Rainbow's End until we reach White Haven. Since the men Piscator has stationed there will be searching quota carriages, I think it safest that you stay disguised until we meet with Lord Callan."

He turned to Ned and Jock. "Have I forgotten anything?"

Ned shook his head, but Jock elbowed him in the ribs and grinned. "Hugo's costumes might be a little tight for this wee laddie, don't you think?"

Ned clenched his teeth, but his expression didn't change.

"Oh, I can help with that," said Giselle. "If you give me Hugo's shirts, I can alter them to fit, and I'll add some panels if I have to."

"Excellent," said Tangler with a clap of his hands. "Now, we have much to do and not much time in which to do it. Giselle, perhaps if you speak with Sister Victoria, I think you girls will need brightly coloured tunics and maybe some ribbons to wear over your usual clothes. Kira and Jenna, you will need to eliminate any sign that you were at the priory, and we will need some fresh supplies to fill my chest. Kira, perhaps if you have time tomorrow you could forage on the woodland and collect the herbs and plants you think we might need. I haven't had a chance in the last week or so to replenish the stock, so that would be a great help."

He started to lean back over the desk, his attention on the map, but Kira held up her hand. "Tangler." She waited until he looked up before continuing. "Any news from River Glen?"

His features softened. "Agatha is safe and well. The soldier who watched her cottage swore that he never saw her leave. She has not been held responsible for your escape."

Kira couldn't speak. She nodded her thanks to Tangler and followed the others from the room.

Sister Eloise met them in the passageway. "All we will need is your cloaks," she said, as though they should know what she was talking about. Nodding their understanding, the girls hurried to fetch them. "Meet me in the training room," she called after them.

When Kira entered the room, cloak over her arm, half a dozen faces looked her way.

Sister Eloise waved her over, "Come, come." She took the cloak and positioned Kira in front of the wall. To the other nuns, she said, "Line up in height next to Kira, let me have a look at you."

As they obediently shuffled into place, Kira took stock of them. A couple of the novitiates she recognised straight away, and two of the older nuns she thought she had seen in the dining hall, but the other two she was not familiar with at all. One was quite short, and the other tall, almost the same height as Kira. She had light brown hair and hazel eyes that twinkled with excitement, despite her serious expression. Kira guessed her to be four or five years older than she was.

"Sister Blythe." Sister Eloise handed her the cloak. "Try this on." The mistress of disguise cast a critical eye over the nun. "Yes. We may need to darken your hair. Can you go and speak with Sister Catherine and ask if she has any chestnut hulls?"

Sister Blyth nodded and went to take off the cloak. "No, no. Keep it on. Wear it and get used to it. It needs to feel as familiar as your own."

Jenna and Giselle entered the hall and Sister Eloise beckoned them over. Sister Blythe flashed a smile at Kira as she left and whispered, "Goddess protect you."

Jenna's match was found easily, they looked so alike they could almost be sisters. "My cousin, Jess," she announced, throwing her arm over the nun's shoulder with a wide smile.

Sister Eloise cleared her throat. "Thank you, Sister Jessica. Keep the cloak. You know what to do."

"Yes, Sister." Sister Jessica bowed her head but before she left, she nodded to the three girls and said with genuine compassion, "Goddess protect you all."

Giselle was an inch or two shorter than Jenna but drew herself up to her full height when she stood against the wall with her arms stiff by her sides and a determined tilt to her chin. The smallest of the nuns was the only one wearing a coif under her veil. She removed them both, revealing a head of thick white hair that was in a tight bun at the nape of her neck. Kira frowned. The nun's face was unlined, apart from the crinkles around her eyes, but her hair and her demeaner suggested someone well past middle-age. She was also the only one to hold a staff, and she used it to balance her weight as she limped towards the wall.

Giselle's eyes widened and she glanced to Sister Eloise in concern. Jenna sidled closer to Kira and muttered, "A bit old for this, isn't she?"

But Kira had been watching the hand that held the staff and noticed that the skin was firm and the fingers strong. She remembered back to the day that they first met Sister Eloise and started to relax. The little nun tripped as she got closer to the wall and Giselle shot out an arm to steady her. The air seemed to blur, and Kira heard the crack of the staff on the floor. The nun used the staff to somersault over Giselle's outstretched arm and land lightly on her feet. Giselle was frozen to the spot with the staff across her throat.

Sister Eloise raised her eyebrows and allowed a wry smile to bend her lips. "Sister Phenella." She pointed to the little nun with an open palm. "Who will never answer to her given name and so we just call her Flynn."

Jenna was staring with open-mouthed admiration. Flynn chuckled and said, "Still think I'm too old?" Jenna closed her mouth with a snap.

"You heard me? But I whispered."

Giselle cleared her throat. The staff was still pressed to her neck. Flynn lowered it immediately and offered her hand. "I hope I didn't alarm you."

Giselle rubbed her fingers across her neck and shook her head. "No. No, not at all."

Sister Eloise walked over to Flynn and draped an arm over her shoulder. "Flynn is my right hand. She will talk to you now about methods of disguise. The trick is not to try to change your appearance completely but to blend into the crowd so that the eye passes over you because you are the same as everyone else." She handed Flynn her discarded veil and coif and left the room. Flynn indicated they should take a seat on the bench and paced back and forth as she addressed them.

"I like those little scarves you are all wearing. I think we could adapt those to look more like a costume. Add some long ribbons, and maybe some bells. You will need to darken your eyes with kohl and add a bit of rouge to your cheeks, especially when you are performing. It's not quite as important when you are travelling, but I suggest you try it now. You will not feel it on your face after a minute or two, but when you see your friends, you need to not show your surprise or your mirth. Just as the sisters are getting used to your cloaks, you need to get used to each other's faces. You will also need to learn how to apply it skilfully."

Kira groaned inwardly. Ribbons, bells, colourful clothes. She couldn't sing a note. What was she supposed to do? Stand still and pretend she was a maypole?

Chapter 24

With all that was happening within the priory, Kira did not feel it was fair to distract Tangler's attention with questions about dream weaver magic. Nor had she heard from Llyr again. She had helped Giselle dye a ream of fabric a lovely shade of blue, and now that it had dried, Giselle and Sister Victoria were sewing them each a tabard. Farren had supplied them with a multitude of coloured ribbons which Giselle planned to use as embellishment on the costumes and head kerchiefs they wore. Sister Victoria declared that Kira's sewing skills were adequate enough to pad the inside of Ned's quilted shirt for Hugo, and Kira had hastily applied her face paint while she waited for him to arrive for a fitting. He stood in front of her now, looking anywhere but at her face.

She tugged at the shoulders so that the shirt sat more squarely across his chest.

"How does that feel? Is it comfortable?"

Hugo stared at the ceiling, "Aye. It's fine."

"Are you sure? It's got to feel comfortable, otherwise you'll be pulling and twitching at it without even realising you're doing it."

"I have been an entertainer for quite a few years now, Kira. I think I know how to wear a costume and not be bothered by it." He finally dropped his eyes to hers and smiled, but looked away quickly.

"My pardon, Hugo. I'm afraid I'm a little distracted. I've seen you on stage and I thought your performance was wonderful. It's me that's feeling uncomfortable." She waved her hand around her face. "I hate all this."

Hugo looked at her again and pursed his lips. Kira realised then that he had been trying not to laugh, and groaned. "Oh, no. Is it that bad?"

"Aye, well you do look a bit of a merry-henry, I have to say." He started to chuckle. "It's just a wee bit heavy-handed. You'd be attracting attention for all the wrong reasons, let me put it that way."

Kira felt the heat rise in her cheeks. "What am I going to do?"

Hugo ran a hand through his hair. "Well, I don't want to boast, but I'm a dab hand with the face paint. I can show you how it's done, if you've a mind."

"I would be in your debt forever, Hugo, thank you." She fished the little pots of make-up from the pocket of her apron and lay them on the table.

He picked up a pitcher from the table and dribbled some water onto the corner of some excess rag that Kira had used for padding. "Close your eyes." He wiped the kohl from around her eyes and the rouge from her cheeks. "Less is more when it comes to face paint. You only need a thin line around your eyes. Draw across the top of your eyelid first, as close to your lashes as you can. Then underneath—not too heavy, mind, or you'll look like a badger."

It was the most words that Kira had heard Hugo say in one telling, and it took her by surprise.

"Now, when it comes to rouge, don't smear it all over your cheeks. Just put a wee bit on your fingertip and blend it over your cheekbone. You can use it on your lips, too, if you've a mind. But yours are pretty rosy, so I shouldn't bother if I was you. Giselle might want to try a little as her complexion is very fair, but only a little, tell her."

He tilted her chin this way and that, rubbed a smudge on her cheek and declared his work done. "Thank you for the shirt, Kira. I hope your travels are safe ones. Tangler has worked harder on this plan than on many of his tricks. He's a devious old so and so when he wants to be, but he's very fond of you. If it wasn't for Ned and Jock and the fact that he gave his word to Lord Callan, I think he would have tried to spirit you away and save you from the quota. But with Piscator so close, it's safer this way."

Kira gathered up the bits and bobs of her sewing kit to hide the rush of emotion she felt at Hugo's words. The kindness and acceptance she had received from people she barely knew overwhelmed her at times and added to the burden of responsibility she felt for the situation they'd found themselves in. Tangler had been an erratic but constant presence throughout her life, she realised, but to hear that he thought of her fondly was a gentle surprise.

"Safe travels to you, too, Hugo. I hope all goes well."

"Oh, it's sure to, lass." He reached into his pocket and pulled out a little box and offered it to Kira. "Just a wee welcome gift to the newest member of Rainbow's End. I heard a rumour that you can't sing, so perhaps these will help you feel like you are part of the entertainment."

Kira opened the box and was delighted to see a set of engraved brass finger cymbals. "Hugo, how lovely, thank you!" She threaded the first knuckle of her middle fingers and thumbs through the leather loops and surprised them both by striking a beat and creating a merry tune that alternated with clacks and rings.

"Whoa! When did you learn how to do that?" said Hugo, clapping his hands.

Kira laughed. "Tangler gave me a set as a birthday gift one year. He said he won them in a game of dice with the King's fool and told me that though the King was most upset, the Queen had thanked him sincerely. Unfortunately, Agatha was of the same mind as the Queen and after a winter of me practicing all day, every day, begged me to stop." She slid the cymbals from her fingers and put two back in the box. She grasped the leather of the other pair between her fingers and tapped the rims together, listening to the bell-like ring resonate around the room. "I played with them outside once the weather warmed, but eventually other things caught my interest, and they ended up in the treasure box under my bed. I hadn't thought of them until just now."

"More's the pity. You have a knack, that's for sure."

"Hugo?" Ned's deep voice called from the doorway. "Time to move."

Hugo acknowledged Ned's instruction with a wave, "On my way." He bowed with a flourish that rivalled Farren's and reached for Kira's hand. He bent his head and brushed her knuckle with his lips. "Stay safe, Kira." He grinned and sauntered across the room.

Kira's embarrassment at Hugo's unexpected show of affection intensified with the raising of Ned's eyebrows. She dropped the box into her basket and followed Hugo at a more sedate pace, giving Ned time to leave, too. He didn't. She fussed with the things in her basket as she walked, glancing at his boots to see if they moved. He waited until she was only a couple of paces away from him before he spoke, "The carriage leaves in an hour. Sister Eloise would like a word with you first." Kira looked up to thank him and met his gaze. His eyes slid from hers, however and studied the rest of her face. He gave the usual growl from the back of his throat that could signify any number of things but qualified it this time when he spoke. "Not bad."

Relieved that she had his somewhat grudging approval, but annoyed that she was relieved, Kira moved forward using her basket like a shield. Ned was forced to move out of the way or risk being rammed in his gut. He moved quickly for such a large man and cleared the doorway before Kira had taken a second step. "She's in the training room," he called over his shoulder as he strode down the corridor.

Giselle and Jenna were already in the training room when Kira arrived. Jenna was standing on a chair, arms out to the side, while Giselle pinned the hem of her tabard.

"Well met," said Kira, "you've done an excellent job there, Elle."

Giselle had a mouthful of pins protruding from between her lips, so grunted both her greeting and her thanks.

"Good job with your face!" exclaimed Jenna. "It looks much better than yesterday's attempt."

"Yes, I have Hugo to thank for that. He gave me a lesson when I was fitting him with Ned's shirt. I'll share his advice with you both later."

Sister Eloise entered from the door that led to the stairs. She was dressed in wide-legged travelling britches and a pale lemon linen shirt, topped with a short-sleeved leather vest. She carried a quota cloak over her arm. Kira felt a shiver down her spine. The similarity to the outfit that Mevis had worn was uncanny.

"Well met and Blessings, Kira. I've just seen Hugo in the courtyard. From my window, at least, he could be mistaken for Ned. Well done." She clapped her hands, "Now, Giselle will fit your tabard and she will get them all hemmed. Jenna, cook has prepared food for our journey, so is a little behind with meal preparation for dinner tonight, so perhaps you can give her a hand. Have you moved all your belongings down to the cells?"

Jenna nodded. "Yes, Sister. The guest rooms are all swept, and the linens stripped from the beds. I'll show you where you'll be sleeping, Kira, all your things are there."

"Well done. If Piscator happens to search the guest rooms, they will need to seem unoccupied. Any visiting nun would have slept with the rest of the priory in the cells, so that is where you will sleep tonight."

The door opened again, and the other nuns filed in. Kira gasped. Sister Blythe wore a nondescript travelling outfit, but she had darkened her hair and when she threw the cloak over her shoulders and turned around, she could have easily been mistaken for Kira.

Sister Jessica looked even more like Jenna than Jenna's sister did. But Flynn was the biggest surprise of all: she looked half the age she had the day before. Her face glowed with good health and her fair hair fell in two long plaits either side of her head. Kira realised now that Hugo was not the only person skilled in the application of face paint.

"The disguises may not stand up to close scrutiny," said Flynn, "but that is not our goal. When we travel through a village, we will be noticed because we are strangers. People will remember a carriage with four women and two guards. Some might recall what we wore, or perhaps our hair colour, or size. Some might think we are members of the quota. If they happen to be questioned by a soldier, or Piscator himself, even those details might elude them if they are frightened. It will be enough to cause doubt and have the soldiers follow, but if they eventually catch up to us, then all they will find will be four Sisters of the Flame, heading to Bishop's Crest."

Kira was reassured by Flynn's confidence as she spoke. If Sister Eloise's right hand was positive this contrivance would work, then there seemed little to worry about. She began to relax.

Sister Eloise turned to Kira, "Sister Catherine has some spare receptacles that you may have for Tangler's supplies. She asked that you call in and collect them after you have eaten your lunch. She will tell you the best place to forage."

"Thank you, Sister. For everything."

"Blessings, child. These are dark times for all of us, you are not alone in this time of persecution and prejudice. The light of the Lady Edalyn will guide you when you need it, remember this." She spoke in hushed tones to both Giselle and Jenna before indicating to the others that it was time to go.

Kira made room for her friends by the window so they could watch the carriage leave, and then climbed on the chair so Giselle could pin her hem.

After lunch Kira met with Sister Catherine, who had decided that she needed some fresh air herself and declared that she should accompany her. The nun led her through a narrow passage that serviced the kitchen and a washroom where the bedlinens and towels were laundered. They exited through a large mud-room and out onto a small, paved courtyard walled only on one side. Kira had never seen the land at the back of the priory before and was filled with regret that she hadn't been before now. The little wall angled away to run the length of the beautiful gardens on the other side and met with the stables about a hundred paces away.

Chickens and geese foraged in the expanse of grass between the wall and a large duck pond, which was partially obscured by the woodland that surrounded it. A pair of brown-and-white goats came gambolling towards them and snuffled at the pockets of Sister Catherine's apron.

"Meet our grass cutters, Nanny and Billy." She rolled her eyes as she said their names delving inside her pockets to produce a couple of apples. She fed them the fruit and shooed them away.

"This is the working side of the priory," she said, and pointed to the pond. "On the other side is a meadow where George keeps some cows and the rest of the goats. He has a small milking shed there, too. The coops are at the back of the stable. See? There with the picket fence around. It's supposed to keep the foxes out, but he built them on stilts, just to be sure."

Kira smiled. "And that?" She nodded towards a small stone hut between the edge of the tree line and the stables.

"Sticks out like a sore thumb, doesn't it?" Sister Catherine shrugged. "It's George's storage shed. It was there long before this part of the gardens was developed. It was probably a cowherder's hut. George is not of a mind to move it. He says he'll build another when that one falls down. That monstrosity next to it is his drying rack."

The rack was a sturdy A-frame construction, with wide gaps between the cross-timbers and lethal-looking nails and hooks attached to the beams. There were no skins or pelts hanging on the racks, and although Kira was not usually squeamish about dead animals, she was oddly relieved when Sister Catherine turned and walked the other way. She took Kira to the small greenhouse nestled between the priory and the hill which sloped away to form the natural wall of the hot spring that supplied the nuns with hot water. The pipes that carried the water to the priory ran beneath the greenhouse and provided enough warmth to grow many medicinal herbs which would not normally have been available as winter approached. They spent the next hour foraging in the woodland and raiding the herb garden.

When Kira's satchel was almost bursting, Sister Catherine decided that it was time for a cup of tea, and they headed back inside.

"I know it's close to a new moon, but the moon spiders love that little grove of holly on the other side of the herb garden. If you get up with the Aurora Cantus, you should be able to gather some webs to take with you."

"Thank you, that's good advice. I might also collect some sphagnum moss by the pond. I have a supply of dried moss, but Jenna had a heavy cycle this month and needed quite a lot."

Sister Catherine opened a cupboard. "Do you have enough rags? I boiled up some bandages and rags yesterday. We have plenty to spare." She took a few rolls from the shelf and dropped them into a linen pouch and handed it to Kira. "Sister Marguerite asks if you would call in to see her before you leave. She has been in bed with a severe migraine the last two days. I've been giving her willow bark and betony, but sleep is usually her best remedy. Leave it until tomorrow afternoon. She should be well enough to see you by then."

"Thank you, Sister Catherine," said Kira as she accepted the pouch, "please give my best wishes to Sister Marguerite. I hope she recovers soon."

Chapter 25

Kira was roused gently from her slumber by the rhythmic chant of the Aurora Cantus. The repetitious melody permeated through the chapel walls and drifted down the passageway, the thick stone muffling the choir of fifty to almost a whisper. It was the first time Kira had heard the nuns' dawn prayers, and she thought that even though her new room was much closer to the chapel, had she not been on the verge of waking, she would not have heard them today, either.

She dressed quickly and placed a few copper pots into a leather pouch that she tied to her belt, along with a string bag. She grabbed Seren, deciding that the staff would come in handy to hold back the branches so she could avoid some of the spiny leaves on the holly bushes. The moon was too pale to see by, so she took the lamp from her bed table and opened the door.

A vision in white floated in the darkened passage and Kira almost dropped the lamp.

"Pus and horehound!" she hissed with a yelp. "Giselle Threadgold, what are you doing out here? I thought you were a ghost!" She leaned back against the wall and tried to calm her breath and thundering heart.

"Sorry, Kira," Giselle whispered. "I didn't sleep well, and when I heard the cantus start, I came out to hear them better." She was dressed in a long white sleep shift and had wrapped the white blanket around her for warmth. Her moonbeam hair was unbound and tumbled around her shoulders in a spectre-like cloud. "What are you up to?"

Kira pointed to the pouch with her elbow. "Collecting webs. There are some holly bushes near the herb garden. I'll get some more blood moss from the pond as well. I'll be back before breakfast."

Giselle shook her shoulders in an exaggerated shudder. "Erk, spiders and pond slime. Rather you than me. I'll see you when you get back—unless you would like some help?"

Kira laughed at her friend's obvious reluctance. "No; thank you for your heartfelt offer, but I think I can manage. You stay where it's warm and keep your pretty hands clean. We wouldn't want pond slime on our lovely new tabards, would we?"

"Hah! I've missed your jibes, Kira. You are very serious these days. We all are, I suppose." She reached up and wrapped Kira's scarf a little more securely around her neck. "It's cold out there. Be wary in the dark."

A midnight breeze had swept down from the mountains and the grass was covered in frost. It crunched beneath her boots as she tramped towards the herb garden watching her breath cloud in the morning chill. She was tempted to gather the moss first as the woodland would be slightly less chilly than the open air, but the webs would be better collected now, before they had a chance to be contaminated. In the light of her lamp the frozen webs glistened like strands of glass, and Kira wasted no time filling her pots.

Daylight was slow in coming, but eventually she was able to extinguish her lamp. The rising sun was hidden behind the mountain, but the sky held a faint blush of pink by the time she had finished her tasks. She walked along the edge of the woodland, taking care to hold her string bag away from her, as it was full of damp moss which left a dripping trail on the frozen dew. The day promised to be clear, the clouds high and of little substance, but the air smelled of snow and the mountain camellia that grew in profusion on the hillslopes. Kira paused by a large beech tree at the edge of the woodland when she heard the screech of a pair of bramblings. She looked up and caught flashes of orange, black and white as the little birds swooped and flitted between the branches. Another sign that winter was fast approaching.

She rested her head against the smooth grey bark, admiring the few determined leaves still clinging to the branches that arched over her head. It had been days since she had been able to be alone outside and just be still. The tree seemed to lean back into her embrace and for the first time since leaving River Glen her body felt full in a way that no amount of food could ever satisfy. She closed her eyes and let her senses absorb the energy from Mother Earth and thereby revitalise her Eiran.

Crack!

Her contemplations were disturbed by the snap of a twig close by. She pressed closer to the trunk, glad that the silver-grey folds of her new cloak would blend with the bark. She smelled stale tobacco and even staler sweat and then the slow, deliberate footfall of someone taking care not to make a noise reached her ears. Beneath the lower branches of the tree, she saw a man in a half crouch, sword in hand, not ten paces away. He turned and beckoned. A second man appeared from between the clumps of bracken. She held her breath and watched as he followed in the footsteps of the first. The second man carried a short bow and a leather quiver full of arrows leaned forward from his right hip. Kira's heart began to pound. Piscator's men.

Kira glanced back the way she had come. Her boot prints were clearly visible on the frosty grass. She hoped the men hadn't noticed. But their focus was ahead, towards the stables. She hugged the tree and watched as they crept forward among the trees for another thirty paces and disappeared. The woodland thinned out there and only the gardener's stone hut and the rack lay between them and the stables.

A thousand thoughts buzzed in Kira's head. She needed to warn the others. Were there any other soldiers here? Was Piscator nearby? How could she get back to the priory without being seen?

Before she could act on any of these thoughts, the door at the side of the priory opened and a figure stepped out. Even rugged up against the cold, Kira recognised the pale blonde braids that escaped the young woman's hood. If she could see Giselle, then the soldiers would be able to as well. Kira stepped away from the tree and waved her arms frantically, but Giselle's attention was elsewhere. She began to walk to where the men were hiding.

"Giselle!" Kira screamed. "Giselle, go back!"

Giselle had not only the hood covering her head, but a warm woollen scarf wrapped around it as well, but she turned at the sound of Kira's voice and began to wave.

"Go back! Go back!" Kira started to run towards her friend, but a movement to her left stopped her in her tracks. The archer had taken his stance and he was aiming at her. He held the bow in his left arm, and she saw his muscles strain as he drew back his right, trained the arrow and let go of the bowstring. Kira heard the snap of release and threw herself to the side. The arrow arced towards her, and they hit the ground at the same moment. The arrowhead pieced the ground only inches from her outstretched hand, and Kira lay trembling in time with the vibrating shaft and goose-feather fletching.

Llyr! Kira screamed the name in her mind.

She glanced back to the archer, but he had already nocked another arrow and was now taking aim at Giselle. As had happened when they were attacked before, time seemed to slow, and the colours blended. She saw the arrow arc towards the glow of buttercup yellow that was Giselle and saw the red stain that bloomed near her neck. Giselle collapsed on the ground.

The swordsman ran towards Giselle with his weapon raised. The archer turned back to Kira and nocked another arrow. Kira was stricken with fear and anguish. She would not let Giselle be killed. Could not. She leapt to her feet.

Dream it, weave it, will it. The words rose, unbidden from the centre of her being. She didn't question or hesitate. Instinct took over. She flung a net of energy towards the archer and simultaneously pointed her staff at the soldier. Her scream echoed off the priory walls and it seemed as though a thousand voices called Giselle's name.

The earth shuddered. Kira was charged with a wild energy that started at her feet and filled her entire being. The air vibrated and spiralled around her. Wind lashed against her back, whipping her cloak against her legs. The hood was flung back from her head and the scarf torn from her neck. Her hair flew wildly about her face as the wind roared and circled ferociously around her. Abruptly all was silent. She stood in an island of calm at the centre of the vortex she had created, while leaves and twigs caught in the whirlwind orbited around her. In the stillness she was at one with the trees, was part of their connection with the water from the lake, the roots and the earth, the leaves and the air. She understood that the forest blessed her with its energy, and she was mesmerised by its power.

Kira. Stop.

The voice in her mind was firm but gentle, and Kira obeyed. The spell was broken. The debris fell to the earth as the wind ceased to blow. Kira looked around frantically. Where was Giselle? The soldiers? She saw Tangler and Farren run towards a mound of leaves and let out a cry of relief when she saw Giselle move her arm from over her head and try to sit up. She was alive.

Kira's legs started to tremble and couldn't seem to bear her weight. Sister Evangeline and Ned were running towards her. She dropped to her knees and bowed her head. She was more exhausted than she had ever been in her life. She hadn't seen the soldiers but didn't have the energy left to care. Giselle was safe, that's all that mattered.

"Kira?" Ned's voice seemed to come from a long way away, but when she looked up he was crouching only a few feet from her. She raised her eyes to his and was startled by the anger etched in his expression. She moved her gaze to look behind him and thought she understood why. The roof had been ripped from the little stone hut and the broken timbers strewn about as if by a spoilt child cross with his toys. Nuns began running from the priory towards the forest, armed with staff and shield. Sister Evangeline waved an arm to Tangler and turned back to Ned. "Let's get her back."

Kira looked at him. "I'm sorry." Her voice croaked like she was suffering from winterfever. She thought she saw his expression soften but was overcome by a wave of light-headedness and just had to close her eyes. She heard Ned growl and then felt herself being lifted. "You're not getting any lighter," he grunted, and shifted her weight in his arms.

Kira tried to apologise again but all she managed was a feeble nod. She was aware of being carried. The smell of his leathers and his unique sandalwood and cinnamon scent told her she was still awake, but it wasn't until she heard Ned mutter "Edalyn's Flame!" in an anguished whisper that she opened her eyes.

The swordsman hung like the pelt of a freshly skinned deer on the beams of the drying rack. Rivulets of blood ran from a dozen wounds where he had been impaled on the nails. The hook was buried in his left eye.

Kira struggled in Ned's arms. "Down, down," she croaked. She dropped to her hands and knees as he released her and was violently sick.

Chapter 26

Kira was so cold that she couldn't stop shivering. She sat by the fire in Sister Evangeline's study wrapped in blankets and nursing a heat stone, but still felt chilled to the bone. What had she done? Her heart ached. She saw the soldier impaled on the rack every time she closed her eyes. But death had changed him from mere soldier to a man. She had killed a man. Possibly two; she had no idea what had happened to the archer. She had used magic and brutally killed a man. What had she become?

She thought of Isaac, whose death she had facilitated with love and respect. She thought of Mevis, who may not have died at her hand, but who she hadn't tried to save when there might have been time. The magic she had been blessed with should be used to heal and help, but it seemed the more she possessed, the more destructive she became. This was why magic was feared. This was why the dispatchers existed: to rid the world of people like her.

The water in the fire kettle finally started to boil and Jenna poured some into the teapot to brew some willow bark tea. The door opened and Sister Catherine entered, her face pinched and pale. She thrust a silver flask towards Kira. "Tangler says to drink some of this. It'll help warm you up."

Kira took the flask, but her hands shook so much that Sister Catherine took it back and held it to Kira's lips herself. It was the same amber elixir he had given her before, and soon its fiery warmth spread throughout her body, and she stopped shivering.

"How is Giselle?" Her voice was still husky, but her throat was no longer sore.

"She is well. The arrow grazed her upper arm. The wound has been cleaned and bandaged. It should heal quickly. She will be down in a minute."

"I'm sorry."

Sister Catherine shook her head. "Don't dwell on it, child. Things could be worse. I must go and help with the tidy-up. You get some rest." She reached out her hand to pat Kira on the head but changed her mind and stroked her cheek instead.

Jenna handed her a mug of tea. "Have this and I'll braid up your hair." She leaned close and whispered, "You have another red streak. I need to gather up the sides to try to hide it."

Kira didn't respond. She sipped the tea and waited for the oblivion she hoped the elixir would bring.

The sound of raised voices roused her, but she didn't open her eyes. Her head rested in the crook of her arm, and she found she was curled on one corner of the couch. Something heavy lay on her legs and she peeped through one eyelid to discover it was Giselle's sleeping head. Jenna sat on the floor with her back resting against the couch, but Kira couldn't see anyone else without moving her head. There was an awkward sort of tension in the room, so she kept her breathing even and pretended she was still asleep.

"Believe me, I wouldn't have brought her here if I had known how great her powers were," said Tangler.

"Of course you would!" exclaimed Sister Evangeline. "You had nowhere else to go. Don't try to douse my anger with an empty glass of remorse."

Tangler gave a rueful chuckle. "Your pardon, Prioress. You speak truly. The only refuge in the whole River Province is this priory. But I would not willingly have placed you all in this danger."

"I know that, you silly man." Sister Evangeline was not mollified by Tangler's apologetic tone. "But you have done so, nonetheless. The question is, what to do now? As much as I care for that poor girl, she can stay here no longer. When Piscator comes sniffing round, Kira and the rest of you need to be far away from here. The guardians are charged to protect all that is sacred within the priory walls, and we cannot fail in this. My sentinels are checking the grounds and the perimeter as we speak. The owls search further afield. So far only the two soldiers who were killed have been found. What of your men?"

"Farren and Ralph have been to the village. There is talk that soldiers have been seen on the road North. Ned and Jock have not yet returned."

Kira, already feeling wretched for what she had done, decided that since she was the cause of all this trauma, she should face up to the consequences and let them know she was awake.

"I cannot tell you how sorry I am," she said as she sat up, careful not to disturb Giselle. "I have no idea how it happened. I just wanted to save Giselle." Her voice started to break. "I didn't mean to kill anyone, but Piscator won't care. He already wants me dead. Protecting me because I have magic is one thing. Murder is another thing entirely. The blame is mine alone for this. You should hand me over to him."

Giselle had woken at the sound of her name. She sat up and grabbed Kira by the hand. "No!"

Tangler and Sister Evangeline exchanged a look and she gestured towards him in mute appeal. He nodded once. She clasped her fingers over her crescent and smiled at Kira.

"Kira, if the blame was yours alone and you had killed with full intention and knowledge of what you were doing, I may agree with you, but it is not the case. You acted in defence of yourself and your friend. You are but a little section of a much larger tapestry, my dear." She shook her head and kissed the crescent. "I am the one who is sorry. There is so much more you need to know, and no time to tell it. I'm sorry, but you will need to leave as soon as possible. Tomorrow will be too late."

Before Kira could respond there was a sharp rap at the door and Ned entered. He cast a glance at Kira but addressed Tangler and the prioress.

"The roads are blocked. Soldiers lie between here and Woodville. We will not ride through undetected." He ran a hand through his hair and across the back of his neck. "I don't know what those two were meant to be doing here, but if they were supposed to report back to anyone..."— he shrugged—"it may already be too late."

Tangler touched the prioress on her sleeve and held her gaze. She looked over at Kira and narrowed her eyes, deep in thought.

"Yes," she said to no one in particular. She paced back and forth several times and then said, "You have half an hour to collect your things and prepare to travel. Ned, Jock, Tangler and Farren will go with the girls. The others will have to ride to Woodville with spare horses and the bulk of your gear. You can only take what is absolutely necessary." She clapped her hands. "Quickly, now. Meet me in the training room in thirty minutes!"

Kira sat on her bed and watched Jenna pack her bag. She chattered non-stop, but although Kira heard the words she wasn't listening. Jenna cast worried glances at her every now and then and Kira knew she was supposed to be making a comment or answering a question, but her mind was so full of fog she couldn't think straight. She couldn't even summon the energy to put the memory of what she had done into her mind room. What if it tainted all the memories that were hidden there? She never wanted to do or see anything like that again.

Jenna touched her on the shoulder. "Kira? We must go now. I've packed what I think you will need. Ralph will collect what's left. Can you stand?"

"Yes. Thank you, Jenna." Kira accepted her outstretched hand and rose from the bed. She followed her from the room and into the passageway. A figure was leaning against the wall a few doors down. It was Sister Catherine. She wiped her eyes on the bottom of her apron as they approached.

"It's Sister Marguerite," she said tearfully. "She had an apoplexy during the night. That's most likely why we had no warning of the intruders." She gestured to the door. "I know you must leave, but I'm sure Sister Evangeline would grant you a minute to say goodbye. She is in the deep sleep, now, and won't wake again. We will start the vigil shortly, but I expect she will be in the arms of the Goddess by nightfall."

Kira's throat tightened. Could more go wrong today? Poor Sister Marguerite. She needed to pay her respects to the nun who had shown her the truth.

"You go in, Kira," said Jenna. "I'll take the bags down and let Sister Evangeline know you'll be a few minutes. Do you need me to come back for you?"

"Thank you. No, I'll be fine. I'll come straight down; I promise."

Sister Catherine nodded at Jenna. "Safe travels."

Kira entered the cell and walked to the bedside. The scent of lavender and rosemary drifted from a bowl of water on the nightstand. Sister Marguerite looked even smaller than she had before, dressed in a night shift and covered only in a sheet. The effect of the apoplexy was clear to see—one side of her face was paralysed, and her cheek blew in and out with every breath. A cloth replaced the gauze across her eyes and Kira used it to wipe the beads of perspiration on her forehead and sides of her face, taking care to wipe the dribble from the drooping side of her mouth. She rinsed the cloth in the cool, scented water and replaced it across her eyes. Sister Catherine moved to stand alongside her and put her hand on Kira's shoulder. "She seems not to be in pain, which is a blessing. And she knew her time was near, and not because she was a seer, she told me, but because she was ninety-three."

Kira looked up in surprise. "I didn't think she was that old." She leaned forward and picked up Sister Marguerite's hand. "I feel privileged to have met her and I am sorry not to have been able to speak to her again before…" Her voice trailed off as her throat tightened with sorrow and regret. She bent her head, closed her eyes, and said a silent farewell to the seer nun and a quick prayer to the angel to gather her peacefully.

She heard a tapping in the back of her mind. Kira entered her mind room and heard it again. She pulled back the trap door and in the empty cellar saw the little wooden door that she had used before. She flung it open, and the room was filled with the orange glow of sunset. A white owl circled around the room in a graceful arc before fluttering down to perch on Kira's shoulder. It nestled its head against her cheek, and she felt the soft warmth of its feathers tickle her skin and a feeling of love and acceptance flooded her body.

Don't cry for me, child. My time on this earth is done but I will sit with The Lady Edalyn and my Sisters in the glade of the Goddess and know a greater peace than I have ever known.

Kira reached up and touched the owl's head with the tip of her finger. Its head swivelled and the large topaz eyes blinked at her, and Kira knew that these were the eyes through which Sister Marguerite had seen the world. The tears slid from her own eyes, and she nodded.

I can't help it. I am sad to say goodbye.

I know. You have had much sadness today. I wish I could be there to counsel you, but I hope you will take comfort in my words, Kira. Your power will be used to do far more good than harm, remember this. Do not blame yourself for what you couldn't control but use it as a lesson. Most importantly, know that you will find a way to control your gift. This is something you need to learn for yourself, but the skills you have already will show you how. The knowledge is inside you.

The light inside the cellar dimmed and the owl took flight again.

Remember the words of your foretelling, Kira, and all will be well. May the Flame give you light in the darkness, daughter of Aeldra. My Blessings to you.

Kira bowed her head and pressed her lips to the back of Sister Marguerite's hand. She laid her hand back down on the bed and made the sign of the angel. Sister Catherine squeezed Kira's shoulder.

"Her breathing changes. Perhaps you would ask Sister Evangeline to ring the chapel bell when you see her. I think we will have Sister

Marguerite with us for just a couple of hours at most."

Kira hugged Sister Catherine, bid her goodbye and hastened from the room. The fog was rising from her brain and her heart felt a little lighter, despite the sorrow she felt at Sister Marguerite's imminent demise. She jogged down to the training room and found only Sister Evangeline and another nun waiting for her.

"I'm sorry—"

"All is well," the prioress interrupted. "How is Sister Marguerite?"

Kira pursed her lips and shook her head. "Sister Catherine asks if you would ring the Chapel bell. Her sleep deepens."

"Sister Freda, could you do that, please?"

The other nun nodded and left.

"Kira, before we go, I want to make it clear to you that I do not blame you for what happened today. Do not think I'm making you leave with such haste because I don't want you here. As I said before, the threads you see are part of a much larger tapestry, and I cannot risk what we have already achieved, as much as I would like to. Be brave and true to your heart and all will be well." She gave Kira a brief hug, then grabbed a lantern from the bench. "Come, the danger increases the longer we tarry. We must move quickly now."

Chapter 27

The peal of the bells accompanied them down the stairs. Sister Evangeline turned in the opposite direction to the way that led to the room where she had chosen Seren. They took only a few paces and seemed to come to a dead end. In the lamplight Kira saw only a large tapestry of the Lady Edalyn hanging on the wall, but Sister Evangeline pulled it aside to reveal a heavy oak door. There was no handle or keyhole, but a small brass flame inset into the wood. Sister Evangeline placed her crescent against it. Kira heard a click, and the door swung open without a sound.

They travelled down four more long flights of steps, cut from the stone, and were stopped by another door. As Sister Evangeline pushed it open, warm moist air surrounded them and from the pungent smell of damp earth, moss and mould, Kira guessed that they had reached the bottom of the catacombs. She heard the murmur of voices below, and as Sister Evangeline raised the lamp, she saw her traveling companions clambering into a narrow boat. Kira followed her down the last few steps that led to a small stone pier, hesitating as Tangler drew Sister Evangeline to one side.

Giselle waved to her, and Kira smiled in acknowledgement, relieved beyond words that Giselle had not suffered serious injury. Farren held out his hand and helped her into the boat. Giselle shifted closer to Jenna to make room, then stroked Kira's cheek with her hand. "All will be well," she whispered, and tucked a stray curl behind Kira's ear.

Kira nodded. She didn't trust herself to speak and cleared her throat.

"Take off your cloak," said Jenna. "Apparently the air trapped in mountain tunnels is quite warm."

Kira heard the apprehension in Jenna's voice and as she glanced around, could understand why. They were floating in a small boat beneath the weight of an enormous mountain. She shrugged off her cloak and folded it. "Where should I…?" She lifted it up.

"Under the seat. It should fit over your bag. Mine did."

Tangler climbed nimbly aboard at the stern and sat next to Farren.

Sister Evangeline placed the lamp on the ground and raised her hands towards the travellers. "Safe travels. May the Goddess protect you and Lady Edalyn's light shine in the darkness. Blessings."

Kira raised a hand in farewell and the boat lurched. Ned stood on the prow of the boat with a long punt pole in his hands. He used it to push them forward, but before long the roof of the cave became too low for him to stand, and they entered a tunnel. The way ahead was illuminated by a lantern on the prow, and their shadows danced on walls which were almost close enough to touch. As soon as Ned sat down, the boat seemed to pick up speed. He and Jock cradled a paddle each, ready to push the boat away from the rock should they move too close. They drifted in an uneasy silence for several minutes, then Kira became aware of a familiar rushing noise in the distance. It gradually increased in volume and Kira felt an uneasy quiver in the pit of her stomach.

"Brace yourselves!" Ned called over his shoulder as he reached for the lantern. "Sister Evangeline said we would reach the drop after ten minutes."

"Drop? What drop?" said Kira, grabbing hold of the side of the boat with one hand and the edge of the seat behind Giselle with the other.

"No idea," said Giselle, and having nothing solid to hold on to, made do with wrapping her arms around both Kira and Jenna.

"Whoa! This! This is the drop!" Jenna yelped.

The boat seemed to hang in the air for a moment and then pitched downwards over a small waterfall. The water splashed high, enough to wet the passengers but not swamp the boat. Kira braced her feet on the floor and squeezed hold of Giselle's vest instead of the seat.

"Flame!" said Giselle and grabbed more tightly onto Kira's waist as the little boat plunged and righted itself.

"Is everyone safe?" called Ned as he raised the lantern and looked around.

"I may need to change my britches later," replied Farren, "but yes. All well back here."

Farren's quip seemed to lighten the mood and even Kira managed to smile as Giselle and Jenna chuckled. The cave was smaller than the previous one, but the water was strangely calm, despite the torrent coming from the waterfall. Still, the current was strong enough to propel them towards another tunnel. A faint blue light flickered in the darkness.

"What's that?" asked Jenna.

"The light?" said Tangler. "It comes from a tiny creature, similar to a glow-worm. They will help light our way for the next few days."

"Few days?" said Giselle. "No one mentioned *few days*. How are we going to eat, and sleep and—well, you know. It's fine for you fellows, but how are we expected to attend to our ablutions?"

"Calm yourself, Giselle," said Tangler, "the nuns have kept these caverns and tunnels for centuries. There are places to stop and rest, a few storage caves and places to…attend to your ablutions in private."

"Oh. Good. Thank the Goddess for small mercies. But no one said we were going to be down here for days. Ooh!" Giselle's voice changed from disgruntled to amazed as the boat rounded a bend.

Thousands of tiny blue–green dots glowed in the darkness, like the stars had fallen from the sky to land on the ceiling of the tunnel. The lights were reflected in the darkness of the water, so the boat seemed to be floating through the night sky. The rock that formed the sides of the tunnel had been worn smooth over time, but in the eerie blue glow Kira could make out intricate patterns in the horizontal layers of stone. She had never seen anything quite so beautiful, and for a moment the wonder of it let her forget why they were there.

They drifted in silent appreciation for about fifteen minutes until Kira's stomach grumbled so loudly the whole boat heard it.

"Oh. My pardon!" she said pressing her arm across her belly. She realised that she had not eaten breakfast and most likely lunch as well. She had no idea of the time.

"Should we lose track of time down here, your stomach can be relied upon to inform us when it is time to eat, Kira. We are all light on meals today, I think. Mid-afternoon approaches, so maybe some bread and cheese would suffice. It will take the edge off our hunger until we arrive at our first shelter, anyway." Tangler fished around in a sack that he lifted from beneath his seat. He took out a roll for himself and Farren and then handed it to Kira. "Help yourself and pass it along."

Kira opened the sack and held it out for Giselle and Jenna to take a roll, then picked one for herself and handed the sack to Jock. She unwrapped the square of cheesecloth and saw the roll was filled with cheese, sliced ham and tomato. The aroma from the fresh bread sent her tummy growling again. The last of the fog clouding her brain receded more with every delicious mouthful, but though her hunger was satisfied, the enormity of what she had done left her feeling empty.

"How is your arm?" she asked Giselle.

"It is just a small wound. Tangler gave me some of his elixir to sip when I need it." She pulled a small flask from the pocket of her breeches. "He said that he has diluted it in water, so it won't be potent enough to knock me out. Sister Catherine told me that I might have a small scar, as though something like that would cause me concern. I told her I would gladly have a hundred such scars than be dead from a sword through the heart." She looked up at Kira and the sincerity of her gaze was emphasised by the blue glow of the tunnel. "I owe my life to you, Kira. Again."

Kira lowered her head and touched her cheek to Giselle's. "Any time," she whispered. But in her heart of hearts, she wondered whether Giselle realised her life would never have been at risk if Kira had not been part of the quota. Fate was surely a double-edged sword. Kira could feel the blade against her throat. If they managed to evade Piscator long enough to get to the Legion Isles, what sort of life would greet them there?

Chapter 28

They reached the first shelter a few hours later. The tunnel wall and roof widened to become a small cavern, just tall enough for Ned to stand without needing to duck his head. A curious rock formation rose from the floor to divide the cavern at one end and Tangler informed the girls that they could use the small closet-sized area for the privacy of their ablutions. Towards the back of the cavern was a stout wooden chest containing dry wood and a flat camp stone, and Jock made short work of starting a fire. It was hardly needed to keep them warm, but Kira was in dire need of a cup of tea, and so was relieved to see Ned haul several wicker baskets from the space under the prow and produce a fire kettle and teapot.

"The stream water is not suitable for drinking," said Tangler, "but there are several places along the way that have spring water available. This is one." He pointed to a darkened area of rock at the side of the cavern, and Kira could just make out the trickle of water oozing from the rock. "Fill up your waterskins once we have filled the kettle as it may be a while before we can access clean water again."

Kira checked Giselle's bandage and was relieved to see no blood-stain.

"It's only a scratch, I promise," said Giselle, pulling her sleeve back into place. "I only fell because I slipped on the wet grass."

In a bid to clear the air, Kira took a deep breath and addressed them all, "Well, I'd just like to say thank you for coming to help us as quickly as you did. I don't know how you knew we needed help, but I'm very grateful you came."

"It might have been something to do with that wee scream of yours," Jock said with a chuckle.

"Certainly woke me up," agreed Ned.

"Yes indeed. You have a fine set of lungs for such a slender frame." Farren opened his arms and sang a note in high falsetto that echoed around the chamber. "Like that, but louder."

"Be quiet, you idiot!" hissed Tangler without any malice. "What if we're being followed?"

"They'll think the tunnels are haunted by banshees and run for their lives," said Farren with a grin. "Besides, if anyone does come, Kira can throw a whirlwind at them and blow them away."

Kira gasped and waited in uncomfortable silence for the recriminations to begin, but none came. Tangler was in the middle of dividing up serves of cold chicken and potatoes but paused and glanced between Farren and Kira.

"We're going to do this now?" he said to Farren.

"Well, the poor girl has been beating herself with a stick since it happened. It's no good letting a boil fester when a simple lancing will let out the pus."

"I am aware of that, thank you Farren," replied Tangler with a touch of asperity, "I was just waiting until we had eaten, and she was feeling a little less empty."

Farren reached for a plate and passed it to Kira, "Here, Kira, eat up. Master Tanglewood would rather fill your belly than ease your soul."

Kira took the plate, somewhat bewildered by the undercurrent she felt swirling beneath the words. Giselle and Jenna moved closer to her, and she was touched by the feeling of solidarity their nearness provided.

"Please just say what you have to. I feel wretched enough as it is; I doubt your words could make me feel worse."

"No, no, dear child, I do not wish to add to your burden, far from it," Tangler placated. "In my haste to prepare for our journey, I failed to ensure you were sufficiently recovered from your ordeal. It was remiss of me, and I apologise."

Kira swallowed against the lump in her throat. She had expected recriminations, not apologies.

"Tell me. What distresses you most—that you killed two men, or that you used your magic to do it?" Tangler had asked the question gently, but Kira felt his words like a stab to the heart. She shook her head, unsure how to answer.

"Let me put it this way, then. If you had done nothing and Giselle had been killed, would you feel better or worse?"

Kira felt Giselle's arm against her back and answered truthfully, "Worse. A thousand times worse."

"So you love your friend and wanted to protect her. Giselle's life meant more to you than the soldiers, correct?"

"Yes"

"So, we understand then that you killed those men before they could kill you or your friend." Tangler looked at Giselle. "Tell me, had it been Kira's life that was threatened, and you had the means to save her, would you do it?"

Giselle straightened. "Yes, of course I would."

Tangler nodded. "Of course you would. I never doubted it. I'm sure Jenna feels the same."

"Yes, I do," she replied quickly. "We have not been training with Sister Eloise for show, let me tell you. If I'd had to use my staff, I would."

Kira appreciated what Tangler was trying to do, but the memory of that soldier impaled on the drying rack still ached her heart.

Farren spoke then: "Kira, no one thinks you took pleasure in killing those men. It's no different to when Ned and Jock and I had to fight those horse thieves when we were ambushed. Evan's blade cleaved the skull of the bastard who tried to get into the carriage. We did what we had to do to keep you girls safe. If we'd had to kill them all, would you think any less of us?"

"No, of course not." Kira's voice shook as she spoke, "It's just…the soldier."

Ned shifted uncomfortably on his seat. "I should never have let you see that, Kira, I wasn't thinking straight. I'm sorry."

Kira bowed her head, overwhelmed by the efforts of her companions to make her feel better. "I guess it's the magic then," she said, her voice thick with emotion. "I hate that I cannot control something that even with the best of intentions, has such horrific consequences. What distresses me, Tangler, is the destruction and devastation I caused just because I willed it so. I am supposed to save lives, not crush them."

The dam that was holding back her despair cracked wide and Kira sobbed on Giselle's shoulder. After a long minute she gathered herself and dried her tears.

"See?" said Farren. "A boil always feels better when you lance it and let out the pus. Now that you've had a good cry, it's time to feed your belly."

Kira could feel Tangler's regard as she ate. She speared the last piece of potato and popped it into her mouth before looking up. He rose from the rock he was sitting on and stroked her cheek before taking her plate. "There is much to discuss and important information you need to know, but not tonight. This day has been arduous for us all, but particularly you, my dear. We are safe for now. What I have to say can wait. Try and get some sleep."

Kira was hit by a wave of exhaustion and yawned loudly. "Thank you again for all you have done. I will be forever indebted to you all and the kindness you've shown me. Since you declare we are safe, Tangler, I will do as you suggest and get some sleep. Good night."

Sleep proved a little harder to come by than Kira expected, but eventually she stowed the memory of what had happened that morning into her memory room. She opened the cellar door, and from the back of a snowy white owl watched her mother kiss her father goodbye until she finally fell asleep.

Chapter 29

Kira slept fitfully and she was glad when the sounds of breakfast preparation woke her properly. She attended to her toilet, then joined Giselle and Jenna by the fire. Jock handed her a mug of tea, then doled out some oats from the pot bubbling on the fire. Tangler was in deep discussion with Ned and Farren in the corner of the cave, but when he saw Kira watching he stopped talking and ushered the other men towards the fire.

"Well met, girls. I hope you slept well? I told you last night there were things that I felt you needed to be aware of, and while my friends here think it may be a little premature to discuss our current political situation, I beg to differ." He waved away Ned's growl of frustration. "The girls do have a right to know, Ned, especially Kira, since she blames herself for much that has happened."

Ned sat down and ran his hands through his hair. He looked at Jock, who shrugged but said nothing. Kira frowned. Ned and Jock may be Lord Callan's guards, but Tangler always seemed to be the one in charge. However, now there was a subtle tension between the men, and she sensed that if Ned really objected, Tangler would defer to him.

"Very well. But choose your words with care."

Kira felt Giselle give her a nudge and knew her friend was as perplexed as she was.

"Always," said Tangler with a nod towards Ned. He turned to the girls and smiled.

"River Province is about as insulated as is possible from Shardial while still being within the Realm, but even so, news from the capital reaches here eventually. You are aware, for instance that King Davic has reached a level of infirmity such that he rarely leaves his bedchamber, but with the same stubborn streak that marked his reign, refuses to hand over complete power to his son, Crown Prince Thomac. Many people believe this reluctance is for two reasons. Prince Thomac is a man of questionable judgement, easily influenced by flatterers and sycophants who cannot see further than next week, never mind plan for the next few decades."

Ned's groan managed to convey his frustration. Tangler held up a hand in apology,

"Your pardon, Ned. But I speak the truth, and you know it." He turned back to face the girls without giving the guard time to reply. "The second reason is a little more complicated. You all know of Prince Rhicard, I presume, the King's nephew who resides in the Northern Province?"

Kira nodded. "That's where Lady Lydia told me she would seek refuge with Mica. She said she would go to Prince Rhicard's court."

"Isn't he a lame-bird?" asked Jenna.

"Jenna!" Giselle censured her with an elbow to her ribs.

Tangler raised his brows. "He is crippled, you are correct. One leg is lame, and his left hand is withered, but the man's brain is as big as Dragon's Doom. The Prince has more wisdom in his little finger than the entire court of Shardial has in their heads and King Davic knows it. Rhicard has no plan to challenge Thomac, but the crown prince is, as I said, easily influenced and fears he will. To make sure Rhicard lays no claim on the crown, there is a price on his head should he ever leave the Northern Province."

Kira heard the admiration for Rhicard in Tangler's voice, and it got her thinking. She had been so wrapped up in her own problems that she hadn't been as observant as she usually was. Tangler was very well informed for a travelling entertainer, even if he did spend time in the Royal courts. She nibbled pensively on her bottom lip as he continued.

"Prince Thomac is under the impression that magic will be used to wrest the throne from him before he even sits on it. Hence the increased diligence from his dispatchers. Why he believes this, we are not sure, but it has resulted in even more incarcerations, torture, and execution. Unfortunately, my dear, you are caught between Thomac's paranoia and Piscator's obsession. The Crown Prince can preach all he likes about saving Cabarac from the return of the Plague, but I believe he looks only to protect his own skin."

"I see," said Kira. "Are there many in Cabarac who would prefer Prince Rhicard to inherit the throne, rather than Prince Thomac?"

Tangler looked at her sharply. "Not enough, I'm afraid. Many prefer the lies of a prince to the truth of a pauper. The hatred and distrust of magic is whipped to a frenzy in the capital. It is an easy scapegoat when things are not going well."

"Sister Evangeline said a similar thing," said Giselle.

"Several staunch supporters of King Davic who feel the prince lacks the foresight and the forbearance to take on the responsibilities of the realm, now find family members accused of either having magic or supporting those who do."

"Edalyn's Flame, Tangler!" Ned glared at the old man. "Be careful what you say!"

Kira picked up the end of one of her braids and ran it between her upper lip and the bottom of her nose as she thought. Her treasure chest was stuffed with trinkets from all over Cabarac, and even the neighbouring kingdoms. Tangler really did have the perfect excuse for travelling the country and the means of hiding in plain sight. It seemed so obvious to her now, she felt a little foolish.

"So," Kira asked tentatively, "do you spy for Prince Rhicard, or simply recruit like-minded people on his behalf?"

Tangler slapped a hand against his knee and grinned his approval. Farren let out a long whistle and Ned just groaned. Judging by their reactions, Kira thought she might have caught the fish by the hook.

"Spying is rather a harsh word," said Farren. "We prefer to call it 'information gathering', if you please. The fact that Thomac uses magic as an excuse to eliminate anyone without just cause is reason enough for Prince Rhicard to help those who are persecuted by the Crown Prince. We help where we can."

"Spreading seeds of your own of misinformation and deception while you're at it," said Giselle, always quick to catch on. "No wonder you always seem to know what's going on."

"But what of Ned and Jock? Don't tell me you're both spies as well," said Jenna, the confusion evident in her tone.

Surprisingly, it was Jock who answered. "Oh, no, lass, simple soldiers we are. Loyal to the King, but not necessarily to anyone who hopes to wear the crown. Lord Callen is King Davic's man, and he is our commander. We know where our loyalties lie."

The enemy of my enemy is my friend? The argument seemed plausible, but Kira wasn't sure if it carried enough weight. She decided to wait and see.

"I don't wish to seem like the minnow in this catch, but what exactly does all this have to do with Kira?" asked Jenna.

Ned stood abruptly and began collecting the plates. Kira was surprised to discover that she had almost cleaned her bowl while

Tangler was talking. She spooned the last bit of porridge into her mouth and handed it to Ned. Tangler waited until Ned and Jock were washing the breakfast dishes before he spoke.

"As you know, the Rainbow's End and I were on our way north when that little accident on the bridge delayed our plans. The Northern Peaks are nigh on impassable after first snowfall, and the only other way is by boat from White Haven. The docks are under the control of the Harbour Master, Anton Garrett, but between Thomac's spies and Piscator's soldiers, hiring a vessel will be risky. Still, I think it is a risk we must take." He lowered his voice and leaned closer, "If I could, I would take you with me, Kira, and ask for Prince Rhicard's protection while you learn to gain control of your magic."

Kira's surge of excitement was doused almost as quickly. Ned's hearing appeared to rival Jenna's.

"You go too far, Tangler!" he growled. "These girls have been gathered for the quota. It is irresponsible of you to give Kira false hope."

"But why? Why can't he help Kira?" exclaimed Giselle.

"Aside from the fact that she is part of the quota and under Lord Callen's detention, and being pursued by Piscator for execution, you mean?" Ned raised his eyebrows and made no attempt to soften the sarcasm in his tone.

"Yes," said Giselle impatiently, "that's exactly what I mean."

"My apologies, Ned. Forgive me, I forget that you are Lord Callan's authority here."

Tangler ignored Ned's snort of disbelief. "Ned is correct, of course, Giselle. Lord Callan would have to agree before I could help Kira this way."

Tangler's apology did little to mollify Ned's anger.

"You cast a long line, Tangler. I suggest you stay focussed on more immediate problems before trying to reel that fish in. We need to get these girls to White Haven in one piece first; their safety is our only priority."

Tangler raised his hands. "Certainly, certainly. I shall say no more."

Kira knew Tangler well enough to realise the old man had achieved exactly what he set out to do. She had no idea whether escape to the Northern Province was indeed possible, but the seed had been planted. With a cynicism most unlike her, Kira wondered just how much Tangler's talk of bluff and double bluff back in Sister Evangeline's study related to their current situation and how much referred to a greater sleight of hand he was contriving.

Chapter 30

Kira had lost track of time. The boat drifted along the tunnel at its own pace and couldn't be hurried. The tunnel walls were too close to use the paddles; the height of the roof so unpredictable that the punt-pole was rendered useless. Even the spectacular light display that illuminated their way had started to pall, its monotonous beauty more of a reminder than a distraction. She thought that it must be late afternoon of the third day but didn't want to disturb the silence by asking. Jenna would do that soon enough.

To pass the time, Tangler had suggested that they change seats every now and then so they could learn more about their travelling companions, and while it had been distracting for the first few hours, the strangeness of the situation meant that conversations had been more a litany of random facts rather than a natural discourse. Kira didn't really mind. They were in such close confinement that any private information would easily be overheard, unless, like Tangler and Ned, they sat close together in the stern and spoke quietly.

She did now have a greater knowledge about her companions than before, she had to admit, but at the same time, wondered whether knowing that Farren could sing the entire six verses of King Olaf's Lament backwards or that Jenna knew seventeen ways to clean, gut, prepare and cook rainbow trout, and had happily shared nine of her recipes before Giselle interrupted her, really counted as deepening her understanding of their personality.

It had done what Tangler had intended, however, and passed the time. Even so, Kira was glad of the silence now. For the last couple of hours, she had heard snippets of song amid the conversations, but when she had tried to listen, the music faded and she thought she must have imagined it. So intently was she listening, when Jock's unspoken thought hoping not to have another meal of smoked fish and boiled eggs brushed against her mind, she yelped in horrified surprise.

"What's wrong?" asked Giselle.

"Nothing!" Kira made a show of stretching her leg. "My foot went to sleep. Pins and needles." She wiggled her foot around and tried to control her dismay. Sister Evangeline had warned her something like this could happen. What a disaster. What was she to do? She thought back to Sister Marguerite's words of advice and wondered how best to use them now. If closing the shutters in her mind room kept people from seeing in, then what could she do to stop herself from intruding on other people's thoughts? She remembered when she had called out to Giselle and how she had turned at the sound of Kira's voice but had not been able to hear what she said because her words had been muffled by the scarf and her hood. If she imagined the same sort of barrier around her awareness, would it suffice? She had to try something.

Thinking of that morning, she remembered the way she had instinctively used Seren to direct the force of her energy, and yet she and Giselle had remained unscathed. Her mind shied away from the aftermath, but she thought that the staff would be able to protect her awareness while allowing her access when needed. Seren was with Ralph and their other belongings, but she could still imagine it, couldn't she?

Dream it. Weave it. Will it.

Kira concentrated and almost immediately heard Jock's thoughts again. She channelled her awareness through her imaginary staff and heard only silence. It worked. The sense of dread that had been gathering around her slowly dissipated and was replaced by a small semblance of control. She leaned into Giselle and grinned.

"'Tis surely a mark of how much the time drags, that the waking of a sleeping foot gives you so much pleasure," said Giselle, returning both her smile and her nudge.

"How much longer?" said Jenna. Giselle rolled her eyes. It was always a surprise when the next shelter arrived, as no one had been in the tunnel before. *Except perhaps Tangler*, thought Kira, although he never admitted to it. Sitting for hours was no fun for anyone, but Jenna seemed to feel it most and always spent the first hour on land practicing her training exercises with an imaginary staff. Even on the boat Kira saw that she would twist and turn her wrists and repeat the blocking moves that Sister Eloise had taught them in their self-defence classes.

Now, Kira had to admit to herself, she needed to train, too. She needed to strengthen her mind so that she improved her control. Just as she had always been diligent in studying herblore and healing skills so that the knowledge was always at her fingertips, she needed to master these new abilities, whether they be a blessing or a curse.

The boat shuddered as it grated against the narrowed tunnel. Ned swore and ordered them all to push against the rock wall to keep the boat in the middle of the stream. Kira pressed her palms against the stone, surprised at the cold roughness of it when the air was so warm and the rock near the water's surface so smooth. Hand over hand they steered the little vessel through the confined space, and every time her skin touched the stone Kira heard another note of the song she thought she had imagined earlier. Suddenly the boat was caught again and wedged in the tunnel.

Ned raised the lantern and Kira saw that the tunnel continued only for a few more yards, then looked to open on both sides. He swung the light to the leeward side, and she could see the top of the boat was about three inches from the rock. He moved over to starboard, and they could see the side cleared the rock by half a hand width. "The rock must catch us on the bulkheads, lower down. We need to push backwards to get free," advised Ned, "On the count of three. One, two, three, push!"

On the third try, the boat escaped the rock's grasp, and they moved back several feet.

"How can we be stuck?" asked Jenna. "Isn't the boat made to go through the tunnels?"

"Perhaps because there's more weight in it than usual? Mebbe the boat sits a wee bit lower in the water," said Jock. "I'm thinking that the rocks do not usually scrape the bulkhead like this."

"Mmm," Ned agreed. He clambered across the thwarts to the stern and took off his boots.

"What are you doing?" said Tangler.

"This," said Ned, and lowered himself off the back of the boat. "Move forward as you did before, but go slow. The boat should sit a tad higher now. If not, Farren or Jock might have to join me."

Kira moved forward to take Ned's place and they tried again. The rock still grazed the bulkhead, but this time they made it through without incident. The boat lurched forward and suddenly they floated on a large pool in an enormous cave. The blue light was absent here.

The roof of the cavern arced into darkness, but as Jock raised the lantern, Kira caught glimpses of wonderous formations hanging from the ceiling like icicles of rock, as though the roof had melted like a candle and the drips frozen in time. Jock swore under his breath and as he moved his arm in a slow circle, Kira saw that other formations rose from the floor of the cave, like mirror images of those above. It felt wild and dangerous, like the teeth of an enormous wolf.

On the opposite side of the pool, the cave was dome shaped and the rock, although rugged, was smoother and more welcoming. She was relieved when Ned called from the bank of a naturally formed pier, asking Jock to throw him the rope.

"Oh, my goodness," said Giselle under her breath. Kira heard the admiration in her voice and had to agree.

"Isn't it amazing? I've never seen anything like it." Kira looked down at her friend, who didn't seem to have heard her. Far from being entranced by the rock formations, Giselle was staring, opened-mouthed, as Ned wound the rope around a small boulder on the pier.

"He's certainly kept that well-hidden," whispered Jenna, apparently as stunned as Giselle by the sight.

Kira looked over at Ned, now shirtless, his muscled chest and arms glistening in the lamplight as he worked. She wondered just which natural attraction would be most dangerous and began to chuckle.

"I thought you were talking about the rocks," she explained, as a flush crept across her cheeks.

"Of course you did," said Giselle, rolling her eyes, and laughing as well. "Only you would look at a half-naked man with the body of a god and be mesmerised by strange, twisty rocks instead."

Before she could think of a suitable reply to Giselle's teasing, Tangler ushered them out of the boat. "According to the map, the cave on this side opens to several others. There's a small rock pool, suitable for bathing, and a spring that brings cold water for drinking. Tomorrow, we will travel most of the day and should reach Meadow Vale by nightfall."

The girls sat together in the rock pool, luxuriating in the steaming water. Kira found she was able to stretch out her legs while resting the back of her head on the stone ledge. It felt wonderful to wash away the sweat and grime of the last few days. Tangler had even managed to produce a bar of scented soap from his satchel and the air was now perfumed with jasmine and lavender. Farren had searched the storeroom and found a supply of candles, which provided a flickering glow in the darkness. For a few minutes, at least, Kira thought she could relax and forget why she was there. But when she closed her eyes, the undercurrent of anxiety that seemed ever present in her life intensified, and the moment was spoiled.

Tangler's words swam in her mind, and she wondered if it really was possible to evade both Piscator and the quota and seek refuge in Prince Rhicard's court. What if she could find someone to teach her about dream weaver magic? What if Agatha could come and stay with her, too, so they could both be safe? How wonderful would that be? But the voice of reason also spoke to her. What of Giselle and Jenna? Lord Callan and the quota? Ned and Jock would never let them all go, even if Tangler managed to secure a ship to take them to Prince Rhicard. Even if Tangler convinced Lord Callan to agree, how could she leave her friends behind after all they had been through because of her? Her life meant no more than theirs, so why did she deserve a freedom they might not have on the Legion Isles?

"What do you think, Kira?" asked Jenna, prodding Kira's foot with her own.

"Kira!" hissed Giselle. "Have you been listening to anything we've been saying?"

Kira pulled herself up to a sitting position. "Pardon me, my friends, I have not," she said apologetically, fully expecting the discussion to be about Ned's physique or Farren's wonderful singing voice. "What do I think about what?"

"If there was a way to escape the quota, would you take it?" asked Jenna,

"What?"

"You heard. Would you try to escape if you could?" Giselle flicked water from her fingers towards Kira.

"All of us, together?"

"No." Giselle sighed in exasperation. "Only you."

Kira wondered if she had been speaking her thoughts out loud. She scooped up a handful of water and splashed it across her face.

"I'm not sure. I think it would depend on where I was escaping to, and what would be happening to you."

"See, I told you," said Giselle to Jenna, then turned back to Kira. "You never want to put yourself first. Well, we want you to know that if you get the opportunity, take it. Because we would."

"Well, I would," said Jenna. "But Giselle wasn't sure." She ignored Giselle's little groan of frustration and continued. "In the end she said yes, but we would both want you to try and not worry about us."

And that's easier said than done, thought Kira, swallowing the lump in her throat as she struggled to her feet. "Thank you, I'll think about your kind advice, should that time ever come, but the way my luck has been running these last few weeks, I think the best I can hope for is to just stay alive."

She stepped gingerly across the rocks to her pile of clean undergarments and shirt and dried herself as best she could with her hands and her hair-kerchief.

The music wove through her dreams, beautiful, but achingly sad. The slow beat of the drum thudded between the haunting melody, like a double heartbeat. The song called her from sleep, whispering across her skin and through her hair like a cool breeze on a summer's day. When she opened her eyes, Kira felt the tears on her cheek, and for the first time in the past few nights, was glad of the darkness. The song lingered in the back of her mind, but as she roused more fully, she realised that the melody came from the cave itself, not from the rock, but somewhere beyond.

She listened to the sleep sounds around her. Tangler's gentle snore and Jock's frequent muttering interspersed the even breaths of the others. All asleep. She eased herself to a sitting position and concentrated her awareness on the music and immediately felt its pull, as though someone had grasped her hand and was urging her to stand. Mesmerised by the tune she tiptoed across the floor of the cave, taking care to step over the legs and feet of her sleeping companions. She grabbed one of the candlesticks that lit the path to the privy and let her awareness guide her towards a pile of rocks near the store cave. Tangler had surmised that they were part of an ancient rockfall, but had warned them all to stay clear, just in case it was unstable.

Kira hesitated, but the call of the song was irresistible, so she held the light in front of her and clambered across the rocks, using her other hand for support. Just when she thought that she could go no further, she saw a narrow gap between the rocks and the roof of the cave. She crawled forward and lay on her belly so she could poke the candle through the gap and illuminate what was on the other side. It was a tunnel. The walls glistened as the light touched them, not like the light that the glow worms provided, more like the way frost sparkled when touched by the first rays of the sun. Kira could go no further; the hole was too small. She pulled back her arm and set the candle on a stone. She shifted her position so the rock wasn't pressing so hard into her ribs, and cradled her head on her forearms. The music swirled around her, the double heartbeat of the drum called to her "Come, come. Come, come."

She entered her mind room and into the cellar. Seren was propped against the wall and Kira took hold of the staff and opened the wooden door she had used with Sister Marguerite. She tethered her awareness to the silver thread. The tunnel glistened before her. The music beckoned.

Chapter 31

The melody swirled around Kira's awareness, the warm low notes reminding her of a viola, but deeper and darker. She followed it down the tunnel, no longer glistening from candlelight but twinkling in response to the music as though the melody pulsed through the rock itself. The notes became words, and the words became memories, and the longer she listened, the more Kira understood. It was a death song. The final lament of a creature once revered above all others, a creature ancient and magical, wise and wondrous, but because of the hypocrisy of man, now relegated to myth and legend. A requiem for a dragon. Zarabesk, the last of the dragons.

The song faded to silence, punctuated by the final double drumbeat. She stopped at the top of a long flight of stairs carved into the rock of a cavern unlike any she had seen so far. Two dragons were entwined on the floor below. One was made of ivory coloured stone, carved from the very rock of the cave with such exquisite care that it mirrored every detail of the dragon beside it, black enough to be its shadow. Both were lifeless, but in the black, Kira saw the magnificence of what used to be. As her awareness moved closer, she saw what ordinary eyes could not. The scales, far from being entirely black, sparkled with pinpricks of red and gold, green and violet. Even in repose the beast was terrifyingly beautiful. The dragon could almost have been asleep, not dead for over two hundred years.

A wave of melancholy washed over Kira, and she was overcome with unfamiliar emotions. Her awareness gathered fragments of memory scattered around the dragon. She tasted the bitterness of betrayal on her tongue, felt the sting of a broken promise across her back and smelled the pungent odour of rot and decay in the air she breathed. But it was the crushing pain of a deep love, destroyed, that pierced her heart and left her trembling, and she knew that of all the things that the dragon had suffered, this loss was the greatest of all.

Kira felt helpless. She longed to give comfort to the creature, to give its soul some ease, but this was a memory, centuries old, and could not be changed. This dragon had once held the most powerful magic in not only Cabarac, but the world beyond, and a tiny ember had survived the dousing of its flame. It glowed brightly in response to Kira's desire to cherish and console. The air around the dragon grew luminous and she heard a deep humming that vibrated through her chest. The dragon spoke in her mind.

I have waited a long time for the one whose blood hears my song. Zarabesk the last is honoured to meet you.

Kira trembled. *The honour is mine, ancient one. I am humbled to meet Zarabesk the Wise.*

Laughter rumbled from the dragon's chest like rocks down a mountain.

Not so wise, little one, or it would be me greeting you and not my shade. Your sadness on my behalf is both pleasing and unexpected. There is much I would like to share with you, yet there is not much time. I would show you these things, instead, if you allow.

Kira's heart pounded. She could not have refused, even if she wanted to.

I would like that very much. Thank you.

Kira's awareness was joined to the dragon's before she took her next breath.

The strange disorientation she had felt on the back of an owl was intensified a thousand times on the back of a dragon. They soared higher than Kira had ever dreamed was possible, higher even than the tallest mountain, so the world beneath was in miniature. She leaned into the warmth of his neck and heard the strange double heartbeat increase its rhythm as the enormous wings fought the frigid air current to change direction and hover above the land below. As her senses adjusted, Kira saw the land through the dragon's eyes. They glided above mountains topped with snow, over gushing waterfalls, and swift flowing rivers, through verdant valleys with fields lush with golden crops. To her it was beautiful, but from the dragon she sensed alienation and regret. This was not *his* place.

As soon as she recognised that emotion, the dragon allowed her glimpses of the land he had once called home. Kira sensed that though it had been many decades since he lived there, it would forever be in his heart. The landscape was different to anything she had seen before, yet was still familiar. Everything was on a grander scale: the mountains, the trees, the open expanse of land, the lakes that teemed with fish the dragon liked to eat. The air was warm, warmer even than inside the mountain, the sun shone more brightly and the sky an endless ocean of blue. The land seemed to pulse with life. The vegetation was lush with rich, vibrant colours that Kira had only ever seen in paintings and tapestries. It was breathtaking.

Before she could do more than take in the beauty, the memory changed again, and Kira thought her heart might break. What had been bright and beautiful and full of life was now bleak and desolate and grey. The air was thick with smoke and ash, and Kira sensed the dragon was labouring to breathe. He struggled to rise above the toxic fumes. Kira watched in horror as a glowing red summit spewed forth deadly smoke and molten rock, devastating everything in its path. The ground rumbled as though in pain and suddenly cracked and split. Fissures formed where the land had been flat before. The mountains trembled and boulders as big as houses crashed to the valley below. Fires pockmarked the land. The lakes were smothered in ash and thousands of fish lay poisoned and bloated on the shore. The dragon's lair and habitat were decimated.

Kira felt only a fraction of the dragon's pain and anguish but knew that had this been more than just a memory, the agony and grief would almost have killed her. As Zarabesk sensed this, the image changed again. They were back in the first land he had shown her. Of the dozens of dragons in his flight, only five had survived both the devastation of their homeland and the journey to what Kira now knew was Cabarac. Images flashed through her mind like someone flipping the pages of a book. She saw the young woman who had saved his life, the magicians who sought his counsel, the King who allowed him refuge in return for allegiance and protection. Faster and faster the pages flipped, and she saw wonderous magic and great deeds, the magical protection he gave to Cabarac, the exploitation of the dragons' strength and power, broken promises, the spilling of dragon blood, the death of his mate, friendship from some, betrayal by others, his grief, and his death from a broken heart. A century and a half whizzed by in minutes and left Kira reeling.

"Do not weep, daughter of Aeldra, descendent of Valethrix, your tears are wasted on memory. That you have witnessed the truth pleases me greatly. What name do I call you?"

The dragon's voice resonated deep within her soul and Kira was filled with an indescribable joy. She couldn't tell where the dragon's happiness ended and her own began.

My name is Kira, and I am honoured to have borne witness. Though I had but a glimpse of your joy and your pain, I will treasure these memories for the rest of my life. I thank you with all my heart, Zarabesk.

Memory is like a reflection in a looking glass, Kira. It does not compare to the real thing; the essence is missing. Yet, I am pleased you have seen some of mine. Though I was betrayed at the end of my life, I had many friends throughout my time in Cabarac. But hold the looking glass towards an enemy and his reflection will be no different to that of a friend. This is a painful truth to learn.

I would give you a talisman if I may. I, too, glimpsed some of your memories as we flew together. You have faced more than one enemy in the short time since you have come into your power, and while my scale will not protect you from every dire thing that may befall you, it will help in time of greatest need.

Kira was touched beyond measure. *Thank you.*

Farewell, daughter of Aeldra.

Zarabesk's lament accompanied her all the way back to the cave.

Chapter 32

Kira lay still for a moment. The music was silent, but she felt the song echo in her heart and knew she would never forget the memories that Zarabesk had shown her. The rock was hard and unyielding, yet she experienced the same sense of comfort that she had from the beech tree in the priory garden and so allowed the ancient stone to give her solace. Eventually her energy returned, and she was able to sit up. Her hand brushed against something sharp, and she winced. She moved the candle a little closer. A thin black object protruded slightly from where it was wedged between two rocks.

Kira's heart pounded. The dragon scale. She put down the candle, grasped the scale with her fingertips and tugged. It didn't move. Convinced it was the talisman that Zarabesk had promised, she sent a thread of awareness through her fingers and the scale was suddenly in her hand.

The scale was almost the same size as her palm. As hard and dark as obsidian, it glistened with the same minute dots of colour as the dragon, and yet, the longer Kira held it the softer it became, until it was like leather. Startled, she dropped it back on the rock and instantly it was hard again.

"Kira?" Tangler's voice drifted towards her in a loud whisper. Kira stuffed the scale down the front of her bodice and felt it soften and mould to her skin. She scrambled as quietly as she could down the rocks. She hastened back to the campsite and waved as she saw Tangler in his own circle of candlelight.

"Is all well, my dear?"

Kira contemplated her answer. Tangler could spot a lie a mile away and most certainly knew far more than he ever let on, that she knew for certain. Deciding that she would follow his example and hope he would be satisfied with half a tale, she assumed a puzzled expression.

"You'll probably think I'm a bit addled, but I thought I heard music."

"Music?"

"A song, really. Not a merry tune, though. A lament."

"A lament?"

"Mmm." Kira lowered her voice. "A death song. A dragon's lament."

"I see," said Tangler, with no disbelief in his tone at all. "So, where were you?"

"I had to follow it. But I only got as far as that rock pile. I know you advised us not to go near it, but the pull of the song was so great, you see, that I didn't have a choice. I'm sorry."

"Go on," said Tangler. "What happened?"

"I climbed to the top, and I think there might be a tunnel on the other side, but the opening was only big enough for me to poke an arm through, unfortunately. I just had to lie there and listen to the music. It was so mournful, but at the same time incredibly beautiful."

"Just as well you couldn't get through. We wouldn't have known where you were or where to start looking. I'm interested to hear more about this song. But not now. Later."

Tangler led her towards the fire and the pot of tea he inevitably brewed whenever they made camp. Ned and Jock were each nursing a cup while toasting stale bread over the fire. The smell made her tummy rumble. Kira wondered just how long she had been gone from the others.

Jock handed her his stick, and she slipped the toasted bread from the end, flinching as she burned her fingers.

"Ouch. Thank you."

Ned poured her a mug of tea. "Snail slime's good for burns."

"Yes, I'm aware of that," she replied, sucking her finger as she took the offered mug and set it on the ground. "It's not that bad, though."

Tangler placed a pot of oats on the fire before hunkering down next to her. He stared into the flames, lost in thought. Kira bit into the toast and wondered whether her incomplete truth had been enough to satisfy the old man's curiosity. Eventually, he looked up and spoke.

"We will leave as soon as the others have woken and eaten. By early afternoon we should have reached our final landing place where the boat can go no further. The stream exits via a narrow tunnel and joins Border Falls, and we will be in Trader's Province. Unfortunately, we will have to travel on foot for several hours, up through the mountain to reach a safer exit. Sister Evangeline assured me that there will be a place to rest overnight and then we will make our way down, and hopefully meet up with Parr and the wagon and the others. If all went well with Sister Eloise, then Hugo and Declan should catch up to us before we reach White Haven."

There seems to be a great deal of ifs and maybe's, thought Kira as she sipped her tea and wondered if Tangler had another plan up his sleeve should things not work out as he hoped. She felt a warmth over her heart, right where the dragon scale lay and rather than admit it came from the tea or her proximity to the fire, fancied that Zarabesk was sending her a message of reassurance that all would be well. She grinned into her mug. Foolishness or not, having a talisman gave her a sense of protection and well-being that had been sadly lacking in the last few weeks and after all that had happened, she was hardly in a position to question whether magic could exist in the scale of a dragon dead for centuries. She stowed the memory into her mind room alongside her other precious memories.

Kira leaned over the fire and stirred the oats that had just began to bubble in the pot.

"It's a good thing we'll be out of this mountain tomorrow; this is the last of the honey," said Jock, scraping the sides of the jar with a spoon and dolloping it into the pot. "I'm looking forward to daylight and some decent food."

"Aye, and some elderberry wine, no doubt," said Ned, passing around the bowls.

The noise and smell of breakfast roused the others and soon they were all sitting around the fire. Tangler repeated the day's plan and added more information.

"As difficult as our journey may seem, there are more immediate things you need to be aware of. We have been in almost complete darkness for several days, so it is likely that your eyes will take a little while to adjust to daylight. This is only temporary, and some of us might have no trouble at all. We will leave the mountain at dawn so the effect should not be so startling as the brightness of midday. It will also be very cold outside, so you won't need me to remind you to wear your cloaks and gloves."

Giselle looked at Kira and rolled her eyes. Sometimes Tangler stated the obvious.

Once the breakfast dishes had been cleaned and stowed in the boat, Kira and the girls attended to their final ablutions and climbed on board. Tangler beckoned her to the stern and patted the seat next to him. Away from the light of the lantern his expression was hard to read, but his question was asked gently.

"Are you well, my dear?"

Kira knew at once that he wasn't asking about her physical health and pondered how best to answer. So much was happening to her that she didn't really understand. It was wonderful and terrifying at the same time. She found it hard to express the thoughts and emotions that swirled around her mind, so she asked him a question instead.

"How is it that you know so much about magic?"

"Aah." He steepled his fingers and tapped his thumbs on his chin. Kira was silent. Tangler glanced around as though the answer might be on the wall of the tunnel, then gathered his beard in his fist and sighed.

"How old do you think I am?" he asked, keeping his voice low so only Kira could hear.

Kira shrugged. "Around the same age as Agatha, I suppose, in looks anyway. You have the energy of someone as young as Ned or Farren, though, so it's hard to tell."

Tangler smiled and inclined his head at her compliment. "Your diplomacy is appreciated, my dear, thank you." He shifted his weight on the seat and crossed one leg over the other, changed his mind and crossed his ankles instead.

"You listened to the death song of Zarabesk, the last dragon in Cabarac, last night, did you not?"

Kira did not reply straight away. She had not mentioned the dragon's name when she spoke to Tangler, and she hesitated to confirm it now. She had made no promises to the dragon but felt his final resting place should remain undisturbed. As fond as she was of Tangler, she wasn't sure that he wouldn't use the information if he had to. Could she trust him? She clasped her hands in her lap, so she wouldn't reach for the dragon scale.

"Tangler, I…"

"All is well, my dear." He patted her on the knee. "I do not ask you to betray a confidence, only to reassure myself that your dream was true. You have answered my question by not answering."

Kira wished that he would stop talking in riddles, and answer *her* question, but held her tongue. She was fast learning that Tangler took the roundabout route when it suited him.

"I was but a young man when Zarabesk and his flight arrived in Cabarac. He was the most wondrous creature I had ever seen, before or since. My life changed that day. For better or for worse, I am not always sure, but that day will remain in my memory forever."

Kira's scalp tingled. Despite her resolve not to draw attention to it, her hand moved to the site of the dragon scale, and she pressed her palm against the material that covered it. Was Tangler telling the truth? That would make him over three hundred years old. Impossible! But was it? The very fact that she hid a dragon scale beneath her bodice gave her pause. She could feel its warmth against her chest and knew with dreadful certainty that Tangler did not lie.

"I see," she managed to say. "So you're a bit older than you look."

Tangler chuckled. "Yes, my dear. Quite a bit older."

Kira heard the relief in his tone, but it was coloured with something else. Regret, perhaps? He started to speak again, but Kira held up her hand to stop him.

"No wait. Please give me a minute."

Tangler had been a much larger presence in her life than she had realised, as memories flooded her mind. Why had she been unable to recall them until now? Sister Evangeline had mentioned something about bindings being placed on her to protect her, Kira had thought they were to stop her from accidentally using magic, but what if they had clouded parts of her memory, too? She recalled her conversation with Giselle and Jenna about the scalper. Was that when the bindings had been put on? Had Tangler done that to her? How? Why? She tried to swallow around the lump that tightened her throat. It was hard not to feel a sense of betrayal.

She looked at him steadily. "You could have saved a lot of heartache if you'd taught me how to control my magic properly."

Tangler pressed a hand over his heart. "Ah! You wound me with your words, Kira, but what you say is not untrue. I'm afraid I let you down in this matter, but even I cannot be in three places at once. Of all the risks I was taking, I considered yours to be the least concerning. I was wrong. Your magic is more powerful than I believed was possible, and you have my sincere apologies for not being there when you needed me."

Kira did not doubt the sincerity of Tangler's words, but they did little to ease her anguish. Still, she regretted her accusation; it wasn't fair to shift the blame to him. She wiped her eyes with the back of her hand.

"Your pardon, Tangler, and thank you. So much has happened in the last few weeks, and I am not used to feeling so out of my depth, and you know, I've actually *killed* people!"

Tangler placed his arm around her shoulders and drew her close. "Hush, child. I know this weighs heavily on you, but you are not to blame. The full extent of magic does not manifest until after the wielder reaches their majority, but even so, a magic such as yours has not been seen since before the purge. No one, least of all me, expected you to display quite this ability."

Kira raised her head to look at him. "Well, you must have powerful magic yourself to have lived this long, surely."

"If only," he said with a sigh. "Once upon a time, I was the most powerful magician in Cabarac. We lived in a golden age. Cabarac had been granted independence from the Maladikkan empire and for the first time in two centuries we had our own king. Zarabesk's magic protected our borders like nothing had before and Cabarac flourished. After his death, the magic weakened, and our enemies saw our vulnerability. We had relied on the dragons more than we should have and our defences were weak. The Maladikkan empire stepped back in to protect its trade routes, but cleverly they allowed self-rule in return for the first choice of any trade. For another century Cabarac lived in their shadow until King Bryon rebelled."

Tangler paused and Kira sensed a great sadness within him. For a moment she thought he wouldn't continue, but he ran a finger beneath his eye and took a deep breath.

"The war lasted many bitter years, and then came the plague. Unfortunately, when the plague was at its worst, sorcery was blamed as the root cause. The decision was made to destroy all things magical, and I and many others sacrificed our power to save Cabarac. Now, I am the same as any other man. Except I haven't aged."

Kira searched his face. In the dim light she could hardly read his expression, yet she sensed Tangler was not being as truthful as he should be. There was a far bigger tale to be told. Without considering what she was doing, she set her awareness free from Seren's protection and tried to read his thoughts. If her mind room was like a little cottage, then Tangler's was like the fortified battlements of a King's palace. She shied back at once, appalled, and ashamed of what she had just tried to do. What was happening to her?

Kira dropped her head into her hands and moaned inwardly. "I'm sorry," she whispered.

Tangler didn't pretend to misunderstand. "There are quite a few strings to your bow, Kira, are there not?"

Kira nodded; shoulders hunched.

"Yet, despite having no formal training, you have learned not only how to protect your own thoughts, but how to guard against intruding into other's. Remarkable."

"I don't want this ability. I don't want to listen to other people's thoughts and know their secrets, I really don't. I am ashamed of myself that I even thought of doing such a thing. I need help, Tangler. I need to know how to stop using magic. It's making me do things that I really don't want to do."

"On the contrary, my dear, you need to learn the full extent of your powers. You need to embrace it and become all you are meant to be. You are possibly the one person who can prevent this Kingdom's slide into oppression and tyranny. You are the key, Kira. The key that can unlock the vault and bring magic back to Cabarac."

Chapter 33

Kira's scalp tingled. A wave of exhilaration was quickly followed by a surge of terror. The lock and the key, that's what Sister Marguerite had called her. Now Tangler, too. She swallowed hard against the nausea churning in her belly. Pus and horehound, all she had ever wanted was a quiet life and to become the best healer she could be. She entered her mind room and took a few calming breaths. Seren stood in the corner and Kira picked up the staff and ran her fingers down the oak shaft. The bronze feathers gleamed in the dull light of the cottage and Kira stroked them with her thumb as she contemplated what Tangler had said.

So far, most of her dealings with magic had been at best distasteful and at worse downright destructive. Zarabesk's scale grew warm against her skin and Kira felt a gentle admonishment in its touch. She wasn't being fair. She had seen her parents and Zarabesk himself, hadn't she? She had Seren and the scale and Gwyneth's herbal, all wonderous things she would never have had if it weren't for magic. Even her mind room was more likely to be as a result of her magic than her good memory, she decided.

So, what was she to do? She needed to control this power which seemed to grow in strength week by week. Had it reached its pinnacle yet? Everything she had been taught growing up painted magic as something to be feared and destroyed, yet here was Tangler telling her that magic was a good thing. In her heart she wanted to believe what he said, but what were the implications for her? And what of Agatha, Giselle, and Jenna?

Kira picked up one of her braids and ran it back and forth across her forehead. Her hair would betray her secret every time she used magic, she was sure, so where would she live? At Prince Rhicard's court? Kira may have lived her life in a small provincial village, but she was not naïve. If she took refuge in his court, there would be a price to pay, and she wasn't sure that she wanted to be a pawn in any political game. Cabarac enjoyed an uneasy peace; if there was an uprising against the Crown, innocent lives would be lost. She didn't want more deaths on her conscience.

Tangler interrupted her train of thought. "You have much to think about, my dear, and there is no urgency to decide now. On the journey to White Haven, I will try to help you control your ability, but to determine the extent of your magic would take far longer, I'm afraid. If Piscator gets wind of how much magic runs in your blood, he will stop at nothing to get you."

"Can't you just put bindings on me again?"

Tangler's head jerked back. "No!" He cleared his throat. "No, my dear, that fish has escaped the hook. You must learn to master this gift; now that it has presented itself, only you can control it. If not—" he paused and shrugged his shoulders—"well, you saw what happened to the soldiers."

Despite feeling that Tangler's low blow had landed exactly where he had intended, Kira knew he was right. But learning to control her power did not mean she had to wield it. She straightened her shoulders. She decided to try to understand as much as she could about her magic, but she would make no promises on how that knowledge would be used.

"Very well. I would be honoured if you would teach me as much as you are able, Tangler, I would prefer to have no more blood on my hands. Thank you."

Tangler let out a deep breath and patted her on the knee, "Excellent. We will start tonight once we have made our last camp. Now, if you wouldn't mind, I need to speak with Ned. Could you ask him to join me back here?"

No time for questions, then, thought Kira with a wry grin. She climbed over the thwart and tapped Ned on the shoulder. "Tangler would like a word," she said as Ned turned around. They did a shuffling sort of dance as he clambered between Farren and Giselle, and then Farren took Ned's place and offered his seat to Kira.

"You and Tangler had much to talk about," said Giselle, nudging Kira with her elbow.

"We did." Kira leaned into her friend. "He's going to help me to control my magic."

"Good," replied Giselle, surprising Kira with the calm acceptance in her tone. "Now, remember what we discussed in the rock pool. If it means that you also get the chance to escape the quota, then you take it. Farren says—" she stopped abruptly and grimaced.

"Yes," drawled Kira, "what did the lovely Farren have to say?" She didn't doubt for a minute that Tangler would use any means at his disposal to convince them to do exactly as he wanted. He was indeed a skilled manipulator.

"Only that there could be more danger for you in the Legion Isles if you haven't found a way to…you know…"

"Stop killing people?" Jenna cut in.

"Jenna!" Giselle flicked Jenna's arm with the back of her hand. "That's not what I meant at all." She turned back to Kira and tugged at her braid. "It's really not. I was going to say hide your magical ability and the way it affects your hair. We know so little about the beliefs and customs there, so who knows how they feel about magic?"

"True," said Jenna, not in the least chastened by Giselle's rebuke. "It could be even more dangerous for you in the Legion Isles than it is here. If Tangler can find you a safe place to hide, I think you should take it."

Kira didn't know whether to feel happy that her friends were so concerned for her safety that they wanted her to escape, or disappointed that they seemed to accept the possibility of her leaving them without any hint of regret. She remained silent while she contemplated what they had said.

She was saved having to reply by Ned's return. He reached between Giselle and Kira and tapped Farren on the back. "Your turn," he growled.

Giselle sat herself on Kira's lap as the men swapped places. "I don't really want you to go," she whispered in Kira's ear, "but Farren is very convincing, if you get my drift."

Giselle moved back into place and Kira squeezed her hand. "Thank you," she replied.

The rush of the waterfall grew louder with every minute. When eventually the tunnel opened into the last cave, it was almost deafening. Ned and Farren secured the boat to the small wooden pier and helped the others disembark. The height of the ceiling lowered dramatically, and Kira noticed that a metal grid had been bolted across the entrance. Even when Jock held a lantern aloft it was too dark to see what direction it took, but the air was noticeably cooler than it had been.

"We'll eat now, then make our way up the track. Make sure you refill your waterskins here. The path has quite a moderate slope, but is steep in places, and thirsty work. I should think it will be a good three and a half, four hours' walk."

"Would have been nice to have our staffs, wouldn't it?" said Jenna, already running through her exercises. "I hope Ralph remembered to collect them."

Kira frowned. She had been in her mind room so often these last few days that Seren seemed to be with her. She realised with surprise that everything in her mind room felt more real than it ever had before and presumed her magic was responsible. If only she could keep the good bits and not have to worry about the bad. Sister Marguerite's last words of advice came from nowhere and spoke to her: *Most importantly, know that you will find a way to control your gift. This is something you need to learn for yourself, but the skills you have already will show you how. The knowledge is inside you.*

Kira shivered as the goosebumps raced across her arms. So far, her skills had been sadly lacking. She hoped that Tangler would help her to remedy that. She felt a tap on her knee and looked up to see Giselle holding out a mug of tea and a bowl of smoked fish.

"Oh, thank you. I'm sorry, I was fathoms deep."

"Thinking about roast chicken and vegetables, no doubt," said Giselle with a grin. "That's what I think about, anyway. If I never eat a piece of smoked fish again in my life, it will be too soon for me."

"Oh, yes," said Jenna with a mournful moan, "and fruit pie with cream, and sausages and brown onion gravy, and—"

"Enough!" Giselle interrupted. "Let's just eat this and get it over with. Hopefully this time tomorrow we'll be in the fresh air and tucking into something hot and flavoursome."

Kira washed down each mouthful of the smoked fish with a gulp of her tea. She hoped Giselle was right.

Three hours into the hike, Kira's knees and calves were aching with the unaccustomed exercise. The path wound gently upwards, hard underfoot and unforgiving. She was surprised how quickly her tolerance for exercise had waned, but Tangler had assured them they would recover quickly. Farren had been singing marching songs for the last hour to keep their pace up and encouraged the girls to learn the words and join in. Kira decided to save both her breath and the others' ears and stayed silent. Ned dropped back to rearrange the pack on his back to a more comfortable position and then moved alongside her.

"Are you well?" His voice was deep even when he spoke quietly. Kira was a little taken aback by his concern. Ned had rarely spoken to her since his admonishment of Tangler.

"Not used to walking on the flat, let alone on a rise."

He grunted. "I meant have you recovered from the incident at the priory."

Kira looked up at him in alarm. She remembered the anger on his face after she had all but destroyed the priory grounds. And killed the soldiers.

"It seemed to take a lot out of you. You looked shattered."

"Oh. Did I?" She wasn't sure what to say.

"You did." He nodded and hitched his pack again. "You're a brave lass. Uncommon brave. Don't dwell too much on the things that went wrong; focus on the things you did right. Not just at the priory, but when the carriage was attacked. You have a good heart, Kira. Stay true to it."

Kira moved her own bag more comfortably across her shoulders and averted her gaze, so her teary eyes did not betray her. She was unaccountably moved by the guard's unexpected praise. Maybe his anger hadn't been directed at her after all. She searched for a change of topic.

"Have you always wanted to be in the military?" she asked, cursing herself for the lack of originality. Ned glanced down at her, then focussed on the path ahead.

"No, not always," he said slowly. Kira heard the note of resignation in his tone and wondered what he would have preferred to be. He was silent for a minute and Kira thought that perhaps that was all he was going to say on the matter, but then he continued.

"Let's just say it's a family tradition. The oldest son carries on his father's work, the others train to be soldiers."

"I guess our heritage dictates a great deal as to who we are and what we do," said Kira, thinking of her own situation. "It's a pity if that's not what we want for ourselves, however."

Ned chuckled. "Indeed. Though, I have learned far more as a soldier than I would have had I stayed at home. I do not regret what I had to do. My father will be pleased, I think."

"How long since you have seen your family?"

"Four years. A long time to be parted from those you love."

A cold chill ran through Kira. How long would it be before she saw Agatha again? Before her friends saw their families?

"Yes," she said, unable to keep the sadness from her voice, "it's an awfully long time."

Ned touched her on the shoulder. "I'm sorry you must go through all this, Kira. Tangler wants what he thinks is best for you, but don't despair if you have to remain with the quota. Life in the Legion Isles isn't all bad. Or so I've heard."

"Ned?" Tangler shouted from the head of the line. "Can I have a word?"

Ned growled deep in his throat, but called out, "I'm coming," and with a nod of his head to Kira, strode up the path.

Kira ran her fingers across her shirt where Ned had touched her. She was perplexed by the whole conversation but felt there was more to the guard's words than appeared on the surface. The dragon scale warmed against her skin just as Tangler called out, "Almost there!" and she quickened her pace at his words.

The last cave was much cooler than the others and although a refreshing change, Kira soon needed to add extra layers of clothing. The air was tinged with the scent of balsam, cedar and the wild winter berries that grew on snowy mountain peaks, and she filled her lungs with the familiar fragrances. Jock built a fire in the small stone pit and Kira fed pieces of dry kindling to the flames until it blazed enough to add wood from a small stockpile at the back of the cave. Ned and Farren disappeared outside once the camp was settled to Tangler's satisfaction and were back in a surprisingly short space of time with two hares that they wasted no time gutting and skinning before roasting them over the flames. Kira had never been particularly fond of rabbit, unless it was cooked in a stew, but the smell of the roasting meat poked her tummy grumbles like a bear in a cage, and the juicy game was preferable to another meal of smoked fish.

"The entrance to the cave is only about fifty yards down the tunnel," said Ned, wiping the meat juices from his lips with the back of his hand. "The snow line ends about two hundred yards below us, but from what we could see in the falling light, the path looks safe enough."

Farren nodded and tossed a bone into the fire. "I think there may be some posts and hand ropes along the steeper parts. As Ned said, it was getting too dark to see properly, but I'm fairly certain I saw some."

Tangler rubbed his hands together, then warmed them over the fire. "Excellent. We will have an early start tomorrow, so best get a good night's sleep."

Chapter 34

Kira drifted on the edge of sleep. The long walk had tired her out and she was comfortably warm, nestled between Giselle and the fire, but anticipating Tangler's arrival she had entered her mind room and waited there. Before long there was a scratch on the door and when Kira opened it, she saw not Tangler but a large snow fox. Its fur was a dazzling white, long and thick, but its ear tufts and bushy tail were a silvery grey. Kira thought that next to Zarabesk, it was the most magnificent creature she had ever seen.

Aren't you going to invite me in? The snow fox tilted its head and Kira saw the twinkle in its remarkable grey eyes. It was definitely Tangler. Kira opened the door wider and gestured the snow fox to enter.

Your pardon. I wasn't expecting a fox. You are a man of many surprises, Tangler! The snow fox leapt onto the small sofa and glanced around the room.

Since my magic was drained, I find it easier to assume a smaller shape. There was a time when I could transform my physical self into any animal I wanted, but the snow fox was always my favourite.

Kira sat down alongside the snow fox and reached out her hand. *May I?* The animal raised its chin and moved closer so she could touch the fur. She ran her fingers along the luxurious pelt, wondering how it could feel so real when it was all in her mind.

Because your dream weaver magic is particularly strong, Tangler answered her unspoken question. *You have a remarkable ability, my dear. Your mind room, or should I say* cottage, *is one of the best I've seen. Certainly, the most impressive in one so young. The fact that you can not only see but hear and touch my projection is almost unheard of. In truth, I would not have believed it if I did not see it for myself. Indeed, this is the main reason you need to come with me to Prince Rhicard's court, for there you will be able to get the help you need. Once we arrive in White Haven, you may only have one opportunity to escape the quota, so you need to be prepared to take a leap of faith.*

Kira couldn't help but feel flattered by Tangler's words, but the feeling was tinged with apprehension as well. Sister Evangeline's lesson had been well learned. The more he discovered about her magic, the more eager he became to steer her in the direction he wanted, and Kira didn't know enough about magic and the so-called benefits it would bring to Cabarac, to just blindly follow. She would need to perform some juggling of her own to persuade Tangler to teach her some control while not making him any false promises about her future plans.

Thank you, but I'm not sure how that helps me.

The snow fox leapt down from the sofa and trotted around the room, pausing to sniff at certain objects and occasionally standing on its back legs to get a better view of the contents of a shelf.

It takes a great deal of patience and control to maintain a mind room such as this. It may be as effortless to you as breathing now, but it wasn't always so, was it?

Kira shook her head. *No, you are right, it did take a great deal of practice, but once I got the knack, it was easy.*

The snow fox sat at Kira's feet and placed a paw on her lap.

It will be the same for you now. You need to practice.

Practice what, though? I don't want to hurt anyone else because I lack control.

Tangler's eyes gazed at her from the fox's face.

I realise that Kira, and there isn't a great deal you can work on while we are travelling. However, just as you did when creating your mind room, you could try to manifest a 'faithful' of your own.

A faithful?

Yes, a projection. Old witches called them familiars, but dream weavers call them faithfuls. Start with something small and once you have perfected it, you can move on to something larger if you wish. You might find that you are drawn to a particular animal or bird and may want to concentrate on that. Just as you have catalogued plants and healing skills and stored the information where you can find it without hesitation, you need to use that talent to build a faithful. It will take time, but eventually the image will not fade away, and remain as you have manifested it. By training your mind to do this, you are also training yourself to learn control.

Kira scratched the snow fox behind the ears and nodded thoughtfully. Yes. She would do as Tangler suggested, she could see how it might help. She withdrew her hand with a gasp.

Your pardon! Your faithful is so very true to life, I forgot it was you.

The animal shook its head, then nudged her hand with its muzzle. Tangler's voice chuckled in her mind.

That is the trick, my dear. Once you have perfected it, the faithful is as real as any animal, but you are connected through the power of your mind. In the olden days, before the Great Divide, a faithful might appear in the physical world and no one would know by just looking at it that it wasn't real. Unfortunately, we will have to make do with the imaginary, at least for the time being. Now, you must forgive me, my dear, this old man needs his rest. It's time for me to go.

Kira ran her fingers along the animal's back and then stood to open the door. The snow fox disappeared as soon as it crossed the threshold and so Kira brought her awareness back to the cave. Her travelling companions all were sleeping soundly, so she turned on her side, drew up her knees and decided to do the same. Despite feeling so sleepy only moments before, Kira now found it difficult to drift off. What animal should she choose? Or should she pick a bird? Robins had always been a favourite, but she did love the frisky cheekiness of red squirrels. She thought of the little squirrel she had rescued back in River Glen and hoped it was managing well. Eventually she fell asleep and dreamed of snow foxes and red squirrels chasing each other through snow covered woodland while a black dragon wheeled in the skies high above.

Chapter 35

Kira followed the others out of the tunnel and gasped. Dawn had painted the sky with streaks of orange and crimson, and the snow-covered trees and hillslopes gleamed with shades of pink. After days of semi-darkness and confined spaces, the vista was breathtaking, reducing the travellers to silence. Gradually the sky lightened, and the snow changed to its usual white. The thunder of Border Falls indicated its proximity, but it would not be visible until the boulders and craggy indents thinned out further down the mountain. The river ran like a silver ribbon through the valley and beside it, a thin brown line of road. In contrast, the land rose gently on the other side, the hills only half the height of the range they were standing on. Between the peaks Kira caught a glimpse of ocean and one or two thin white spires, indicative of the architecture of White Haven.

A lump formed in her throat. Her future lay just across those hills. She had arrived at a crossroads and in less than a week needed to make the most crucial decision of her life. She felt a nudge at her side as Giselle came to stand alongside her. Kira glanced down at her friend, but she too was transfixed by the view. Kira watched as Giselle's smile was replaced by a frown and the clenching of her jaw, and Kira guessed that she wasn't the only one who was contemplating her future.

"Take care, now," instructed Tangler. "Single file, I think. Farren, you first, then Jenna, Jock, Giselle, me, Kira and Ned. Ned, make sure you keep an eye out for anything untoward behind us."

Ned swore under his breath but said nothing. Jock was standing next to him and muttered, "Like taking a whore to a brothel." He slapped his hand across his mouth when he realised Kira had heard him and then grinned at her. "Pardon, Kira. But the old man forgets sometimes that we are soldiers of the Realm and do know what we're doing."

Kira returned his grin, then took her place at the end of the line. The snow crunched beneath her boots as they cautiously descended the slope. The trees were blanketed in white, lending them a heaviness that had been missing in the autumn. After the darkness of the tunnels the brightness of the landscape and the fresh, crisp scent of pine and cedar was cleansing in a way, and Kira relished the changes.

After about half an hour of slow progress, their path took them past the large boulders, and they could finally see Border Falls. It gushed down the mountainside, wild and reckless, pounding the rocks so hard that sprays of water arced high into the air, forming rainbows as they caught rays of sunlight. The snow line had ended fifty paces before, and the rocky path was now made more treacherous by the icy spray from the falls. Farren slipped on a flat stone and as Jock bent forward to lend him a hand, he too lost his footing and tumbled forward, striking his head hard against the rocks. Kira moved forwards as quickly as she dared and was relieved to feel Ned's steadying hand at her elbow.

Tangler and Farren had managed to sit Jock up by the time Kira reached them. Blood flowed from a large gash above his right eye and there was a nasty graze on his cheek. Tangler fished around in his bag and handed Kira a bundle of clean rags, which she placed over the wound, pressing firmly with the heel of her hand.

Jock said a few choice words then clenched his teeth together and closed his eyes.

"Sorry, Jock. I'll have to apply pressure for a few minutes, then I'll check to see how bad it is."

Kira glanced at Tangler and raised her eyebrows. Head wounds were likely to bleed profusely when the cut was deep, and she had seen how deep the gash was in those first few seconds. She handed a large rag to Ned. "Could you pack a handful of snow in this for me, please?"

Ned made his way up the slope and was back in a few minutes. Kira nodded her thanks and turned to Jock. "I'm going to put this snowpack on your cut. The cold will help reduce any swelling. Be brave."

Jock opened the one eye he could see from and managed to roll it at her. Kira released the pressure and was not surprised to see blood gush from the wound. She hastily replaced the blood-soaked rags with the snowpack and wrapped a bandage firmly around his head.

Kira? She recognised Tangler's mind speech after his visit the previous night.

Yes?

We do not have the time to manage Jock's wound in the usual manner. We cannot afford to waste time here. You need to use your Eiran to seal the blood vessel.

Kira knew it was pointless to argue. Tangler was right. If Jock lost too much blood, he would feel faint and be unable to travel. Even if she mended the wound, he would no doubt have a nasty bruise and a black eye. She pursed her lips and nodded.

"Jock, the cut is deep and needs more treatment than we have here. Spider webs and moss won't be enough, especially since we must keep moving."

"Aye, I guessed as much. Can you sew it up?"

Kira shook her head. "I'm sorry, we didn't pack needles in our kit." She hesitated, unsure what to say.

"Kira can use her magic, if you let her," said Tangler matter-of-factly.

"Aye, as long as she doesn't blow my head off with one of those whirlwind things." Jock chuckled. "I'm jesting, lass. You do what you have to."

Kira was touched by Jock's calm acceptance and grabbed his hand in hers. He squeezed it gently. "I trust you, lass. Just get a move on, my arse is starting to go numb on this cold ground!"

Kira breathed deeply. She had no fire to draw energy from, but as the forest had provided before, the tumbling waters did now. She withdrew her awareness from Seren's protection, linked it to the silver thread and placed her palms either side of his face. She felt the warmth flow from her fingers and followed it beneath his skin. She absorbed the blood from the gash and around his eye into her awareness and saw that it would be impossible to knit the jagged edges of the blood vessels together, so badly were they damaged. Instead, she drew the heat from within herself, focussing the energy to cauterise the ends. As blood flow ceased, she could see a faint crack on his skull and strengthened it with layers of gossamer thread, then gradually withdrew her awareness. Kira carefully removed the bandage, exposing the gaping wound. Her healing had worked, the blood flow had stopped. The rest of the wound could be tended the usual way.

"Did we use all the honey?" she asked.

"Um, no," said Jock with a rueful chuckle, "there's a little pot in my pack that I held back for emergencies."

"Emergencies like your next bowl of porridge, you mean?" Ned fished about in Jock's pack and opened the little tin. He handed it to Kira. She poured the honey into the gash. "Honey will help keep it moist as well as stick the edges together. It's the best we can do for now."

Kira cleaned the dried blood from Jock's face, then fixed another clean rag over the wound and retied the bandage. As soon as she had finished, she was hit by a wave of nausea and only just managed to turn her head before being sick.

"Goddess! Are you well?" Giselle glanced between the blood-stained vomit and Kira.

Kira took the waterskin Tangler offered her and rinsed out her mouth. "Yes. It's not my blood." She grimaced and took a drink. "The blood has to go somewhere, and unfortunately, that somewhere is me."

"Erk, that's disgust—"

"Shut up, Jenna!" Giselle interrupted.

Jock moaned. "Thank you, Kira. I didn't know you would have to go through that when you said you'd fix my head. I'm sorry, I shouldn't have said yes."

"Nonsense. I'm fine. Let's get you up. Let us know if you feel sick or light-headed. I don't want you passing out."

Chapter 36

They reached the bottom of the mountain by mid-afternoon. Jock was starting to look pale, so Kira was pleased when they could finally rest and build a fire. They made a makeshift camp between the road and the riverbank, beneath a grove of larch trees. Kira looked back to where they had started, but though the tunnel was less than a quarter of the way up the mountain, the entrance wasn't visible. She wondered just how and when this escape route had been discovered.

Ned and Farren made quick work of the campfire and soon the water was bubbling in the pot, ready for Tangler to brew some tea. Kira checked Jock's bandage and was relieved to see that it remained clean and dry. She changed Giselle's dressing while they waited for the tea to brew and was doubly happy to see that her arm was healing well.

"I can hear hoofbeats," hissed Jenna, who was practicing her fighting moves in a clearing closer to the road. She threw down the stick she had been using as a staff and ran to the others.

"You girls hide down there. Behind those trees," Ned instructed. "Remember what I told you before. Quick as you can."

Kira grabbed her bag and ran with Giselle and Jenna to the safety of the trees. She lay on the bank and peeped over the grassy verge to see who came. Within seconds of their hasty scramble, Kira also heard the clatter of hooves. The men sat around the campfire, but Kira noticed that Ned and Jock had each taken his sword from its scabbard and placed it on the grass where they sat.

"Only one, I think," whispered Jenna.

The rider eased his horse from a canter to a trot once he saw the campfire. The sunlight caught his hair, so it glowed in a red halo around his head.

"It's Donald!" Jenna started to rise, but Kira placed a warning hand on her back.

"We'd better wait. Just to be safe."

Jenna dropped back to her belly. "Yes, we don't want a tongue lashing from Ned!"

They peered over the grass again and watched as Donald dismounted and embraced Farren. He clasped forearms with Tangler and the others, and then Tangler turned and waved to the girls and called out "Cabarac!"

Donald bowed low as the girls approached. "Well met, ladies. I'm pleased to see you all, safe and sound. Parr and Ralph are about an hour away in the wagon. I thought I'd ride up and keep a look out for you."

Once the girls had made their greetings, Tangler passed around the tea, and Donald produced a sack of honey oat biscuits. "Courtesy of Parr, he's a dab hand at baking."

Kira had to agree: the biscuits rivalled Agatha's in both taste and texture.

"Did you have any trouble?" asked Tangler.

"Not much." Donald washed down his biscuit with a mouthful of tea. "We borrowed a cart from George and covered your bags, and your staffs with firewood." He grinned at Jenna, who had clapped her hands as soon as she had heard her staff was safe. "The soldiers on the road to Woodville barely gave it a glance, then when we met up with Parr, Evan drove the cart back to the priory again."

Tangler nodded. "Excellent."

"Parr did a good job with the wagon. He's built a false bottom so the extra bags can be stowed away, but it's big enough for the girls to hide if need be." He shrugged and grinned at Kira. "It'll be squashy, mind, but hopefully we won't be needing to use it."

"Don't suppose you've heard anything about the others?" asked Tangler.

"Matter of fact, we have. Had to call in to the blacksmiths at Cobbler's Creek, because Lonny here tossed a shoe." His horse was grazing on the grass but raised his head when he heard his name. "Half a dozen soldiers came in, demanding to be served first because they were on important business for the Crown Prince. Terry, the smith, wasn't havin' it at first. He's not a fan of the Crown, ever since his youngest lass got gathered for the quota, but I slipped him a coin, and he shod their horse first. No doubt it'll be needing to be re-shod in a day or two!"

Kira exchanged a look with Giselle.

"Anyways, I was sitting in the corner, waiting, and I heard the soldiers complaining. Seems three of them had been sent on a wild goose chase after some girls who escaped from the quota—that's what they'd been told, anyways—but when they caught up to the carriage, they found a group of crusty-faced nuns. All het up, they were, since this had been the second time they'd been stopped. Little white-headed one had given them a right telling off, apparently. The men were not happy, let me tell you!"

"Ha! That'd be Flynn," said Jenna, clapping her hands again. "Good for her!"

Tangler stroked his beard. "Hopefully, Hugo and Declan will catch up with us by the time we get to White Haven. I think we should probably make camp here when the wagon arrives and then make an early start in the morning. We should reach White Haven in five or six days."

"One more thing," said Donald, his voice full of regret. "One of the other soldiers said that Piscator was on his way to the Northern Province. He sets a trap to catch a witch. The rest of his command have orders to search all the quota carriages before they can embark on the ship to the Legion Isles."

Kira's mouth went dry, and her throat tightened. She felt like a rope had been wrapped around her neck and was slowly being pulled in two directions. She bit down hard on the pad of her thumb and closed her eyes. What was she going to do?

Jenna was overjoyed to be reunited with Ailith and as soon as she could, she began practicing with her staff and urged Kira and Giselle to do the same. Jock perched on the back step of the wagon and called out occasionally with tips and gentle criticisms, but overall seemed impressed with what they could do. Although she had been reluctant to join in at first, Kira soon lost herself in the exercise routine and began to enjoy the work out her muscles received. It felt strange having Seren in her hands again. She hadn't held the real staff since she had used it to wield her magic, but any misgivings she may have had, vanished as soon as the oak was in her hands.

What had surprised her even more was the warmth she experienced from Zarabesk's scale. As soon as she had touched Seren, the scale had tingled against her chest, and she had to check that the glow she felt was not visible through her clothes. The staff had responded with a thrill of recognition and Kira was filled with an inexplicable charge of jubilation. The sensation dissipated almost as soon as it had begun but left Kira feeling slightly more optimistic than she had been.

The mood around the campfire was quite festive, considering the danger they were in. Kira leaned back against the wheel of the wagon and listened to the others sing. Farren had taught Giselle and Jenna the words to two of the songs in the Rainbow's End repertoire and she was impressed at how quickly their voices blended into the male vocals. Parr had made a delicious chicken and vegetable stew and had baked a loaf of crusty bread in a clay pot under the coals, and the aroma still lingered in the air. The tent gave them reasonable protection from the wind and frigid night air, but the hole in its top, made for the smoke to escape, also prevented it from being as cosy as it could have been. Kira was thankful she would be sleeping in the wagon with the other girls, even though she had been able to find some warmer clothes in the bags Ralph had collected.

Ned and Tangler were deep in conversation on the other side of the fire, but then the guard stood and left the tent. He was back in about ten minutes and Kira felt the cold radiate from his leathers as he hunkered down next to her.

"Cold out there," said Kira, stating the obvious.

"Aye, it's a bit nippy. Bit of a change from the last few nights. The sky is clear, so it'll be cold, but I don't expect rain or snow overnight." He blew into his hands and stretched his long legs out towards the fire. "I've had a quick look around. All seems quiet out there. Did Parr show you how the false floor works?"

Kira nodded. Inside the wagon, Parr had built what looked like a cupboard, behind where the driver would sit. The floor inside slid to one side, leaving a gap wide enough to wriggle through. The space beneath was probably only two feet in depth but was almost as wide as the wagon and long enough for the three of them to lie side by side without squashing each other. There was another crawl space at the back of the wagon which was accessed from under the steps, and into this their bags and many of the troupe's belongings had been stowed, leaving more room inside the wagon. Kira had smiled to herself as Parr was showing them his handiwork; their costumes and instruments still took up a fair share of space.

"Yes, we did a couple of practice runs while you and Ralph were collecting firewood and water. We have to sort of roll into the hole, but Parr has kindly lined the floor with sheepskin, so it's a soft landing and pleasant to lie on."

"Aye, and will muffle the noise as well. He's a clever one, that Parr."

Ned stared at the fire for a moment, then turned to look at Kira. "Thank you for what you did for Jock this morning. I've seen head wounds like that before and know how hard they are to fix properly. He's lucky you were there."

Kira was taken aback by Ned's words. It always came as a surprise when he spoke to her rather than issuing orders. "My pleasure. It was nice to be able to do something to help, rather than wreaking havoc."

Ned raised an eyebrow. "You sound a wee bit bitter. Count your gift as a blessing, Kira, and nurture it. A talent such as yours should not go to waste."

Before she could reply, Tangler clapped his hands to get their attention.

"Ned, a word if you don't mind. Everyone else, I think it's time to call it a night. Sleep well, we have an early start. Kira, Giselle and Jenna, remember the signal, but if you are woken by anything untoward, don't hesitate to get under the floor. I'm not expecting any trouble tonight, but the closer we get to White Haven, the more alert we'll have to be."

Kira listened to the sleeping sounds of her friends as she lay in the unfamiliar but welcome comfort of the wagon. The straw mattress was topped with sheepskins and after the last few nights felt like luxury. She snuggled deeper into the warmth of the blankets, and once she was settled, entered the cellar of her mind room. She had decided on a red squirrel as her first faithful and thought back to the little family that inhabited the pine trees not far from Agatha's cottage.

The tricky part was to see it not in her imagination, but as though it were in front of her, so she pictured it first in profile, small sharply clawed front paws clutching a nut beneath its chin. It sat on a log, its long bushy tail following the contour of its rounded back like a furry letter *S*. Kira painted the underbelly a creamy white and decided she preferred the dark red coat of winter best and added longer ear-tufts. Something wasn't quite right. She added eyelids of a slightly paler colour around the dark brown eyes and made the nose a little smaller, but still wasn't satisfied. She thought back to the baby squirrel she had rescued and realised that she had forgotten to add whiskers. That was better. The tail hairs needed to be thinned out more at the edges and she needed to blend more colours into the coat, but she was pleased with her first attempt. She let the image go and it slowly dissipated.

It was much easier now than when she was a little girl. Kira remembered her screams of frustration when she was first learning what to do. Eventually, her control had improved, and she had no longer tested poor

Agatha's patience. Kira felt a pang of remorse. She must have been quite a handful growing up. Agatha was already an old woman when Kira was born, so it can't have been easy for her. She hoped her grandmother was safe and well; Agatha deserved only peace and kindness in her winter years.

Aware that her thoughts were becoming maudlin, Kira imagined the squirrel again. It appeared exactly as it had before, and she was content with the result. Gradually she would add more detail, but she was satisfied for now. Over the next few days she would bring her faithful to life and start to make it move. She yawned loudly and felt sleep calling to her, so she let the image go again and surrendered to her tiredness.

Chapter 37

By the third day of travelling in the wagon, Kira had become accustomed to the face paint and the blue tabards she and her friends wore. Giselle was in her element and spent most of her free time embroidering flowers and trees onto strips of material that she fashioned into belts. Jenna pestered anyone who listened into mock battles with her staff and would often jog alongside the wagon, rather than sit in it. Kira noticed that her friend had become so proficient with her staff that even Ned raised a sweat when they practiced. Tangler had put an end to her staff-play this morning, however, since they had started to encounter more people on the road, and the little villages they passed through were more frequent.

Kira had expected Jenna to protest, but she had accepted Tangler's direction without question and was now helping Giselle sew ribbons onto headpieces that the girls would wear when they performed. Kira was privately dreading it. Farren had declared that morning—with a little too much enthusiasm, she thought—that the Rainbow's End would be performing that evening in Freeman Pass, a large market town spanning the river, and the gateway to the coast.

"We play at a large inn called the Ship and Sail every time we pass through," he explained with a grin, "and it would bring more attention on us if we didn't perform, let me tell you. It'll be fine. You girls sing well." He glanced at Kira and winked. "Well, your friends do, but you do have a talent with the finger cymbals, Kira. If Hugo makes it back in time, you two would make a fine duo."

Kira had flashed him a smile that didn't quite reach her eyes and said, "Thanks, Farren."

She perched on the back seat of the wagon and spent the rest of the morning working on her faithful, who she decided to call Cheeks, while listening with half an ear to the troupe practicing their songs. She was the only one who couldn't sing. Jock had a lovely lilting tenor and Ned a rich baritone, and they were both singing the harmonies in no time at all. Cheeks was waiting in the cellar of her mind room and began scampering around as soon as she appeared. Kira had perfected his little frame and his colouring and was now working on his speed and movements. She was grateful to have so many memories to look back on. Agatha had always had a soft spot for squirrels and left a supply of walnuts on the windowsill, so the little creatures were a familiar sight, particularly in the winter months. Satisfied with her progress, she allowed him to scamper up her side and perch on her shoulder while he nibbled a walnut. She reached up a finger and stroked him behind the ears and under his chin. Cheeks nuzzled her hand with an approving chirp. Suddenly, he stiffened and twitched his ears.

Kuk-kuk, kuk-kuk, he squeaked in alarm.

Kira was non-plussed, but then she heard Farren call out.

"Kira, get yourself out here and get your cymbals on. Quick as you can!"

She withdrew her awareness and reached for the little pouch that dangled from her belt. The wagon had come to a halt. She jumped from the step and trotted to the front.

"Soldiers ahead. Just got the wink from a fellow traveller." Farren waved towards a horse and cart retreating down the other side of the road. He gave her a leg up onto the bench behind the driver's seat next to Giselle and Jenna and climbed back onto his horse. Donald and Ralph were perched on the roof of the wagon holding a fiddle and a hand drum. Ralph gave a little drum roll as she sat down, and grinned. Parr flicked the reins and the wagon moved forward again. Kira glanced around. Ned and Jock rode either side of the wagon, but Tangler was nowhere to be seen.

"Tangler's ridden on ahead," said Giselle in answer to her puzzled frown. "He said he'd distract the soldiers, to give us a few minutes to prepare."

"There's a checkpoint less than five minutes up the road. Just remember, stay jovial, smile often, and keep singing and playing until I signal you to stop." Farren pulled out a silver baton from the side of his boot and began making a beat in the air, "We'll start from the third verse of 'Nelly Barnes and her seven husbands'; Kira, take your cue from Ralph. And go."

There were sixteen verses of the ballad of Nelly Barnes, documenting the inventive ways Nelly disposed of her husbands, each one slightly bawdier than the last. The troupe were on the last verse about Baker Mick and his spotted dick, when they were pulled over by the soldiers on roadblock duty. Tangler winked and joined in the chorus as he juggled five balls and danced in time to the music.

The soldiers were all grinning by the end of the song, but still gave the wagon a thorough look through. Not enough to find the false floor, Kira was relieved to see.

"All clear, Master Tanglewood," said the Sergeant of the Guard after his man waved a hand to indicate all was well. "No doubt you'll see a few of us in the Ship and Sail tonight. The Rainbow's End have a fine reputation, and after that performance, I can see it's well deserved."

"You told them we are playing at the Ship and Sail?" asked Kira once they were out of earshot. "What on earth for?"

"Routine," Tangler replied. "We would normally invite anyone who'd listen to come to the show. Coin is coin, no matter whose pocket it comes from. Besides, you never know what you might overhear when a man has a few ales under his belt. The barkeep's an old friend of mine, he'll make sure any soldiers who come tonight have a regular supply of ale at their table. Don't worry, my dear, all will be well."

Kira looked at Giselle and raised her eyebrows. She wasn't sure she shared Tangler's confidence, but Giselle grinned at her, eyes sparkling. "That was slightly terrifying, but also very exciting, don't you think? The soldiers barely gave us a second glance, so I think our disguises worked well. I feel much better about singing tonight."

"Me, too," said Jenna, bouncing in her seat. "I almost forgot who Nellie's sixth husband was, though. For some reason the fiddle player from Brent wanting to tune her instrument always slips my mind!"

"You'll need to keep practicing, then," said Giselle. "We can go through it again if you like."

Kira groaned inwardly. Her friends obviously didn't share her trepidation. She slipped the cymbals from her fingers and dropped them back into the pouch. Ralph tapped her on the shoulder and beckoned her to join him on the roof. She watched Donald somersault to the ground with an easy grace, then took his place next to Ralph.

"You lasses all did well," he spoke quietly, so only Kira could hear. "Jenna and Giselle are feeling the buzz of success just now. It'll give them a boost to their confidence for the performance tonight. They don't think they're as brave as you, you know, so allow them this little victory."

Kira stared at him. "But I'm not brave. I'm terrified most of the time."

Ralph grinned. "What do you think bravery is, Kira? It's doing what needs to be done when all you want to do is run and hide. If you don't fear what you're doing, then you aren't being brave, are you? From what they've been telling me, you have more to fear than most, but look at you: you're here, aren't you? And so are they, thanks to you."

Kira was lost for words. She met the smile in his eyes with one of her own, then nudged him with her shoulder. "Could you teach me how to play your drum?"

"Indeed, I could," he replied, "it'd be my pleasure."

He picked up the bodhrán and handed it to Kira. She ran her fingers around the circular frame. "Is this willow?" she asked.

"Aye, you've a good eye. And the drum skin is goat hide." He picked up a carved stick, slender down the shaft with rounded knobs on each end. "This is a tipper."

Kira held the bodhrán like she had seen Ralph do, with the frame upright, resting on her thigh.

"Aye, that's it, but a little closer to your body, sort of cradled with your left arm." He nudged the drum back a little. "That's better. Now place your left hand and your fingers quite firm against the skin to hold it steady, and you will also use that hand to change the tone of the drum when needs be."

Kira positioned the drum as Ralph had instructed and nodded.

"Right, now shake your right hand in front of you, but point your fingertips towards your chest. Loosen up a bit. Aye, that's better." He pushed down on her shoulder and moved her upper arm closer to her body. "Just shake from the elbow. Good. Now, flick the back of your fingers up and down against the drum. One two, one, two."

Once Kira had mastered the timing to Ralph's satisfaction, he handed her the tipper, showed her how to hold it correctly and had her strike the drum to the same beat. Gradually he increased the tempo and began to sing a simple ditty that she could keep time to. Once she found the knack of it, she found herself grinning with happiness and her heart felt lighter than it had for days.

Tangler brought her back to earth with a thump. "Freeman's Pass!" he announced as they crested the small hill they'd been travelling up for the last half hour. The trading town was bigger than any other Kira had seen. It nestled in the valley below, split in two by the river. A large bridge spanned the river near the centre of the town and from where she sat, Kira could just make out the small stone archways that protected the entrance and exit.

"It's a toll bridge," explained Ralph. "Locals don't have to pay if they are on foot. But there's a charge for horse and cart, as that usually means a trader and they've coin to spare. We have an exemption, since we are entertainers, but Tangler always pays the toll to maintain goodwill and keep the guardsman sweet." He pointed towards the road that led from the bridge to a gap in the hills on the other side of the river, "That's The Pass Road. We'll travel on it tomorrow and should reach White Haven by late afternoon. It'll seem like we are going back in the direction we came from, only on the other side of the hills, and indeed we are, but this is the only place to cross this far south."

Kira felt a shiver run through her. One day to decide her future.

The applause thundered around the front room of the tavern, accompanied by the good-natured hoots of tipsy revellers on their way to becoming completely inebriated. The first half of the performance had gone better than Kira expected. The group performed well together, and while not as polished as the real Rainbow's End, only they seemed to notice. The crowd was far more forgiving. Not for them, the dance reels and romantic verses that were played at the Merryman Ball, the locals of Freeman's Pass preferred lusty ballads and drinking songs. Tangler took centre stage now, to give the musicians a well-deserved break to catch their breath and quench their thirst. Kira thought that the crowd might become restless, but she was wrong; they loved him.

He was dressed as a court jester, in brightly coloured costume and cap'n'bells, and he pranced around the stage on his hands as though he was as young as Kira. He completed his entrance with a somersault from his hands to his feet and produced a pinwheel from thin air and tossed it into the crowd. He pointed to a table in front of the stage and the drinkers had evidently seen his act before, because almost as one, they downed their ale and began tossing their empty tankards to him. Tangler caught each one and sent it up into the air, juggling one after the other, until he had eight of them spinning in a circle from one hand to the next.

"Get ready," he called after a few minutes, turning his back to the table. He tossed each tankard over his shoulder and every one of them landed within easy reach of the person who'd thrown it. The entire room cheered, and fists pounded the tables in appreciation.

Farren tossed him three balls, and as Tangler threw them higher and higher in the air one-handed, he downed an ale he'd accepted from one of the patrons. Farren placed three stools on the stage and upturned one of them, so it rested on the seat, legs in the air. Tangler set the empty tankard back on the table and sauntered over to the upturned stool. He bowed low to the audience, then leapt up in the air to land gracefully on two of the legs of the stool. The balls remained in motion, but now, he used two hands to juggle, and they moved faster. He leapt to another stool and somehow the balls moved with him. Kira held her breath.

He balanced on one foot and slowly pointed the toes of the other in Farren's direction. Farren flipped a wooden hoop onto Tangler's foot and with a flick of his ankle, the hoop began to spin. The crowd roared.

But Tangler wasn't finished. He leapt from one stool to another, keeping the hoop spinning and the balls tumbling in the air all the while. Eventually, he kicked the hoop back to where Farren was standing and caught all the balls, which he also tossed back. As soon as the last one left his hand, he moved so quickly that the colours of his costume blurred, and he was upside down balancing on his hands on the legs of the upturned stool. He let go with one hand and balanced on the other. Gradually he bent his knees in towards his chest, then with an explosive burst of energy thrust them away, only to land on his feet on top of the stool, which was now, incredibly, the right way up.

Kira and her friends clapped as loudly as the rest of the amazed onlookers as Tangler took his bow.

"Oh, that was wonderful!" Giselle grabbed hold of Kira's sleeve. "I can't believe how clever he is. Just brilliant!"

Ralph began beating his drum before Kira could reply, and the girls danced back on stage to take up their positions. Kira stood next to Ralph and joined in with her finger cymbals to play the introduction to 'Nellie Barnes'. Donald joined in with his fiddle and soon the audience were tapping their feet and slapping their thighs as the Rainbow's End began to sing.

True to his word, the barkeep had kept the soldiers well supplied with drink and Kira watched as Tangler circled their table with his hat collecting coin from appreciative patrons. The Ship and Sail would pay them a share of the night's takings as well as supply them with free lodgings, so Kira suspected Tangler's wanderings were more to do with gathering information than collecting extra coin. Her bladder was fit to burst, so she decided to nip out to the privy before the final song.

On her way back, she paused for a moment to watch the others on stage, admiring how well their costumes and voices blended in with the troupe's. Even Ned and Jock didn't look out of place. The performance had worked out much better than she had thought possible. Kira was so distracted by what was happening on stage that she didn't notice the man in front of her push back his chair and block her path until it was too late. She knocked her knee on the edge of his seat and lurched forwards.

She was gripped by her forearms, but rather than her tumble being halted by a steadying hand, his fingers dug into her skin, and she gasped in pain. He pulled Kira down and around, so she landed in an ungainly heap in the man's lap. His leathers were filthy and ingrained with the stench of unwashed clothes. Before Kira could say a word, he grabbed her braid in a meaty fist and pulled her head back so roughly she yelped. She glimpsed dark eyes and yellow teeth as his head lowered to her mouth. Zarabesk's scale flared as his other hand groped at her breast. Time seemed to slow, and she could see the colours around her start to meld as her lips were crushed against his, and he shoved his whisky-tainted tongue down her throat.

Chapter 38

*D*on't use magic. Don't use magic.

Kira clung to the words as she endured the assault on not only her body but all her senses. His coarse whiskers scraped against the softness of her cheek as his foul-tasting tongue penetrated her mouth with an aggressive disregard for her airway. Stale tobacco and alcohol lingered on his moustache, and she was forced to inhale the disgusting smell through her nostrils. She heard the shouts of encouragement from the other men at the table over the harmonies of the Rainbow's End and when she opened her eyes she could see the light from a lantern hanging from the rafters behind her attacker's greasy hair.

Don't use magic. Don't use magic.

Kira gave up trying to shove his hand from her breast and let go of the man's sleeve. She focussed her energy as Sister Eloise had taught her and elbowed him as hard as she could in the ribs. He threw back his head with a roar. Kira inhaled deeply and simultaneously flicked back her arm and smacked him fair across the bridge of his nose with the back of her closed fist. He let go of her breast and clamped a brawny hand over his nose to stem the blood and snarled, "You cock-sucking whore!"

Kira lurched to her feet, but he still had her braid in his other fist, so she was caught in a half-crouch, unable to move forward. The panic flared again, and her heart thundered against her ribs. She felt the heat of Zarabesk's scale against her skin and focussed again. Then, somehow, she twisted in her attacker's grasp so that she was now facing him but bent low from the waist. She braced her hands against his thighs and thrust herself upwards, slamming the back of her head into the point of his chin. A bolt of pain spasmed down her neck and her eyes began to water, but his head snapped back, and he let go of her hair. Kira pushed away from him, but not before he delivered a backhander that stung her face and made her ear ring. She was free.

The man might have let it go, his nose was bleeding, and he had got the last slap in, but the other men were laughing at him. They pounded the table with one fist while raising their tankards to Kira with the other. He lurched to his feet as Kira backed away. Her cheek throbbed and her ear still buzzed. She could feel the anger coming off him in waves and saw the threatening glint in his eyes as he drew back his arm and closed his fist. She snatched a tankard from the man alongside her and threw the contents in her attacker's face. It wasn't enough to stop his blow, but it blinded him for a second and threw off his aim. His fist missed its mark and glanced off her shoulder.

Kira turned to run but slammed into a wall. Only it wasn't a wall, it was Ned. He frowned down at her face, then thrust her behind him and into Ralph's arms.

"Take her to the rooms," he growled.

Ralph gathered her close and forced his way through the growing crowd of patrons who had sensed the start of a fight and were eager to see more. Kira heard a loud crash and turned her head in time to see her attacker land on his back on the table. The spilling of drinks seemed to provoke more of a call to action from the men seated there than her assault had, and they jumped to their feet. Ned had set three of them back on their behinds before Ralph found the door. Jock and the girls were waiting outside. Ralph nodded at Jock and ran back inside.

"Edalyn's flame, Kira, are you hurt?" Giselle reached up a hand and touched Kira on her cheek. "What happened?"

"Drunken idiot groped me." Kira adjusted her bodice and grabbed her braid in her fist before her hair could escape its confines. The shock hit then, and Kira began to tremble. Her legs gave way, and she slid down the wall to land on the cobblestones with a thud. She looked up at Giselle's worried face and tried to smile. As dreadful as it had been, she was filled with a strange elation. She had fought off that snake and hadn't used magic.

"Did you blow his head off?" Jenna gestured with her hands and grinned.

"No," said Kira with a note of pride in her voice. "I used some of the self-defence moves Sister Eloise showed us instead."

The sound of breaking glass and men behaving badly drifted outside. Jock gazed at the doorway wistfully. "Love a good fight, I do, but I have orders to take you girls to the rooms. Come along." He offered Kira a hand and helped her up.

"Just as well, that cut on your head isn't anywhere near healed enough," replied Kira as she tested her balance. Their lodgings were situated behind the stables that housed both the horses and their wagon. She was suddenly conscious of how cold the night air was and began to shiver.

"Where are the others?" asked Kira as they hurried across the courtyard.

"Farren and Donald were helping Parr with the instruments, and Tangler stayed back to parley with Billy, the barkeep."

"You mean Ned and Ralph have to face that mob alone?" Kira felt a little sick.

"Nah, the boys will have gone back. Not that Ned needs help, mind you, he could take on most of that motley crew with one hand behind his back." Jock grinned at Kira over his shoulder and opened the door.

Parr threw a blanket over her shoulders and led her to the fire. He handed each of them a small tankard. Kira felt the warmth of the pewter as she accepted the drink and looked up at Parr in surprise.

"Hot toddy," he said with a wink, "that'll warm your insides."

Kira sniffed at the drink and wrinkled her nose. The scent of whiskey made her stomach churn.

"Ooh, it's lovely," said Jenna. "We often have this in the winter months. Dad says it's good for you."

Kira took a small sip and was pleasantly surprised by the flavour. The whiskey had been diluted with hot water and honey, so it was deliciously sweet. She sipped again and tasted lemon and cinnamon as well. The inside of her cheek stung a little and she explored the inside of her mouth with the tip of her tongue. She guessed that her teeth had grazed it when she had been slapped. She didn't care. She hadn't used magic and she hadn't killed anyone.

Tangler arrived when they were on their second drink. He examined Kira's cheek and tilted her face with a forefinger under her chin. "Are you well?"

"I am," she replied, "but what of the others?"

"Fine and dandy. Just helping clean up the mess." Tangler accepted a hot toddy from Parr and stood with his back to the fire. "No doubt you haven't seen many bar fights, my dear, but don't concern yourself. If you hadn't been the spark that started this one, there would've been plenty others." Tangler paused as Giselle tutted loudly, but when she said nothing he continued. "Most times when the ale runs freely, there's some sort of scuffle to be had at the end of the night. It's almost expected."

"But what about the damage?" said Kira, thinking about the broken tables and chairs.

"Nowt to worry about there," said Jock, "the barkeep's likely got a carpenter nearby, if he's not handy himself."

Tangler grinned, "Jock's right. Billy's brother is a shipwright, and his carpentry skills are second to none in Trader's Province. Billy's not bad either. And there's no shortage of timber."

"Do we have to pay for breakage?"

Tangler looked at Kira as though she had grown two heads. "Of course not! The Rainbow's End brings more coin to the inn in a night than he usually sees in two or three weeks. We just help with the tidy up and all is forgiven."

"Well what about the muckspout who attacked Kira?" asked Giselle, eyes flashing, "I hope he wasn't just tidied up and forgiven!"

"No my dear. He was well and truly tidied up, if you get my drift. Last I saw he was cooling off in the back of a prison wagon."

Kira stared at Tangler. "What? Surely not?" As awful as it had been for her, Kira knew that men did not usually get imprisoned for groping. More's the pity.

Tangler chuckled. "Indeed yes. But not for his scrabble at you, my dear. Ned punished him well and truly for that. No, he drew his weapon inside a reputable establishment, and in Trader's Province, that is against the law. The soldiers stepped in and locked him up. If Billy doesn't want him charged, they'll let him out in the morning, once he's sober. But, if he does, then he'll have to go before the magistrate."

Giselle snorted. "Aye, that'd be right. You can ravage a woman against her will, and no one will raise a hand, but woe betide if you draw your sword!" Her eyes glinted with fury, and she pummelled the air with her fist.

Tangler blinked and grabbed his beard. Jock raised his hands in mock surrender.

"Steady on, lass. Ned and Ralph both leaped over a few tables as soon as they saw what was happening. That bastard will have got more than a raised hand, let me tell you. Ain't that right, Tangler?"

"Rest assured, my dears. Although I acknowledge the point you are trying to make, Giselle. It might have been a different story if Ned and the others weren't there."

Only slightly mollified, Giselle sat back down and muttered, "Yes, Kira might have been forced to use her magic after all." She rubbed Kira across her shoulders.

"Ouch." Kira flinched. "Sorry, Elle, that's a wee bit tender."

Giselle frowned. "Can I have a look?"

Kira nodded and eased her sleeve down her arm, exposing a bruise already starting to purple on the tip of her shoulder. There was a raw area in the middle where his knuckle had broken the skin.

Giselle glared at Tangler. He raised his eyebrows at her and smiled. "I'll get my chest."

Jenna leaned closer to get a better view. "That'll be painful for a day or two." She glanced up at Kira. "Can't you, you know, just fix it? Like you mended Jock."

Kira shrugged, and immediately wished she hadn't. "No, it doesn't work like that. I have to suffer like everyone else." She didn't actually know for sure but having managed to not use magic to protect herself before, she wasn't going to try it now.

Giselle was rubbing a salve of yarrow and henbane onto Kira's shoulder when the rest of the troupe arrived. Ralph entered first, sporting a huge grin and a swollen eye, which Kira knew would be purple by morning, "Don't put that salve away just yet," she said to Giselle. "I think we're going to need it." He sat on the sofa next to Jenna and made himself comfortable.

Giselle rolled her eyes. "What is it about men and fighting? They look as happy as pigs in mud."

"I think that may have more to do with the ales they had when they were tidying up," muttered Jenna, as Donald plonked himself down on the floor next to the fire. He looked a little dishevelled, his shirt was torn, but apart from a graze on his knuckles, was otherwise unhurt.

"Are you well, Kira?" asked Farren, his concern marred somewhat by the fact that he was having difficulty trying to focus his gaze. Kira tried not to smile.

"I am, thank you, Farren. And you?"

"Good as gold. Gold as good." He tried to rest his elbow on the mantle and missed. Kira noticed a smear of blood on his shirt, but as she saw no wounds on him, decided it must have come from someone else. He tried again and this time his elbow stayed put. "Billy gave us some of his mulberry gin. It's very good."

"Must be to get you this blootered so quickly," Jenna grinned. She looked at Kira and Giselle. "Mind you, I suppose they haven't had a drink for a while."

Kira glanced towards the door and saw Ned frowning at her. She pulled up her sleeve and said to Giselle, "I think Ralph could do with a bit of that salve on his eye." Giselle nodded and sat on the other side of Ralph who was now leaning drowsily against Jenna's arm.

Ned nodded at Tangler and then strode across the room to Kira. She was relieved to see no obvious wounds on him apart from some bloody grazes on his knuckles. He didn't even look like he'd been in a fight. Nor did he appear inebriated.

"Are you well?"

"Thank you." They both spoke at the same time. Kira held up her hand, "Yes, I'm well, thanks to you. I hope you didn't injure your hands?"

Ned frowned and flexed his fist as though noticing for the first time that there was anything wrong. Much as Tangler had, he placed his fingers under her chin and tilted her face to the side. He ran his thumb across her cheek, but so gently she barely felt it. Then he ran his hand over her head until he found the lump. "That sore?"

"Yes, a bit."

"Aye, I bet. Not as sore as that bastard's chin will be, though, you can be happy about that. And his nose. You have many hidden talents, Kira, do you not?"

Ned's expression was as stern as ever, but Kira heard the teasing note in his voice and was so taken aback that she didn't know how to answer. She nodded instead.

Tangler clapped his hands. "This has been a most eventful night, and apart from Kira's distressing encounter, one I think was sorely needed. However, tomorrow we need to be up by cockerel crow if we are to be in White Haven by mid-afternoon. I overheard the soldiers talking and they said that the quota carriages would be arriving in three days, so we must take care. Billy told me the ship will set sail at high tide the following day. He's asking his brother to find a boat willing to take me and the Rainbow's End to Prince Rhicard's court,"— he winked at Kira and stroked his beard—"but if he can't, the boys and I might have to winter round here. Ned, can I have a word?"

Kira heard the rumble in Ned's throat and saw his jaw clench, but he followed Tangler to the other room without saying any more to Kira. It was no wonder she never learnt any more of Ned than just the basics; Tangler always seemed to require his attendance whenever they began a normal conversation. Giselle knelt in his place and laid her head in Kira's lap. "Four days," she whispered. Kira stroked her friend's hair, "Yes. Four days." Suddenly her heart ached more than either her shoulder or her head.

Chapter 39

They were on the road by sunrise. Kira watched as the clouds, heavy with rain, blazed crimson and gradually faded to a dull grey. Her head no longer ached, although the lump was tender to touch. Jenna had braided her hair for her, noting with some satisfaction that the strands of green that had appeared after Jock's healing had faded enough to be less noticeable. Kira had some stiffness in her shoulder, and it pained to lift her arm above her head, so she was grateful for Jenna's offer to help. There was a small red mark on her cheek, but the face paint disguised it well enough to pass Giselle's inspection.

They sat on the bench behind Parr, protected from the bitter sea breeze by a thick woollen blanket over their knees, munching on warm egg and bacon pies, courtesy of Billy's wife, Jean. Farren's eyes were a little bloodshot, but he was as jovial as ever as he handed out the pies. As Kira had predicted, Ralph's eye was purple and his lid so swollen he couldn't see from it, but he wore it like a badge of honour and accepted the taunts about his inability to duck with good humour. Ned and Tangler rode ahead of the wagon in close conversation and Kira wondered why they always seemed to have so much to talk about. Jock and Donald rode behind and Kira heard snippets of Jock's tuneful whistling when the breeze dropped.

If it wasn't for the fear of the unknown looming over her head, Kira might have been able to enjoy the ride, but she was plagued with doubt. Should she do as Tangler wanted and sail to Prince Rhicard's court, or stay with Giselle and Jenna to face whatever fate lay across the sea in the Legion Isles?

The Pass Road wound between the rolling hills to reveal a landscape of rugged beauty. To the left lay the hills and behind the hills, the mountain range, snow topped and somehow more formidable at this distance. It was hard to believe that they had travelled through the centre of it. To the right the land was almost flat, gently undulating towards the sea. The trees were straggly and bowed to the mountain, buffeted by the almost constant ocean breezes. Far in the distance the coastline curved, and the land stretched out into the sea like an accusing finger. White Haven. The city flowed like a wave from the jagged cliffs to climb the hill slopes behind.

Ralph leaned forward from his perch on the wagon roof and pointed out to sea. "See there, just past the point, that's Bannister's Lookout. Tallest lighthouse in Cabarac. Treacherous rocks all around this part of the coast; many a ship ran aground before the lighthouse was built. Plus there's no beach to land, it's all cliffs to the harbour. The only safe way into White Haven is on the opposite side to where we are now."

Kira squinted to where he pointed and thought she could make out the lighthouse.

"It looks a fair way out from the mainland," said Jenna.

"Aye, it is. Barren rock of a place. Full of sea birds, mind. They come there to nest. Puffins' paradise, we used to call it."

Kira looked at him. "You've been there?"

Ralph turned to face her so he could see through his good eye and nodded, "Aye, I was born there." He leaned in closer and whispered, "Dragons helped build that light house more than two centuries ago. Not supposed to say things like that, are we? But our family knows it's true and I can tell it to you. No one of any importance comes to visit, so they don't see it, but the mirror is actually one of the chest scales from a white dragon. It was gifted to my ancestor, the first lighthouse keeper, and it works just as perfect to this very day." He leaned back and touched his forefinger to the side of his nose.

Jenna nudged Kira in the ribs and rolled her eyes, but Zarabesk's scale had warmed at Ralph's words, so she believed that what he said was true. Kira leaned back against the wagon and gazed at the white city. Even from this distance Kira could see the famous white spires that the most powerful sorcerers and magicians had once called home. She frowned and stared back out to sea, contemplating why some things had survived the Purge when most things magical had not. If she was feeling cynical, she might believe it was because if those in power thought it was useful to them, then it was protected from destruction.

Giselle put the final stitch in the rip in Donald's shirt and snipped the cotton with her scissors. She held it up for inspection and gave a nod of satisfaction. "It'll do."

"I'm amazed that it dried overnight," said Jenna as she practiced her arm exercises.

"I'm amazed he was sober enough to wash it!" Giselle gave the shirt a flick and then folded it neatly. She brushed some errant pie crumbs from the blanket and sighed. "I'm going to miss these merry men."

"Yeah, me too." Jenna dropped her hands into her lap. "I hope the men on the Legion Isles are as nice."

Kira's breath caught in her throat. Jenna had put voice to what Kira was sure they had all been thinking since the night of the Ball.

Parr swivelled in his seat and looked at them over his shoulder. "Men are pretty much the same wherever you go, lass. Some are good, others not. Legion men are fighters, to be sure, but they have a strong honour code that they live by, so I would guess they would also conduct themselves honourably around women."

"Then why are the women never heard from again?" muttered Jenna.

Parr shrugged. "Sorry, Jenna, that I can't answer. Maybe ask Ned or Jock, they've had more to do with the quota than I have. I'm just sayin' what I know, myself, and any man would be happy to have you lasses in their company, let me tell you."

Kira and Giselle exchanged a look as Parr turned back to the horses. The lobes of his ears glowed red beneath his knitted cap. Giselle's face dimpled as she said with a smile, "Thank you, Parr."

Jenna looked at them and shrugged. She screwed up her face and mouthed, "What?"

Kira understood her confusion but had no words of reassurance. It was the unknown that caused the most trepidation. If only they were told what to expect. Not knowing made things a hundred times worse. So much had happened in the last few weeks that had prevented Kira from properly confronting what her future held, but now, as she watched White Haven inch ever closer, she wondered if it could really be any worse than what had already occurred. Unwilling to contemplate the possibilities even now, she called herself a coward and retreated to her mind room to take solace in the cheeky antics of a red squirrel.

They stopped for lunch at The Mermaid's Tail, a small tavern with a spectacular ocean view. The limestone cliffs that cradled the shore were a stark white in the midday sunshine. Rain clouds that looked so threatening at dawn had been blown inland and only a few white clouds remained, high in the sky. The sea had been a constant pulse as they travelled, and now Kira could see the waves crashing against the rocky outcrops, spraying a white arc of seafoam high into the air.

Ralph fetched them each a bowl of steaming soup and a crusty roll and sat down at the table opposite Kira.

"Mm, smells delicious, what is it?" Kira's belly made its usual grumbles as she inhaled the fragrant steam.

"Fish chowder," replied Ralph as he broke off some bread and dipped it into the soup. "This tavern's speciality. Fish, mussels, shrimp, potatoes…" His voice trailed off as he stuffed the bread into his mouth. He gave a thumbs-up and managed to say, "Good. Hot."

"Lovely," said Kira after she had tasted the chowder, "reminds me a little of my grandmother's fish pie."

"Aye, but this is made with ocean fish. Little tastier than freshwater fish, I reckon."

Kira rolled her eyes but was enjoying the soup too much to argue.

"Where's Farren and Ned?" asked Jenna, between mouthfuls, clearly enjoying her chowder as much as Kira.

Kira glanced down the long table, and saw that Parr wasn't there either.

"They'll be along in a minute," said Ralph, "just helping Parr with the horses. They'll bring the instruments with them, too."

Giselle stopped eating with the spoon halfway to her mouth. "Pardon?"

Ralph grinned. "Free food in exchange for a few songs. This place is one of our regular stops. Don't worry, it won't be like last night. We'll sing a few sea shanties, but this barkeep's partial to ballads. Ned'll have to step up, this time. The keep's favourite is 'The ballad of Widow Maguire', and Declan's not here to sing it. Always sounds better from a baritone."

"What about us? Will we need to sing? We haven't learned any ballads." Giselle frowned.

"Oh, you'll know a couple. Remember 'The Mountains of Tarlee' and 'The Flower that Blooms in Winter'? We sang them at the Ball. Everybody knows them. You'll just have to sing the chorus." He looked at Kira and grinned. "You can whisper."

She resisted the urge to poke out her tongue and smiled sweetly instead. "Remind me to bathe your eye with some salt water after we've eaten. It's starting to look a little crusty."

Kira was cleaning the bottom of her bowl with the last of her bread when the others joined them at the table. She looked up when she felt a nudge in her ribs from Giselle and was surprised to see that

Farren's hair was damp and had been neatly trimmed. The fullness of his beard was gone too, and he now sported a neat goatee. Giselle turned to glance at Kira and lifted her brows. She was impressed. Kira had to agree, Farren was a handsome man and exposing more of his face didn't make him less so. Ralph didn't seem to be quite of the same mind and took the opportunity to pay back some of the barbs he'd been receiving.

"Buckets of blood! What happened to your face? Did your whiskers get caught in the axel, Farren?"

"Orman, the barber, just pulled up in his wagon," Farren replied and ran his hands up and down his newly exposed cheeks. "He says this is the latest beard style in Shardial and it's now all the rage in White Haven."

Ralph snorted, "Aye, and you've arrived on the first boat if you believe that, my friend!"

"Say what you like, but Orman knows his stuff, and that pretty barmaid liked it. She was all for having a wee feel, wasn't she Ned?"

"Aye, she was. Couldn't keep her hands off." Ned leaned forward when he spoke, and Kira saw that he'd been to Orman as well. His hair only just brushed his collar at the back, but very little had been taken from the long waves on top. Nor had he gone to the same extremes with his beard, but it had been shaped and his moustaches expertly trimmed.

"Really?" said Ralph, and promptly stood up from the table. "Your pardon, ladies. I'll be back momentarily."

Parr turned his head from one side to the other, "Notice anything?" His long beard was in its usual braid, and he still wore his knitted cap.

"Can you give us a hint?" said Jenna.

Parr waved his beard with one hand and removed his cap with the other, "Can you not see it? He took an inch from ma whiskers, and polished ma noggin for free!" He bent his head to display his shiny bald head.

"Oh, yes," said Jenna, starting to chuckle. "I can see it now. We'll know where to come if we ever need a spare mirror, won't we, girls?"

Parr grinned and pulled on his cap and returned to his soup. The good-natured teasing and chatter continued through the meal, which was topped off nicely with apple pie and cream.

The barkeep propped himself against the edge of the bar and wiped a tear as he listened to Ned sing. Kira understood how he felt. The lilting melody filled the inn with a melancholy air as Ned's mournful rendition of The Widow Maguire captured the crowd's attention. He sang the chorus and last verse for the second time and encouraged the audience to join in.

She walks the shore, does Widow Maguire
And searches the waves for her heart's desire
Her song on the breeze, flies over the sea
Wind and wave, bring him home to me.

Her dress is black, and her face is pale
As she searches the waves for his ship's white sail
Ten long years she's walked this shore
'til her love returns, she'll walk ten more.

Kira's gaze wandered over the crowd as they sang the chorus once more, grateful that the atmosphere was more relaxed and cheerful than at the end of last night's performance. As she scanned the faces she locked eyes with a man watching her from across the room. He smiled briefly and touched a finger to his head in a kind of salute. Kira smiled automatically and continued her sweep of the room, but his dark hair and sallow complexion was vaguely familiar. She had seen him before, but where? She turned back for a second look, but Ned was singing the last line of the ballad and the crowd were on their feet, clapping and cheering.

"Wind and wave, bring him home to me."

The man was nowhere to be seen.

"Is something amiss, my dear? You look a little pensive." Tangler pulled her aside as they were loading up the wagon.

"No, all is well," Kira shrugged, "I saw someone in the crowd I thought I recognised, but for the life of me, I can't remember where I know him from. I think he recognised me, too. Well, he smiled at me."

"Maybe he just fancied you," said Jenna as she walked past. "You're quite pretty when you smile, you know."

Tangler looked at Jenna and then back to Kira.

"One of the patrons from last night, perhaps? Or one of the soldiers we saw on the road? With your memory, I'm sure if he was important you'd be able to recall."

Kira shook her head. "Perhaps, but I don't think so. I had the feeling that it was from a while ago, and not someone I've ever spoken to. But you're probably right, he can't be that important if I can't remember."

She accepted Tangler's offer of his arm and climbed up onto the wagon. Ralph asked if she would like to learn another beat on the drum and Kira put the stranger from her mind.

Chapter 40

The port of White Haven gleamed in the afternoon sun, but as they approached the city gates, Kira saw that not everything was made from the stone mined at the local quarry. The buildings and spires that towered above the town centre were constructed from limestone, but most of the houses were whitewashed mud brick or timber, especially the dwellings that barnacled up the steep hillsides. The main streets were wide enough for two carriages to pass each other travelling in opposite directions and still leave room for travellers on foot to walk in comfort on the narrow paths. Kira's head swivelled from side to side as first Giselle then Jenna nudged her ribs to point out sights none of them had ever seen before.

The noise was chaotic after the relative quiet of the open road. Vendors called from shop doorways, entreating passers-by to try their wares, and the sound of hooves and carriage wheels clattering on the cobblestones, bounced off the building walls and echoed down the street. Parr pulled the wagon to the side of the road to allow for a platoon of three dozen soldiers, marching four abreast, to pass more easily on the other side of the road. The sun glinted on the gold of their breastplates and the breeze caught the bright red panaches that plumed atop their helmets. Kira saw the red shield and black lance on the long capes they wore, which, like the rest of their dress uniform, were black.

Ned reined his horse close to the wagon and kept his face averted, though Kira saw that he watched from the corner of his eye.

"Royal guardsmen," he muttered. "More than usual even at quota time." He shot a worried glance at Tangler, who shook his head.

"I've not heard that the Crown Prince has left Shardial. Let us hope they are here simply to escort a chest of valuable trade back to the palace."

Ned growled. "Valuable trade? That's one way to name it, I suppose." He nudged his mount and trotted forward. Kira sensed an odd tension between the men, but Tangler ignored the barb and smiled at the girls.

"Come, we have only a few minutes to go to reach our lodgings. With a bit of good fortune, Hugo and Declan will already be there and have started the fires."

They turned down a side street that tapered as it left the bustle of the city centre and meandered up the hill. Kira nibbled at her lip as they climbed. The houses were two and three stories high, with a genteel elegance about them. Fit for noble folk, perhaps, but not them, surely? She was wrong. Parr drove the wagon down a narrow lane alongside a whitewashed house with shutters of pale blue. There was a small garden out the back and a stable big enough to house all the horses.

"Blimey," exclaimed Jenna, "this is a bit posh, Parr. Are you sure you have the right house?"

Parr chuckled. "I do indeed. Belongs to a very dear friend of ours."

There was a fire blazing in the large sitting room Kira found herself in. It was larger than Sister Evangeline's generous study, and grander than even the mayor of River Glen's front room, which Kira had only been in once, but the elaborate décor had left an impression. Alongside this room, however, the mayor's parlour paled in comparison. The walls were painted a deep turquoise and the woodwork and shutters a pale grey. If that wasn't fascinating enough, floor length curtains hung from gold-painted rods. Giselle had been unable to stop herself from stroking the fabric, and even now cast longing glances at the birds and flowers depicted on the drapes.

Dozens of paintings in all sizes adorned the walls. Most were of ships at sea or mountain landscapes, but there was an occasional portrait of straight-nosed men or full-bodied women with delicate hands, reading or gazing out of a window towards a summer field. All were hung in ornate gilt frames. The oak floor was highly polished and thick woven rugs scattered upon it in threads of blue and grey. A small flotilla of glass-bottled ships decorated the mantle above the fireplace, and above the ships hung a portrait of a handsome man, with dark eyes and hair, holding a quilled pen above a map. Despite the opulence in much of the room, the furniture was sturdy and beautifully crafted, and Kira nestled into the soft leather of the couch she shared with Giselle and Jenna.

Hugo and Declan had the floor, recounting with glee their journey to Bishop's Crest with Sister Eloise and the other nuns. Hugo had enveloped Kira in a huge bear hug as soon as he had seen her, startling her and annoying Ned, whose shin she had kicked when Hugo twirled her around so fast her feet left the ground. He had greeted the other girls just as warmly, but not with quite the same exuberance, Jenna pointed out with a smirk.

They had been stopped twice by Piscator's men but had been allowed to continue their travels once the soldiers saw that it was nuns in the carriage and not the escaping quota girls they had been expecting. Hugo knelt on the floor and flicked the back of his shirt over his head, gathering the material under his chin, and in a very creditable impression of Flynn, began berating imaginary soldiers, using a knife he produced from his pocket as her staff.

"What do you think you're doing? Interrupting the sacred pilgrimage of the Sisters of the Flame! How dare you! Have you nothing better to do? Well, let me suggest your mighty brawn would be put to better use repairing roads and bridges damaged by the storms, instead of waylaying Sisters with legitimate business in Bishop's Crest."

Hugo exaggerated his breaths and patted his chest. "Look what you've done, I'm having an attack of the vapours. Get away with you now." He waved the knife in a vaguely crescent shape and called out, "May the Light of Edalyn's Flame guide you in the darkness!"

Kira chuckled. She could just imagine how Flynn had reacted. She was relieved to know they had made it to Bishop's Crest without further incident, however. Hugo returned to his usual lanky self and tucked in his shirt.

"Aye, we didn't tarry at Bishop's Crest," continued Declan. "We had a wee bite to eat with the Sisters and made our way here as quick as we could. We were stopped on the North Road and questioned, which turned out to be fortunate, because Hugo overheard the soldiers saying that they were fixing the bridge at Maryport, and it was easier than tackling the pass at Mount Leopold."

Hugo nodded. "Didn't much fancy crossing that poor excuse for a bridge again, but the soldiers had mended the hole and most of the loose timbers, so it was a much easier crossing this time."

"Saved us a few days' travel, it did. Mind you, we didn't expect to see you for another day or two." Declan glanced between Tangler and Donald. "What's the story?"

The room was silent. Kira took a deep breath and said, "My fault. Two of Piscator's men came to the priory the morning after you left and I…" She straightened her shoulders and looked at Hugo and then at Declan. "I accidentally killed them."

Hugo's eyes widened. Declan gave a snort of disbelief and grinned. "A wee lass like you? How do you 'accidentally' kill two soldiers? Were they asleep? Did you trip over them in the dark and smother them?"

Giselle and Jenna sprang to her defence and explained what had happened. Farren filled them in about their journey through the mountain and then Parr chipped in with what had happened with the wagon. Ralph bragged about how he got his black eye defending Kira's honour and was immediately derided by the others for his embellishment of the tale.

Kira let the chatter wash over her, relieved that her confession had garnered congratulations rather than condemnation from the two men. Still, her conscience didn't allow her to take pleasure from their words. She stared at the portrait above the mantle, admiring the way the artist had captured the intelligent expression on the man's face. The lace cuff exposed by the drawn back sleeve of his jacket was painted with such incredible detail that it seemed to froth from his jacket to pool over his withered hand. Kira's mouth went dry. She stared at the hand a moment longer, then slowly turned her head towards Tangler. He was already watching her, and seeing the comprehension dawn on her face, raised his glass and winked. Kira looked back to the painting. The 'very dear friend' who owned this house, was evidently his Highness, Prince Rhicard. Suddenly, Tangler's claim that the Prince would provide refuge for her and Agatha, didn't seem quite so unrealistic.

Kira paced the floor. She was filled with a strange restlessness that not even Cheeks could tame, and didn't know why. Giselle and Jenna sat at the table teaching Jock how to play 'Hook, Line and Sinker' with the deck of cards they had found on the bureau. Tangler and the reunited Rainbow's End had gone down to the harbour to sing at their favourite tavern called 'Time and Tides' and glean any information they could from local gossip. Ned and Jock stayed behind to keep the girls company, and though nothing had changed on the surface, Kira felt a subtle shift in the current, and was more keenly aware that she, Giselle and Jenna were captives, rather than friends. She turned from her fourth circuit of the room to find Ned watching her rather than bent over the map of White Haven he'd been studying since the others left.

He stretched his arms over his head, then twisted from side to side so his back cracked. "Do you want to go for a walk outside instead of wearing a path on this fine floor?" he said quietly. "I don't know what's worse, watching you pacing back and forth like a caged bear, or listening to Jenna squawking like a chicken every time she lands a fish."

Kira smiled and nodded, "Yes please. I'll just grab my cloak and gloves."

The sky was dark and thick with clouds that obscured the stars. The moon rose above the sea, visible only as a halo of silver behind the haze of cloud. Kira looked down towards the harbour, more brightly lit than any other part of town, and fancied she could hear snippets of song and laughter drifting up the hill on the salty breeze. Beyond the harbour lights the sea was an inky black, darker than the night sky. She shivered. One way or another, she would be crossing the sea in less than three days, but in which direction?

"East or West?" asked Ned.

"What?" Kira asked more sharply than intended. Had he read her thoughts?

"Do you want to walk up the hill or down?" he replied patiently.

"Oh." Kira rolled her eyes, glad that Ned couldn't see. "Up, I think."

"East it is."

They walked in companionable silence for a few minutes and then Kira stopped and looked back down to the harbour.

"You and Tangler seemed a little tense with each other when we saw the Royal Guards earlier. Is anything amiss?"

Ned made a sound between a chuckle and a groan. "Nothing gets past you, does it, Kira?"

"What did he really mean when he said, 'valuable trade'?"

Ned continued walking and she thought at first he wasn't going to answer, but then he sighed and looked down at her.

"Legion fiscals."

"Ooh! La-de-dah! I wonder what could possibly have been traded to receive fiscals as payment. They're the most treasured coins in the Realm, aren't they?"

Kira didn't expect an answer; she was stating the obvious. The prized gold coins from the Legion Isles were studded with a small emerald at the centre. She had only ever seen a painting of one; nothing in River Glen was worth that much coin. Even a small chest might warrant that many guardsmen.

Ned growled and rubbed the back of his neck, "Your pardon. I speak out of turn. Tangler is no doubt correct." Kira heard the remorse in his voice and was about to let it go, but then a thought occurred to her. She went cold.

"Us? Payment for us? I thought the quota was a tithe to the Legion Isles? Edalyn's Flame. The Crown gets paid?" Kira bent forwards and rested her hands on her thighs as she tried to regain her breath. Was that why the quota had been increased in River Province? Money changed everything. The bitter taste of truth soured her mouth.

"No wonder you and Jock try so hard to keep us from Piscator's clutches. We're worth far more alive than dead."

Ned grabbed her by the forearms and held her in front of him. "We helped you escape because you *are* worth more alive, but not for the coin! The fiscals are supposed to be given to the families of the girls gathered for the quota as recompense for their sacrifice. It was never meant for the coffers of the Crown."

"What do you mean? I don't understand. And you're hurting me."

Ned released her at once. "Your pardon. I should not have said anything."

"Well, it's too late. You have. Please, tell me what you mean."

"No."

"Is that why the women sent to the Legion Isles never return home? Does the Crown get more money if they stay there?"

Ned sighed. He didn't speak for a moment, and then she heard the soft growl deep in his throat. "No. Money has nothing to do with it."

"Then why? There must be a reason. Why all the secrecy?" Kira reached out and touched his chest. "Please, Ned."

"It can't be helped," he said reluctantly, "it's because of the curse."

Kira's scalp tingled. "What curse?" She had only ever thought it a figure of speech. When someone had a run of bad luck, they were said to be as cursed as the Legion Isles.

Ned turned and continued walking. Kira hurried to catch up.

"Ned? The curse?"

"I'm sorry, Kira. I cannot speak to you about this. Forgive me. I should never have mentioned it."

"But you did." Kira didn't even try to keep the accusation from her voice. "I'm sick of being kept in the dark about this. How would you like it if you didn't know what your future entailed?"

Ned whipped his head around as though he'd been slapped. Kira took a half pace backwards, but his voice was gentle when he answered.

"I'm honour bound not to speak of it on Cabarac land. This is one vow I cannot break. You will hear about the curse if you go to the Isles."

"*When* I go, you mean."

Ned stopped this time and faced her. Kira could just make out his frown in the light from a nearby house. "Tangler wants me and Jock to turn a blind eye and let you go to Prince Rhicard's court."

Kira's heart pounded. "He can't ask that of you."

Ned gave a short bark of laughter. "He can, and he has."

"Lord Callan would not allow it. Besides, you'd get the blame."

"Lord Callan could be persuaded. Mevis died on the journey. No reason that you couldn't have died at the same time. Prince Thomac's greed will be appeased somewhat by the extra coin he gets for the River Glen Quota. Callan cannot be held responsible for an attack by brigands."

A wave of dizziness washed over Kira, and she thrust out a hand to steady herself. Ned grabbed hold, then threaded her arm through his. He placed his other hand over hers and the warmth and strength in his touch was reassuring.

"It couldn't be that easy, surely?" she asked, bewildered. For days she had been wondering how Tangler would whisk her away from the quota if Piscator didn't find her first, never really believing it would be possible.

"Why not? Jock and the girls would vouch that it's true. Tangler says he has a boat lined up to take you to the Northern Province. The quota would be none the wiser."

The irony was not lost on Kira. A few minutes ago she was despondent because her future on the Legion Isles was unknown, and now she was being offered the means to remain in Cabarac. Why did she not leap at the chance?

"What would you do, if you were in my boots?"

"Kira, there's no way I can answer that. Only you can look into your heart and decide what destiny will be yours. Tangler and the Northern province or the quota and the Legion Isles? The choice is yours alone."

Kira pondered his words for a moment. Ned was a soldier of the Crown, and a man of honour. He was supposed to uphold the law. What was Tangler thinking? It was unfair of him to put Ned's loyalty to the King to such a test, not after all Ned had done to help them. The mere fact that Tangler discussed his plans with Ned was a risk in itself. Or was it? Was Ned also a spy? Her curiosity aroused, Kira kept her voice even,

"And would you let me go, Ned? Could you turn a blind eye?"

He altered his stride and crossed the road, so they were facing the way they came and began walking down the hill. Her question hung in the air like a hawk preparing to swoop. They reached the garden gate before Ned finally answered. "It would go against every vow I have taken, Kira, but yes. I would if that's what you really wanted." He tilted her chin with his forefinger and gently brushed his thumb across her bruised cheek. "But only if *you* asked me to do it."

Chapter 41

Tangler was frustrated and it showed. His fingers tapped a staccato beat on the table, and his brow remained furrowed as he stared at one of the few bits of blank wall not covered by paintings. He had been like this all through breakfast. Kira had said good morning, but he hadn't replied. She looked at Farren and raised her brows, but he had turned down the corners of his mouth and shrugged. She wondered which of the balls Tangler always seemed to be juggling was causing such consternation, and with a slight touch of mean-heartedness hoped it was her. She shook her head, cross with herself. It wasn't Tangler's fault she had slept poorly. Not completely.

While Ned hadn't exactly avoided her company when she sat down to eat, he was back to his old taciturn self, and Kira had the distinct impression he regretted last night's candour.

As the rest of the troupe wandered down to breakfast, Tangler's mood lightened. Whether due to the company, or because he had worked out a solution to his problem, Kira wasn't sure, but she was glad to see the frown leave his face.

"Anything amiss, Tangler?" she asked as he poured a cup of tea from the ornate silver pot. "You seem troubled this morning."

He cradled the cup in his hands and blew gently across the rim. He took a sip of the tea and then set the cup down on its saucer.

"We have less time than I thought," he said regretfully. "Lord Callan and the quota will arrive tomorrow. The last ship will leave White Haven at first light the following day."

Giselle fixed Tangler with her gaze. "We've known this day was coming for weeks. What does it matter that it comes a day early? Truth be told, if it wasn't for the weather and the trouble at Marybank Bridge, we'd already be on the Isles by now."

Tangler chuckled. "Ah, Giselle, ever the pragmatist. I will miss the directness of your speech, my dear." He raised his teacup towards her in salute and took another sip.

"If Piscator wasn't so hell-bent on finding Kira, we could simply reunite with the quota when they arrive. Lord Callan could complete the official paperwork and it would be done. However, our current circumstances are unusual, to say the least. The quotas from the other provinces met their ships and sailed more than two weeks ago. As you rightly point out, Giselle, if we hadn't been delayed you would have sailed with them. Hiding you amongst twenty, instead of two hundred, is far more difficult."

"Nineteen," said Kira. "There's only nineteen of us."

"Eighteen if you tell Lord Callan that Kira was killed at the same time as Mevis," said Jenna, then promptly clapped her hand across her mouth.

Giselle groaned. "Jenna!"

Really? Kira glared at Tangler. Was she to be the last to be told everything? The man had no shame. He was a master puppeteer. He stared back, grey eyes wide and innocent. "No use getting your hopes up before everyone agreed."

She looked across the table to where Jock was sitting, but he kept his head down and avoided her gaze. Ned was standing by the window and though she only saw his profile, could see that he clenched his teeth by the way his whiskers moved across the angle of his jaw. Kira turned back to face Tangler, acutely aware of the tension in the room, but still reluctant to make her choice.

"What else are you worried about?" she asked.

A flash of emotion crossed his face, but Kira wasn't sure if it was amusement or annoyance at her lack of response to his plan. There was no hint of either when he continued speaking.

"A merchant friend of mine told me that one of his empty storehouses will be used to accommodate the quota overnight. Piscator's men will be on guard. I think the only way to join them will be as they board the ship."

Kira was struck by a thought, "How? We gave our quota cloaks to the nuns. The soldiers will notice straight away."

Hugo stood up from the table. "No, no. I forgot to tell you. We have your cloaks. Sister Eloise packed them in a satchel for us. It's up in our room. Shall I go and fetch it?"

Tangler waved him back down.

"My friend also told me that the soldiers rented another, smaller storehouse. Three large wooden crates were offloaded from a cargo vessel last week. The dock hands weren't allowed to help. Soldiers did all the work. The crates were stamped with the dispatcher seal."

Ned strode across the room and paused at the end of the table. He spun the chair around and sat astride, with his forearms resting across the top of the backrest. "What's in them?"

"He doesn't know. The storehouse is guarded day and night. The soldiers regularly patrol the docks."

"How does that affect us?" asked Giselle.

"It doesn't directly," replied Tangler, "but it means we will need to be extra diligent. If we had the time, I'd like to have a little peek at what's inside those crates, but never mind."

"Maybe you can take a look after we've gone," said Jenna, finally removing her hand from her mouth.

Tangler looked at her as though he wished she'd kept it there.

"No time, I'm afraid. The fishing boat that takes us to Prince Rhicard sails on the same tide as the quota."

"And what of Piscator? Any news about him?" Kira pressed the top of her thumb against her teeth. Why did it seem that she had to choose between bad news and more bad news? What if she did go with Tangler to the Northern Province, only to walk straight into Piscator's clutches?

Tangler shook his head. "Not a word. We can only assume that he does indeed lay in wait at the Northern border. Hopefully, he won't be expecting us to come by boat. Prince Thomac has spies planted in Cottcar Harbour, but he doesn't realise that there are plenty of hidden coves a small vessel can anchor in."

"And if your plans don't work and I am captured, what happens then?"

Tangler didn't answer straight away. He drank the last of his tea and looked at Kira.

"You won't be captured, my dear. I'll make sure of it." He held up a hand as Kira started to protest. "Very well. Should it be here in White Haven, then I assume you would be imprisoned until Piscator returns. If, in some bizarre twist of fate, you were taken before you could get to Prince Rhicard's court, then I imagine Piscator would…" His voice trailed off and he waved his hand in a gesture of apology.

"You could just use your magic, couldn't you? Blow them all away and escape?" Jenna waved her hands around her head and flicked her fingers.

Kira wondered if Jenna would ever learn to think before speaking and shook her head sadly.

"Kill anyone who gets in my way, do you mean? Murder soldiers who are following orders? Destroy anyone who doesn't approve of magic? I'm a healer, not a monster, Jenna." Kira was shocked at her own bitterness and stopped talking.

Jenna's face flushed and she bowed her head. Kira immediately regretted her harsh words and reached her hand across the table. "I'm sorry, Jenna, forgive me. I feel like no matter what decision I make, someone is bound to get hurt. I want to tread the path of least danger, but they are both as treacherous as each other. I'm sorry."

Jenna pressed her eyes with the heel of her hand. She squeezed Kira's fingers and shook her head. "Fish and pickles, that didn't come out the way I intended. I'm sorry, too. I don't want anything to happen to you. To any of us. And I want us all to stay together, but I also know, if I had the chance to stay here in Cabarac and become a Guardian, I would take it. I think you should have that chance, too."

"But there are no guarantees, are there?" Giselle said with some conviction. "We'd all like to return to River Glen and live a normal life, but that's not possible. Tangler hopes that Kira will be safe in Prince Rhicard's court. But how can he know for sure? And they have to get there in one piece first. It's just not that easy."

Jenna nodded. "I know. Nothing seems easy these days. Edalyn's flame, I wish it were."

"I know you do, but the time is looming. We're all on edge." Kira patted Jenna's hand and sat back in her chair. "What's your plan, then, Tangler?"

Tangler grabbed his beard in his fist and tugged at it several times. "We need to get our bearings and work out the best places to hide. I'm familiar with White Haven, but these days when I come back, there seems to be gaps where there were buildings before, and buildings where there used to be gaps. Houses are built where there used to be fields and shops where there used to be houses. Fortunately, the docks see little change, but I need to see exactly where these storehouses are."

"We'll need to work out what route the quota will take to get to the ship, as well," said Farren, "and whether they will be on foot or taken in carriages."

Ned growled. "Most likely on foot. Carriages get in the way when the dock hands are loading the ships. Their bags are usually taken in hand trolleys and loaded afterwards."

"We might need to work out a distraction, then, and get the girls to join the quota as they reach the docks."

"What about Lord Callen?" asked Kira. "He'll have to agree with what's going on."

"I'll catch him when the quota first arrives. He won't be under guard, and he'll be expecting to meet us. I'll have to fill him in with what's been happening, if he doesn't already know."

"How could he possibly know?" Jenna frowned.

"Same way we know that he's due tomorrow," said Farren. "Riders will have been sent to check on his progress and report back. He'll no doubt have been told that the quota will be searched before they leave."

"Hope he doesn't get into trouble because he helped me escape," said Kira, realising that Piscator would hold Lord Callan responsible.

"Piscator has no proof that you escaped with the quota," said Tangler, gently, "though he might suspect that's what happened. It would take either a very brave or very stupid man to accuse the High Sheriff of law-breaking without proof, and Piscator is neither."

Farren nodded in agreement. "Besides, if he actually believed you were heading to the Legion Isles, Piscator would be here in White Haven, wouldn't he? Not setting traps in the Northern Province."

"I think a stroll along the docks might help you to get your bearings. Piscator's men will hardly be looking for you. They'll be expecting you to be arriving with the quota," said Tangler.

For once Kira was glad of the drizzly weather and icy sea breeze. She was bulked up with extra layers of clothing and the hood of her cloak covered all of her hair and shadowed the half of her face that wasn't hidden by her scarf. She walked arm-in arm with Hugo, wandering along the harbourside markets with a basket filled with the fresh fish they had purchased for dinner. Her coin purse and a spare string bag were stowed in a pouch on her belt. Ned followed about twenty paces behind. He'd been closer at the start, but twice he'd been mistaken for a dock hand and been asked to help unload crates of fish. Hugo prattled on about inconsequential things, but Kira noticed his head turned regularly from side to side as he chattered, so she knew he was scanning the docks as they walked.

Farren and Giselle approached from the other direction, and she only recognised them because of Farren's distinctive green cloak and Giselle's prominent belly. She had stuffed a round silk cushion from the parlour under her belt and looked about six months gone with child. Jenna had gone with Parr in the wagon, marking the changes on

Ned's map as he drove slowly around the city centre, pointing out the local sites of interest.

"That's the quota ship," said Farren as he shook hands with Hugo, and kissed Kira on both cheeks. She glanced over his shoulder at the sleek, two-masted brigantine, looking as bare limbed as a tree in winter, with all its sails furled. Though it dwarfed any boat she had ever sailed on the River Ryder, it still looked far too fragile to cross the wild straights of Whaler's Bay, let alone the turbulent currents of the Unnamed Sea.

"Goddess of Light, protect us," muttered Giselle as she stared at the vessel. "How long are we on that thing?"

"A week. Ten days at most," said Farren. "Depends on the wind and the tides."

"Thank you, Farren," she replied tartly. "I am aware of how boats work."

Farren chuckled and took hold of her hand. "Come, Mistress Threadgold, your hands are frozen, and you need to rest your weary feet. You obviously need a hot drink to restore your good humour. Sour moods are not good for the baby."

He winked at Hugo and said, "We'll meet you at the Time and Tides shortly."

Kira saw a splash of red from the corner of her eye as she waved her friends goodbye. She turned and saw a tiny stall about ten paces away, almost hidden from view, nestled as it was between the larger fish sellers.

"We might as well go, too," said Hugo. "Ned's beckoning and I think it's about to rain again." He waved back to Ned in acknowledgement and began to walk back the way they came.

"Hold on. I just want to buy some of those winter-apples. I'll make apple pie for pudding tonight." She thrust the basket of fish into Hugo's hands. "Wait here, I'll only be a minute."

Kira trotted over to the stall before Hugo could object, pulling the string bag from her pouch as she went.

"Kira!" She heard Hugo call, but when she turned she could see that he'd stopped and was gesticulating to Ned.

"Well met," she smiled at the young girl behind the stall. "I'd like two dozen of your delicious looking apples, please."

Kira's voice trailed off as she heard a plaintive wail at the door of her mind room. Her scalp suddenly tingled and the hairs on the back of her arms stood to attention. Her awareness called to her like it never had before and her heart began to pound. Oblivious to the concerned,

"Are you well, Mistress?" of the apple seller, or Hugo's shouting of her name, Kira ran. Faster than she had ever run in her life. She followed the urgent pull of her awareness, as fast as her legs could carry her. She pounded down narrow alleyways. Shopfronts passed in a blur. She dodged people and lampposts with the agility of a deer. She splashed through puddles that soaked the hem of her cloak, and not once did she stumble. She gave no thought to Hugo or to Ned and didn't know or care if they followed.

Eventually, the streets opened to a small square. Kira looked around frantically, chest heaving. Here somewhere. Squat buildings lined the square on two sides and an imposing town hall stood opposite her. She glanced to her right and was drawn towards a tall white spire. She ran again. The spire towered above her, so perfectly constructed that the rain flowed down the smooth, seamless walls like the sea from a dolphin's back. No door, no window. She flung her arms around the stone and sent her awareness soaring, searching for a way in.

It was like trying to swim against the tide. Her awareness spiralled around the surface probing for an entry until finally, almost at the top, she sensed a weakness. She sent her awareness through and then plunging down to the depths, beneath the ground on which she stood. Down to dark and dismal passageways that led to prison cells with doors made of metal bars.

Here. She moved more cautiously now, pulled towards the flickering light of a thick white candle. She paused at the cold iron bars. A figure was huddled on the floor of the cell, moaning softly. Outside, Kira's body clung to the walls of the spire as if sheer desperation would let her melt through the stone. She sobbed as though her heart would break. But inside, her awareness called a name, as gently as the fluttering heart of a baby bird.

Agatha.

Chapter 42

Agatha?

Kira wrapped her awareness around Agatha like a warm blanket and tried to calm the emotions that swirled around her grandmother like angry bees. She was hindered by a strange lethargy of her own, but gradually she was able to penetrate the haze of pain and anguish and sooth Agatha's sorrow.

Kira? Goddess of Light. Is it you?

It's me, Gran. It's me.

Agatha struggled to sit up, and it tore at Kira's heart. In the dim halo of candlelight she could see the bruising on her face and the back of her hands. Agatha flinched and clutched her side. Kira guessed that a rib might be broken. She longed to mend her grandmother as she had done for others, but her awareness felt as insubstantial as the smoke from the candle, and all she could manage was comfort.

Gran, what happened? Who did this to you?

Soldiers. Piscator's men. Be wary, my brave girl. He wants you. Your blood.

Stay strong. We'll get you out of here somehow. I'm sorry, my Eiran is weak. I cannot stay much longer. I love you, Agatha. Hold on.

Don't give him what he wants. Save yourself. I'm older than I've any right to be. Save yourself.

Agatha!

Zarabesk's scale burned a warning against her chest. Kira lost her tenuous grip on Agatha's awareness and felt her own hurtling back to her. Her hands lost their grip on the slick white walls of the spire and her legs gave way. Someone called her name, but she couldn't answer. She fell into the darkness.

Nothing seemed to break her fall. She sank down further and further into the blackness, like a pebble thrown into the middle of a lake.

Eventually, she stopped falling and simply floated. She heard Tangler call her name from far away. She couldn't answer. She was too tired. Again and again he called, but Kira just wanted to sleep. She drifted further down.

Zarabesk called to her. At least, she thought it was the dragon, but how could it be? He was dead. She dreamed of black dragons and a white snow fox. She didn't want to wake up. There was something she had to do, though, wasn't there? What was it? Something to do with Agatha? She loved Agatha. Tired. Too tired. Someone else began calling her name with a persistence that irritated her.

Kira

Go away I need to sleep.

Kira. You need to wake up now. You've slept too long.

I'm so tired, Llyr.

I know, but you must. It's very important. Please, Kira.

Llyr?

Yes, little dove?

You are very annoying.

I know. That's why you love me.

I love you?

No…but you might one day.

One day.

Come back now, spread your wings and fly home.

Kira floated towards the sound of his voice and gradually the darkness became grey and then the grey became light.

When she woke, Kira was lying on the sofa in the parlour. She felt someone stroking her hair and thought it must be Giselle. Her eyelids felt as though they were glued shut. She tried to just open one and saw Ned on the seat opposite her. He sat with his head in his hands, slumped forward with his elbows resting on his thighs. His eyes were closed, and his hair poked through his fingers in clumps. He looked so dejected she wanted to tell him that all would be well but decided that since she didn't actually know what had upset him, it would be best not to.

She heard Jenna blow her nose. No one blew their nose quite like Jenna, and Kira was able to see from the corner of her eye that her friend was kneeling by the fire. She leaned into Jock's embrace as he stroked her back in a comforting kind of way. What on earth had happened? She forced open her other eye and tried to sit up.

A wave of giddiness washed over her, and she immediately felt sick. Giselle threw an arm across her shoulders and thrust a bucket under her chin. The speed of her response told Kira that this wasn't the first time she had vomited, but she had no recollection of waking earlier. Her stomach spasmed, but must have already purged its contents. She lay back, exhausted.

"Edalyn's flame," she croaked. Her mouth was as dry as sand.

"Kira?" Giselle was suddenly on the floor in front of her. "Are you awake? Truly awake?"

Kira nodded. "Drink, please."

"Oh, Kira," said Giselle with such sadness that Kira shot a look at her. She'd been crying. Her nose was red and her eyes puffy. Why was she so upset? Kira's heart constricted with fear. Memories began crowding her mind and she struggled to get herself up on one elbow. Something had happened to her grandmother.

"Agatha!" she rasped.

"Settle, lass. Agatha's alive as far as we know. Try and drink this, it's only just warm." Jock poured a willow bark tea from the teapot and handed it to Giselle. "I'll go and freshen the pot and put some bread on to toast. I'm pleased you're awake, Kira. You gave us a nasty scare."

Ned stood so abruptly that his chair rocked on its back legs. Some other emotion seemed to have replaced his earlier dejection, and by the way he clenched his teeth, Kira thought it might be anger, but when he spoke his voice was gentle.

"I'll let Tangler know you're awake."

The memory hit her with the force of Traitor Falls. Agatha. Her grandmother was hurt and in prison. She had to free her.

"Agatha," she tried again.

"We know, Kira. You don't remember much, because you used too much of your power. You fell into such a deep sleep. We were so frightened. Tangler said that if you woke up, you should drink as much tea as you can, and if you no longer feel ill, have something to eat. He says it will help." Giselle held the cup to Kira's lips and encouraged her to drink. Her belly rumbled, but the tea stayed down.

"Thank the Goddess, you're alive," said Jenna, bending down to kiss Kira's cheek. "I'll go and get the toast. Tangler says you need to eat as soon as you can. He says your mind needs nourishment to help you focus properly." She wiped her eyes and nose with her handkerchief. "We were so worried, we thought we'd lost you."

Kira's eyes filled with tears. She took the cup from Giselle and drank some more tea. She still couldn't grasp what was going on. Why were they glad she was alive? Agatha was the one in trouble.

"What happened?"

"To you?" Giselle laid her hand on Kira's arm. Kira nodded.

"Hugo said you took off like a rabbit when it sees a fox. He thought at first the apple seller had said something to upset you, but he couldn't understand why you ran away from him. He and Ned chased after you—"

"He said he'd never seen anyone run so fast," cut in Jenna, back with a plate of toast and honey. She had sliced the toast into fingers and offered one to Kira.

"Yes, so fast that they lost you a couple of times, but fortunately they saw you in the Town Hall Square."

"Hugging the spire," said Jenna. "Lucky it was raining; no one was about."

"Hugo wanted to grab you straight away, but Ned stopped him, even though you were sobbing. 'Look at her hair,' Ned said."

"Your hood had slipped back, and your kerchief had come undone," said Jenna helpfully.

"He said a strand was glowing…silver, like a moonbeam. And as they moved closer they saw tiny threads of silver leaving the tips of your fingers and spiralling all around the spire like a spider's web. And then, suddenly, it was gone, and you collapsed." Giselle's voice cracked with emotion.

"Ned caught you and sent Hugo to find the wagon. And lucky for us, because of the rain, we were headed your way. Ned carried you all the way, which was lucky for Hugo, because I think Ned would have punched him into next week if he didn't have his arms full," said Jenna.

"Farren and I were waiting at the Time and Tide, when Hugo ran in to fetch us. Tangler was at the wagon by the time we got there. I've never seen him so grim. He was truly concerned about you, Kira, and the longer you slept, the more worried he became."

"It was awful. You were sick as a dog and moaning about Agatha, and then you just fell deeper and deeper asleep."

Giselle squeezed Kira's hand so tightly it hurt. "Sometimes we had to check to see if you were even breathing".

"I couldn't find a way in," said Kira, her voice husky despite the tea. "It seemed to take forever to reach Agatha. On the docks I felt her pain and her fear like a stab in my heart; but only a glimpse, mind, and I just had to follow. But I couldn't get in." She stared at the fire, too weary to cry.

"No one could get in, my child. Or should I say, no one but you."

Kira turned at the sound of Tangler's voice. He stood in the doorway, shoulders stooped and face pale and drawn, looking every one of his three hundred years. He shrugged off his cloak, spraying droplets of water across the floor, then pulled off his boots wearily. He shuffled across the room to stand with his back to the fire, pausing only to rest his palm against Kira's cheek. Ned wasn't with him.

"What do you mean?" she asked.

"The spires are warded. From the time they were built. Spells of protection are woven through the stones themselves. Sorcerers and magicians lived and worked in the spires. They often worked with powerful magic, so the spires were warded to keep the people outside safe, and to protect the people inside safe from outside attack. Magical attack." Tangler ran his hand over his thick, white hair and seemed surprised to find it damp. He accepted a cup of tea from Jock, gulped it down and held out the cup to be refilled.

"I thought anything magical was destroyed in the Purge," said Giselle.

"The spires are the backbone of White Haven; destroy the spires and you destroy the very fabric of the city. Besides, once the magicians were gone, very few people remembered that spells had helped build them."

"It's been over a century. Maybe the magic faded. Maybe that's how I was able to get in. I don't really care, Tangler, I just want to get Agatha out of there. What did you find out?"

Tangler grimaced but didn't argue the point. He set his teacup down on the table.

"Eat some more toast and I'll tell you what I know."

Kira obediently shoved more toast in her mouth and began to chew. He was right; the fog in her brain was beginning to lift.

"Agatha and the other women that Piscator accuses of magic, or witchcraft, have only just arrived in White Haven. Whether by good fortune, or divine intervention, I don't know, but at the very moment Agatha must have been led from the prison wagon to the cells, you were on the docks and close enough to hear the distress in her Eiran. Once inside the spire it would have been blocked completely. She could only have been in the cell a few minutes when you found her."

"I was terrified." Kira shuddered at the memory. "I couldn't get to her. I didn't know what to do."

"You have a rare gift, my dear, but even so, the effort cost you dearly. You could have died."

Kira stared at him.

"Even in the most knowledgeable of magicians, the complete draining of power can be fatal. If you had not called back your awareness before your collapse, the power would have continued to flow out of you like a haemorrhaging artery."

A cold shiver ran down her back, but she had more important things to worry about. "But what about Agatha? Why is she here? And how do we get her out?"

Tangler bowed his head. His shoulder sagged and there was such an air of dejection about him that Kira's throat tightened.

"Tangler! What are we going to do?"

He raised his head and locked his eyes on hers. They were dark with sorrow.

"Kira, you have been asleep for a day and a night and almost another day. The ships sail in the morning."

The air left her lungs with a rush. "No," she said once she could breathe again. "No." Her voice grew stronger and more determined with every word. "No. No. No." She glared at Tangler and said, "It's me Piscator wants. I'll trade myself for her."

Four voices spoke at once,

"Kira, no!"

"You can't. I won't let you!"

"Y'canna do that, lass."

"My dear, that will simply not work."

Kira balled her fists so tightly her nails almost pierced the skin. "Why not?"

Tangler spread his arms, palms up, as though he was a supplicant before a magistrate.

"Agatha would not want it, Kira. You know this as well as I. Your sacrifice may salve your misguided need for restitution, but it would pain Agatha more than anything Piscator could do to her."

Though his voice was gentle, Kira felt the sting of his words like a barb. She closed her eyes to stem the tears and Agatha's parting words echoed in her mind: *Don't give him what he wants. Save yourself. I'm older than I've any right to be. Save yourself.*

Her chin trembled. "I have to do something. Please, Tangler. I'll do anything you want. I'll go to Prince Rhicard's court with you. I'll help you with my magic. Anything. Please, there must be something we can do?"

Giselle broke the silence that followed with a question of her own.

"Why is Piscator going to all this trouble? Why bring Agatha all the way from River Glen to White Haven, when he can't possibly know for sure that Kira is here? And why does he want Kira so badly?" She unfurled one of Kira's fists and held her hand in hers. "You had barely come into your magic when he saw you. How could he know how powerful you've become? It doesn't make sense."

"He's a fanatic," said Jenna, as though that explained everything.

"Yes he is," said Tangler, almost to himself, "but Giselle is correct. I have been so busy concentrating on the bigger picture that I have neglected these small but important details." He looked between Giselle and Kira. "Tell me, my dear, did Agatha speak at all when you were in the cell? Can you remember?"

Kira nodded. "She said that Piscator wanted me, and then she told me not to give him what he wants."

"Do you think she meant don't give him yourself, or don't give him something you possess?" Tangler tugged on his beard.

"I'm not sure. No, wait. She said he wanted my blood, but that's the same thing, isn't it?" Kira's heartache intensified as she recalled the memory. Poor Agatha.

"No," Tangler said slowly. He steepled his fingers and tapped his forefingers against his lips, "Think back to the night of the Ball, my dear. When Piscator tested you, what exactly did he do?"

Kira would not forget that moment as long as she lived. "He put his hands on my head and then he clutched his pendant. He whispered something like 'Dragon's blood' and then yelled at Lord Callan to arrest me because I had magic in my veins."

Tangler sighed. "And this is why the man pursues you with such vengeance. His dragon shard must have sensed the awakening of your Valethrix blood, not just your Eiran. I have been a fool. I should have realised that Piscator would never give you up. As much as the man despises magic, he craves the power he sees in his fragment of dragon scale."

Kira stared at Tangler. Should she tell him about the scale Zarabesk had bequeathed her? Would Piscator want her even more because of it? She brushed the thought aside. Her grandmother's safety was more important now.

"And Agatha?"

"To ensure your co-operation, my dear. If by chance you were travelling with the quota and his men discovered you here, what better way to ensure your cooperation? Piscator would assume, quite rightly, that you would not dare to use magic if Agatha's life was threatened. You could be held in the Spire quite safely until he arrived. On the other hand, if he found you in the Northern Province, I'm sure he would have proof of Agatha's capture to show you also."

Kira grimaced. "Tis a good thing he cannot see me now, then. I have not the energy to swat a fly, let alone try to kill one."

A wave of exhaustion swept over her, and though she fought valiantly against it, she just had to close her eyes. Her last thought was that Tangler had neatly managed to avoid answering her question. What about Agatha?

Chapter 43

Kira woke at the clop of hooves and the crunch of the wagon wheels on the gravel path outside. She looked out of the window and was shocked to see that the sun had almost set.

"Ned went to fetch them," said Tangler. Kira assumed he meant the Rainbow's End and wondered where they had been.

Jenna stood up and drew the curtains. "The boys will be looking to eat. There's a fish pie in the oven for dinner."

Jock took his boots from under his chair and pulled them on. "I'll give the lads a hand with the horses." He flashed a grin at Kira and winked. "They'll all want to come and see you for themselves, but there's one who'll be more than relieved to know you're alive, let me tell you."

"I think he means Hugo," Giselle whispered. "Ned did threaten to kill him if you didn't recover, but I don't think he was serious. I think he blames himself for not keeping a better watch over you."

Kira didn't have time to ponder Giselle's thoughts. Hugo was the first one to come in and rushed across the room to kneel next to her and beg for her forgiveness.

"Don't be ridiculous! There's nothing to forgive. It's not your fault I took off like a lunatic. I should have waited for you, but I just couldn't. Nothing would have stopped me, Hugo, you must believe me. Truly, if my ankles were in chains, I would have cut off my feet and still tried to run."

He bent his brow to her hand, which he was holding, then kissed her knuckles.

"Thank you," he said hoarsely, and his face lost the haunted expression she had seen when he first walked in. One by one the others had come to kiss her cheek or stroke her face and offer both condolences for Agatha's plight, and heartfelt relief that Kira herself was alive and well.

Farren was not satisfied with a mere kiss on the cheek and sat himself on the sofa next to Kira and pulled her into his embrace. "Don't scare us like that again, Kira of River Glen," he whispered. "Neither Giselle's heart, nor my own, could take it. I am so glad you are well." He held her away from him and said more loudly, "My life was quiet and peaceful until you girls came into it. I've had more twists and turns in the last few weeks than in the last ten years. I'll have to write a song about it!" He winked and rose to his feet with a bow that had her smiling in response, but she had heard the genuine emotion in his private words and was moved almost to tears. He offered his arm to Giselle and led her to the table.

Ned stood back, arms folded across his chest, watching as the others came and went. Kira had felt his gaze when Farren took his leave, but when she looked his way, his expression gave nothing away. She closed her eyes. He moved quietly for such a big man, but she heard him pick up Giselle's chair. He moved it so it was directly in front of Kira, and he sat down with a sigh and rested his elbows on his thighs.

"I'm sorry," said Kira.

"Are you well?" Ned asked at the same time.

He growled and bent forward to rest his chin on his clasped hands. Kira had never seen his eyes so close before and as they searched her face she saw that his irises, though grey from a distance, were flecked with green and blue. He had a small V-shaped scar, almost hidden in the hairs of his left eyebrow and she wondered if it was that, as much as his frequent anger or frustration, which made him frown.

"Are you well?" he said again.

"Yes. I am. And I'm sorry for running off. I couldn't help it."

"Aye, so I assumed. Nearly killed yourself, nonetheless."

Kira was a little taken aback by the accusation in his voice and tried to defend herself. "To be fair, Ned, I didn't know that was going to happen."

He dropped his gaze to the floor and growled. "Aye, I know. But, Kira, I'm not always going to be around to pick you up when you fall. You need to take more care."

She grimaced. "Easier baited than hooked, I'm afraid. Besides, I'm more concerned about Agatha."

Ned leaned back in his chair and ran his hand across the back of his head. "Lord Callen will be here after dinner. Maybe he'll know what to do."

Kira had no appetite but ate because she knew it was the only way to regain her strength. She stayed on the sofa while the others dined at the table, but it was a sombre affair with little conversation. She accepted a second bowl of fish pie from Jenna and didn't try to correct her friend's assumption that it was because it was so delicious. She needed to clear this brain fog and try to think. She was running out of time.

Eventually, the gallon of tea she had drunk sent her messages she could no longer ignore, and Giselle and Jenna helped her to the privy.

"I don't know how we're going to disguise this," said Jenna. She pulled a curl of hair about the thickness of her forefinger from the loose braid they had managed to plait when Kira was asleep.

Kira groaned. "I see what you mean." The long curl was silvery white, and from the tug she had felt when Jenna loosened the strand, came from just above her right temple. She redid the braid more securely, thinking that a hair comb would help hide the silver and wished she had not lost her own. She made do with an embroidered hair kerchief instead.

When they returned to the parlour, Lord Callan was warming his backside by the fire. His dark eyes found hers and he raised an eyebrow. "Well met, Kira, Giselle, Jenna." He nodded to each of them in turn. Kira managed a curtsy without overbalancing and then dropped onto the couch. "Well met, Lord Callan. Are you well?"

He gave a short bark of laughter. "As well as any man can be, escorting sixteen sullen and resentful young ladies on a journey that took nearly three times as long as it should have. My nerves are shattered and my patience so far past breaking point that I may never recover."

He began a litany of misfortunes they had had to endure with such a sardonic wit it made Kira smile.

"Torrential rain, bogged wheels, blocked roads, distressed females, poor accommodation, frustrated and angry guards." He paused and held up his hands in mock horror. "Monthly cycles! Snow, lame horses, bitter cold."

Eventually, he stopped and looked at Kira. "These dreadful tragedies, Ned informs me, pale into insignificance when compared to what he and Jock have had to contend with while watching over you. Do you agree?"

"Well, I wouldn't put it quite like that!" Giselle retorted.

"It's not Kira's fault," said Jenna.

"Yes." Kira nodded.

Lord Callan raised an eyebrow, but his eyes twinkled. "I see." He turned to Ned and nodded. "You win."

He glanced at Tangler and back at Kira. His voice was suddenly hard. "The quota has been searched by Piscator's men, but despite finding no sign of you, they will sleep under guard in the temporary accommodation so kindly provided by the dispatcher. Until they are handed over to Legion Captain, Lord Campion, tomorrow morning, they are still my complete responsibility. After their departure, however, I will be free to resume my duties as High Sheriff. I believe Agatha Stillwater has been wrongfully imprisoned. She has committed no crime in Trader's Province that I am aware of, and since Piscator is not here to demand otherwise, I will seek her immediate release."

Kira launched herself at Lord Callan, threw her arms around his neck and thanked him a hundred times.

"You'll have to go to Prince Rhicard's Court now," said Jenna when Lord Callan had taken his leave, pricking Kira's bubble of euphoria. "If Lord Callan does manage to get Agatha released, it won't be safe for her to return to River Glen. Not for a while, anyway."

"Jenna's right. He has a soft spot for you, Kira; you saved his son's life, after all. But Piscator will be furious if he loses both you and Agatha. She won't be safe here. Lord Callan will not always be able to protect her," Giselle agreed.

Kira knew what they said was true. If Prince Rhicard would protect her and Agatha from Piscator, then that's where she would go. Her heart was torn, though. Tomorrow she would have to say goodbye to her dearest friends and likely never see them again.

Lord Callan had made it clear that the earliest Agatha could be released would be mid-afternoon, long after the boat had to set sail. Tangler was adamant Kira had to leave. No sailor would travel North once the wind changed. The winter seas were treacherous and unpredictable.

"We'll take Agatha back to the priory," said Farren, "and bring her north with us once spring is in the air. Sister Evangeline will take good care of her, you know that."

Kira did, but it didn't make leaving any easier. She couldn't even say goodbye to her. She would have to write her a letter instead. She drank the hot toddy Parr made for them all and ate a handful of his delicious honey oat biscuits. Her appetite had returned with a vengeance.

Kira fell asleep the moment her head touched the pillow. She dreamed she was skating on a frozen lake, skimming across the surface as quickly as a bird in the sky. She heard the crack only a few seconds before she felt the ice tremble beneath her feet. A thin black fissure snaked towards her like a bolt of lightning. She knew she had to choose a side to jump, but the crack was already between her feet. Too late! The chasm opened and Kira fell into the abyss.

The dragon saved her. Zarabesk swooped beneath her and caught her on his outstretched wing. She climbed onto his back, and he flew high into the mountains and into his cave.

I called to you before, but you didn't answer, daughter of Aeldra.

I'm sorry. I drained all of my power and fell into a deep sleep.

Yes, I am aware. The one you call Llyr told me.

Oh? How can that be?

Through you. And my scale.

Your scale saved me, Zarabesk. Had it not called me back, I would have died.

I am aware of that, too.

Thank you, my friend.

I regret I cannot help you more, dear one, but though your power is weak now, you will be strong again. My scale will protect you. Remember this and remember that sometimes the illusion of power can be as great as power itself.

Kira felt someone shake her gently on the shoulder. It was Giselle. Her moonbeam hair tumbled about her shoulders and her pale blue eyes were sad. There was a resolute set to her chin, however, and Kira knew her dearest friend would be determined to put on a brave face.

"Time to get up. We leave in less than an hour."

"Well met, my friend. I'm going to miss your plain but kindly face."

Giselle squeaked, "Plain?"

"But kindly," said Kira, her eyes filled with tears despite her smile. Suddenly Giselle was in her arms, hugging her like she would never let her go.

They wore their quota cloaks beneath the others they had been wearing. There had been a forced sort of cheeriness at breakfast that told Kira that she wasn't the only one not looking forward to saying goodbye. She would miss the Rainbow's End. And Jock. And

Ned. Tangler was nowhere to be seen.

"He's gone to check all is in order down at the dock. He says he'll meet you down there." Farren grinned. "He's as jittery as I've ever seen him."

She was surprised when she had come down to breakfast to see Jock and Ned back in uniform. Jock had hugged them all fiercely and told them to behave themselves. Ned had said little, except to remind them to listen to his instructions when they got to the docks. And here they were, now, hiding behind a stack of pallets, waiting for Tangler.

"What's keeping him?" asked Jenna for the thousandth time.

"There must be a problem with the quota," said Jock. "Do you want me to go and check?"

Ned growled. "No, I'll go. If the quota comes, you know what to do. Signal Lord Callan, and when he gives the all-clear, Giselle and Jenna, you join the end of the queue. I should be back with Tangler before then. Stay put and do as Jock says."

He trotted back to where Farren and Parr waited in the wagon, taking care to stay in the shadows. Though dawn was only just painting the sky, several streetlamps were lit along the length of the wharf, providing a sickly yellow gleam in the early morning mist. The wharf was far from quiet. The quota boat wasn't the only ship preparing to leave at first light, and the sounds of fishermen calling to each other and sails being unfurled echoed along the cobblestones.

A scream pierced the air. The hairs on the back of Kira's neck stood up.

"Edalyn's Flame," hissed Jock, "somebody's bein' murdered."

They crowded together and looked over the top of the crates. The fishermen had already started to run to the sound. Again and again the agonised cry rang out. Kira grabbed hold of Giselle's hand. But the skin wasn't smooth, or soft. It was hard and far too large to belong to Giselle. Another hand covered her mouth, and she was hauled off her feet before she could do more than register what was happening.

"Scream and I will gut your friend like a fish. Do you understand?"

Fear clawed her belly and ripped it open. Her lungs refused to breathe, and her heart pounded in panic. Bluff and double bluff. Piscator must have been here all the while. With a flash of intuition, Kira knew exactly what was hidden inside the wooden crate in the storehouse.

The brazen dragon.

Chapter 44

Kira couldn't see. She was blindfolded, her hands tied behind her back. The same calloused hand that had been over her mouth was now clamped around the back of her neck, urging her forward. The air changed. She could smell a heady blend of spices that at any other time would have delighted her senses. Now, she was simply terrified. She guessed that they were in a spice storehouse. She cracked her knee against something hard and stumbled. Unable to break her fall, she landed awkwardly against a hessian sack and was assailed by the scent of cinnamon.

"Get up!" Her assailant yanked her arms up behind her and a spasm of pain shot through her shoulder. Kira scrambled to her feet and stood, trembling.

"Gently, Scarrow, gently."

A frisson of fear ran down Kira's spine. Piscator. She would recognise that rasping, reedy voice anywhere.

"I would remind you, Kira of River Glen, the lives of not only your grandmother but your friends, are in your hands. Try your little whirlwind trick here and their throats will be slit before you can point your staff." Piscator laughed. "If you had one."

Kira's mind reeled. How could Piscator possibly know about what had happened at the priory? Goddess of Light, what was going on?

"Remove her blindfold".

Scarrow's nails raked down her cheeks as he pulled the rag from her eyes and let it hang around her neck like a noose. She blinked, trying to adjust her eyes, and scanned the area in front of her. She had guessed correctly: it was a warehouse, almost empty but for a scattering of sacks and upturned crates. The only light came from several lanterns on the hard stone floor, but it was bright enough for her to see Tangler tied to a chair. His head lolled to one side so the blood oozing from his nose stained only one half of his beard. Behind him Giselle and Jenna were also bound, mouths stuffed with rags. They stared at Kira, wide-eyed and full of fear. Behind each of their chairs stood one of Piscator's guards holding a blade to their throats. Jock lay at their feet, unmoving, a dark pool beneath his head.

Kira's heart pounded. She turned her head slowly, stifling a scream as Piscator's smiling face seemed to float in the darkness, his body hidden within the black folds of his robes. The menace in his smile chilled her to the core. Scarrow walked slowly to stand at Piscator's side. He was dressed as a fisherman, but as he lifted a finger to his head in a kind of salute, Kira had a flash of recognition. It was the man she had seen in The Mermaid's Tail. Now that he was standing next to Piscator she realised where else she had seen him. He was one of the dispatcher's personal guards that had been at the Merryman Ball.

The lanterns gave only partial illumination to the cavernous storehouse. The upper part of the walls was shrouded in darkness, but as her eyes adjusted to the light Kira could see enough. Perched on top of the crates were two archers with their arrows aimed directly at her. Her bladder weakened.

"The archers were Scarrow's idea," Piscator rasped. "He lost his brother at the priory, were you aware of that, Healer? Found his boot and an arrow, but nothing else. Scarrow himself was blown clear across the pond and into the reeds. Saved from destruction by a call of nature, weren't you, my friend?"

Kira's stomach churned. There had been a third soldier? Edalyn's Flame.

"I was. Never thought taking a piss would save my life, but it did. Hid for hours in them reeds watching nuns run back and forth like headless chickens. They never saw me, and I never saw my brother again. Nor my Sergeant. Blew them away to kingdom come, you did."

Kira bit down on the inside of her lip. Thank the Goddess he hadn't seen what had actually happened to his brother and his sergeant.

"I'm sorry," she whispered.

"Don't be. Scarrow will have his redress. An eye for an eye, blood for blood."

Kira could feel the rope tightening around her neck.

"Where's my grandmother?"

Piscator smiled and Kira shivered. He reminded her of a feral boar.

"Why, right behind you, Healer."

Kira turned and the blood froze in her veins. Agatha lay at the feet of the brazen dragon between two guards. The points of their swords hovered dangerously close to her throat, but she lay unmoving. The flickering lantern light reflected on the bronze hide so the beast seemed set to take flight. It was both beautiful and terrifying. Kira dropped to her knees and moaned. "No. Stop. Please. Don't hurt her. It's me you want. Please let her go."

Piscator smiled coldly.

"It is far too late for bargains, Healer. You sealed your grandmother's fate as soon as you escaped from prison. Now, you will watch her burn." He glanced towards Giselle and Jenna and back to Kira. "It will be up to you who burns after that."

He signalled to his guards, and they hauled Agatha to her feet. She sagged between them, unconscious. Purple bruises covered her face and hands and the sight of them tore at Kira's heart.

"You're mad! Let her go!" Desperation made her voice harsh and Piscator's eyes darkened with fury.

"You dare to speak to me in this manner?" Piscator spoke with deadly calm, as his fingers clutched his silver pendant. Zarabesk's scale flared a warning. Kira ran her tongue across dry lips. She was on her knees, with her hands tied behind her back. Helpless. Without her power she could do nothing. But Piscator didn't know that.

The door in the dragon's flank opened with a clang. Kira whipped her head back to see what was happening. Piscator leapt forward and grabbed at the rag around her neck. He swung Kira around with more strength than she thought possible and held a knife to her throat.

"Move more than an eyelash and your guts will be opened quicker than you can blink. Your friends will follow."

He motioned Scarrow and between them they manhandled Kira into a chair. Scarrow threaded a length of rope through the bindings on her wrists and used it to tie her feet to the legs of the chair. Only then did Piscator take the knife from her throat. Kira felt a sting under her chin and then a warm trickle ran down her neck. He stared at the drop of crimson on the point of his blade.

"Does magical blood taste any different to ours, I wonder, or is it tainted with poison?" He brought the knife up to his lips. Kira's stomach churned. He stared at her as he licked the droplet of blood from the blade with the tip of his tongue. His eyelids fluttered and he shuddered. The bile rose in Kira's throat. The dragon shard in his pendant flickered.

"Bind her mouth!"

Scarrow forced the rag between her lips and over her tongue and secured it with a knot at the back of her head. Kira breathed heavily through her nose and struggled to swallow.

"Much better," Piscator rasped. He leaned close to Kira's ear and whispered, "The dragon beckons. Every time my pendant senses magic, I hear his call. Many witches have been sacrificed to raise this dragon from the dead, but to no avail. I know the dragon blood is strong in you, Healer, but first we will offer your grandmother. If her blood is not enough to raise Zarabesk from his slumber, I will offer him yours."

Kira knew the words were for her ears alone. The man was mad. She shook her head and tried to deny his claims. Piscator may as well have sliced her heart in two. He snapped his fingers and Agatha was thrown into the belly of the dragon.

As the flames caught beneath the dragon, Zarabesk's scale warmed again. What was she to do? She didn't have enough power to kill Piscator and save her grandmother at the same time.

I am here, daughter of Aeldra. Choose wisely.

My grandmother. I cannot let her suffer this.

I will watch over you.

Kira steadied her breath and entered her mind room. She reached for Agatha's awareness and prayed that what little power she had would be enough. She opened the door in the cellar and found herself inside the cavity of the beast. Agatha was barely breathing. Kira wrapped her in a fine gossamer mist and cradled her to her breast.

Agatha?

Kira? I told you not to come.

Shh now. Did you think I would leave you to die alone? I love you too much for that.

I know, child. Stubborn to the last, just like your mother. I'm glad you're here.

We haven't much time, Agatha. The metal grows hot, and the water inside starts to boil. I would give you a death dream if you'll let me.

Agatha nodded and opened her memories.

I'll let you choose which one, my brave and beautiful girl. My favourite memories are all of you.

Kira walked in a cottage garden filled with flowers. Winter blooms nestled alongside blossoms from summer and spring, trees were dressed in autumn finery and the russet leaves murmured on the summer breeze. Perfume filled the air, jasmine, rose and lavender: daffodils and jonquils when she turned one way, lily and hyacinth as she turned another. Each bloom revealed a precious memory when plucked. She saw her first steps as a chubby legged toddler, giggling with delight when she wobbled from chair to chair without falling, scooped up in Agatha's arms, kisses raining on her face. She felt Agatha's pride when Kira managed to build her first mind room, and her thrill of delight that Kira had chosen the stag quilt she had sewn as the first memory she stored there. Cooking lessons that ranged from disaster to success were remembered fondly and with great affection. Small acts of kindness were treasured more than Kira had ever realised, and Kira was glad that she had always tried to put Agatha's needs before her own. Kira's skill with healing had been the greatest source of joy, however, and Agatha's love and pride in her granddaughter's achievements brought Kira to tears.

She wove the blooms together in a coronet.

Acacias for friendship, daffodils for regard, ferns for sincerity, gladioli and honeysuckle for affection, roses for love. She threaded Agatha's favourite wildflowers and herbs through the crown and laid it gently around her head.

The heat was becoming unbearable now and Agatha began to moan.

Are you ready, Gran?

Yes, pet. Always remember, I love you.

And I you.

Kira kissed her gently on the cheek. She placed her hand on Agatha's chest and willed her heart to stop. At the moment of her death, Kira sent Agatha's spirit forth into the garden, and the sun shone from the clouds and the birds sang in welcome. She made the sign of the angel and asked her to gather Agatha gently. Kira felt a breath of cool air and heard the sweep of an angel's wing, and slowly withdrew her awareness.

Through bitter tears she watched the dreadful beast hiss and spit as the steam was forced through its nostrils while the fire roared beneath it. Piscator stared at the dragon with a fascination that bordered on the obscene. A white-hot anger raged inside her, searing the grief that tore at her heart.

Chapter 45

Kira had never wanted to hurt anyone as much in her whole life. The fury whirled around the centre of her being, wilder than even her whirlwind had been when she killed the soldiers. She wanted Piscator dead. Yet Zarabesk sang in her mind and the warmth spreading from his scale calmed her, like words could never do. Gradually, her anger stilled, and she listened to what the dragon told her to do.

As we are linked through my scale, so I will link to this corrupter through his pendant. In this way, his thoughts will be filled with me, and you can slip unnoticed into his place of memories. His fate will be in your hands. I will lend you what strength I can.

Piscator stood in the centre of the arena, basking in the glory of the brazen dragon. He opened wide his arms and strolled around the statue, revelling in Agatha's death. Madness gleamed in his eyes. Kira hated him. Her death would be next, but not if she killed him first. She hoped she had enough power left. Piscator clutched his pendant and bowed his head. She knew he called the dragon.

Zarabesk spoke, *Are you ready, dear one?*

I am. But are you sure? His madness should not be rewarded with visions of you.

Illusions and ghosts of the past are all he will see.

Zarabesk linked his awareness to hers and suddenly she was on the dragon's back. The bronze dragon gleamed beneath them, and Kira wondered how she could both love and hate something with equal passion. Zarabesk felt her pain.

Had I the power I was born with, yon beast would be but a molten puddle on the ground. That the form and memory of a creature loyal and loving to the Crown is used this way tears at my soul.

Mine, too, whispered Kira.

My shade will appear before this craven fool, and let him think what he will. Do what you have to, daughter of Aeldra, I will give you what strength I can.

The dragon snarled as Piscator grasped the pendant, and then suddenly they were in the swirling chaos that was Piscator's mind. Kira dropped from the dragon's back and watched as Zarabesk announced his arrival. Piscator's thoughts reached her, too, as he crowed with triumph.

I did it! I did it! I have summoned the mighty Zarabesk, last dragon of Cabarac.

Exultation and disbelief swirled around Piscator in equal amounts. Kira sensed this confliction was a constant torment within him. On one hand he was jubilant that his plan had worked, but on the other he was ashamed of his own actions. His deep hatred of all things magical was palpable, yet he had an overwhelming craving for the power he thought it would bring. Tangler was right. The power in the dragon shard had seduced him. Zarabesk spoke.

Who calls me from my slumber? I would speak with this powerful mage.

Kira felt Piscator's confusion. He didn't know what to do.

Grasp hold of your pendant and invite me to link my thoughts to yours.

Kira held her breath, but Piscator did not hesitate. Zarabesk linked his awareness to Piscator, and once Zarabesk had him enthralled, Kira had access to the memories she needed. She gathered the shreds of her courage and started her search.

In the dark dungeon of his mind, tiny pinpricks of light gleamed red, like fungus on the walls of a damp cave. The stench made her gag. Unlike Agatha and Isaac, she knew Piscator's death dream would bring him no comfort. Reluctantly, Kira began siphoning through his memories. The touch of the fungus made her shudder. She plucked the darkest one of all.

A young boy cowers in the corner of a filthy room, his thin arms no protection against the boot aimed at his frail body. It is his father's boot. The boy watches him stagger from the room. The boy has no name. He is starved, abused and bullied. His mother feeds the dogs before she feeds him.

He is sold to a man in a black robe, rescued from a life of poverty and shame. The man is cruel and kind in equal measure but doesn't beat him. The boy has food to eat and clothes to wear. Gradually the victim becomes the bully and Kira sees the cruel satisfaction he gets from tormenting a poor woman he calls the witch of Brackenridge. Vengeance is his.

Sickened at heart, Kira continued her search and in the dark recesses of Piscator's mind found another fungus which still gleamed brightly. It reeked of poison and decay.

The boy is in a large arena, crowded with people and noisy. The man he loves dearly, his saviour and protector, parades around the statue of a bronze dragon as the boy lays a fire beneath the belly of the beast. The dragon fascinates him. He wishes with all the hope a young boy can muster, that he might see a real dragon one day and fly across the world on its back. He would send flame raining down on anyone who had ever hurt him and live in a cave, high in the mountains. But he knows this is a false hope. And besides, his master loves him, too. Hadn't he told him that only last night?

Kira hears the chants of the crowd through the ears of the boy.

"Kill the witch, kill the witch."

The boy watches impassively as the soldiers manhandle the sobbing woman towards the dragon. He feels no sympathy, just a vague curiosity. Kira hears the clang of the door slamming shut and the whoosh of the fire as the wood catches alight.

Kira cannot bear to look but has no choice. Pain spears her heart.

The boy feeds more wood to the flames, then, disconcerted by the woman's screams inside the belly of the dragon, joins the dispatcher at the beast's head. The man throws his arm across the boy's shoulder and draws him close.

"This is it, boy. The King will appoint me as Grand Dispatcher, just wait. You will follow me in the glory of righteousness. Together we will rid Cabarac of the evil that is magic and the women who pretend otherwise. Show them no mercy, boy, for they will take advantage of your kindness. Women are not to be trusted. Especially women with magic in their veins. If ever you are tempted to show leniency, remember your own mother. Remember every beating, remember being forced to sleep on the floor, remember the scraps fed to the dog before you got to lick the bowl. Remember every unkind word, every cold night without a blanket. Remember and grow strong."

Together they turn to admire the beast. The boy is transfixed. The dragon seems to come to life. Its hide of burnished bronze now glows red and it breathes with each flicker of flame. It snorts and snuffles with each exhalation. The boy is sure it will unfurl its massive wings and take flight. Steam spews from the dragon's snout and the air is filled with the scent of incense and herbs. The crowd roars and the dispatcher steps away from the boy, hands him his cloak, and bows to the Royal box. The boy is happy for his master. With this success, his promotion to Grand Dispatcher is assured and he has promised the boy a name.

Suddenly, a deep growl rumbles from the belly of the beast, and the boy and the dispatcher turn to look. The dragon's eyes flicker. A flare blazes from its snout and arcs towards his master. The dispatcher is drenched in flame. The boy screams. He runs to help his master as he writhes on the ground, howling in agony. The boy throws the cloak over the dispatcher and then falls on the cloak and tries to bat the flames with his hands. The fire is too fierce. It catches the hood of his own cloak, and his head is engulfed in flame. He smells burning flesh, and pain, a thousand times worse than any beating, rips through his skull. Worse than death, even. He loses consciousness and welcomes the darkness.

Kira wiped the tears from her face. She has witnessed the death of one monster and the birth of another. Though she understands tragedy and circumstance have shaped the life of the man called Piscator, she cannot forgive him. She might mourn the loss of innocence, but how many women has he put to death because of his warped sense of justice? How many more will suffer if she does nothing?

Heart sickened by what she has observed, Kira sought guidance from the teaching of the Eiran. Torn between vengeance and her healer's ethics, she weighed her options with care.

Agatha was gathered in the arms of the angel, her body consumed by the flames that Piscator fanned with his lies, but Kira knew her soul was at peace and would soon dwell in the glade of the Goddess. Did Piscator deserve such peace? The boy, perhaps. But the man? Kira thought not.

She felt Zarabesk's presence and knew she must decide quickly. Her energy was fading. With Zarabesk's help she had the power to kill him. Surely she would be justified. Her heart ached for vengeance, but Agatha's death weighed heavily on her mind. Piscator's death would bring no recompense.

You do not kill the evil one?

One death is enough, Zarabesk.

Yet he will not go unpunished?

Oh, no. He will not go unpunished. He will become the instrument of his own torment.

Kira heard the rumble of appreciation from the dragon as he understood what she was about to do. She brushed her hand across the fungus and left a trail of spores to the mouth of the cave.

Dream it, weave it, will it.

It was done. Exhaustion claimed her. Doomed to relive the anguish and horror caused by the brazen dragon whenever he slept, Piscator's dreams would haunt him until the day he died.

Chapter 46

Zarabesk spoke again. *Are you done?*

I am. Even if he kills me now, I will not regret my choice.

I have told him I need no further sacrifice, but I cannot control his actions.

I know, and I thank you with all my heart.

The enormity of what she had just done hit like a small avalanche and Kira broke the link. The fire still smouldered beneath the dragon, so Kira knew that only minutes had passed. It seemed like days. A pall of smoke drifted above the floor, stinging her eyes. The faint aroma of burned flesh made her want to retch. Exhaustion threatened to overwhelm her, and Kira knew that if Piscator decided to kill her now, there was nothing she could do to stop him. She was spent. Part of her would welcome the oblivion. The person she loved most in all the world was dead because of her. Grief and self-loathing settled on her shoulders like a cape.

Piscator stood immobile in front of the dragon as if entranced. She twisted her head to look behind her and saw Giselle and Jenna. They were still alive, thank the Goddess. Tangler groaned and raised his head. Kira couldn't even use mind speech. The small amount of energy she had managed to regain since she had drained her power was depleted.

Scarrow glared at her, and she felt his hatred as surely as a blade.

A loud crash split the silence, and with it, the sound of splintering wood. The doors flung open and in marched Lord Callan, Ned and two dozen Harbour Guard.

"Drop your weapons!" Lord Callan's voice cracked across the room like a whip. No one would dare to challenge his authority, thought Kira, and she was right. Accustomed to obeying orders, the soldiers complied at once. Kira heard the clatter of bows, arrows and knives as they were dropped to the floor.

Piscator suddenly came to his senses and seeing his men's subservience, screeched at them.

"What are you doing! Arm yourselves!" No one moved.

He strode to Lord Callan and hissed, "What is the meaning of this? You dare to interrupt dispatcher business. I work with the authority of the Crown Prince!"

A small man detached from the row of Harbour Guard and stood next to Lord Callan.

"And I am Captain Anton Garrett, Harbour Master of White Haven, and I work with the authority of the King. My word is law on these docks. You show flagrant disregard for public safety, dispatcher! Fires are not permitted in storehouses under any circumstances." He flicked his fingers as he spoke, and a Harbour Guard hastened to douse the smouldering fire beneath the dragon with a bucket of sand.

"As well, you violate regulations of Trader's Province by drawing weapons in an establishment sanctioned by the sovereign himself. These are punishable offences. You and your men will be held in custody until your case is heard by the Magistrate."

He signalled his guards, and they marched forward to arrest Piscator's men and collect their discarded weapons.

Piscator was livid. "No!" he screeched, "This man has no authority, I tell you. The Crown Prince will hear of this!" He pivoted on his heel and pointed an accusing finger at Kira. "She is the one you should be arresting. The witch is evil! She has dragon blood in her veins. She is tainted with forbidden magic!"

Ned stepped forward and ended Piscator's diatribe with one well aimed blow to his chin. The dispatcher collapsed to the ground, out cold.

"Untie these people at once," ordered Lord Callan.

Kira's relief at seeing Ned and Lord Callan was cut short by Piscator's agonised shriek. He writhed on the floor, slapping at his robe like a madman. He pulled the hood from his head, raking his hands over tufts of greasy brown hair and his puckered, burn-scarred scalp. He screamed and yelped, his face contorted into a rictus of pain as he thrashed about, unaware of the stares of the horrified onlookers.

Kira stared at him in horror. Bile rose in her throat, and she was flooded with remorse. What had she done? After a long minute of harrowing torment Piscator woke from his nightmare and looked around, dazed. The fear left his face and he scrambled to his feet. He glared at Kira and snarled, "Scarrow."

Kira saw a movement from the corner of her eye. She turned her head in time to see the blade leave Scarrow's hand. It danced through the air in a graceful pirouette straight towards her heart. The light flashed on the silver blade as it rotated on its trajectory of death. Kira counted the flashes. One. Two. Three. Four. Five. The point of the blade reached its target. She closed her eyes and braced herself.

Kira felt the hit like a punch to the chest. But Zarabesk's scale absorbed the impact and the blade shattered on contact. She glanced down. Her clothes were ripped by the blade, but there was no blood. She heard Ned growl and looked back up in time to see him launch across the room and bring down Scarrow with a tackle to his knees. The crack of Scarrow's skull against the flagstones was the last thing that registered before the room started to spin.

"Kira!" Ned's voice came from far away. The rag around her mouth loosened and she took a deep breath.

"Kira?" he said again, and this time he was closer. So close, she felt his breath on her cheek and his hand over her heart. She raised her head and tried to focus her gaze.

"What are you doing?" she croaked.

"Edalyn's Flame, Kira," he replied hoarsely. "I thought he'd killed you. But there's no blood. You're alive."

She looked at him and nodded. His frown was more pronounced than ever, but she could see the worry in his eyes. His fingers fumbled with her restraints and suddenly she was freed. The giddiness returned and she put a hand on his chest to steady herself.

"Are you well?" he asked, concerned.

"No," said Kira, fighting her exhaustion and her grief. "No, I am not."

He picked her up, carried her to the wagon, wrapped her in a warm blanket and held her until the shivering stopped. She stared at the wall. Poor Agatha. Kira was sure her heart could not hurt more than had it been pierced by Scarrow's blade. In the distance she heard Piscator's furious complaints as he and his men were escorted down the docks, quieting only when Anton Garrett threatened to have him gagged. Eventually, Giselle and Jenna were allowed to join her in the wagon and Ned took his leave. She let her friends fuss over her, too weary to object.

"This is getting to be a habit," said Jenna. "Who will do your braids when you are in Prince Rhicard's court?" She tried to laugh, but her voice broke, and she wrapped her arms around Kira. "I'm so sorry about Agatha. That vile, disgusting man should be made to get a taste of his own punishment. No one deserves to die like that."

Kira looked over at Giselle as Jenna sobbed on her shoulder. Her face was as pale as snow and her eyes bright with unshed tears. She reached for Kira's free hand and gripped it tightly in hers. She didn't need to speak. Kira sensed every bit of Giselle's anguish and pain and sorrow in her touch, but most of all she felt her friend's deep affection.

"I killed Agatha," she said softly. "I stopped her heart."

"You gave her a death dream?"

Kira nodded sadly. "Yes."

"So she didn't suffer, Kira. You saved her from a horrible, horrible death." Giselle's voice started to break. She cleared her throat and continued. "You cannot blame yourself for this. Agatha loved you. She would not blame you. You did it out of love, Kira, because you loved her, too."

Kira knew Giselle spoke the truth, but still her tears did not come.

Tangler poked his head through the curtains to check that all was well. His face was ashen and his eyes full of sorrow.

I am profoundly sorry, Kira. I feel your pain as deeply as my own. Agatha should not have died like this. I should have been more diligent. Forgive me.

Kira could not answer him. Agatha had been his friend for countless years. She knew he loved her, too. She looked into his eyes and made the sign of the angel.

Tangler may have been upset, but Kira heard the fury in his voice when he talked to Parr and Farren outside. Unused to being outmanoeuvred, he fumed over Piscator's clever ruse. The brazen dragon had not been the only thing to arrive in a crate: the dispatcher had, too. To add injury to insult, Tangler had been ambushed when he had gone to find Lord Callan.

"Jock lives," he told them. "The blow on the back of his head knocked him out, and the gash he got on the mountain opened up again when he fell on the cobblestones, but it'll mend. The ship's doctor is attending to him."

"The ship's what?" asked Jenna.

"Doctor. Like a healer, but on a ship." Tangler looked at Kira. "He thought perhaps he should check on Piscator after that strange seizure he had when Ned knocked him out, but I told him not to bother. It was a simple blow to the head, and he was in fine fettle when he woke up."

He waved a hand over his beard. "I'm going to wash this blood out, then I'll start loading provisions on the boat. Lord Callan has gone back to get the quota. Anton Garrett has given permission for the boats to sail, but we need to make haste. The tide turns in less than an hour."

He gave Giselle and Jenna a brief hug and kissed them on the cheek.

"Thank you and farewell," he whispered and quickly left the wagon. He was gone only a minute when Parr knocked and called out softly.

"Can I come in? I have willow bark tea and honey oat biscuits."

Giselle opened the curtains and took the tray of cups. "You are a magician. Thank you, Parr."

He swept his cap from his head showing the top of his bald head. "You are more than welcome. Deepest condolences to you Kira, I'm sorry you lost your grandmother. But you need to get back your strength now. You drink as much of that as you can and eat up. Tangler said it could take weeks for you to recover from the incident at the spire."

Kira's belly grumbled in response. *If only you knew*, she thought, but she tried to smile. "Thank you, Parr."

Parr pulled his cap back on. "Been my pleasure, lookin' after you lasses, though I did have a full head of hair when I met you!" He winked and backed down from the step. "You take care, now."

"Wait. Parr, do you know what happened before we were taken?" asked Giselle.

"Mebbe not really my place to say," he said, his voice low even though they were the only people there. "Ned told me that Lord Callan was spittin' chips. When he went to collect the quota this morning, they were locked in. No one had a key, and the dispatcher's guards weren't being helpful. By law, the Harbour Master has to have a duplicate key, so Callan hot foots it over to his house. Anton Garrett is nobody's fool and comes back with Lord Callan. Ned has heard the scream in the meantime and comes back here to check you were all safe. Sees a pool of blood and follows the trail to the storehouse. Tells me and Farren to watch out for Tangler and runs back to find Lord Callan." He paused to take a breath. "Nowt much more I can tell you. You probably know the rest."

Farren came next. He kissed Kira's hand and said, "My sincere sympathy, Kira."

He looked at Giselle and Jenna. "Lord Callan has asked that you wait near those crates until he gives you the signal. Kira, he asked that you wait here. He wants a word in private."

He saw their faces drop. "Kira will be able to come and say goodbye, don't fret. Parr will give you a hand with your things. I'll bring Kira along in a minute."

Farren promised he would take Agatha's ashes to the priory. He placed an arm across Kira's shoulder and pulled her close. Kira ignored the ache his gesture caused and leaned into his warmth. They sat together on the back step of the wagon watching as the last of the quota boarded the brigantine in the early morning mist. Though it felt like a day had passed, it was only three hours past sunrise. Thick grey clouds leached the colour from the sun and the sea mist lingered over white caps beyond the harbour. The overcast weather suited her mood.

Lord Callan approached the wagon. Kira eased herself away from Farren and sighed. "It must be time."

"I'll get your things." Farren nodded to Lord Callan and disappeared inside the wagon. Lord Callan bowed to Kira, and she saw sadness in his dark eyes.

"Little did I know how things would turn out when I asked you to tend to my son, Kira." He glanced up at the sky, then back to her face. "Yet, if I am honest, had I known what lay in store, I would still have asked. You saved Mica's life." Regret made his voice husky, and he clenched his jaw. "I am sorry beyond words that I was unable to repay your kindness and save your grandmother."

Kira could barely speak. "Thank you."

"We found this in Piscator's crate. I think it may have belonged to Agatha. It's old and battered, but I thought you would want to have it." Lord Callan withdrew a package from beneath his cloak and handed it to Kira. She recognised the shawl at once, and as soon as she felt the weight of the book, she knew without having to unwrap it that it was Gwyneth's herbal. She hugged it to her chest, nodding her thanks as she blinked back her tears, only to find a strange comfort in the unexpected warmth emanating from Zarabesk's scale.

Lord Callan bowed. "I have made an enemy here today. Piscator is a vengeful man and a fool. But he does have the ear of the Crown Prince. Had I the means to keep you safe, I would allow you to return to River Glen, but Piscator will never stop his vendetta against you. I'm sorry, Kira, but it's time for you to go. Tangler waits aboard the Fortuna."

Farren handed Kira her travel bag and she placed the herbal inside.

"I think Jenna has taken your staff. She and Giselle are waiting to say goodbye."

Kira glanced about as they walked. The mist was thicker than ever. She couldn't see more than a few feet in any direction.

"Looking for Ned?" Farren nudged her arm.

"I just wanted to thank him. And say goodbye."

"He sends his apologies and his condolences to you. He had to stay with Jock. He asked me to tell you that he will think of you fondly the next time he has to pick up anything heavy. You have prepared him well, he says. He also gave me a letter to give to you to read once you have set sail. I've put it in your bag. He wishes you well, Kira, and safe passage to your future."

The future. It was time to sail to Prince Rhicard's court with Tangler and seek refuge there. Keep her promise. Learn about her magic and how to control it. Help Tangler with his political machinations. Forget about healing and her life in River Glen. Avenge Agatha's death. Leave her friends. Heavy-hearted, she tightened her grip on her bag and squared her shoulders.

Last night's dream came to mind. She was skating on the ice and heard a crack. This time when the ice split, she knew which way to jump: down into the abyss with no one to save her but herself. It was a leap of faith. The choice was hers to make, and she would accept the consequences that followed.

She opened her arms as Giselle and Jenna ran towards her and hugged them tightly. She whispered to one and then the other and they said their goodbyes.

Chapter 47

Kira sat on the stairs which led from the main deck to the forecastle and stared over the sea to the horizon. The Captain had given up trying to coax her inside, and once he was sure she wasn't about to throw herself overboard, had let her be. She was grateful to him. Below deck felt crowded and closed in, and she much preferred being outside. The weather had been kinder than expected and they were making good time.

Kira folded the letter and tucked it back into the pouch she wore on her belt. She knew the words off by heart, of course, but she liked looking at Ned's surprisingly neat handwriting.

> Kira,
>
> Firstly, I give you my sincere condolences on Agatha's death and my apologies that we arrived too late to save her. I know her death will wound you deeply and I am sorry I could not prevent this suffering for you. I would say you shouldn't blame yourself, but I fear that advice will fall on deaf ears. Your heart is too big. Perhaps that is what weighs you down. I jest. You have heavy bones.
>
> Forgive me for not coming back to bid you farewell in person. I cannot. My allegiance to my country pulls me in another direction. I hope you fare well in Prince Rhicard's court. I hear they have many a strong gentleman there who will, no doubt, be able to pick you up when you fall.
>
> Good wishes,
>
> Ned.

The letter always made her smile. She wished that his sense of humour had been more evident on their travels, but she supposed the times for that had been few and far between.

She heard footsteps, and a shadow fell across her face. She didn't need to turn to see who it was. On this boat, only one person sought her company. She made room on the step and Giselle sat down next to her.

"Do you think Tangler will have forgiven you, yet?" asked her friend.

Kira smiled and shrugged her shoulders. "I don't know. I think it is more important to know that I have forgiven myself. Well, I'm starting to."

She had done a great deal of soul searching out here on the deck. The vast expanse of sea and sky had overwhelmed her at first. Not a tree or a mountain in sight. But gradually, her energy had returned, and the pulse of the sea had eased her doubts and the wind had blown away her tears. She hoped Tangler had not been too hard on Jenna when he discovered they had swapped places.

Giselle leaned into her. "I knew you would choose this path."

Kira laughed. "Oh you did, did you? Do you have the sight like your Aunty?"

Giselle grinned. "No. I just knew. We're sisters, remember?"

"Aye, I do. Family first."

They sat in companionable silence for a while, lost in thought. Giselle took out her ever-present embroidery and began stitching. Kira looked down at her work and frowned.

"Elle?"

"Mmm."

"Remember back when we first met in the quota carriage? You told me that you refused Colac Proctor's token because of something he said."

"Mmm."

Kira nudged her friend. "Well… What did he say?"

Giselle sighed. She threaded the needle into her work and set it down on her lap.

"He told me that once we were married, I had to act like a Lady of the Guild. No more associating with the River folk. He had a reputation to uphold. And I must definitely cut ties with the likes of that healer I was friendly with. If the dispatcher was interested in her, then goodness knows what sort of trouble she could bring. He would not have his good name besmirched by even the slightest hint of scandal and nor could I."

Kira didn't know what to say, but Giselle continued, and her eyes flashed with indignation. "So I told him what he could do with his blasted gold token. He, nor any man, would tell me who I could or could not choose as my friend. If my best friend wasn't good enough for him, I told him, then he wasn't good enough for me. I gave it back to him, and that was that."

Kira shook her head. Why she had been blessed to have a friend like Giselle in her life, she didn't know, but she gave thanks to the Goddess and to the Lady Edalyn that she did. No matter what happened on the Legion Isles, they would have each other She took the needle from Giselle's sewing and pricked her thumb. As a small droplet of blood formed on the skin, Giselle grinned and poked her own thumb with the needle. They pressed their thumbs together and let their blood mingle.

"Family first," said Kira.

"First and last," replied Giselle.

Epilogue

Jenna pulled another sheet of parchment in front of her and began to write.

Dearest Kira and Giselle,

I have no idea whether this letter will ever reach you, but Sister Evangeline told me to have a little faith, so I am writing to you in the hopes it finds you.

I hope you are both safe and well.

I have been at the priory for six weeks now and the snow is thick on the ground. Six weeks, you're probably thinking. Why has she waited six weeks to write to us? Forgive me, life has been hectic. I have been accepted as a novitiate, and I can't tell you how happy that made me. Well, I can, I'm absolutely thrilled! Sister Eloise tells me that my skill with the staff has not diminished, and that I'm one of the most talented novitiates she has had the pleasure to teach. I shouldn't really tell you; it makes me sound immodest, and she frowns on that.

Sister Victoria and Sister Catherine send their Blessings to you. And Sister Eloise and Flynn, of course. And Sister Evangeline. Everyone, really. Even Tangler. He's been a frequent visitor to the priory. And Farren sends his love to you both. He did as he promised, Kira, and Agatha's ashes have been laid to rest in the crypt. A great honour for someone who is not a nun.

You would have expected Tangler to be furious when he found out it was me and not you who climbed on board the boat, wouldn't you? But he wasn't. In fact, he hadn't even turned around when he said, "Well met, Jenna, welcome aboard."

"Fish and pickles," I said. "How did you know it was me?" But he just gave me a sad sort of smile and shook his head.

That wasn't his only surprise, let me tell you. Instead of sailing to the Northern Province, we pulled in at a little cove that very afternoon. We stayed at a charming little inn that night, and the next day he hired two horses and we travelled to the priory. It took us quite a few days, but horseback is much quicker than by wagon. Tangler was truly kind to me, and not once did he chastise me for talking too much or for changing places with you, Kira. I still can't thank you enough for that.

Sister Evangeline has promised to have someone take care of Agatha's cottage, so you don't have to worry. She was so pleased to see us both. She rang the bell and asked Sister Eloise to run me a bath and get me a hot meal, which I was so grateful for, since it was bitterly cold and my backside was aching. I was on my way out of the study when I heard her ask Tangler if it all went well. He said "Yes. She sails to the Legion Isles." Sister Evangeline said, "Of her own free will? She chose to go?"

Tangler said, "Yes, it was her choice." Then the door closed, and I didn't hear what else was said. But that was a strange sort of conversation, wasn't it? I'm sure I heard it right, but Sister Eloise was talking to me as well, so maybe I didn't.

I will end now. Farren promises that he will try and get this sent on the next ship that sails to the Legion Isles. I don't know that it ever will, but just in case, I will send my fondest thoughts to you. You are the best friends anyone could have, and I miss you both, even though I do love it here.

May Edalyn's Flame forever light your path.

Blessings always,

Jenna